Sarah (S.K.) Neilson's writing is influenced by her experiences living and travelling in rural Australia.

Her themes explore animal behaviour and the human-animal bond, coming from working in the animal industry for 30 years, and with over 40 years' experience riding and owning horses.

She has an Advanced Diploma of Arts in Professional Writing, is an alumna of Bryce Courtenay and Fiona McIntosh's masterclasses, and is a member of the Australian Society of Authors.

Her articles have appeared in the Australian Veterinary Nurses Journal. Writing as Faran Silverton, her short stories have been published by Deadset Press, and the Canberra Speculative Fiction Guild.

# Singing Down the Sky

by
S.K. Neilson

Singing Down the Sky

All Rights Reserved

ISBN-13: 978-1-923382-21-3

IFWG Publishing International
Gold Coast

www.ifwgpublishing.com

*To Jen, for reading more of my words than anyone else in this world.*

# Acknowledgements

I owe endless thanks to my family - Mum, Dad, Olivia, Travis and Zack - for their support and unwavering belief that one day my obsessive scribblings in notebooks would be published.

To Bryce Courtenay, who made me believe that I could. I am a writer! You told me to make it absurd, so I do.

To Fiona McIntosh, whose unstoppable energy and encouragement that writing fantasy is my thing kept me on track. Your ability to make me see that no-one cares has helped me in the very best of ways.

This story wouldn't exist without my fellow writers, who've helped beta read my stories and submissions, answer questions, and support me along every step of the way. Big shout-outs to Briar, Marian, Louise, Dev, Meghan, Annabelle, Listya, Shelley, and my best friend, Jen.

Thank you to Gerry and the team at IFWG Publishing for believing in me and transforming my story into a real-life book. I pitched this story to Gerry in a conference room at Adelaide Zoo with Fu Ni the giant panda sitting in a tree right outside the second story window. She was clearly an auspicious sign.

And to everyone else who's played a part in this story finding its voice – thank you. You rock.

# Chapter 1

The moment she saw the mercenary lounging across the table from her, Tali Sarsega knew she'd found the husband she'd buy today.

She settled opposite him as he rested his elbows on the cheap wood, leaning forward to study her. A cocky one, sure of his looks, sure of the scarred forearms he'd positioned under her scrutiny. A fighting man. Then again, this was Iskarlia, so they were all fighting men—except the ones sitting in this row of tiny rooms were fighting to leave the poverty of their drought-stricken country. Poised, Tali waited, meeting his stare until his blue-eyed gaze wavered with uncertainty.

"So, Eulo Juke," she said in Vernese, glancing at the name card on the table. "There are forty-seven other men in this building looking to sail to Vernesia with a new wife. Tell me why I should choose you." Scars didn't bother her; his personality might.

Juke drew his brows down. "'Cause I'm loyal, hard-working, and I will worship my wife like a goddess." Her language sounded stilted through his deep voice.

Tali sat back in her chair, lips crooked into a faint smile. "Do you know how many times I've heard that today? Thirty-nine." Her smile deepened. "Come on, you look like a man who can think for himself. If I'm wrong, tell me, and I'll move on to the next room." Where she'd cram in knee-to-knee with another hopeful, inhaling more stale sweat and desperation in the humid air.

Her elderly escort from the binding agency shifted against the wall behind her, the squeak of his boots and drawn breath signalling his unease with Tali's manner. He probably wouldn't receive any commission unless she selected a husband. She ignored him—he wasn't the one making a big decision here, was he? Instead, she arched an eyebrow at the bronzed man across the table. His gaze burnt into hers, stirring a renewed flutter in her belly. The air between them danced with energy, like that preceding a storm.

"Juke?"

"I do work hard, and I know how to please women," he said, his Vernese smoother now, more genuine. "So how 'bout you tell me why I ought to pick you?" A wild-dog grin split his face.

"Insolent." The escort sprang past Tali's chair. His thin cane whistled against Juke's hands where they were spread palm-down on the table. Raising the cane to strike again, the escort's eyes bulged when Tali caught him by the wrist.

"Idiot!" she said in fluent Iskarlian. "Why would anyone want a husband who can't use his hands? If I decide to buy him, I'll have his price lowered to reflect the damage. Now get out so I can talk to him without you lurking there all pissy-pantsed." She stabbed a finger towards the door.

The escort hesitated, under strict instruction not to leave any of the Vernese women alone with the men. Maybe he expected Tali to offer him a bribe. She'd heard stories about women handing over coin to be left alone with their prospective husbands for a while, stripping them naked, poking and prodding, testing the men's prowess in sex, and more.

Her expression darkened. "If your superior grizzles about it, he can come talk to me himself."

He curled his lip with a sniff and stalked out, slamming the door behind him.

Juke hadn't moved. A thin line of blood brightened the scars on the back of both hands. He grinned. "You talk our tongue."

"Of course. I want a husband who can hold a half-sensible conversation, not just a man who fights and thinks pleasuring his woman involves pawing at her breasts." Tali sank into the hard-backed chair again, flipping her black plait over one shoulder. She pushed down the doubt chewing at her. "And if that doesn't answer your question, I know you'll be sailing to Vernesia with me because I've seen the other women here in the market for a husband." Most of them were older, less glamourous, some desperate to get themselves a young, handsome man to take back to their estates and submit to near-slavery, both physical and sexual. Rumour had it plenty of bought men didn't survive their bindings.

Juke's smile cut deep into his cheeks. He must've seen enough of the other buyers to know Tali was right.

She let her slender fingers uncurl in her lap, dark against the turquoise silk skirt. He wasn't the most handsome man she'd met today, but she was hooked by the sharpness of his eyes above that perpetual half-smile. "I'm offering passage to Vernesia, a comfortable cottage, work and a wage, decent food in your belly, and good coin. For a one-month binding."

"One month?" The grin fell from his face.

"With my family, it could feel longer, but afterwards you'd be free to go your own way, with gold in your pocket and your papers declaring you an honorary Vernese citizen," she said, smiling. He wouldn't be offered a better deal in this flesh-market, or anywhere else.

Juke drew his hands off the table, flexing the muscles through his arms. "What do you get out of it?"

Good: so he was at least a little cautious, not stupid. Still, Tali's reasons were none of his business. She shrugged. "I'll treat you well, so I'd expect you to do the same for me. Or the deal is broken and you leave with nothing."

"I don't hurt women."

Plenty of other Iskarlians would. She'd have to take him at his word. She held her hand out. "My name is Tali Sarsega. I'm offering you a binding then, on those terms."

His cocky smile returned. He shook her hand with firm, rough fingers. "You got yourself a deal."

With that, Tali had a husband-to-be, and cause enough to keep her estate while destroying her family's plans to fob her off to wretched Loy Myrtis. It seemed so simple.

A strong breeze leapt off the waves, ruffling Eulo Juke's dark blond hair before skimming past the other men waiting on the waterfront. He slouched against the timber wall of the passenger terminal, slitting his eyes against the bright Iskarlian sunrise. None of the women were here yet, but Eulo reckoned every single new husband was, as though arriving too close to the mid-morning launch might leave them standing on the docks watching their chance for a better life sail off towards the horizon.

The binding agency had put the new husbands up in a nearby boarding house for the night, where they'd sat shoulder to shoulder in the dining hall, laughing and bragging about their—and everyone else's—new brides. Eulo brooded over his keerfish and boiled squetch dinner in the darkest corner, not feeling the slightest bit emotional about leaving behind the Iskarlian cuisine. The bland rat-of-the-sea and even blander seaweed probably wouldn't be as nasty if it didn't have to be cooked into oblivion for your guts to handle it. There was a lot an Iskarlian gut had to handle.

He hadn't laughed or bragged about his bride, even though the others were all bent on finding out whose finger the pretty young woman had slipped her ring onto. Eulo turned his right hand, catching the sun on the binding band on his middle finger. If he angled it the right way, a vein of green glimmered in the metal, disappearing in the next breath. An extravagant gift, considering Tali was only binding with him for a month. He grinned. Finding a good supply of valuable *kilili* silver might be easier than he'd expected.

A woman shrieked somewhere down the way, her cry picked up by a flock of seagulls startling into the cloudless sky. She tottered onto the waterfront, her sturdy legs torturing two narrow-heeled sandals. She shrieked again, arms outstretched, reaching for the Iskarlian who now belonged to her. Beaming, she clapped him into her bosom. More women followed close behind, cawing with the enthusiasm of gulls squabbling over a keerfish head as they sifted their husbands out of the crowd.

Eulo scratched his crotch, bemused by the mob of scoundrels edging along the gangway to their vessel, escorted by these overfed, middle-aged Vernese women. The *Seadancer* bobbed in its moorings, proud and well-maintained, its crew readying the auburn sails. The captain probably made a fortune off such desperate women paying passage to raid the Iskarlian flesh-market.

No wonder the men all liked the look of Tali. No wonder she hadn't liked the look of them. He smiled, smug she'd picked him out of all the candidates. He wouldn't get complacent though, not 'til he knew what she was up to. Of the women who'd interrogated him, it'd been obvious why they'd come to Iskarlia to buy themselves a husband. Old, shy, unhinged, ugly. Not Tali Sarsega. No, his new wife had another plan, for sure.

Eulo dug an apple out of his pack. He dusted it on his tan-clad thigh before biting into its red skin. Savouring the crispness on his tongue, he figured he could afford to buy new apples now. While it was strange to have a wife, she was really just hiring his skills, same as everyone else he'd worked for. She must want a baby, to only need a husband for one month. Eulo grinned. He'd kissed her full lips on impulse yesterday when they'd placed rings to complete their binding ties. He could put her in foal no problem if that was what she wanted.

He ate the apple to its skinniest core and ate that, too. Better than tossing it to the loitering gulls, or they'd never leave him alone. He stood up, pacing to stretch his legs. The movement made his right knee grumble in the protest song it sang most mornings, a memento from his time as a warrior.

A parade of newly-bound moved aboard the *Seadancer*. Were they all looking at each other, reckoning they'd made the wrong choice? Eulo snorted. As if the Iskarlian men had any other option to escape this blasted chunk of rock and sand.

If they weren't watching their crops wither and die without rain, they were scratching out a wage digging gemstones out of the ground, or fighting as a disposable soldier in the warlord's army. They were better off taking their chances with a fat-pursed woman from across the ocean. Anyone who didn't have a family back home to send money to would at least be leaving for the land of plenty.

"Eulo bloody Juke, eh?" a gravel-scraped voice said behind him.

Eulo faced the big man, squinting as the sun flayed his eyes. "What are you doing here, Krike?" How'd he missed this goon amongst all the rest?

"Same as you, 'less you found some other way to get off Iskarlia," Krike sneered, his face all angles and shadows with the sun behind him. "Burnt too many bridges, huh?"

Eulo stared him down, unwilling to talk about reasons with this traitor.

"Don't reckon I'd fancy being in your wife's shoes," Krike said. "D'you tell her how bad luck walks in your shadow, how you got a habit of losing people?"

Eulo's hands clenched into fists. "Your sister's gone. You still so bent up about it?"

"If you'd looked after her like you ought've—"

Eulo glimpsed an older woman marching across the wharf towards them. Her silk blouse strained against her broad shoulders, like a farm labourer who'd stolen her mistress's best shirt. "Your wife's coming. No wonder she bought you, eh? Needed someone her own size."

Krike glanced over his shoulder at her. He turned his dark gaze back on Eulo. "You reckon I care about her looks if it gets me away from here? Soon as we get to Vernesia I'm off to find kilili. I'll be gone so quick she won't even remember my face."

"You reckon? It don't look like it'd be easy getting out of her grip."

"You done better, did you?" Krike worked his jaw, thinking for a moment. "You sneaky maggot. You got her, didn't you?"

"The black opal in a gibber desert."

"We'll see. Once we're on the boat, half these grubs will be begging her to swap you over." Krike jerked a thumb at the handful of men still waiting on the waterfront. "If she bothers coming to get you. Time's running out, Jukey-boy."

Krike swiped lank hair away from his sneer before turning to meet his new wife. She babbled at him, her smile stretched wide as she wrapped her fingers around his arm. Shades, wasn't it a sight, the war-hardened soldier following his soft, round woman onboard the ship. She'd just as like turn up dead once she'd served his purpose.

Eulo toed a stone in the dust. Not his wife; not his problem. He scanned the wharf again. Near empty. Maybe his own binding was over, not even a day after starting. He booted the stone away, checking the sundial in front of the warehouses for the hundredth time. Sunlight edged the spire's shadow into the morning quarter. Before long, the *Seadancer* would raise anchors and be gone, together with Eulo's chances of repaying his Scabmen debts.

Nerves weighed heavy against his bladder. Fidgeting, he glanced around. Not much choice aside from the narrow laneway behind the warehouses. Eulo snatched up his pack, sure if he didn't some bastard would do it for him, and headed around the corner. He pissed against the wall, staring at the peeling white paint, trying not to breathe through his nose. The breeze ruffled the hair on his nape, blowing from the wrong direction now, burdened with the decaying stench of Port Garnet.

Once he'd finished and left the laneway, Eulo faltered to a standstill on the wharf, alone except for the sailors getting ready to cast off. He threw his pack on the ground, pale dust rising in a cloud around it. "Fuck." He kicked the bag, hard enough to spin it across the dirt, even with his blades wrapped in the bottom.

He'd been gammoned.

"Morning."

Tali Sarsega's smoky voice stroked his ears. Two braids hung down her slender neck, twin stripes against her blue vest. A streak of loose hair skipped on the breeze, blowing in a thin black vein across her smile. Caution clouded her gaze, though she seemed genuinely pleased to see him. He knew she was the wrong target for his anger when she spoke in her unassuming manner.

"Having second thoughts?"

"Too late for that," Eulo said. Of course he bloody had though, when everything in his bones warned him against signing up to the binding agency and getting on a wifeship. He'd been a mercenary too long not to trust his gut feeling. Until now when he'd left himself with no other choice.

Tali blinked at him with the striking green eyes that'd caught his attention yesterday. Her sober expression revealed nothing. "If you want to stay, now's the time to say so."

He glanced at the scrub-tangled hills behind her. Staying here— selling his skill with fist and blade, keeping the bad company he did, wondering when he'd end up with someone else's knife between his shoulder blades—wouldn't help him. He needed entry to Vernesia to find enough precious kilili to pay his debts. He'd be stupid not to take Tali's offer.

"Eulo?" she asked, her accent curling around the word.

He bent to grab the strap of his pack. "Better get on this boat then, eh?"

# Chapter 2

The slab-armed Vernese loitering on the docks beside the *Seadancer* took a sheaf of papers from Tali. His eyes disappeared under his forehead as he squinted at the pages, verifying the identity of this last couple to board. If the big brute didn't accept the papers or let go of them so they blew out across the water, Eulo would be on his arse back on the wharf.

A trickle of sweat ran down his spine.

All he could read on his card of entry to Vernesia was the X where he'd made his mark beside what must've been Tali's own name, above a red stamp marking the card an authorised paper of the Vernese Kestrine's offices. He guessed two smaller papers in the man's hand were their tickets to get aboard the *Seadancer*. It eventually passed the man's scrutiny, because he returned the papers to Tali. She tucked them into her pocket, taking ownership of the formalities. Of Eulo, and his permission to be in Vernesia.

He shuffled up the gangplank in her wake, shouldering past other voyagers in the passageways leading to their cabin on the lower deck. He gripped the handrail with white knuckles. There were too many bloody people and not enough solid ground under his boots. No wonder Tali hadn't rushed to get on board. She unlocked the cabin, screwing up her nose as she went in. Behind her, Eulo trailed into a fug of stale sweat and sex, salt and timber. He squeezed in with Tali between a table and bunk.

She thumped open the porthole, frowning. "Seems they gave our cabin to someone else, to reward us for being last to board."

"Or they saw the size of the other wives." Eulo sprawled on the narrow bunk. He laced his fingers behind his head. They were in for a cosy voyage.

"And I thought you agreed to my proposal because it was the best deal you'd ever get." Tali pushed her bag under the table with one foot.

Eulo grinned. "Well, it don't hurt that you're a pretty girl too, eh?" Now they were here, he'd use some of his charm on her, just in case Krike and these other grubs reckoned they might try to pinch her away.

Tali didn't seem to be listening, though. She bent over the table, unwrapping a scrap of cloth. Extracting a gnarled stick from the bundle, she snapped it between her hands, releasing a sharp tang into the air. "This bilah root will help if you get seasick."

He blinked at the way she'd ignored his flirting. The thumb-sized lump she offered reminded him of an old man's knuckle. He frowned, unwilling to admit he'd never sailed out beyond the Fawney River that licked its big brown tongue down Eastern Iskarlia.

"Take a bit now, before we get out on the open seas and you can't keep your breakfast down. I found that out the hard way, coming over." Tali grinned wryly, still holding the pale lump out to him. She put the other half between her teeth, bit off a chunk and rolled it around her mouth, her gaze steady on him.

Eulo sat up, squaring his shoulders. The tuber couldn't be as bad as gecking up his guts in front of his new wife for the next day and a half. It squeaked against his teeth like a raw yam, bursting pungent flavour across his tongue. He grimaced.

"I know, it's strong when you're not used to it." She rewrapped her remaining piece. "We cook with it a lot, with meat and in teas and cakes. It's good for settling your belly, and maybe your nerves too, eh?" She cocked her head, drawing Eulo's eye to her neck.

"I ain't nervous." Eulo stood up. The overhead pressed in on him, only a handspan above his scalp. The *Seadancer* wasn't a ship made for Iskarlians, or anyone else who liked space around them.

"I would be, to leave my homeland and sail to a foreign country with a complete stranger."

"There ain't much to leave behind on this stinking lump of sand and snakes. Armed men, deserts, broken dreams, broken people," Eulo said. "You're lucky to make it past your fortieth year in Iskarlia." He ground his teeth, silencing the demons. It wasn't Tali's fault he'd ended up in such a mess, getting into one debt too many with the Scabmen.

A horn sounded above, loud and long. Eulo startled, cracking his skull against the overhead.

Tali sighed, the warmth ebbing from her face. "I'm going to watch as we leave port. It's the last interesting sight we'll see until tomorrow." Her voice grew soft as molasses as she paused in the doorway. "You could come with me, if you wanted."

Eulo wasn't going to stay below without her. He thudded up the hardwood stairs onto the upper deck, shading his eyes against the glare. Could be his wife had never laid with a man. Maybe she wished she'd picked out Krike, or one of the scrawny non-soldiers, anyone except Eulo Juke.

"Come on, we'll see better from the side," Tali said, pushing him in front of her.

He barged through the crowd with her darting in his wake, her fist knotted into the back of his shirt. He stopped, bracing himself against the rail with one hand. Tali edged in between his chest and the wood. The top of her head came just level with Eulo's chin, and he inhaled the perfume of flowers on her hair. The freshness made a welcome change from the warm, fish-scented air that hung squalid over the harbour, and the sweating crowd surrounding them.

People jostled and shifted around Eulo, bumping him against his wife. Her lithe body fit well against his. She didn't move, so he snugged in good and close to show the other men Tali Sarsega was his. He bristled at the way they leered at her, while trying to ignore the hungry stares their wives were sending him.

The ship lurched away from the dock, the wind catching the sails, snapping them against the masts. Turquoise water slapped at the hull, sending whitecaps rushing across the waves. Port Garnet shrank into the distance, dwarfed by the scrub-tumbled mountains beyond. Eulo's chest tightened: a good hunter went prepared, but he knew nothing about Vernesia. Hadn't bothered to find out before he left, just took the first chance he could.

His hand rested beside Tali's, the waist of her vest soft against his forearm. Even with his deep tan, he was still shades lighter than her. The breeze blew cool against the sweat on his skin. It didn't matter how many of his layers got stripped back, nothing could shift the scars and marks on him, the legacies of his decade as a fighting man. First as a soldier, then a mercenary, now a lump of man-meat bought by a woman. A Vernese woman. His lips peeled away from his teeth into a half-grimace. Tali tilted her chin at him, her eyes bright as fire. She'd caught him with that look yesterday when she'd strolled into his life to make her stupid-generous proposal.

"You really aren't sad to be leaving?" She nodded at the shore.

He shrugged. "The Iskarlians starve while our Cove gets fatter and richer on his spoils of war. If the hard labour don't kill you, a blade in the back probably will." The only difference between whether it belonged to a soldier or outlaw would be how well polished the blade was.

"It's your country, though."

Eulo nodded. "My uncle used to say a man won't ever change the colour of the sand in his veins."

"Maybe not, but we all bleed red."

"He sure did, when his time came." Trading a cut throat for a stolen scythe, before Eulo relieved his uncle's attacker of the scythe and opened the thieving maggot's belly with its tip.

"Saltwater for his soul." Tali pressed the two forefingers of her left hand flat on her right eye-socket, then the left. She shifted, edging out of Eulo's shadow.

He wanted to move with her, keeping touch with the first woman he'd be having in his bed in at least three months. Funny how Mako, the wretch god, made life take these roads. His last woman had hassled him, wanting a binding and a baby. Maybe he'd loved her in some way, beyond her temper. Shades. He rubbed his forehead, recalling how he'd spent the past year lurching between her nagging, his half-deranged mercenary mentor, and the guileless people he hunted down to put coin in his purse. That was right back when he began looking for something more, making stupid bets with even stupider people.

Then, being the stupidest of them all, he'd borrowed money he couldn't repay and gotten himself tangled in the middle of a Scabman stew.

Port Garnet waned on the horizon, its peaks jagging up from the ocean's surface like desert dogs' teeth. Eulo gazed out at the disappearing chunk of island, bemused by the lump under his breastbone. He'd be back soon enough, though, with the prized kilili he needed. The Scabmen's threat resounded in his mind: *you got sixty days, or else.*

Above the ship, white-bellied sea eagles soared with freedom—the very foundation forming the beliefs of the country Eulo was heading to.

Plus, they shit down on everyone below them.

With the excitement of setting sail over, other passengers drifted away from the deck. Eulo shuffled his feet, catching his heel and lurching into Tali. She hissed as her right shoulder bumped his chest. He leapt back, surprised by her reaction at their bodies touching, muttering an apology as she moved farther along. Frowning, he rested both palms on the wooden rail, sank his weight into them. It was easier to eavesdrop when you seemed to be doing something else, like choking up at the sight of your fading homeland.

The women within earshot all spoke in Vernese. Their new purchases replied in broken, guttural accents, most having some grasp of the trade tongue. The men grunted to each other every now and then in cautious mutters of Iskarlian, although Tali was the only woman who'd spoken Eulo's language to him yesterday. The rest had interviewed Eulo in jabbering Vernese, as though it hadn't even crossed their minds he might not understand their demands for him to strip naked for their inspection.

"Well, I didn't choose him because he was smart," an older woman said to her friend, on Eulo's right-hand side. Both women smirked at the brawny lad fidgeting behind them, their parrot-screech laughter filling the air. The friend's much younger husband stood by, picking a scab on his elbow.

Eulo sniffed. He'd swapped a life of killing people to become a plaything for rich, exotic women. Was Tali talking about him too, like he wasn't even standing there? He glanced to his left where, sure enough, she spoke to another Vernese woman, the sun highlighting her smile.

Tali glanced at Eulo, her lips crooking into a grin. Her fingers butterflied over his elbow, while she extended her other hand towards her friend. "Eulo Juke, meet Kardia Riole."

Kardia's smile faltered. She looked down as she swivelled to greet Eulo, dropping a curtain of dark hair over her left cheek. An ugly burn jagged from her ear to her nose, though not a mark blemished the smooth, high cheek on the right side of her face.

He stepped forward to offer his hand. "Miss Riole."

"Mr Juke. Or Sarsega, as you'd be now." She shook his hand after a moment of hesitation, her scarred mouth lisping out the words.

During the binding ceremony, they'd told him of the Vernese custom for the man to take his wife's name. He'd ground his jaw, saying nothing. He was Juke, always would be. Nobody would take his identity, not even for one month.

"Eulo, this is my husband, Alvic." Kardia motioned to the man hovering beside her.

He shook Eulo's hand, without extending his wet, pudgy grip to Tali. Another custom Eulo must've trampled on.

Alvic grimaced, looking Eulo up and down. "You're of fighting background?" he said, his tone nasal.

Eulo stared at the man's tailored shirt and pants. Even Tali's fingers were more work-worn than this goose's. Eulo let his biceps bulge as he raised his scarred forearms. "I didn't earn these fighting off my master's housecats."

Kardia laughed, though her husband didn't crack a smile. "All our scars tell a story," she said in a low voice, spidering long fingers over her ruined cheek. Her gaze met Eulo's for the first time, then skittered away. She reached for Alvic's hand. "Come, let's give Tali and Eulo some space to get to know each other." They wandered down the deck, her maroon skirt billowing in the wind.

"I met Kardia on the way over," Tali said. "She's very smart." She smiled after the retreating couple. "I'm glad she chose Alvic over some of the men here." Her gaze shifted in Darley Krike's direction.

Glimpsing the soldier, Eulo's skin prickled. "You ought to stay away from Krike."

Her sloe-eyes unblinking, Tali said, "Perhaps you should too."

He nodded, relieved she hadn't asked why. Still, he'd be stupid to believe she meekly accepted everything he said. Having Krike around didn't sit easy with him, not with the bad blood between them. Not that Eulo really trusted any of the men onboard; any one of them might be working for the Scabmen.

"Krike got bound to the richest woman on the ship," Tali said, grabbing the handrail and stretching her body backwards. "How many of these other men do you know, Eulo?"

"A few. Not all by name. Not all are bad. Do you know all these women?"

"Should I? Because we're on the same ship together? You know how big Vernesia is, don't you?"

"No. They don't let men like me in very easy. Not 'less we sell ourselves to coin-heavy Vernese who can't convince anyone to bind with 'em in their own land." Eulo said, brash, although inside his heart sank. Finding forty-thousand kistars worth of kilili would be hard enough even in a small country. He leant out where the sea-spray could hit his face, avoiding the crimp of Tali's mouth.

"I didn't mean any offence," she said.

Eulo studied the wake furrowing white trails into the ocean behind the ship. He had, but he'd regretted his words the moment they'd left his tongue.

"I know a few of these women, some by face. And a fair lot more by their reputation. Not all by name. Not all are bad." Tali propped a hip against the timber beside him, her arms folded. "You might be surprised to know I don't have much in common with them when we're not rolling around in all our gold coins."

"Sorry." He flinched under the heat of her glare. "I didn't bind with you because I want money." Just passage to Vernesia. Though money would help.

The bow of the ship bounced up on a wave, slapping back down with a rush that stole his breath away. None of the couples lingering in the sunshine paid Eulo and Tali any attention. At least she kept her anger controlled, not becoming a shrieking mess.

"The tall woman on the bench there, they say her hunger for sex is insatiable. Her last husband choked to death, naked with a silk scarf around his neck, some sort of game gone wrong." Tali spoke in breakneck Iskarlian. "The big lady attached to your greasy friend is onto her fifth binding. Her last four husbands vanished. Ran off into their new world, she says." Tali snorted. "More like ran into the mouths of her boars. She farms the best-fed pigs in the region. So if you prefer to try your luck elsewhere, I'll tear our binding papers up and you can go do it instead of wasting my time."

Eulo's gut churned, sending a wash of clammy nausea through him. He closed his eyes, drawing a deep breath in through his nostrils. The ship rocked under his feet, pushing, pulling, swirling. Shades, he was going to geck. He stumbled over Tali in his rush to leave without chundering up his breakfast all over her. Worse than a drunk, he lurched to the stairs, desperate to swap everyone's judgemental gaze for the stifling darkness of his cabin.

Inside, he fell to his knees on the worn timbers, hugging a bucket to his chest as he retched so much his stomach hurt. What in shades was happening to him? Eulo Juke, great warrior and ruthless mercenary, reduced to a whimper.

# Chapter 3

Tali gaped at her husband's broad shoulders as he bolted down the deck. Her toes throbbed from being trampled over by his huge boots. Blazes, she'd tied a binding to the world's biggest toddler. The charismatic man who'd agreed to her deal had become exactly the pigheaded, blunt thug she'd vowed to avoid. She should cut him loose now, save herself the fight her father and sister would hurl at her. Tali sighed. Maybe this binding hadn't been such a good idea, after all.

She hugged her arms around her chest, tilting her face to the vast blue expanses of ocean and sky behind the ship, welcoming the rush of fresh air over her skin and the wind scattering the stench of the cabins below her feet. Few vessels shared this open stretch of water between the two islands. The Vernese wouldn't let many in, and there wasn't much demand for people wanting to go to Iskarlia.

When she'd stared out across the dancing waves for so long her mind felt numbed, Tali abandoned the hole she'd fretted into the hem of her vest. She pushed away from the rail, straightening her spine. Time to find out what her husband had been doing while she'd lingered up here.

Several couples strolled the deck, weaving around thick coils of hemp rope and sun-darkened sailors. It'd been good to get back onto the *Seadancer*, with its familiar crew. Some of them had gotten friendly with the women on the way over to Iskarlia, but they'd been happy enough chatting to Tali about their work once they realised she wouldn't entertain them in her cabin. A boring journey with easy money, they'd said. Much less dangerous than near-slavery on the merchant traders that ran up and down the Kelp Strait, carrying stock between Vernesia, Iskarlia, the Threelands, and the ship's homeland further north in the Saltspit Islands.

Tali descended to the passengers' quarters, bristling when a man stepped out of the gloom. He stretched his arm across the narrow passageway, leaning into his hand so she couldn't get past. Her nostrils flared at the reek of perspiration.

Darley Krike grinned, lowering his ginger-stubbled chin to her. "It's Tali Sarsega, ain't it?"

"Is it?"

He laughed with the same rasp that gravelled his speech. "I made it my business to find out."

She stood taller. "Get out of my way."

"Lost your husband, eh?"

Her eyebrow shifted a smidgen. She wouldn't dignify him with a response.

"It near broke my heart to see you picked Eulo Juke. Now couldn't I tell you a tale or two about him." He ran his tongue slowly across his top lip. "For a cost, of course."

"You're still in my way," Tali said again, this time in Iskarlian. She stepped forward, pointing at the limb blocking her passage.

Krike sniffed, his face hitching into a snigger. He let his arm drop, muscles rippling as he flexed his fingers.

Tali forced him to step back as she passed, without reacting to his trailing leer and bully's stance. At first, he'd caught her attention in the interview rooms, until she'd seen the dark streak in his eyes.

"I like you, Tali. Don't give up on me too quick, eh?" His coarse whisper trailed after her into the depths of the ship.

She stalked along the worn timbers, rubbing at a twinge in her right shoulder, her irritation rising. Muffled laughter and voices floated out beneath the doors along the passageway. A rhythmic, gasp-studded thumping grew louder as Tali neared her cabin. She caught her breath, letting it out when she reached the door from where the noise emanated — her neighbour's. She frowned at her own door, listening. Nothing. No sounds to suggest Eulo was even in there. He might be pleasuring the neighbour. Tali rested her fingers on the brass handle. Too bad for her, if he'd decided to lock her out. She turned the handle, clicking the latch open, and stepped into the darkness.

Hot, vomit-laced air hit the back of her nostrils. Grimacing, Tali relocated the sick bucket and its sloshing contents out into the passageway. She shut the door and kicked off her boots beside it. Padding over to open the shuttered porthole, she let light and fresh air spill into the cabin. Eulo lay sprawled naked on the bed, snores rattling out of his open mouth. No wonder he'd been tetchy. It was hardly her bloody fault if he felt seasick, though. She studied the black ink flared across both his collarbones, Iskarlian symbols which wound down his chest and abdomen. Her gaze dropped lower to the golden curls around his talents. No harm admiring such a well put-together man when his ego wasn't awake to notice.

Tali dragged her bag out from under the table. Her mouth hitched into a smile. The two strands of long black hair she'd planted on top of her clothes were gone, confirming Eulo had searched her possessions. Not that he would've found anything exciting amongst her moleskin pants and vests. After settling onto the bench closest to the porthole, she slid a roll of thick paper out from the bag and unfurled it on the table-top, revealing a map of the Opalline, the greater ocean region they were bobbing around in. Behind her, Eulo rolled over, cutting off his snores. The couple next door continued thumping and moaning their way into the early afternoon.

The straw mattress rustled as Eulo stretched, yawned. The neighbours drummed against the wall, the woman's cries intensifying in what Tali hoped was the end of their prolonged session.

"Righto, darl. Ready to come get your money's worth out of me?" Eulo said, deep and slow.

"Darl?"

He winked. "Ain't that what the bound do? Have names for each other? Y'know, darl—darling?"

She blinked at him, stretched out with his head resting on one hand and his elbow propped on the mattress. The gleam in his dark blue eyes sent heat rushing between her legs. She turned her attention back to the map. "You can call me Tali, and even if I wasn't sitting here breathing in the stink of your vomit, I still wouldn't have sex with you, Eulo."

He snorted. "What? Don't you like men? Or have you just never taken pleasure with one?"

Aha, that bruised ego again. "If I wanted to pay to fuck someone, I'd have done it at home instead of wasting my money sailing across the Kelp Strait." She shifted on the bench, stabbing him with her gaze. "Besides, you didn't strike me as a whore."

Next door, the woman finally shrieked out her climax. At least, Tali assumed it was the woman.

"Every man on this fuckin' boat has whored himself," Eulo growled, rolling out onto his feet. He hunched to avoid hitting his head on the overhead while he pulled his pants up.

Tali dragged her attention off the smooth muscles in his legs and arse and refocused on the squiggles on the map. Heart-shaped Vernesia lay in the west, full of carefully painted forests and the mountainous divide that ran north to south, roughly halfway between the east and west coasts. The Heartbreakers.

"Plenty of women on this ship have already asked to pay for you to screw them," she said. She loathed the idea of a man only having sex with her because he was in her employ. "If you want to earn some extra money, I can't stop you."

He sat edgeways on the bench opposite her, his presence filling the tiny room. "My deal is with you."

"Good." She meant it. The less to worry about, the better, but she'd be hanging on to his Vernese papers until the end of their agreement, just in case. She watched the tattoos on his torso twist as he reached for a water flask on the floor beside her bag. Nudging the bag with her foot, she asked, "Did you find what you were looking for in there?"

"Only some fancy lace undies."

"I'm afraid they'll be too small for you."

"Search mine, it don't worry me."

Tali shook her head, refusing to give in to her curiosity.

Eulo scratched his bare chest. "So, if you didn't tie a binding with me to fill your belly with a child, what do you want from me?" He eyed her as he swigged the water.

"Aren't mercenaries supposed to take on jobs without asking their employer why?"

"Are you my employer now?"

"I'm paying you to pretend to be my husband for a month, aren't I?"

"It'd make more sense to me if you were paying me to kill your husband."

"Well, not all us Vernese have a pig farm handy," Tali said. She smiled at his careless chuckle. "If you have questions, ask them. I'll be honest."

Eulo leant against the wall where the shadows tipped off the angles of his face. He splayed his fingers on the table, drumming them against the wood. "Righto. It's obvious enough why most of these women are here. Why are you?"

So he wasn't willing to trust her by offering his own honesty in return. Tali swept up the water flask, tipped it into her dry mouth. Shame it wasn't rum. She rubbed the back of her hand across her lips.

"What do you think?"

"I reckon you need to hide your relations with another woman. You're too mad crazy for any Vernese man to have you," he said, "or you really like big white men."

Tali shook her head, watching his knuckles bunch. "What if I said I had a dirty job I needed you to do?"

"Then I'd say I'm the best man for the job. If I knew what you were up to." He leant closer, his gaze inescapable.

Blazes, she'd blundered straight into her own trap. A chill stalked her spine. Sometimes it wasn't only the new husbands who got fed to the pigs. Tali glanced away from his sudden intensity.

Eulo blew a deep breath out through his nose. "Righto then, I'll assume it was a drunken bet." He pushed forward on his hands to rise from the table.

"I didn't go to Port Garnet to buy a husband." Tali ran her thumbnail across a notch in the pale wood. "It was for a business transaction I did this morning. I bought passage on the *Seadancer* because it's considered the safest ship for women travelling alone. When some of the others told me why they were buying themselves husbands, I thought maybe I would, too."

"Just like that?" Eulo sank back onto the bench, his brow etched in disbelief.

"Just like that." She bit her lip, wishing she hadn't mentioned her business dealings. Her shoulder burnt under its dressings, but she resisted the urge to press a hand over it. She'd already inadvertently drawn Eulo's attention to it earlier when they'd jostled against each other above deck.

"It must be nice to have so much money you can buy someone when it suits you. Don't anyone in Vernesia bind for love?"

The vessel lurched, shuddering sideways and back. Tali flung her hands out to steady herself. Her knees collided with Eulo's under the table. She didn't move them away.

When they'd resettled, she said, "Love? You know Vernese society gives women a higher status than men?" Eulo nodded. "I'm firstborn, so I carry the burden of upholding the Sarsega name." She tangled her fingers together in her lap, every word bitter on her tongue. "My parents always planned for me to offer a binding to the son of a wealthy Vernese family. So, I'll be showing them there's a different way to secure our future." By picking who she tied a binding with, even if it meant destroying her reputation.

Eulo raised his eyebrows, his expression easing out of a scowl. "I don't reckon your parents will be too pleased to meet me." He twisted his head from side to side, cracking the tendons in his neck.

Tali rose from the table to squint out the porthole at the endless blue sky and water. She sucked in a breath of fresh salt air to steady her dizzy head.

"My father will be ropeable. My mother walked out on us nine years ago, after an argument about mustering cattle, so I doubt she'd care." She didn't bother mentioning how her father still blamed Tali and her aunt Cyska for insisting the saltwater muster had to be done that morning, causing her dissenting mother to leave in a huff and never come back.

"Your father brought you up?" Eulo said.

"Mema, my grandmother, raised my younger sister and me. When her mind wandered, I became head of the family." She twisted her plaits into a knot, fastening them with a silver pin. It chafed that the goddess could steal all Mema's knowledge instead of letting her pass it on to Tali. "I'm going above deck. I can barely breathe down here. They'll be serving lunch soon if you can stomach it."

Eulo shrugged his shirt on, hiding his tattoos but not his muscular physique. His big hand landed on Tali's shoulder. Her own half-healed tattoo should've burnt. Instead, its silver spirals and kilili curls cooed at his touch. She pressed her tongue to her top lip, disconcerted. Maybe her kilili was calling a connection to his binding ring—she couldn't find any other reason why the tiny auras would react to him.

"I'm not a learnt man," he said, "but I'll help you out as best I can."

In a heartbeat, he'd moved to open the cabin door, the warmth of his contact lingering on her skin. She watched him stagger down the passageway.

He had no idea what he'd gotten himself into.

# Chapter 4

The ocean stretched as far as Eulo could see, its relentless waves chopping into the *Seadancer's* hull, toying the ship with love pats, a small warning of what the water could do if the mood struck it. He gnawed on another lump of the bilah tuber Tali had given him, begging it to tame the lunch coagulating in his gut.

"Look there," she exclaimed, nudging him with her knee, unguarded for the first time since he'd met her. She sat forward on the narrow bench, pointing to a huge black object breaching the waves. Water spumed from its blowhole. A hemiwhale, probably worth ten thousand wings to a hunter.

Eulo smiled, fascinated by his new wife's crooked grin. Her astonishment reminded him of his brother, when Remmy was a little tacker discovering something new. He rubbed his thumb along the blemished skin on his left hand, unable to recall a job he'd taken that didn't involve spilling blood. Still, it didn't sound like the Sarsega family would be too happy to meet him, and sometimes families fought worse than anyone. He clamped his hands into his armpits. It'd be stupid not to use his time on the ship to learn about the battlefield he'd be walking into.

"Tell me about Vernesia, Tali."

"Do you know much about it?" She turned her catlike gaze on him.

"It's an oasis with lots of rain, run by beautiful, iron-fisted women with lots of goods to trade and lots of money."

She smiled. "I guess." She stretched her legs out, tapping the scuffed toes of her boots together. "The Kestrine's Five Feathers, her council, is made up of women called Loresses, with a few men in high-ranking advisory positions. They're all elected by the people to help reduce corruption."

"That's something Iskarlia could learn a few lessons about," Eulo grunted. It'd be hard to find a leader more crooked and sly than Cove Vasker, for sure. The last worry on the self-proclaimed warlord's mind was his poverty-stricken people. So long as money kept trickling into Jarrison Bay, the bastard didn't give a toss about the drought-ravaged outposts.

To come within a wrinkle of finding enough kilili, Eulo needed to know if the dealers were as cut-throat as Iskarlian Scabmen. "They reckon there ain't much crime in your land," he said in an offhand drawl.

"There are crooks and thieves from the bottom all the way up. Perhaps not as openly as in Iskarlia," Tali laughed. "Why? Are you thinking about joining them?"

"Not bloody likely." Joining them, no. Finding them, however, was a different matter entirely. A thought struck Eulo. "I mean, not 'less I already have?" He gave her a pointed look.

Tali clicked her fingers. "Oh no, you got me." She rolled her eyes at the wake driving up in the water behind the vessel. "Sarsega is a good name in Vernesia. Our integrity is essential for trade."

"Trade?"

"Cattle and horses grow well in mild summers and cold winters."

"Not like Iskarlia. Rum and rogues grow best in hot summers and hot winters." He rested his hands on his knees. "Everyone in the Opalline speaks Vernese, but you learnt Iskarlian. Why?"

"My two favourite people taught me when I was little. It's good for business," Tali said. She rolled her shoulders back. "You know what? For all your tough talk, I think you're after a better life, same as your countrymen here." She waved a hand around, gesturing to their fellow passengers.

Eulo squinted at a cracked board in the deck. He liked how forward she was. Shame he couldn't offer her the same honesty. Too many times he'd seen how truth didn't stop a man's throat being slit, or a knife sunken to its hilt in his ribcage. Tali would have no idea what it was like to live with someone's next pay wagered on your lifeblood. He almost envied her naivety as he spun the greensilver band on his finger. Still, if she wanted him to upset her father, he'd do it. It was what he'd been paid for.

Chatter and laughter echoed through the mess, sounds that should've been warm and comforting. Eulo scraped the last spoonful of sago porridge out of his bowl, hunching over his meal, hoping it would stay in his belly. Even the beer mug beside his hand shone silver. Fussy, fancy details for the new couples' first dinner together. Finishing, he flattened his shoulders against the timbers behind him. Tali chattered across the table to Kardia Riole, while the scarred girl's husband sat on her other side, talking to another Iskarlian man. No one spoke to Eulo, which suited him fine.

Men and women lined the long rows of tables and benches, leaving barely an empty seat in the room. A couple of groups didn't seem to suffer any seasickness, judging by the speed they swigged down kegs of ale. The husband-strangler sat with her legs around one man's waist, while another fondled her breasts through her unbuttoned dress. Her husband's hands were full of someone else's wife.

Tali didn't pay any attention to the near-orgy going on down the way. Then again, she wasn't much interested in Eulo, either. He lurched to his feet, the abrupt movement causing Tali and Kardia to stare at him.

"I'm going to our cabin," he said.

"Alright," Tali said, without reacting to his gruff tone. "I'll head up to get some air while the sun sets."

Inside the cabin, Eulo faltered to a stop, dragging a hand down his stubbled cheeks, alone in the thick, stale air, listening to the neighbours. Again. He kicked his pack. Women liked him—they always had—so why didn't Tali? He snatched up the water flask. Warm water met his tongue. He spat it out, spraying the wall. No sense making himself sick again. He'd go find a fresh barrel where he could refill the flask. Gripping it in one hand, he headed out the door. He'd find Tali while he was at it, too.

He'd watched boats from the solid Iskarlian coastline skimming the water in serene harmony, flimsy crafts defying the ocean's might, but the *Seadancer's* passageway lurched under Eulo's feet, its timbers groaning in chorus with his guts. Fuck knew how sailors lived in the cloying darkness below deck, swaying around their days on the water's relentless roll.

The ship's shadows drifted with their own cadence too, black ghosts morphing and whispering around the corners and doorways. One drew away from the darkness cloaking the foot of the stairs. It approached Eulo with tresses and skirts flowing behind.

"I've been watching you ever since I saw you in Port Garnet." The woman's breath tickled Eulo's throat, her breasts pressing against his arm. "I'll pay good coin for you." Her hand slid down to his groin, rubbing, rubbing.

"No." He pushed her off in a gauze of floral scent and skirts, slapping back her groping hands as he charged on through the passageway gloom.

The ship bounced from one wave to the next, worse than earlier. He steadied himself on the stairs, his boots clunking onto the upper deck. His guts grumbled, tamed only by the bilah root.

Sunset sprayed the clouds pink and yellow, glittering along the water to silhouette a slender figure against the far rail. Her chin was lifted, her long hair streaming out on the wind. Behind her, the shadows moved, becoming a man with scraggy ginger stubble, creeping up on her.

Krike.

Eulo's nerves, lust and bruised ego merged into a flare of anger, warming his veins with familiar, comforting power. He sprang across the deck, a growl rumbling in his chest as he collided with the man he'd once called friend. Unprepared, the big goon fell face-down. Eulo landed on top of him, punching one fist against his jaw, then the other. Krike flipped his elbow, jolting blackness into Eulo's left eye. He bucked, the surge of his twisting body knocking Eulo aside. Krike rained blows on him, his strength compensating for his blundering style.

A woman's hysteria pierced the dullness smothering Eulo's head. A fresh wave of adrenaline flooded his veins. He'd been waiting a long time for this chance.

He head-butted Krike, crunching the bigger man's nose into his face. That caused more screaming, but not from Tali, or Krike. Eulo's muscles bunched and flowed into each clout. He'd break the rest of the maggot's face, too, smash him to a pulp.

Water rained down, burning Eulo's eyes and lips. Both men gasped, sliding and twitching on the deck like netted fish in a puddle of saltwater.

"Oh, my love." Krike's wife slipped as she ran over. Arms flailing, she crashed onto Krike, knocking his breath out better than any of Eulo's efforts had.

"I wouldn't fucking laugh if I were you," Tali said, cutting through Eulo's amusement. She loomed over him where he sat on the deck, her feet planted apart, the water bucket still hanging from her hand.

"You ruffian, you'll pay for this," Krike's wife shrieked at Eulo. She sat with her thick legs splayed, nestling Krike's head in the drenched skirts on her lap.

Eulo couldn't tell if the big man lay prone because of the blows to his head and body, or because of his wife's unrelenting hold.

"Don't," Tali hissed, jabbing her toe into his thigh, crushing the retort on his tongue and the laughter bubbling into his chest.

He sobered. Laying about was never a good position to be in a fight. He sprang to his feet, his clothes dripping onto the planking. It'd been one of the strangest bloody tussles he'd ever started.

Krike moaned, clapping his hands over his nose while his wife stroked his forehead. Then she screamed for the captain.

*Drip. Drip.*
A wet patch spread under the table, darkening the Iskarlian starwood floor. Hard as iron—a perfect wood for shipbuilding. And for making cabins to hold rebellious husbands. Eulo sank his head into his hands, beside the wet pants slung over the edge of the table. They'd been his better pair before his angry wife broke up the scuffle with Krike. After she'd banished him to their cabin, he'd pulled on another pair, deciding it wasn't worth stirring Tali even more by waiting stark naked for her return.

When she burst in, shoving the door back so hard it slammed into the wall, she didn't even glance in Eulo's direction. Peeling off her shirt, she squeezed past the table. At the basin under the window, she washed her face, quick and brisk, with her back to him. Eulo stared at the alluring curve of her ribs and hips, the chain looped around her waist—greensilver like the band she'd put on his finger. Tali held his identity papers *and* kilili; the very treasure he was hunting. His pulse quickened. Maybe he'd find what he needed in Vernesia more easily than he'd first reckoned.

When she lifted her arms to pull on a clean shirt, he glimpsed a bandage around her right shoulder. The shirt drifted down, hiding her brown skin, the bandage, and the chain.

"Filia Tartula wanted to have you charged with attempted murder," she said. "Lucky for you, her stupid husband's skull is as hard as sandstone."

"Lucky for him—"

"No, Eulo. Do you have any idea what I've done for you? What I paid the captain so he wouldn't arrest you?" She planted her hands on her hips.

Heat traced his veins again. "What did he make you do?"

"I hired you as a husband, not a guardian. I'm not going to hand out money whenever you behave like a lunatic."

Eulo blinked.

Tali slapped the table with both hands. "If you fuck up enough, you'll be deported straight back to Iskarlia without even getting into Vernesia. And I won't see a single splinter of my money again." She scowled at him, her eyes burning with fire and fury. "Nor are you any use to me in a prison cell."

His chest lifted with a deep breath. He'd be no use to anyone else, either. He struggled to hold his anger. "I'm sorry. I don't know how to do this."

"I can tell." She closed her eyes. "I made a mistake picking you, didn't I?"

"I'm a mercenary. I fight and I fuck," he drawled, wanting to shock her, to see how far he could push her.

Tali pinched her nose with a forefinger and thumb, as though to veil her anger and disdain. Turning around, she unbuttoned her pants with long fingers. "While you're with me, you don't fight. We've already talked about the fucking." She kicked the pants off, tugging the shirt down over her thighs as she stomped to the bed. Flinging the covers aside, she climbed in, shrugging her way across to the wall with her back turned on him.

For a moment, uncertainty pulsed under Eulo's jaw. He dropped his pants and stepped out of them. He extinguished the oil lantern hanging above the table, pitching the cabin into darkness. Tali didn't move when he eased in beside her. His left arm hung out of the narrow bed, the right one as close to his overseer as he dared, without touching her. Muttering, he rolled onto his right side. The image of a greensilver chain around a toned waist tugged at his mind. His groin stirred. Prodded her.

"Roll the other way, mercenary," Tali said.

Eulo flipped over, dragging the blankets with him, sprawling across as much bed as he could. Next door, the thumping started again, building in tempo with the neighbour's moaning. Tali's back trembled against Eulo's. He cursed under his breath. Kind-hearted wretch he was, he'd made her cry. Guilt punched him in the guts. As he opened his mouth to ask if she was alright, she snorted, an explosive sound that ripped apart the tension in the cabin. She dissolved into huge brays of laughter.

"Shades, woman, did you just drop your guts on me?" Tentative, Eulo sniffed the air. "You wouldn't, would you?"

That set her off into a fresh wave of hysterics, pure and unrestrained, the best sound he'd heard since she'd proposed their binding. He smirked at the dark cabin overhead.

A shriek of ecstasy interrupted Tali's chuckle, the neighbours drowning out the beautiful madwoman beside him. Eulo burst out laughing. When both they and the neighbours subsided into composure, he edged across the cabin to retrieve his water flask. He dove under the bedsheet, relishing its soft warmth against his goose-pricked skin. Drinking deep, he passed the flask to Tali when she sat up beside him.

"Alright?" she asked.

"Enough," Eulo said, even if he still had no idea how to handle her. He took the flask from her outstretched hand, dropping it beside the bed. They resettled under the covers, resuming their back-to-back standoff, although Tali wriggled in against him. His skin drew tight with arousal, too conscious of every place her hair and body touched his own.

"Enough?" she repeated, her words thick with sleep.

"To agree you made a mistake," he said softly.

Her only response was a throaty snore.

# Chapter 5

The *Seadancer* crested and raced each breaker on its path to Vernesia, rocking and rolling Tali in the bunk. Her guts shifted in nausea-swirling discord with her body. It was time to swallow the remaining nub of bilah root, just enough to get her home. She stretched her leg out, striking nothing until her toes breached the blanket's hem.

No Eulo.

She wriggled over, opening her eyes a crack. He sat at the table, studying what must've been her dog-eared map. Bare-footed, bare-chested, at ease. Tali widened her eyes, taking in a clear view of the curling symbols inked on him: a fishhook, a circle of fire over his heart, a sharp-winged bird soaring across his collarbones, and three others she didn't recognise, stretching right down past the muscles on his abdomen.

"You want to come touch them?" he said, slow and deep, without looking at her.

She did, but instead she said, "You're not very good when you don't get your own way, eh?"

"We can't all afford to buy our way out of trouble."

Tali rolled over to blink at the rows of planks overhead, all jammed and hammered into place like good Vernese daughters. Eulo, the idiot, still had no idea how hard she'd fought to save his arse last night, or how much money she'd handed over to stop him getting arrested. She blew a deep sigh out her nose. Let him think she was rich and spoilt if he wanted. He'd work it out for himself once they got home to Glimmers Gap.

She rubbed her shoulder, wincing at the cloth grazing over raw flesh. It'd been her own fault, harvesting the kilili too far from the full moon. She'd had to, though, to finish making the flickerblades she'd sold in Port Garnet. As her grandmother used to say, gifts always came with a cost.

"I've been looking at this map," Eulo said, "trying to guess which part of Vernesia we're heading to."

He glanced at her. She got out of bed, padding across to retrieve her pants, conscious of his gaze following her. When she stood beside the table, fully dressed, Eulo slid the map across to where they could both look at it. Tali tapped a broken fingernail onto a stretch of ocean off the south-east Vernese coast.

"We should be about here. The helmsman told me we'd be able to see land this morning."

"Good."

"We'll sail up the coast to the capital, Silveraine. My horses are stabled there." Hers was, at least. Getting Flame back for her unplanned husband might be a little harder.

"Horses?"

"I'll teach you to ride. Flame's an excellent horse. I bred and trained him myself."

"You reckon I'm lower than a desert dog, don't you?"

"What?" Tali bit her lip. Most Iskarlians couldn't afford to own horses.

"I done an apprenticeship for a hunter, spending every day with his bitch mares. I'll get by with your nags."

Nags? Tali shifted away from him, reeling in her disappointment. It shouldn't matter if Eulo didn't share her passion for the animals.

For a long moment, neither one of them spoke, until he said, "Where do we go on these flash steeds?"

"From Silveraine," she said, dragging her finger down the inked lines, "south to Oyster Point, where we'll overnight before we head over here to Glimmers Gap." She tapped a blank expanse where the Sarsega estate sprawled along the tail of the Starsfall Ranges.

"Don't people like it there?"

"I like it fine," Tali said.

"Most of the towns and cities are in the north, yeah?" He pointed to the dots radiating away from Silveraine along the north-east coastline.

Her lips twisted. "It's warmer there, and Silveraine is the main trade port." She hesitated, expecting him to give some scathing reply about knowing the capital's significance. When he didn't, she continued, "Vernesia is a strong country, despite the unease between north and south. Us southerners believe in the simple ways of working hard and honouring the goddess. The northerners can easily sell their harvests because of their proximity to Silveraine, so their values have changed." She fell silent, doubting Eulo cared about local politics.

"And the Kestrine cares more about her own money and pleasures than her people's?"

Tali lowered her voice. "Sovann is inexperienced and takes advice from the wrong people. But it would be stupid for us to say so too loudly, and especially not in Silveraine or on a ship full of Vernese dignitines."

"Dignitine? Is that what you're called?" His broad Iskarlian twang mangled the word.

"They are; I'm just a southern savage," Tali laughed. She swatted the back of her hand against his taut belly. "Come on, mercenary, let's go get some breakfast before the rest of this lot wakes up."

Down in the mess, Tali was relieved to see Krike and Filia Tartula weren't among the diners. Their fellow passengers spoke in low tones, demure compared to the previous evening's revelry. Eulo strode past rows of empty seats to choose a table in the darkest corner.

"One with some ambience, hmm?" she said.

"Ambi-what?" Eulo propped himself against the wall. Unyielding.

Tali set her bowl down and climbed onto the bench opposite, so he could watch the room beyond her. Everywhere he went, he tracked their surroundings, ever-watchful, ever-suspicious. Of what, though? She dipped a spoon into the bowl, swirling honey through the pale pudding.

Eulo chomped into a piece of bacon, his teeth clicking and grinding without finesse. He furrowed his brow at Tali. "If you want some, you ought've gotten it while we were at the servery." Another tearing bite, with no offer to share.

"I'm happy with what I've got, thanks," Tali said. She scooped pudding into her mouth, questioning her decision to take this man home. No doubt her sister Vivi would become a meddler. And Ranson? Her father would be furious. She might as well enjoy the break from her family while she still could; they'd cause trouble for her soon enough.

"Do you know much about my people, Eulo?"

He glanced at her, jaws ruthless on his food. "Some of you like to fight, and a lot like to fuck," he replied, so straight-faced Tali couldn't tell if he was joking. His goading mood was bad enough without such comments.

She kicked the table leg, wishing it was his shin. The motion caused pudding to slop off her spoon onto her red shirt. Cursing, she used her spoon to scrape food off the cloth. Eulo wasn't the only one lacking refinement.

He grinned at her and said, "A place that worships women sounds alright to me."

Teasing, or indulging her? "I thought you might find it easier to adjust if you understood our culture better."

"I'd be a bad mercenary if I didn't."

An iron streak flashed through his eyes as he spoke, not quite the response Tali expected from a man looking for a better life—more of a man with a job to do, and not the one she'd paid him for.

"I reckon your goddess Lolani used up all the beauty and equality making Vernesia," he shrugged, "so she had none left when it came to Iskarlia. Left us in Mako's mad hands."

"If Lolani had anyone chewed up, it was Mako." Tali scraped carefully at the traces of pudding clinging to her bowl. Every Vernese knew the legend of the goddess triumphing over the demon.

Eulo laughed a hard, humourless bark. "Better hope you don't spend time in Iskarlia again, or you might find out otherwise."

Tali licked her spoon clean. "Do you believe everyone in Vernesia swims in money? We don't get poor, or sick?" she asked. "Surely it'd be worse living in poverty in a stinking gutter while the rich pass you by like you're not even there."

"Bit like Iskarlia and Vernesia, yeah? Is that why you're here—because gold-hearted Tali Sarsega don't walk by? You reckon you help people, don't you, like tying a binding with a poor, downtrodden Iskarlian so you can show him off to your friends, and stir up Mummy and Daddy?" Eulo shook his head. He shovelled pudding into his mouth.

Tali sprang to her feet, stung by his callous words even though he knew her mother had deserted her. She slid off the binding ring she'd whispered and wheedled into shape, the cause of the pain stabbing her right shoulder. "Sort out your own affairs in Silveraine." She slapped the ring onto the table. "Sell them. You'll have enough to last you a whole year before you need to take death money off anyone again."

He gaped at her, spoon halfway to his mouth. She swung her leg over the bench to make her final exit.

Except she didn't.

Her bootlace caught on a bolt hidden under the edge of the seat. She pitched sideways, sprawling across the floor with her leg hung up. Agony screamed through her back.

"Miss?" One of the crew hurried over. He cast a horrified glance at Eulo, who hadn't moved to help her, just sat there grinning over his meal.

"She's alright," he told the man. "Aren't you, darl? Had too much to drink last night, she did. Now she's sick."

"Uh..." The man glanced at Tali as she contorted up to untie her boot. The storm on her face must've said enough because he ducked his head and scampered off. Eulo loosed deep, rich chuckles.

Tali scrambled up, panting, her cheeks burning. "In this together, are we? Or only when you thought you had half a chance of getting your leg over?"

"The trick is to get it high enough," Eulo winked. When she spun to leave, he said, "Wait Tali, please."

*Please?* His beseeching tone made her waver.

On his feet now, he offered her his hand, outstretched past their breakfast bowls. Her ring glimmered in his palm, silver and pale green in the low light. "Come on," he beckoned to her, all charm and handsome smiles again. "Let's go watch Vernesia from the deck, so I can see it before I do what I need to do there."

Her mouth went dry. "What exactly would that be?" She shifted from one foot to the other. An ache throbbed in her right calf, promising a bruise.

His amusement faltered, like he'd said more than he'd intended. Tali shook her head, doubting he'd tell her the truth anyway. Eulo rolled her binding ring between his forefinger and thumb, studying the light through it. He flicked it with his thumbnail, watched it flip through the air. "The job I been paid for." He caught the ring and dropped his hand to the table, where the greensilver chimed against the wood.

"Then do it without being such a bastard," Tali said. "I don't need you enough to tolerate your rude shit, Eulo, and whatever your reasons, I'm not going to spend the rest of this voyage with you, let alone a whole month, if you can't muster some manners. No matter what you've assumed, most women on this ship aren't naive and desperate." She leant closer to whisper, "The husband-strangler has already offered me twice what I paid for you, and I'm half-inclined to let her have you."

He rubbed the disfigurements on his left hand. "I don't believe you." But his brash edge was gone.

Tali gave him a long, stony look. She swept up the ring. "I don't care."

Despite her anger at her new husband, Tali's heart soared when they climbed out into the overcast morning. The tedious ocean had at last found its end at the foot of dolerite cliffs which stretched two hundred paces above the water. Dark waves battered the rock in an ancient battle lost by neither land nor sea, only the occasional boat which ended up shattered beneath the surface.

Eulo whistled at the sheer wall. "Not much chance of invading from here, is there?"

"Is that what you're doing?" Tali raised an eyebrow at him, sobering when she glimpsed Krike further along the deck. The red-haired man smirked at her, licking his top lip in a deliberate motion. Ignoring her better judgement, she caught Eulo's shirtfront in her fist, using it to pull herself onto tiptoes. His eyes widened as she kissed him full on the mouth. He nestled her into his chest, his tongue soft, cautious. Bolder. Tali's heart galloped against her ribs. Blazes, look at her now, being intimate with this brash man, caught in his scent of musk and spice.

Conflicted, she pulled away. Eulo tilted his head, tipping his gaze at a now-scowling Krike. So, he was more observant than Tali expected. She tasted salt on her tongue, wanted more.

Eulo's lips brushed her ear. "Me and you are in this together, Tali Sarsega."

She stared at the passing coastline, hoping she could trust his alliance. A brisk wind caught the ship's sails, scooting them closer to Silveraine. Cliffs blurred past, iron-grey against the deep blue sky. The colours of Vernesia took Tali's breath away, so rich and vivid after Iskarlia's sun-bleached stretches. Gannets and shearwaters soared above with wings outstretched. One by one they'd drop, spearing into the water, then emerging, victorious, with fish shimmering silver in their beaks.

The ship angled into a wave, its oblique slap showering the deck with saltwater. Tali dipped her head against the stinging droplets. In her eagerness to see land, she'd left her coat behind in the cabin. Rubbing her palms together, she lingered on the unfamiliar feel of the binding ring on her finger. Goosebumps prickled her arms, not altogether from the wind shearing off the water. She glanced at Eulo's big hands, where scars cobwebbed his golden skin. She'd heard the weight of the steel in his bag when he'd moved it in the cabin. What sort of hunter earnt scars like those?

# Chapter 6

Rude, cocky bastard. Eulo fired a gob of spit into the water stretching from the ship's hull towards the endless cliffs. He tapped his foot against the planks, unsure what to make of his blue with Tali. She'd left with an excuse to go down to their cabin, so maybe she did hope for more from him than he'd offered. Tali didn't seem the sort to expect him to follow, begging her forgiveness, and she didn't shy from being honest. Yet here he was, goading her to the point where she wanted to palm him off to some lunatic.

No one made Eulo Juke nervous. No one except for the young woman he'd tied a binding with. He studied the ring on his finger. If what Tali said was true, it'd go a long way toward paying his debt to the Scabmen. It alone could've paid for his passage ten times over, and she'd offered him *two* of them. But passage to Vernesia, or anywhere else, was pointless without entry papers. Papers that Eulo had only gotten by selling himself into a binding, like every other Iskarlian on the ship. The very papers he would've taken from Tali's bag, if she'd been naïve enough to leave them there.

Around him, his fellow Iskarlians took in their first glimpse of Vernesia, watched over by these women who snorted when they laughed, who reduced their new husbands to meat and muscle. Women who'd never have to go hungry, or beg or steal, or sleep in fear, or sell their body or have it stolen. Dark, familiar anger pooled in his heart. His frustration, the rage and regret about his troubles with the Scabmen, pulsed outward at these women and all they represented. He braced himself, ignoring the splinters digging into his palms.

"Mr Sarsega?"

Eulo almost didn't realise the lisping woman had spoken to him. Kardia Riole steadied herself on the rail, positioning her scarred cheek to the far side, apparently giving up on trying to tame her hair over it in the strong wind.

"Eulo will do. I don't reckon I'll ever get used to being called someone else's name," he said.

"Where's Tali? I'm surprised you've let each other out of sight."

"She went to get her coat." What felt like an aeon ago.

"Well, tell her you'll both have to visit my estate in Oyster Bay someday. It's not far from the Sarsega's property."

"Righto," Eulo said, distracted. His real adventure would begin when the voyage ended, bringing him one step closer to redemption, and revenge.

"She's true-hearted, Tali, and I can't say that of many people I know," Kardia said. "Kind people are always the ones who get hurt the worst, though." She paused, her hazel eyes piercing. "Don't let her get hurt, will you, Eulo?"

Eulo marched along the decks searching for Tali. All he'd found in their cabin was a breeze sweeping through the open porthole, disturbing the map on the table. The rumpled bedsheets lay empty. As much as it galled him, it'd serve him right if he'd pushed Tali so far she'd ended up with another man. Of all the places to be, though, he found her standing at the helm. Eulo hung back, watching her whoop and laugh, spinning the wheel under the helmsman's eye. She relinquished her control to the sailor, grinning as she drifted across to Eulo. Her red shirt contrasted with the darkness of her skin and the black hair escaping out of its plait.

They rambled down the deck, sidestepping ropes and sailors with an effortless unity. Plenty of the crew greeted Tali by name, nodding acknowledgement to Eulo as though he'd earnt their approval by association. No other Vernese spoke to the crew, despite Tali saying some women had taken lovers on the outward voyage. She might've been one of them, for all he knew.

A projectile flew into Eulo's vision from his right side, something solid, blue-black and the size of a cat, heading straight for Tali. His fighting senses woken, he leapt towards his wife, yanking her out of the way. He pressed her against the wall, shielding her with his body. The projectile hit the timber two paces away, flicking drops of water as it fell to the deck. Before Eulo could figure out what it was, another one struck. Then two more to his left. One slammed into his back, knocking the breath from his lungs. Nearby, someone screamed.

"We're under attack," he shouted. Another missile collided with his boot.

Tali shivered in his arms. Mako's teeth, she was laughing again.

"You're mad as a cut snake," he said in disbelief.

She grinned at him, her hair tickling his throat as she stood on her tiptoes to shout into his ear, "Fish."

"What?" He flinched as three more objects careened into the wall beside them. He had to get her out of there.

"Fish," she repeated, placing the flat of her hand against his cheek to guide his gaze down.

She was right. Huge fish flopped around on the deck, their scales brilliant in the sunshine. Eulo had never seen anything like these creatures thrashing near his boots, fins splayed open. A fine web of skin sprouted from either side of their bodies.

"They're called flyers," Tali said. "Don't let them bite you." She ducked under Eulo's arm and scooped up the nearest animal, dumping it overboard in one swift movement. She reached for another, its serrated jaws opening and closing as it fought for breath.

Tali danced along the deck, rescuing one fish after another. Dozens of the animals shot out of the waves, flying a good thirty paces and splashing back down beside the ship's hull. A new fish landed with a thump between Eulo's boots. He gripped it around the base of its tail, holding tight when it twisted in his hands, its open mouth full of spiked teeth. He flung it out to the water, the sun muted through its bright blue wings.

When they'd thrown all the creatures back, Eulo stood beside Tali, watching the flurry of wings and shimmering scales fall behind the ship. Her cheeks curled with that lopsided grin, her eyes bright with excitement.

"It's good luck to touch a blue flyer," a gruff voice said; it was one of the older sailors, come to join them.

"So why were we the only goons doing it?" Eulo said. The crew had all stood aside, laughing and cheering as he and Tali scrambled over the deck after the strange animals.

The sailor surveyed him through half-lidded eyes. "'Cause they weren't coming to us. They chose youse."

"Chose us?"

"The Vernese believe Goddess Lolani is of the sky, and the birds are her chosen." Tali gestured to where the fish frenzy became smaller and smaller in the distance. "The sea and sky are brought together by the fish with wings."

"Luck, eh?" Eulo rubbed at a patch of the scales on his palm. Black and dark blue, the same colours he guessed his spine would be, where two of the flying fish had collided with him.

The sailor caught Eulo's wrist. He coaxed loose one perfect cobalt scale with the tip of his little finger. "Luck indeed. I'll give this to me daughter." He walked on, whistling.

"On the burnt lands, there's no way we'd have chucked those fish back," Eulo said to Tali.

"It's bad luck to eat a sacred animal."

"Worse luck to starve 'cause you're precious about old stories. Some of the places I've been, you eat what you're given even when you don't know what it is, and you be bloody grateful to have anything on your plate at all," he said. He stuck his hand in his pocket, wiping the rest of the scales safely into the cloth.

"You won't starve at my home."

Eulo spread his arms wide, stretching out his shoulders. The muscles tugged in protest. He'd have to do his exercises tonight, to stay fit and flexible, and remind him he wasn't really in a better pasture.

He frowned as Tali resumed her watch on the coastline, her expression bland. The ironclad part of Eulo argued he'd be better off pinching his papers from her and slipping into Silveraine by himself. He liked this fish-rescuing girl though, even if she reckoned she'd rescued *him*, a poor savage facing certain death on the Iskarlian plains. Not Eulo. He'd be gone when the month was up, when he'd figured where to fill his pack full of kilili to take home to the Scabmen.

The sheer cliffs subsided into emerald green pastures dotted with vines which grew world famous Vernese wine grapes. Pastures sloped to white beaches where aqua waves fondled the sand, a world at peace with itself. Plenty more ships and fishing vessels shared the water here, too. As youngsters, Eulo and his best mate Speer had sat on the wind-scoured dunes above southern Iskarlia, dreaming of sneaking onto a trader and leaving their hard childhood behind for the riches across the Opalline. Eulo's guts somersaulted. He'd finally done it.

The helmsman set the *Seadancer* scudding through Silverlip Heads, the rocky outcrops guarding the entrance to Silveraine. Passengers crowded the deck now; wives happy to return, husbands eyeing their new country with either caution or cheer. Eulo reckoned the lot of them would be glad to escape the suffocating closeness of the ship. He squinted at the whitewashed stone buildings above what Tali had called Iluka Bay, their vivid red and blue rooftops splashed through the trees.

Tali brushed her fingertips over the back of his hand, reminding him she was there.

"Happy to be home?" he asked.

"This isn't my home. Not yet."

Silveraine's streets stretched along the escarpment, the lines of elegant domed houses impressive compared to the random sprawl of Iskarlian towns. A statue of Goddess Lolani looked down from a hilltop above the city, her long hair and dress rippling around her, arms outstretched to her people. Some passengers made a tribute to the statue, including Tali, who dipped her head for a moment in unspoken entreaty. Eulo studied Lolani's smooth stone cheeks, willing her to let him finish this job quickly.

The sailors scrambled in the rigging high above, readying the *Seadancer* to dock. Excitement buzzed through the passengers as the ship slid past other vessels in the bay to come alongside the pier. Striking land unsettled Eulo as much as taking to the seas in the first place. Men threw thick coils of rope across to hitch the ship to the pier, before a gangplank was lowered.

Tali gripped Eulo's hand as the eager passengers pressed forward in a rush to disembark. He tottered down the gangplank onto the waterfront, struggling to adjust to the sudden loss of motion under his feet.

"Don't reckon I'll rush onto another boat again," he muttered, glad to leave the ocean to the fishermen and Vernese husband-hunters. He let go of Tali's hand to shift his pack from one shoulder to the other.

"Don't you want to return to Iskarlia one day?" Tali looked at him, surprised.

"I don't know," Eulo said. Now he knew what a golden land he'd come to, maybe he and Remmy could both live here. It had to be better than trying to scratch out a living on the Potch Plains, where money only went to the tyrants whose labourers struck it lucky in the gemfields.

Bodies surged against him, pushing him a six-step sideways. He snarled, resentful of the people all squashed in together with no room to move. When the squeeze eased off his ribcage, he scanned the black-haired crowd. Where was Tali? Even towering over everyone, he couldn't pick her out.

Eulo staggered backwards, overwhelmed to be caught in the relentless chatter of the crowd, smothered by the stench of unwashed bodies and strong perfume on the saltwater breeze. Were there Scabmen here, watching him, waiting? He reckoned they'd have at least one spy on the waterfront to see who came and went.

"Get out of my way, you filth-caked lout," a woman shrieked behind Eulo.

Someone elbowed him in the ribs, trying to force him aside. He turned slowly, baring his teeth. The woman lounged on a litter carried on the shoulders of four solid Iskarlians, preceded by a set of gold-uniformed escorts. Eulo braced himself, noting how the unruly masses parted to let the harpy through. Almost. One old codger didn't move fast enough, so the golden goons swept into him, flinging him out of their way like a leaf in a whirly-whirly. He rolled onto the stone pier, sprawling on his back while the crowd stepped over and around him.

With a growl, Eulo barged his way over. He offered his hand to the beggar, who peered at him through milky eyes. Eulo hoisted him upright, together with the reek of his grimy body.

'Blessed, blessed,' the man gabbled, his mouth a circle of toothless gums in a grime-greyed beard.

"Best keep out of the bitch's way next time, eh?" Eulo said, extracting himself from the beggar's clutching hands. His day wouldn't improve if the old wretch pinched his last handful of coins.

"She shines on you. Her luck, my friend." The beggar held his arms out like wings.

Eulo dug one of the remnant blue flyer scales out of his pocket and offered it to the man. "Here, I reckon you need it more than me," he said. The beggar lurched back, his eyes rolling white.

"No, oh no. You have it all wrong. The only luck you'll get from a black scale is bad. Very bad."

Eulo cast another glance over the mob. Still no sign of Tali. Maybe the beggar was right, but when he turned back, the old man had disappeared. He frowned at the scale on his fingertip, like a disc of haematite. Surely someone somewhere would buy it. He brushed it back into his pocket.

Tali would be itching to get her precious ponies and trot home to the Sarsega estate. He scratched his cheek. This was his chance to walk away, to scarper into the melee and go searching for kilili without having to wait for his pact with Tali to end. He glanced around.

From here, the only way into the city was to join a long line of people and carts waiting to pass through a gated checkpoint, where two women clad in purple officials' vests viewed papers under the watchful eye of a dozen Goshawk guards. The Goshawks weren't just there for show, either; they sauntered up and down the line, eyeballing people and searching the carts. A curved blade hung from each guard's belt.

"Hey." The shouting and ruckus of the waterfront continued behind him. "Hey!" Louder now, together with a prod in Eulo's side.

"What in shades is it with you people?" Eulo said, glaring at the purple-clad soldier behind him, barely old enough to shave but standing there slapping a truncheon against one palm, his face twisted in disgust. Eulo sighed. What now?

"You bin reported for unruliness." Purple bounced the tip of the truncheon against Eulo's chest.

"Me? Why don't you go talk to the slave-squashing bitch up there about shoving people around?" He flung a hand in the direction of the golden debacle, which continued to force its way to the front of the gate.

"Swine." The soldier smacked his truncheon across Eulo's bicep. "You don't speak that way about a Loress."

Eulo's brow furrowed. He stared down at the self-righteous little grub. "Touch me again and I'll show you just how dirty I get."

"Show me your papers. Now." Purple held out his hand. He didn't lower the truncheon, apparently confident his status outweighed the Iskarlian's size.

"Papers," Eulo repeated. His card of entry into Vernesia, his permission to be here.

The papers in Tali's safekeeping.

"Trying to sneak past the border, hmm?" Purple hawked back and spat in Eulo's face.

Eulo drew his right arm up, curling his hand into a fist. Saliva dribbled down his cheek. Slender fingers slid across his inner elbow, catching his urge to slam his knuckles into Purple's nose.

"There you are. I thought you'd gone without me." Tali's greeting honeyed Eulo's ears. Worry pinched the corners of her smile. She held out a packet to Purple. "This is my husband's card of entry."

Purple snatched it from her. A red sheen coloured his face as he read the two pages. Tali waited in front of him, tapping the fingers of one hand against her other elbow.

Eulo used his shirt-tail to wipe the gob of muck off his face. If they'd been in Iskarlia, he'd have left the grub with a broken arm.

Purple stuffed the papers into their packet. He sneered at Tali, lips curling off his broken teeth. "It's ridiculous, you rich cows on your wifeships, bringing this filth into our cities."

"Isn't it, when we could have our pick of local charmers like you." She extracted the packet out of Purple's hand, fixing him in a stare granite enough to make him shuffle like he'd shit his pants. Dipping her head towards the mass of people pressing to get through the gate, she said, "I suggest you get us to the front of the line, to make amends for the insult of spitting on my husband." She stepped to the side, turning her palm up to him. "Unless, of course, you'd rather I let him sort it out with you." She smiled, shocking Eulo with her hard, cold expression. "Shall I go ask the other wives and the Loress to put a wager on who'd win?"

With his face frozen in a rictus of contempt, Purple escorted them between the wall and crush of bodies to wait in line behind the Loress's entourage. He barged past on his way to leave, only to rebound off into a group of unimpressed older women when Eulo swatted him aside.

Tali shook her head, curling one side of her mouth. "Krike was right about you, wasn't he? Trouble follows you like a smitten woman."

A shadow fell over Eulo's volatile mood. What else had Krike said? "You oughtn't listen to any drivel coming out of his gob."

"I've already worked that one out for myself. You really don't like each other, do you?"

He didn't reply. Above the crush, the Loress fanned herself, looking beyond the wall rather than at the people jammed into the narrow space below her pallet.

Eulo said to Tali, "Once you collect yourself a few more Iskarlians, you can ride around like that too."

"Three more of you would be enough to send me mad. Anyway, only Kestrine Sovann's advisors become Loresses. Luczia, up there, is the Vernese treasurer."

Tali dropped her pack off her right shoulder. Eulo wanted to ask what was wrong with her, but instead he said, "So that's why she's trampling over the unworthy masses on her way to the Kestrine's mansion, eh?"

"They're not all the same."

"Loress Tali wouldn't be."

"I'm too busy diluting the Vernese bloodlines to be a Loress." She raised an eyebrow. "Come on, we're next."

Luczia and her underlings trundled through the gateway. Eulo and Tali pressed into the gap left in their wake, crushed by a wave of bodies. Eulo grabbed for Tali's hand. If she fell, she'd never get up again. Somehow, though, she slipped ahead, leaving him in the wake of her self-assuredness.

"Morning," the purple-vested official nodded at Tali. She cocked her head at Eulo, scrutinising him through heavy-lidded eyes, and let out a long, low whistle. "Best one I've seen all day. New, or home from a visit?"

"Oh, he's new," Tali said, winking at her.

Eulo clamped his jaw while the official checked their papers. She smiled and passed them back to Tali, who tucked them away in her clothes.

"Sarsega, eh. Not the singer?" the official said, taking their payment for the gate tax.

"No, that's my little sister, Vivica. She'd love to become a lyricene."

"She should—she's good enough. I saw her perform at Oyster Point a while ago. Everyone in the audience thought she was incredible." The official smiled. "Well, enjoy." Her gaze lingered on Eulo. "I know I would."

"Indeed." Tali said, smirking. She elbowed Eulo in the ribs, nudging him through the gateway into the free land. Into the greatest city in the world.

# Chapter 7

Tali strode out beyond the Seaport Gate, glad to escape the jostling elbows and intrusive hands on the waterfront. Eulo matched her pace, his movement fluid for such a big man. From the corner of her eye, she watched how his attention darted up and down the stone-walled alleys where the people of Silveraine lived, laughed and cried. She had to admit, after Port Garnet, this city shouted with colour, from the bright hues of the locals' shirts to the doors obscured behind masses of climbing saltvine.

Eulo stretched out to tear a handful of red flowers from the nearest vine. He crushed them in his fist, sniffing the sweet mass the way a mastiff scouted out its territory. He cast the petals free, his heavy boots trampling them into the white flagstones as he continued on. The aroma cloyed in Tali's nostrils.

"Where are these nags?" He glanced at her.

"On the far side of a meal and a pint?" she said. "There's a workers' pub in the fourth quarter, close to the stables." Workers were far less likely to worry about having an Iskarlian in their midst, let alone be stupid enough to try picking a fight with one.

"If you say so, darl. Lead on, eh?"

Later, full of ale and food, Tali drifted along the laneways, past children playing in the dirt and mothers stringing washing in banners alongside tumbledown fences. She sensed Eulo's absence rather than saw it, and turned to find him standing atop a wall, looking out over Silveraine. The city stretched from his feet all the way back past the jumble of houses clinging like limpets to the cliffs above the aqua-green water. The mosaic of red and blue rooftops curved and swirled to the foot of a bastion on the northern escarpment.

"That's Kestrine Sovann's mansion," Tali said, pointing out the whitewashed walls, her outstretched finger tracing the gold-tiled ridge caps and winged statues standing vigil.

"Look at it all, the diamond of the islands, eh?" he said. "I wonder how different life would've been, to be born here."

"You'd probably be the size of a house, swilling wine and cheese on your front porch while your pretty little wife rolled you from one side to the other so she could wash your spotty arse and please your every whim, while your men broke their backs in your shipyard, making you rich."

Eulo locked gazes with her, his sapphire eyes hard and glittering. "Are you taking the piss?" He jumped down from the wall, landing beside her. "Although I like the sound of being pleasured by a pretty little wife."

"Of course I'm joking. Your spotty-arsed wife would be the one doing the swilling and rolling." Tali punched his arm. "All I meant was, it's in people's nature to expect the things they don't have would make them happy, even though that might not be true."

His stubbled face unreadable, Eulo scrutinised Tali for so long it triggered butterflies under her breastbone. She coughed, startled by her reaction to him, and pointed to another expanse arcing above the treetops beside Sovann's mansion. "That building there is the Academy."

"What Academy?"

"It's Vernesia's school for artists, where my sister wants to train in singing. Once she graduates as a lyricene, people will hire her to perform at their formal dinners and parties. Rich people, like the Kestrine." People who'd pay Vivica's wage so Tali wouldn't need to.

Eulo drew his brows together. "People in Iskarlia sing for free. For the love of it."

"Imagine getting paid for doing what you love. Lyricenes in Silveraine are held in such high esteem they influence what society wears, how people cut their hair and what they believe in."

"A *singer*?" he scoffed.

"It's better than having angry men with weapons dictating what we can or can't do. A lot of people weren't happy when the Vernese matriarchy and Five Feathers formed during the Sunless War. Regardless of whether it was men or women ruling Vernesia, everyone agreed they didn't want the country run by brutes. The Academy was established much earlier, though, to protect our stories and history. To give our people the means to dream."

"We got stories and history too," Eulo said. "We don't need to write 'em down, not with our storytellers and singers."

"Doesn't the Cove value your history enough to keep records of it, though? There must be books, paintings?"

"I dunno. Maybe in his compound in Jarrison." He shrugged. "Our country ain't as complicated as yours."

"Why? Because you're either a killer or the person being killed?" Tali ducked under a sweeping tree branch. "I don't believe that, do you? Even if the Vernese are empowered and the Iskarlians oppressed, the Cove should still embrace your people's culture."

He glanced at her. "Maybe he don't embrace culture. Maybe the rest of us do. How much farther?"

"The stables are just ahead," Tali said, leading him into a laneway heavy with the tang of manure, animal and leather, the mingled scents of her happiness.

She left Eulo under the archway outside Tath's boarding stables, slouched in a fall of sunshine, suspended by the breathtaking views and smells of the city. Inside, the bustle gave way to cool air and velvet muzzles over half-doors, welcoming and inquisitive. A familiar, high-pitched whinny echoed in the aisle. Tali smiled as she hastened to the farthest stall. Her mare leant over the door, brown head bobbing as she pawed at the door.

"Hello, Sepher," Tali cooed, laying her hand on the mare's forehead. She swept strands of blonde forelock out of the horse's eyes. "I hope you haven't been causing trouble again."

From behind her, a man said, "Always. She started that racket up a little while ago."

The newcomer's profile sharpened into focus as Tali turned to greet him. She could've seen the familiar sharp lines of his face with her eyes closed: the perfect cut of his cheeks and jaw, the dark brown eyes. Her nerves strung tight. Blazes, what had she done?

Rithisak Tath, the livery owner's son, clapped her into a hug, his smile broad. "Safe home, Tali."

She breathed in his lemon scent, which she'd always found so irresistible. Now, it suffocated her. "Safe home, Rith." None of her own family ever bothered with the blessing.

"Went well, did it, your business in Port Garnet?"

"It did. I sold a few things. Made an...er...purchase."

He didn't notice her hesitation. "I rode the gelding almost every day. I hopped on your mare, too. Don't like her anywhere near as much."

"You never do." But he exercised her anyway, whenever Tali left her there.

"I have my pride. I'd hate to think there's a horse I can't win over."

She smiled. Rith wasn't the Kestrine's Horsemaster for nothing.

"I'm impressed with that gelding. I knew I'd buy him within a heartbeat of getting on."

"Oh," Tali said. Shit. "Well, I've decided not to sell him, after all." She followed his glance to a sudden movement in the doorway, his mouth already open to protest.

"I'll be with you in a moment," he called out to the man who'd sauntered in, all muscles and charming smiles.

"No need. I belong to her," Eulo said, pointing to Tali. He stopped near the doorway to scratch the cheek of a pony which had stuck its head out to investigate what was going on.

"Does he now?" Rith's expression froze. He raised an eyebrow at Tali, his voice strained as he asked, "You bought an Iskarlian?"

She sighed. "I told you we wouldn't be together." Every time he'd proposed a binding with her.

"Don't I know it." He rolled his sleeves up, slow and deliberate. Contemplating, he stuck his tongue in his cheek. "He's a big bastard, isn't he? Built like a bull. He must be satisfying. And he can even talk, too."

"You're the one being the bastard, Rithisak. Swallow your bruised pride a moment to come meet him."

Eulo rocked back on his heels, all his attention on Tali. Her belly fluttered. She smiled at him, too aware of Rith at her side, taut with anger.

She held a palm out towards him. "Eulo, this is my friend Rith."

"Rithisak," he corrected, pointedly tucking his hands into the pockets of his pants.

Eulo dropped the hand he'd offered in customary Iskarlian salutation. "Pleased to greet, friend," he stammered in broken Vernese, his face splitting into a smile. He faced Tali, impishness glimmering in his eyes. "And wife, beautiful wife. Please for when I should lick boots again?"

Her jaw dropped. What was he playing at now?

"Eulo," she said, through gritted teeth. Her cheeks flamed under Rith's wide-eyed stare.

"I say good, how you teach me, yes?" Eulo nodded eagerly.

"Keep it up and you'll be learning how to remove my boot from your arse," she said, folding her arms. "How 'bout you go saddle your horse? Flame's the chestnut gelding, back down by the doorway."

"Yes. Wife," Eulo enunciated, as though the words were difficult, foreign. "And saddle?"

"Oh shit." Tali twisted a straw wisp between her hands. "I didn't bring a second one." She hadn't expected to take the gelding home, let alone with a sun-blasted husband on his back.

"Take the one on the left." Rith pointed to a rack of saddles on the far wall. "I've been riding him in it." A lemon-sharp sting touched his words. Eulo scooped the saddle up in one arm on his way to the gelding's stall.

"Thank you. I'll return it," Tali said.

"I'd rather you didn't." Rith gave her a flat look. "Have Huon bring it back when he delivers that mare and gelding you showed me. Four hundred kistars each."

She nodded, giddy with relief at securing the sale. "Thank you."

His expression didn't change. "We're going to Jikah's next week. He's selling youngstock, too."

"Not like mine." Tali's tongue stuck to the roof of her mouth. Her biggest competitor was now, as she'd feared, becoming a threat.

"Well, I thought I'd ask if someone else would screw me in exchange for buying their horses."

"Oh fuck off," she growled.

"The Kestrine demands more Rangers to protect our borders. I need horses for them, and it'll take enough to placate her now you've whipped Flame out from under her."

"Rith." She let out a long breath. She'd promised him nothing.

"What a man, eh. He's taken the best horse you've ever bred and the woman I love."

Each word stabbed and twisted in Tali's gut. So much for her deluded hopes he'd forgive her binding to Eulo. Men and their egos. She tipped her head at him. "Don't stamp your foot at me like a toddler who's had his favourite toy taken off him."

He sniffed, wrinkling his nose as though something smelt bad. "Do you really think that man deserves to sit his arse on a seven hundred kistar horse?"

Tali's composure faltered. She was cracked to walk away from so much money by deciding to keep the chestnut gelding.

Rith rested his elbow on the stable door. "What does he do?"

"Argues, fights and makes a pest of himself, mostly." She unlatched the stall door. Slipping in beside Sepher, she ran her hand over the mare's gleaming neck.

"A good match for you, eh. What did your family say?" Rith passed Tali a wisp to curry the horse down.

"I haven't told them yet. Mema barely knows what's going on at the best of times, and Vivi probably hasn't even noticed I've been gone." She sniffed back a tickle of dust in her nose. "All Ranson will care about is that I've ruined his plans to bind me with Loy Myrtis."

"You're the woman of the house, not Ranson."

"I know." Tali's shoulders bowed under the weight of it all. It'd be different if her mother was still around, or if age hadn't addled Mema's mind. She gripped the rail in both hands, its wooden bones smooth under her fingers. "I'm going to lose it all, Rithisak."

"You could've lived with me in the quarters over the Kestrine's stables. Sovann would've agreed in a heartbeat to have you in her employ," Rith said, his eyes wet. "We would've been happy together."

Grief swelled in Tali's chest. She wanted to tell him the binding was all a ploy, that Eulo Juke would ride out of their lives in four weeks. They could keep fooling around, galloping the horses in the hills, rolling together in the summer pastures, swimming naked in the ocean, and he could still sneak her into the Kestrine's stables. But she'd severed all of that now.

So instead, she said, "I did what I had to do to keep the Myrtises off Glimmers Gap. I owe it to my grandmother. You of all people ought to understand."

He kept staring at her with those beautiful, wounded eyes. "I told myself the reason you kept refusing to bind with me was because the Tath bloodlines flow too far below a Sarsega dignitine's, and you have an image to uphold. Well you did, until now."

"Don't be ridiculous. You know I don't believe those archaic northern Vernese attitudes to caste," she snorted.

"So instead you got bound to some money-grubbing Iskarlian thug. Some killer straight out of the Cove's army, still with fresh blood on his lunatic hands." Rith grimaced. "You think he'll be hanging around to help when Glimmers Gap slips through your fingers? The big fucker'll be galloping off into the sunset on your best horse, with what's left of your money and valuables stuffed in his saddlebags."

"You're making a lot of assumptions about someone you don't know," Tali said, because she couldn't say anything else.

"Look at him." Rith kicked at a post. "He's a man's man who likes to drink and gamble. Typical bloody soldier."

"All those plans you made, the things we'd do... You never once stopped to ask me what I want," Tali said. "And I want to breed and train my horses. I want Glimmers; it's my flesh and bones. It's where I belong." She swung her saddle onto Sepher's back and buckled the girth, taking care to tighten it slowly. "I won't be bound to please someone else."

Rith cast a pointed glance down Eulo's way. He waited beside his saddled mount, murmuring to the horse as he fed it something he'd retrieved from his pocket. Apples, probably, from a market stall he'd stopped at on the way to the stables.

"Your Iskarlian there wants to please you."

"No. He wants to embarrass me." Tali rolled her eyes. "I never asked him to say anything—he already speaks fluent Vernese."

"He's after your approval. Looks like he's got it, too."

Tali bridled the mare and led her out of the stall, pausing to face Rith. He picked up the kistar Tali offered, spiriting it out of sight with his long fingers. More money gone in a heartbeat. There was nothing left to say, their past already a mile behind them, and stretching further away with each step. They embraced, arms wrapped tight around one another, the limber familiarity of his body pressing against hers, his smell filling her nostrils. Choked by the emotion of a last goodbye, tainted already by the changing, she turned away.

Tali rubbed a hand down her face. Blazes, how she ached to confide in someone, to be reassured she'd made the right decisions. After buying a husband, bribing the ship's Captain not to throw Eulo overboard for fighting with Krike, and refusing to sell Flame, she'd just about emptied her purse. Considering she also hadn't sold the binding rings on the wifeship as intended, it was just as well she'd got such a good price for the two flickerblades in Port Garnet. She needed to make more, though, and fast.

# Chapter 8

Eulo toed his boot into the ground outside Tath's stables, pushing up a mound of rich brown dirt. Goddess-blessed soil, not like the thin, fragile sand he'd grown up on.

"Ready?" Tali said, coming to join him. Her mare pinned her ears flat and squealed when Flame tried to sniff noses. "Cut it out, Sepher." Tali raised a finger, pointed it at the mare's chest. "Back up." The mare obliged, not stopping until her mistress dropped her finger. Leaving Sepher standing with the reins loose on her neck, Tali moved to check Eulo's tack.

He rested one hip. "Alright?" He knew it was.

She nodded. "Good. Your hunter taught you well."

"He wasn't the type you wanted to upset." Drunk and nasty, at the best of times.

"What did he hunt?" Tali hooked a stray lock of hair off her face. Her eyes shone with expectation.

"Rebels." Eulo turned away from her curious intensity, from bad memories of men without morals in a cruel land sucked dry of water, pride and life.

Tali checked her packs were securely buckled to the saddle. She mounted her horse, as soft and light as a sunbeam. "I'm ready to get out of the city. Let's go."

"As you wish, wife of much beauty."

"Stop it." Tali swung her foot in his direction, pretending to kick him. She pouted. "Any more of that talk and I'll feed you to the pigs."

"Then who'd lick your boots?" Eulo said, winking at her. He laughed when she couldn't stop herself smiling. He mounted Flame, settling into the saddle with a sense of awkwardness. How long had it been since he'd ridden? Shades, he'd be knowing about it tonight.

They rode south, letting the horses pick their way through the muddy laneways. Buildings teetered in overhead, crooked as a handful of broken fingers. It was a far cry from the smart estates lining the streets in the first few city quarters. A dark-haired urchin squatted in the filth of someone's doorway, his finger buried to the knuckle in one nostril, gaping at Eulo as his horse squelched past.

Eulo glanced around, his spine itching between the shoulder blades. People scurried along the narrow way, stepping over and around the puddles, trying to stop the mud flinging up on their threadbare clothes. They all stared at Eulo with distrust and wariness swimming in their eyes. With the Scabmen on his mind, he turned to check for Tali, in time to see a pock-faced youth slagging her off for having Iskarlian company. She didn't flinch, though she caught Eulo's eye immediately, warning him off with a shake of the head.

An old biddy pulled on the youth's arm. Grey hair tangled in her eyes as she jabbered at Tali in Vernese. Eulo didn't understand the dialect, but he could guess what she said from her beseeching tone. Calm as ever, Tali replied in the same jargon. The old woman backed away, urging the youth with her, his hands full of her bags. He glowered back over his shoulder at Eulo, who raised his lip in a sneer, cracking his neck from one side to the other.

"Leave it be," Tali said, nudging her mare on.

"I ought've broke his fuckin' jaw."

"Why? To prove you aren't the Iskarlian thug he thinks you are? To force his grandmother there to care for him, or watch him die? And if he died, who'd care for her?"

Eulo shook his head, said, "Mako's teeth, you don't seriously reckon they'll respect you for showing them mercy, do you?" The idea left him dumbstruck.

"It doesn't matter if they respect me or not. It's respecting myself that matters because I can only control my actions, no one else's."

"Where I come from, it's pretty rude to spit abuse at a woman."

"If someone spits on you, you can be offended. I'll make up my own mind about what offends me." She stared between Sepher's ears.

"If this were Iskarlia, that grub and the old biddy would be dead in a gutter. Prob'ly you too, with your sand-skulled kindness." The words scrambled out before Eulo could bite them down on his bastard tongue.

"Well thank the goddess for Vernese decency, then." Tali shortened her reins, urging Sepher into a trot. She rode with straight-spined pride, moving as one with the horse.

Eulo bunched his hands. How many times had they chosen death over kindness? How many times had he been rude to this woman, then found reassurance in her crooked smile, while she brushed off his blunt comments without losing her temper? Opening his fists, he vowed to do better by her. Her sand-skulled kindness had brought him here, after all, and he *liked* her. Deep down, he wanted her to like him, he wanted his banter to keep making her smile.

He pushed Flame faster, trotting past drop-post shacks pressing in on the laneway, five hundred miles from home, past people with skin of all colours from every country in the Opalline. Doubt flared in his chest. He had no idea when he'd stop feeling like he was scrambling to find control.

Before long, Tali had to rein Sepher in to meander along behind the traffic choking the way. The mare jogged and fussed, throwing her fine head in impatience. Tambo Tarch would've loved her—high-strung and fiery like his stable of Mako-kissed steeds. That's if Tarch wasn't dead; the last time Eulo saw the hunter, he'd left the bastard lying pretty still in a pool of his own blood.

Eulo rubbed his forehead, trying to lose his bad thoughts. He'd rather be thinking about his wife, still riding ahead while he trailed behind like a drudge, and how her shirt clung to the curve between her ribcage and hip, where the silver thread looped around her waist. He snorted. The way he was going with his idiot mouth, daydreaming about Tali's body was the closest he'd ever get to touching it.

He breathed a little better when the narrow laneways led them out onto the paved trading route. Heavy horses trundled past, throwing their broad shoulders into leather collars, towing carts up the incline. The loads ranged from fish to lemons to wads of silk, with a chaos of smells and colours in each one. Eulo pushed Flame alongside the nearest cart so he could peer over the side at unfamiliar, bright vegetables. On his other side woolpacks were stacked high on a bullock cart. Those at least he recognised from the trade ships leaving Jarrison Bay.

The procession of traffic slowed, choking around a gate in the sheer walls ahead. So, for all her would-be tolerance and fairness, the Kestrine wasn't above a little self-preservation. They were too far past the lip of the escarpment now to see her fortress or the jagged coastline where the *Seadancer* had docked. There could've been stockpiles of kilili on the other side of any number of walls or doors they passed, and Eulo would never have known. He'd only seen a whisker of the massive city, and now he was about to leave it behind for some southern backwater, to stir up trouble like a swarm of bees in the Sarsega family.

They got out of the city quicker than they'd gotten into it. Beyond the gate, traffic snaked along a white gravelled road past a shanty town which had mushroomed around the city walls. Eulo scanned the hovels, looking for a clue why the inhabitants had been shunned from inside the city perimeter. It only took a moment to realise most people flitting between the shacks had one thing in common: utter poverty.

Eulo's language floated on the breeze, more words than he'd heard since stepping off the red lands back in Port Garnet. Homesickness closed around him. He recoiled like he'd been kicked in the guts. Flame responded immediately to his weight shifting in the saddle, coming to a stop in the roadway.

"You like, Master?" a girl called out to him. She wound her curly blonde hair on top of her head, wriggling her shoulders to show Eulo immature breasts through her open shirt. A red-haired baby crawled between her bare feet, reaching its grubby hands up to her.

Bile slicked Eulo's throat. He extracted some of the remaining splinters in his pocket and flung them on the ground where she stood. He didn't stay to watch her scramble in the dirt for the coins, ignoring the wailing baby beside her.

Tali waited ahead, her face unreadable. When Eulo neared, she spun her mare around, off into a brisk trot.

"Come on fella, let's go catch 'em up." Eulo rubbed Flame's wither. He clicked the horse on, away from the camp of broken hope and crushed lives.

Tali turned her mare off the road. She leant low over Sepher's neck, letting the mare stretch out in a flat gallop. Not wanting to be left behind, Flame bounded out from under Eulo, throwing him off balance. He fought to bring his flapping arms and legs into unison with the horse's movement. The wind slapped his cheeks with a saltkiss sting, dragging tears out of his eyes. Tali blurred into the distance ahead. Flame's hooves thundered into the earth, drumming Eulo's heart into his throat. Blood surged through him. He crouched low over Flame's neck, finding harmony with the gelding's stride. Shades, how long had it been since he'd felt the magic of galloping across a hillside?

The Scabmen had come for the horses though, when Eulo couldn't pay back what he owed. First the horses, then his best weapons.

Flame eased to a canter near the top of the rise, blowing hard. Sepher waited further along, silhouetted against the hilltop, her banner tail held high. Tali watched as Eulo drew alongside her, fierce pride in her gaze.

"He's a good horse, isn't he? He looks after you."

Eulo lay a hand on Flame's damp neck. He shrugged, nonchalant. "He does the job, without the hysterics." He flicked a finger towards the mare. Tali's mouth twitched, and he caught the ghost of a smile forming.

"Sepher was born two days after my mother left. She means more to me than most people can understand." Her smile turned wistful, and she went quiet as they rode on.

The hillside unfurled beneath them, Silveraine now a good stretch behind. The sculpture of a bird rose from a clearing on the tallest hill; a hawk with wings stretched for take-off, carved into limestone which matched the statue of Lolani greeting ships into Iluka Bay. The bird balanced on its feet, one of which was curled into a perfect circle.

"That's Ava, Lolani's protector," Tali said. "She captures the setting sun in her claws and keeps it safe for the night."

Eulo shaded his eyes to get a better look. Copper-hued kilili threaded the stone, creating an illusion of the bird moving in the sunlight. What would it take to chip the kilili out of that rock?

"Why's it all the way out here?"

Tali circled the forefinger and thumb of her left hand and splayed the other three fingers, holding the circle to her heart as she dipped her head to the statue, similar to the entreaty she'd offered Lolani's statue back in Iluka Bay. "Silveraine and the north are following the Threes' trend of worshipping inside temples, but the southern Aves are outside, where they should be. It makes no sense caging the winged." She peered in the direction of the road. "Come on, the traffic will have thinned out now. That hill always slows everyone down."

For a moment they rode on without speaking.

"You were kind to the girl back there," Tali said.

"Hmm," Eulo grunted. The stink of the hovels still lined his nostrils. "What is that place?"

"The locals call it the Dross; the leftovers no one wants."

"Some of them are my people," Eulo said. They'd be better off at home, where at least no one would spit down on them. "How did they get there?"

"On the wifeships, or with the mine owners or the gem traders, or born to parents who didn't care, didn't want them, or couldn't keep them. Not everyone likes having Iskarlians here."

Eulo sniffed, thinking of the young bloke who'd cursed Tali. "At least in the burnt lands no one cares what colour you are." Only if you had money or not.

Tali stared between her horse's ears. "Some Vernese see Iskarlian men as a threat, stealing their wives and jobs. They don't understand how newcomers need to buy food and houses, or horses, clothes and medics. How our country can become richer by accepting and learning from other cultures." She took her feet out of the stirrups and let them hang loose.

"It don't stop 'em stealing our gems and people and leaving a broken land behind them."

"The people in the Dross call themselves Vernese. Most of them have never set foot anywhere else in the Opalline. The ones who have will tell you this is their country now. The golden land," Tali said. "I'm sorry, I should've warned you before we rode through."

"I've seen worse, just never reckoned it'd be like that here." Eulo rubbed his jaw. "How'd you know so much about 'em?"

"Because I ask."

"And they tell you?"

"Uh-huh." Tali shrugged. She unfastened a water flask from the front of her saddle, chugging a good swig of it, then passed it to Eulo.

"Cheers."

"It was good to go for a gallop, eh? I couldn't wait to get out in the open again." Her eyes sparkled.

"Yeah. I reckon I'll pay for it tonight," Eulo said. His thigh muscles were already protesting at being in the saddle again. He felt like he'd passed a test, though, by not falling off.

An army of ancient gumtrees stood watch over the roadway. It would've taken ten men to reach all the way around just one of those sentinels. They must've stood here for eternity itself, even before the Vernese men went to the Sunless War and came home to find their women had taken over the country. Eulo played with his binding ring, spinning it on his finger. If Tali knew the right people, she could be more than just his pass into Vernesia—she could help him find the kilili he needed.

The road curved away from the coastline, cleaving a hairline part into a rainforest. Ferns and undergrowth huddled close to the eucalypt trunks, their stems and leaves muting the roadside. Birds sang and squawked in the canopy of branches and long leaves, hidden by the dappled sunlight. Goosebumps pricked Eulo's bare arms, the fine blonde hairs standing on end in pathetic defiance of this chilly world. He reined Flame in to dismount on the verge, his boots landing without sound. Letting the horse graze, he untied his pack from behind the saddle.

The damp grass soaked dark stripes into his canvas pack. He rummaged through a few sleeveless shirts and one threadbare coat he'd carried since joining Vasker's miserable bunch of warriors. Even Flame's saddle-blanket was cleaner than his yellowed clothes. He dragged out the least-offensive long-sleeved shirt and tugged it over his head. Stupid goon, reckoning he'd make do leaving Iskarlia with this handful of rags. Still, he didn't exactly have money to buy more.

He picked at the fraying sleeve of his shirt. With his half-grown beard and shabby clobber, he'd fit right into the Dross. The irony was, in Iskarlia, worn clothes were a sign of hard work and honesty, while the well-dressed men were the ones to be suspicious of. Here, it seemed the well-dressed were people of high standing, to be respected. He snorted at the reminder of Loress Luczia and her golden goons.

Eulo remounted Flame and clicked the gelding into a fast trot to catch up with Tali, who hadn't bothered to stop and wait. He'd buy some new clothes when she flicked some coin his way. He frowned. Maybe she didn't trust him not to scarper once he had money. Maybe he didn't trust himself, either. The dirt ingrained in his hands was black to match the dirt ingrained in his soul. It didn't matter what he wore, Eulo Juke would always be the same Mako-cursed bastard on the inside.

# Chapter 9

It'd be easy for Eulo to sink into this ridiculously soft bed and go to sleep, maybe after a tumble with his wife. He rested a forearm over his eyes, wriggling his shoulders against the mattress. A heartbeat later he was sitting up, trying to fathom the noise he'd just heard. His heart stuttered into a canter. He scanned the hotel room, his gaze coming to land on the split-wood door separating the wash chamber from the bed.

"Tali?" Eulo crossed the room, the floorboards smooth under his bare feet. He tapped a knuckle on the door, probably breaking every bloody rule about Vernese women's privacy. "You alright?"

"Leave me be."

He leant his forehead against the cool wood, trying to sound gentle. "You shrieked. Like you were hurtin'."

"Do I look like the sort of woman who shrieks?" she said. "You might bloody shriek if you don't move away."

Eulo muttered under his breath, relenting. He settled on the floor rug at the foot of the bed, stabbing his finger into a web of pale-yellow teardrops embroidered into the violet weave. Made of Iskarlian wool, Tali had said, like the hall-runners and blankets in this mid-end Oyster Point hotel. He stretched one leg out, extending his torso over it to grab his toes. His muscles protested, tighter on the right than the left thanks to his bad knee.

He'd worked up to his back stretches by the time Tali emerged. She stopped beside the bed, watching him contort his shirtless body.

"What are you doing?"

"Impressing you with my tattoos again." He winked at her, although he couldn't ignore the alarm flickering around his senses. "You don't look so well."

"I'm tired, is all." She perched on the edge of the bed, wrapping her arms around her knees, rubbing her eyes with a forefinger and thumb.

Eulo unfurled his limbs. It must've been the shoulder injury bothering her. No point asking what had happened to her, when she was so guarded about it already. She'd tell him if she wanted him to know. "Nothing a good brew and food won't fix, eh?"

"I suppose," Tali said.

She barely spoke in the dining hall, only picking at her food before excusing herself for an early night. Eulo's concern was pacified a little by the six brews' worth of coins he'd been left with. When he staggered up to their room an hour later, he found Tali sleeping black-eyed and hollow-cheeked in bed.

In the bar, he'd managed to find out ships from Iskarlia did sometimes sail this far south and beyond. No one offered much information about what they carried, other than confirming the Kestrine enforced border checks on any vessels, goods and people entering Vernese waters.

He collapsed in under the covers, settling into place with a satisfied burp and fart. He barely sensed Tali beside him in the huge bed, across a gap as wide as the Kelp Straits.

Fingers brushed over Eulo's chest, stirring him awake. He lay for a moment with his eyes shut, waiting for the hand to move. It didn't. Tali snored softly into his ear.

His eyes snapped open to see the sun streaking across the hotel wall. Shame. She must've crept over to him in the night, while he lay oblivious in a half-pissed stupor. He'd let her sleep, so she didn't have to wake face-to-face with an unshaven wretch who stank like the bottom of a keg. He slid his fingers under her wrist, gently lifting her arm off him, not wanting to disturb her when she looked so serene.

"Laah?" she shouted, waking. Her flailing hand smacked him in the mouth.

They sprang back from each other in alarm. Eulo grunted, rubbing his face.

"Sorry. You scared me." Tali rested her hand on his cheek. She skimmed her thumb along it, looking at him through eyes of silver green. After a moment she turned away.

Was she embarrassed by the intimate gesture?

"It's still a bit sore. Reckon you'll need to kiss it better," he said, pointing to his cheek, hoping his morning breath smelt better than it tasted.

"Aw, my poor big soldier. What were you fighting against in the Cove's war? Puppies?"

"You're cruel," Eulo laughed, relieved she sounded better. The dark circles under her eyes hadn't faded though, and she crawled out of bed like an old woman.

From Oyster Point, they continued south, where the sheer cliffs crumbled into boulder-strewn shores and long white beaches. Eulo spotted the Aves statues along the road, almost always up on a high point of land close to the towns and villages, or elevated on a boulder or pile of rocks. Each bird looked north, so its circled talons would catch the sun setting in the west. None were as big or ornate as the statue in Silveraine, and some were mere outlines with an east-west facing hole bored through the base.

Eulo shivered along in his threadbare clothes until Tali insisted she'd buy him some more at the outfitter in Bintau. The sun had tipped past midday when they reached the village, tucked between rolling green hills and tall blue gum forests. Eucalypt smoke rose from chimneys sticking up from the shingle-roofed bluestone cottages, carrying the scent of cooking meat into the crisp air.

The horses walked side-by-side through the mud-slicked laneways to the marketplace, passing people dressed in black and brown work clothes. They greeted Tali by name, polite and friendly, shooting curious glances at Eulo. She nodded to them without stopping or introducing her new husband. In Eulo's experience, small towns were all alike, so word would get around about him quick enough. The marketplace was pretty much the same as any other small town, too, with a blacksmith flanking a carpenter, grain store, saddler, butcher, and an apothecary. The painted verandahs and shopfronts indicated business here was good. The smell of bread from the bakery convinced Eulo, anyway.

Hoping they'd buy something to eat, he shambled inside the general store with Tali. The clothes racks hung along the far wall, forcing him to edge past shelves of cooking pots, tools, and sacks of grain and flour. He slammed his thigh into a bench stacked with rolls of colourful cloth, frantically clutching at them to stop the lot cascading onto the floor.

"Can I help you there?" the shopkeeper called, his mouth dropping open when he came face-to-face with Eulo. "Oh. What do you want?"

"Good afternoon, Kylas. Eulo here needs some winter clothes," Tali said from the next row over. She peered around the shelf, holding a book in one hand and a ball of wool in the other.

Kylas, the shopkeeper, darted a glance at her. "Ah. Miss Sarsega, I didn't see you there." Scratching his thinning hair, he squinted at Eulo.

"Well, I'm not sure we stock anything big enough. We don't get many his size down here, but I'll do my best."

"I wouldn't expect anything less," Tali said, raising an eyebrow at him. "I'll gather a few supplies while you two are busy here."

When they were done, Kylas wrote up the charges in a book at the front counter. He spun it around to Tali, marking the last squiggle of writing with one thumb. "This is the total, here."

"Right." She patted the vegetables and sack of flour stacked on the counter. "I'll put it on my account, thanks."

"Ah…" Kylas shifted, his gaze darting to the clothes heaped in Eulo's arms. "Your account has been over the limit for the past two months." He shook his head a little. "No more."

"But I've been paying." Tali stood straighter.

"Not enough to keep up with everything your family buys." Kylas side-eyed Eulo again.

Tali muttered under her breath, tapping her fingers on the edge of the counter. Caught short, something Eulo knew about all too well.

"What if we just took the clothes, then?" she tried. "Some of them?"

"Look…" Kylas blew a long sigh out his nostrils. "Take what you have. But this is the last time."

"**A**re you uncomfortable?" Tali twisted in her saddle to scrutinise Eulo. He resisted the urge to tug at the crotch of his new, plum-crushingly small pants. The thick cloth was unforgiving. He managed a smile. "I'll do." He'd have to, for what she'd just gone through to leave the store with anything.

"If you'd told me earlier that you didn't have any warmer clothes, we could've gone to the store in Oyster Point," she said. "At least the oilskin coat fits you, and maybe Huon can loan you some clothes while we're waiting for Kylas to get the rest in."

"Huon?" Eulo repeated the unfamiliar name.

"He helps run our estate. His wife was my mother's best friend. He's part Iskarlian."

Eulo's eyebrows hitched. As they'd ridden further south, he'd noticed less of his people around. The Iskarlians probably found it too bloody cold here, where green pasture and forest raced up from the road into sky-piercing mountains.

He raised a finger towards them. "Are we heading up there?"

"Not quite. That's the Starsfall Ranges. Glimmers Gap runs from the foothills down to the coast." Tali gestured in a sweeping arc.

"Mako's teeth. If this were Iskarlia, you'd be the Cove," Eulo said. Or not. She'd probably be stabbed in the back by someone she should've been able to trust. No wonder she'd hardly blinked at the extortionate price they'd been charged for his new clothes. At least the grey wool overshirt fit well and kept him warmer in the chill air. Energy fizzed in his limbs. Not knowing what to expect from this job made him jittery. He said, "So how does this go?"

"Go where?"

"How do I meet my end of the deal?"

"Just do what you do. I'm not asking you to pretend anything different," Tali said. "You'll drive Ranson berserk just by being here. He'll hate you, I'm afraid. Not you, personally. More what our binding means for him."

Eulo shrugged. "Being hated don't worry me." It hadn't yet, and not many people in Iskarlia were happy to find a hunter on their tail. "It won't be hard keeping out of his way if the property is as big as you say." He fumbled for the water flask tied to his saddle.

"That's why you'll be out working the cattle,"

Eulo spat out his mouthful of water. "Me? A cattle herder?"

Tali levelled her luminous gaze at him. "Well, it's not like I have any use for a mercenary, and my sister won't relinquish her place as resident layabout. Someone has to watch the cows during calving, and I can't do it all myself. Besides, I did employ you." Weariness greyed her features as she pinched her right shoulder. "After you meet my family, you'll be glad to stay away from the house."

The horses picked up their pace as they neared home, striding beside brush fences that stretched into the distance. They hadn't crossed paths with anyone since leaving Bintau. Satisfaction coloured Tali's cheeks as she pointed out the Sarsega property boundaries to Eulo: a stand of blue gums to the south, a green belt of shrubs following a creek to the north, and a cluster of granite boulders along the western ridge.

Eulo couldn't see the ocean, but salt brindled the fresh eucalyptus in the air. Vernesia's fertility couldn't have been more of a contrast to his homeland.

A wooden signpost creaked on its hinges at the roadside, the squiggles etched on it presumably announcing their arrival at Glimmers Gap.

"Almost there, eh girl," Tali said to Sepher, rubbing the mare's neck.

The horses passed through the property's stone entranceway with their ears pricked, sidestepping potholes and crumbling edges along the driveway. Glossy black cattle with small ears and no dewlap observed their arrival.

Eulo tilted his head, attempting to read the sights and sounds of this strange land. "Dogs," he said, picking up on faint barking.

Tali looked up sharply. "Blazes, I can't even go get bound without the place falling into chaos." The corner of her mouth curled as the barking got louder. "Here they come."

A stream of heelers poured over the rise ahead, calling out a harsh tune of warning—or welcome, judging by Tali's smile. Eulo counted six dogs coloured either red or blue, square-headed like the Iskarlian desert dogs but stockier, with stumpy tails. The baying subsided into a frenzy of wide-mouthed, tongue-lolling grins. The pack massed around the horses, making it hard to tell where the end of one dog stopped and the next started. Tali greeted them with loving but slightly disapproving murmurs.

"Shades, I wouldn't want to be facing 'em if they weren't in a friendly mood," Eulo said. Strange bloody beasts, staring at him through deep-set eyes.

"They won't hurt you. They can sense my aura on you," Tali said, riding on through the squirming mass.

"Your aura?" Eulo frowned at her. "What's that—something you rubbed up on me last night while I was too half-cut to remember?" The mention of rubbing brought his attention back to the torture-pants he'd stuffed himself into. Thank fuck they were almost at the end of the road.

He forgot his irritating clothes the moment they breasted the rise. Just like the backwater goon he was, gaping in disbelief at the bluestone house towering over a coach-house and stables. Even the Cove might've felt a flash of envy, and that bastard's digs were plenty fancy, too.

"Is that…" his voice came out high-pitched, strangled by the seam of his pants. He coughed and tried again: "Is that where we live?"

"Not quite. My house is in the forest, further up. It's a bit fancier than this," Tali said, straight-faced.

"Fancier?" Eulo rubbed his jaw. A week ago, it'd been beyond him why a man would sell his soul to a woman from across the ocean. This made it blindingly obvious. He smiled to himself. Was Krike's new life on the pig farm like this?

He craned his neck at the house as they rode past. Flowerpots edged the wide stairs leading to the door. What would his wife say to whoever had let the flowers shrivel into death? He spotted movement upstairs, someone at a second storey window. A ghost observing his arrival, cursing the big Iskarlian goon in his too-tight pants.

The horses carried on past the house, to where their hooves whispered into a white, gravelled yard outside the stables. Tali dismounted, disappearing in the swarm of dogs, laughing at their pink-tongued greeting.

A slope-shouldered man emerged from the stables. "Off you go, you mangy pack o' runts," he shouted, waving dismissive hands at the dogs. His voice hardened. "Alright, enough. Go now, the lot of you." He pointed to the side of the stables, sending the dogs streaking off around it, leaving the yard in sudden peace.

"Who let them run loose? They ought to be out working cattle, not mugging visitors," Tali said, clapping the bearded man into a hug. When she let him go, he surveyed Eulo through creased eyes.

Wiping his hands on his work-stained pants, the man nodded, and said, "So, it's true."

"If only my coin flowed as fast as the local gossip," Tali said. "Huon, this is my husband, Eulo Juke. Eulo, this is my head stockman."

The sound of his name broke Eulo out of his daze. He leant forward, swinging his right leg over the back of the saddle to dismount. That was the moment his new pants gave way. The sound of tearing cloth stunned them all speechless. Eulo's plums fair sighed with relief not to be squashed up anymore, filling with blood again at much the same speed as his cheeks. Cold fingers of air tickled his arse through the burst seam.

Tali lifted a hand to her mouth in a weak attempt to stifle her amusement. She snorted, doubling over, laughing soundlessly with tears rolling down her cheeks.

"Don't worry 'bout her, mate. Serve her right for forcing you into such silly-lookin' pants to begin with." Huon's face contorted, struggling to stay straight. Ignoring Tali, who leant against Sepher, hooting, he offered Eulo a handshake.

Eulo gripped the stockman's hand, a strong fellow about his father's age, with eyes like the morning sky under sun-bleached black hair. Back home, they would've called him a bitsa—bitsa Iskarlian and bitsa Vernese.

"I'll go find you a pair o' strides to borrow while you two sort these horses out," Huon said.

"Isn't that what I pay you for?" Tali asked him, her grin full of mischief.

"As if you'd let anyone touch your mare." His bushy eyebrows rose. "Besides, I know you're dying to perve at this poor bloke's bum the moment my back's turned." He wandered off down the stable aisle, his left boot scuffing the dirt on a skewed angle.

Eulo busied himself unsaddling Flame. He wisped the gelding's neck, scrubbing at patches of drying sweat in the chestnut hair.

"Here y'are. I found a few pairs." Huon reappeared with an armful of pants. "You may as well keep 'em. They're a little snug around the waist for me these days, and too long to fit anyone else here." He shrugged the clothes into Eulo's arms in exchange for his thanks and Flame's lead rope. Smiling at the gelding, he said, "I knew Tali liked this horse too much to sell him."

"Of course you did." She pulled a face at him. "When did Cyska leave?"

"The morning after you," Huon said. "She reckons she'll be home in a few days."

"My aunt is a librarian," Tali said to Eulo. "She takes books to the outstations, where people are too far away to get into town much, along with mail and news." She chewed her lip. "She's gone west, higher into the mountains. I hope she's alright. It'll still be snowing there."

Snow? Eulo shuddered.

"Cyska will be fine. She's got a good horse to look after her." Huon clapped Tali on the shoulder.

She turned away but Eulo glimpsed the grimace of pain she hid from the stockman.

"Well," Huon said, "I s'pose you'll get to meet the rest of the Sarsegas soon, Eulo. They ain't like our girl Tali here. Good luck." He reached for Tali's mare and led both horses away.

Eulo threw the new pants over a nearby stable door. He bent over to unlace his boots, on full display to Tali, only glancing at her when he straightened up. It didn't matter that she crouched over her own packs, not looking at him as he got changed.

The smile across her flushed cheeks said enough.

# Chapter 10

Eulo trod the path beside Tali, breathing in damp loam. Did the Sarsegas know how lucky they were to live on land rich enough to grow whatever they wanted, to be able to feed more livestock on a single ayr than on an entire Iskarlian station?

He scratched the three-day growth on his jaw, gawping back at the imposing bluestone house. As composed and graceful as Tali, down to the same worn edges. She marched with her lips pressed together in a thin line.

Her stalking pace slowed as she and Eulo climbed the incline. She carried the pack across her chest, hands tangled in its shoulder strap, her breath coming out in short, sharp bursts although the slope wasn't steep. Eulo reached out to take the pack three times, and each time he pulled his hand back, empty.

Tali stopped on the crest of the hill, where vast blue gums crowded out the sky above the track. She let her pack fall to the ground.

"Nearly there," she said, her breathless voice almost lost on the breeze.

"Good," Eulo said. "I nearly reckoned I'd have to carry you the rest of the way."

Tali closed her eyes and winced.

"I'm joking, darl. Obviously, you'll be carrying me."

"I don't need anyone to carry me," she said softly, although she didn't protest when he scooped up her pack to continue on.

A stone cottage appeared through the trees, its walls glowing in the afternoon sun. A verandah sagged over the doorway like a crooked grin. Eulo liked its welcoming warmth. Three red hens pecked and scratched in the garden. He clumped onto the verandah, breathing in the scent of bright flowers set in pots on the steps.

He started at a sudden noise under the timbers. A ginger cat miaowed as it ran to wind itself around Eulo's legs. He picked the beast up in one hand, surprised by the strength of its radiating purr.

"Just a baby, eh?" He tickled the cat under the chin with a dirt-stained finger.

"This is Chance; the runt who never grew, not even with all the mice in the stables, and the milk and scraps Huon feeds him," Tali said.

"He's a mouthful compared to the scrubcats at home. They're as tall as your waist."

She arched her eyebrows. "I'm sure they are." Shoving the door open, she went inside.

Eulo lingered on the verandah with the cat in his arms. The path continued past the cottage into the forest, where it was swallowed by green ferns and white-brown tree trunks. Funny how these huge trees dwarfed him as much as the saltbush plains under the Iskarlian sun did. Eulo Juke was as insignificant in this forest as he was standing on the red earth that stretched to every horizon in his own homeland.

The silence was absolute—no, not silence, not with the shiver of gum leaves overhead, and parrots chittering on a nearby branch. The blissful kitten in his hand. And the cursing woman inside his new home.

He stooped under the low doorway, squinting to let his eyes adjust. A table was snugged beside the window, separated from the tiny bedroom by a folding wooden screen. It took him a moment to spot Tali kneeling in front of the fireplace, coughing in a mist of ash. He shrugged free of the packs, leaving them where they fell on the floor, and plonked the cat beside them.

"What are you doing, woman?"

"Need to light the fire. Too cold," she spluttered, sending more plumes of ash into the room.

"How 'bout you sit here on your arse before you fall down, and I'll get it sorted." Eulo guided her into one of the hard-backed chairs at the table and pressed a water flask into her hands. Worry seeped into his bones. "You're sick."

"I'm alright," she said, uncorking the flask with shaking hands.

He opened his mouth to ask what was wrong with her shoulder, but she frowned, waving him off. He retreated to spark a flame into the stack of kindling in the hearth, leaning forward to blow life into it. That was when she stabbed him above the right kidney.

"Gah." Eulo leapt up, cracking his head on the mantle, arms flailing behind him as the stabbing climbed his back. Tali laughed.

"Maw," Chance said indignantly, pricking his claws into Eulo's flesh as he clung on to avoid the man's thrashing hands. Tali wasn't stabbing him at all—it was just the fucking cat scaling him like a tree.

"Shades." He plucked the cat off his shirt, wrestling for a moment to separate beast and cloth. Tali grinned as he dumped Chance into her lap. "Glad you find it so funny," he said, hitching one side of his mouth in mock offence. At least it'd put some colour into her cheeks.

"Darley Krike would've been funnier, but he was already taken." She winked, although the easy air between them faded. "I'm going to have a rest. I need to muster some energy for dinner with Vivi and Ranson." She rubbed her sleeve across her eyes.

"You're worrying me."

Tali gave him a thin smile. "Don't go soft on me, mercenary." She rummaged in her pack by the door, dumping half its contents on the table before dragging the rest in beside the bed. There, she curled up on the bedspread, fussing at her shoulder again.

Eulo unfolded himself into one of the chairs. He tapped his fingers on the table. Since when did hired men care about their employers? Maybe she was right—maybe he was going soft. Mako's teeth, it wasn't like he'd ever had an employer laugh at him while he was getting attacked by a kitten.

Chance snuggled into a neat ball beside Eulo's pack, hiding his nose in his fluffy ginger tail. Eulo snorted. 'I got your approval, eh.' The cat didn't move, although he purred a duet with the crackling fire. Eulo lifted a good-sized log out of the wood box and tossed it onto the hearth. He picked an apple out of the mess on the table, knocking Tali's pile of belongings onto the floor.

"Shit." He retrieved a handful of shirts and a belt. Pausing, he squinted at a knife lying exposed on the old floorboards. He ran his fingers around the leather-wrapped hilt, weighing it in his hand, impelled to draw the blade free from its sheath. His scalp prickled. Firelight ran along the gleaming flickerblade, turning its reflection from silver to red, except where a grey-green tinge swirled through the metal. The same hue as the eucalyptus leaves outside the front door.

Eulo lay the blade flat on his right palm, beside the binding ring on his middle finger. The greensilver was identical. He tapped the blade against the ring, intrigued by the chime. Like a little boy doing something he'd promised his mother he wouldn't, he glanced through to the bed. Tali hadn't moved. What was she doing with an expensive fighting knife?

It sat well in his hand, light and balanced. Too light, though, surely, to do much damage. He tested its edge with his thumb. Tali kept it sharp, anyway. He chopped the knife into an uneaten apple on the table, expecting the blade to jam halfway through the core. It whispered through and bit into the wood beneath. Stunned, Eulo let go of it. Both halves of the apple rocked on the scarred wood. He picked the knife up again, cautious this time as he sliced the fruit into pieces. He wiped the blade clean before returning it to its leather sheath. Chance slept on at his feet.

Eulo's mind raced. Two kilili rings, a flickerblade and a belly chain. Where had Tali got them from? And how much more did she have?

Crunching into a slice of apple, he wandered around the room, taking in sips of Tali's life. He ran his hand over leather-bound spines on the bookshelf, tracing stamped words he couldn't read, no matter what language they were in. A motley of objects captured dust on the windowsill. A tiny horse carved out of dark timber, mimicking the proud head and flagged tail of Tali's mare, Sepher. A silver teardrop pendant and dried flower whose crumbling petals across the splintered sill might've been gifts from a lover. Eulo rolled the perfectly shaped pendant between his finger and thumb, struck by its dullness beside his binding ring. He replaced it beside the window. Just as well him and Tali had only agreed to this for one month. He had nothing else to offer her, and nothing that would impress her.

The cottage held a collection of practical items. No paintings, or vases, or painstakingly crafted furniture. Bits of bridle and scraps of leather were scattered over an armchair layered in fine ginger fur.

Eulo padded into the sleeping nook. Tali still hadn't moved, lying on her side with her hair strewn across the red quilt, her chest rising and falling quick as a bird's. Eulo stretched a wool blanket from the foot of the bed up to his wife's chin. Her hand rested beside her throat, the ring almost luminescent in the filtered light. Black hair brushed soft as a cobweb against Eulo's fingers. His pulse quickened, same as when she'd first whirled into his life in that tiny Port Garnet room. He dragged his gaze away from the strong lines of her cheeks and nose. It wasn't right to stand over her like this, staring at her while she slept.

He scratched his chin, touching the road grime caught in his whiskers. He'd have a wash and shave so he wasn't quite so foreign in the big house tonight. The old stockman's clothes were clean and presentable, and the rest of him ought to be, too.

Eulo caught Tali's elbow, stopping her as she rested a foot on the first step of her family's house. "Don't forget, me 'n' you are in this together."

Her surprise eased into a smile. "Thanks, Eulo. I'm sorry for laughing at your bum."

"It takes a fair bit to offend me after five years in the Cove's ranks. Much better to have a pretty girl lookin' at me arse than a mob of stinky soldiers." He winked at her.

"Oh, I wasn't looking." She wrinkled her nose and darted up the stairs.

Eulo laughed to himself, clumping in her wake. He dumped his coat and boots beside hers while she reached for the door handle. He edged in behind her onto a green and cream rug, trying to shake off the sensation of entering a trap. The great room was empty, except for a carved wooden horse staring at them from a centre table, and an immense staircase stretching to the second floor, where it parted left and right. A floral hint couldn't hide the smell of age and stale air.

Tali glanced at Eulo, chewing her lip. She started down the hallway on their left. "Come on, let's see who's around."

A woman's voice floated clear as a bird out of the rooms beyond. Eulo didn't understand the lyrics, but the tune suited the distant, sober mood of the house. A golden wash of lamplight caught Tali for a moment, framed in the doorway at the end of the hall.

The singing stopped. Eulo missed it immediately, as though the melody had filled a hole he didn't know was empty.

A black-haired beauty rose off a couch under one huge window. She flowed across to greet them, smoothing her dress with slow deliberation. Gazing at Eulo, she curved her lips into a smug smile and purred, "Oh sister, what have you done?"

"Vivica, this is Eulo Juke. My husband," Tali said. She didn't smile or move to embrace the other girl.

"Husband," Vivica repeated, without looking away from Eulo.

He nodded, staring openly, drinking in the lines of her cheeks, the wave of tresses curling past her arse, how the silk flowed from her breasts down her curves. Magnificent.

Tali stalked through a maze of couches to the middle of the room, where a pile of books lay haphazard on the table. Bookcases lined the whole room from ceiling to floor. Vivica could've easily glided over the green rug, radiating money, privilege and the same elegance arched in the house's walls. Eulo glanced at Tali. With her loose hair and unmade face, his wife looked like a stray from the stables who'd snuck her way inside.

"Where's Mema?" she said, cool as the slip of a blade between the ribs.

"Upstairs, in her room," Vivica said. "Blazes, Tali, you're not going to force this poor man to meet her, are you?" She whirled to face her sister, planting her feet on a jaunty angle. The movement perked her round arse at Eulo in a way that made him want to rub his hand over it.

"Why has she been left upstairs?" Tali folded her arms. Her lips thinned. "Vivi?"

"Daddy said Cailene is too busy doing her maid's work to deal with Mema as well." Vivica glanced across the room, where a Vernese man stood motionless, staring out the big window there.

Tali waved her hands in his direction. "Ranson?" She turned back to Vivica. "Who else is going to look after her, then?"

"Not me. Spend my life changing the old bitch out of her piss-stained sheets? I don't think so."

"Of course, I forgot you'd never actually do work." A shadow darkened Tali's frown, stormier than any time Eulo had stirred her up.

"How would you know what happens in this house? You're never even here," Vivica said. "Too busy going off as though you've got a reason to be important, wasting our money on luxuries like a new husband."

"I'm busy running our estate." Tali slapped the chair beside her.

"Yes, running our estate into the ground, with Mema watching every mistake you make. Imagine the shreds she'd tear off you if she still could."

The skin under Tali's right eye pulsed. She glanced at Eulo, her lips pressed tight. He sensed she was holding back from starting a full-on blue in front of him.

Vivica tossed a cascade of curls off her neck. She peeped through her fringe at Eulo, her voice turning smoky. "I hope you didn't think you were binding into money. Family love isn't the only treasure missing from this soulless shithole."

"We'll discuss this later, along with how Kylas has blocked our account at the store because you're both taking goods without paying him." Steel edged Tali's tone. She turned her attention on the man frowning at the window. He held a tumbler of liquid amber against his belly, still not prepared to face or greet his visitors.

"Ranson," she said. Her gaze bored into his back. "Ranson!"

He turned slowly, nursing the drink in one hand. The sketch of his cheeks mirrored Vivica's, not Tali's, even down to the hazel eyes and sneer.

"This is my husband, Eulo Juke," Tali said.

Eulo stuck his hand out. "How ya' going?"

Ranson shook his head, sneering. "Don't insult me with your dirty Iskarlian gesture. I don't welcome you into my house, or my family."

Eulo shrugged, letting his hands fall loose by his sides. He left his flat stare on Tali's father though, to let the bastard know he wouldn't be intimidated.

"This is Mema's house," Tali corrected, her voice sharp. She stood taller, staring her father down.

The top dog stepping up.

Vivica watched, head cocked to one side and hands planted on her hips. Amusement perked one corner of her mouth.

Ranson's nostrils flared at Tali. "Do you think your grandmother will be impressed you've brought a money-grubbing Iskarlian here? Let alone anything else you've done with the estate lately. How in skies will you earn more from your horses than our cattle?"

"Since when did you care what Mema thinks?"

He downed his drink with the flick of a wrist. "Cyska put you up to this, didn't she? That madwoman won't be happy until she's destroyed the entire family. No wonder your grandfather took to his heels first chance he got. If he's got half a brain in his head, this Iskarlian will too."

"Unlike you, Father, Cyska believes in following your heart, not your purse," Tali said.

All of a sudden, Ranson stretched his arm out and flung the tumbler at the fireplace, cracking the brittle air in the room. "That's because no one here has anything to fill their purse with," he said, flushed. A grin pulled his mouth into a slack, gaping hole. "Go on, tell me how much you want to be rid of me, *daughter*. Do you know how happy it makes me knowing you can't break your mother's vow that I'd always stay here?"

"Then you should be grateful I won't be binding with Loy Myrtis. You're deluded if you think his mother would let you keep living here, leaching off her coffers."

"*Your* mother would never forgive you for what you've done; binding with some stray from across the ocean." Ranson's eyes bulged. "You shame this family by tainting the good Sarsega name. You threaten all your sister's dreams."

"Of course, because she's the only one who's ever really mattered to you, isn't she?" Tali said, her gaze flicking over to Vivica. "Clean up your mess, Father. Take care not to cut yourself though, because I won't help you and you know how squeamish Vivi gets when blood is spilt." She bunched her hands. Tension filled the cords of muscle in her neck. "I'll go get Mema ready myself. Make sure there's a place set for her at the table."

Eulo trundled out in Tali's wake, not quite managing to avoid the appearance of trotting after his new wife like an obedient cur. He glanced back at the library, where Vivica rested her forearm against the doorframe. She waved to him, a rippling of long fingers. Shades, she was a woman he'd beg for.

On the ship, Tali had made it clear her interests in him weren't sexual. She'd also told him he was free to go to other women if he wanted. And when it came to Vivica Sarsega's lush pout and body, Eulo wanted.

What harm could it do?

# Chapter 11

"Spoilt bitch," Tali said, as she marched into the great room. Stopping, she rested one hand against the wall. "Blazes..." she sighed. "See why I can't stand living under this roof."

He could. The family was as cold and unwelcoming as their house. Maybe the colour and chaos of his own home weren't so bad after all. "It don't worry me. I've met worse." They were the ones he never felt too bad about killing.

"We'll see my grandmother. Who knows what they've been doing with her while I've been gone," Tali said.

They climbed the staircase to the second floor. Eulo ran his hand along the rail, admiring the polished wood under his fingers. Someone had built this place with pride, smoothing the edges against each other, making sure no rough angles stuck out. That's what families were, though—rough edges against smooth—no matter how fancy their house was.

He loitered in the doorway to the grandmother's room, tracing pale flowers in the wallpaper. Someone had embroidered the same flowers onto the bedspread, matching the leaves to the green paint dressing the lower half of the walls. He screwed up his nose at the tang of old rosewood. The place needed a bloody good airing out—there were enough windows to've done it.

Tali knelt before a silver-haired woman hunched in a chair beside the bed, her mark of respect before she said, "Mema, I'm home, with Eulo, my husband." Her voice quavered when she said his name, like a small tot looking for her elder's approval.

The old woman took an age to lift her chin off her chest. She peered at Eulo through faded green eyes and smacked her toothless gums together.

Tali curled her fingers around her grandmother's knee and glanced at Eulo. "Mema taught me almost everything I know about running this estate. A year ago, Ranson and Vivica would never dare talk the way they do in front of her. Just 'cause she doesn't speak anymore doesn't mean she can't hear and think." She sat on the yellow bedspread and held the old woman's hand. Her anger melted into a sad softness. "You're the one reason this family still has its bloody estate, and all they do is bitch and moan."

The room crowded in on Eulo, too small and stuffy, smothering him for invading this home and family. He couldn't have been more relieved when the dinner bell interrupted Tali's story about her voyage to Iskarlia and binding to him.

Eulo put his spoon down, rolling the last mouthful of trifle over his tongue, savouring the alcohol-soaked cake and soft cream. Sweet, not like the anger smouldering off Ranson Sarsega. He refused to acknowledge Eulo at all, let alone look at him, the man he blamed for apparently ruining the family's plans for Tali. Ranson chewed with the emotion of a condemned man who couldn't taste a single mouthful of the most decadent food Eulo had ever touched.

Beside Eulo, Tali leant away, helping Mema scoop the last spoonful of trifle out of her bowl. The old woman slumped in her wheeled chair at the head of the table. Her liver-spotted hands gnarled around the silver cutlery, always with the knife angled towards Ranson, on her right-hand side. As though she sensed Eulo watching her, Mema raised her chin to stare at him.

Vivica reclined in her chair opposite Eulo, pushing away her half-finished dessert. He eyed the bowl, pulling his brow down. There was no such thing as wasted food where he came from, with all the hungry mouths. In Iskarlia, you ate whatever you could, or you starved.

She wriggled her bare shoulders, her gaze skimming past Eulo's. She'd barely looked his way since swanning into the room in red silken glory, although she'd rested her foot in his lap during the main course, hidden under the table, rubbing up against his crotch. He'd strangled a cough when she'd first touched him. He ought've pushed her away, if not for the burn of Tali's disinterest and the endless cups of wine he'd drunk.

He'd dressed in Huon's barely worn clothes, together with the new oilskin he'd left beside Tali's on a peg at the front door. He liked how the new shirt felt, its uncuffed sleeves soft against his arms, snugged in under a woollen waistcoat. Something close to respectable, he hoped.

Tali stacked her grandmother's empty bowl onto her own. "I'm going to take Mema back to her room," she said.

"Good, get her out before she wets herself again. I swear she does it on purpose," Vivica said, grimacing when Mema giggled. "Isn't it ironic, Tali, how you're the one who insists she is wheeled out on display. Maybe if you were ever actually around to wrestle her up and down the stairs yourself, you'd be more realistic about it."

"Why don't you put her in a downstairs room?" Eulo said. "You got plenty to go around."

"So, you *can* understand us?" Vivica said to him. She tossed her hair back, tinkling out a laugh. "See, Father, maybe he is more than a thug taking advantage of Tali to get his papers into Vernesia." She glanced at Eulo and smiled.

Tali wheeled Mema out from the table, turning the old woman's gaze away from Eulo. She said, "Come help me, Ranson."

"Help you?" Ranson said. "Isn't that what you bought this uncultured pig for?" Now he did look at Eulo with hatred deep in his ember eyes.

Eulo flattened his hands on the table, pushing himself up in a slow exaggeration of his strength. Vivica's foot fell away, unseen by anyone else. He stared at Ranson the whole while. *Ain't nothing to be scared of in you, little man.*

"No, Eulo," Tali said, "Ranson will help his matriarch upstairs."

Eulo straightened to his full height, unsure if she aimed the bite in her words at him or her father. "It ain't no problem. Where I come from, we measure ourselves by how well we take care of our weakest." He curled the corner of his mouth, knowing it didn't hide his disgust.

"Keep telling yourself that, Iskarlian. Your Cove and his arse-lickers sit in their mansions surrounded by decadence and gold while your people raise arms at each other so they don't starve. You fool." Ranson snorted. "You think you'll bring your whole family to live here, don't you?" Spit flecked from his mouth. "Why *are* you here? For money?"

"Of course I bloody am, aren't you?" Eulo boomed out laughter, shaking his head at the older man's surprise.

"You're a killer, like the rest of the Iskarlians coming off the boats. Go on, how many people have you killed?"

*Enough*, Eulo thought, however many that was. But that didn't mean he wouldn't do it again, especially not if it meant it would get Remmy back alive.

Ranson opened his mouth again but Tali spoke first.

"Enough!" She stabbed a finger towards her father. "We are not having this conversation." She navigated her grandmother's chair out from under the table.

"Why not? Lyselle probably wishes she had, before her Iskarlian cut-throat left her flayed body on her dining table and fled with all her coin." Ranson flung his arms up. "This thug will deny considering it, but I bet he has."

"Keep pushing and you might find out the hard way, eh?" Eulo narrowed his eyes above a wolfish grin, before walking out of the room behind Tali and Mema. Tali's blue silk dress traced the lines of her body from neck to ankle. It suited her, especially the slit exposing black, heeled boots laced to the knee.

At the foot of the stairs, she glanced at him over the top of her grandmother's tousled silver head. Fatigue pinched the corners of her eyes. She said, "I'm sorry. I tried to warn you how obstinate they are."

Mema giggled.

"Ain't no worry to me. He's all riled up over nothing. Maybe he ought to come stand on the plains sometime and meet some folk who really got it hard." Eulo squatted beside the old woman. "I reckon it'd be easier if I carry you without the chair, does that sound alright to you?"

She held her arms out, giggling again.

"Mema likes you, anyway," Tali said, although she gasped when Eulo scooped her grandmother up.

He carried the husk of a woman upstairs, her grip weak around his neck. Tali lugged the wheeled chair in their wake, her curses echoing in the huge foyer. Eulo followed the oil-lamps down the hallway to the room where they'd met the old woman earlier.

"All lit up to chase away the shadows, eh?" He pushed the door open with his foot. Mako knew, nothing would chase away all the shadows in this unhappy house. He settled Mema on her bed, as gently as he could. Being in this room felt like an intrusion.

"Bloody rug," Tali shouted from the hallway. Wood scraped on wood for a jarring moment. She stomped in, red-cheeked, pushing the chair. To Eulo, she said, "It will take me a while to settle her. I appreciate you bringing her upstairs." A dismissal.

He cleared his throat. "Then I might go out for some air," he said. And to empty his heavy bladder. It wasn't as if he liked their wine much, but he'd swilled down plenty enough of it during the awkward dinner.

"Alright." Tali's eyes glowed through a stray fall of hair. "And Eulo? Thank you."

Walking out into the night lifted the tight band around Eulo's chest. He wove his way past the pots imprisoning dead flowers outside the front door until he spotted a cluster of bushes edging the lawn. It looked as good a spot as any. Cicadas roared in the vast blue gum forest, chanting the relentless hum of night.

When he'd finished, Eulo dawdled back to the house. Give it a few days and he'd start looking around, see what he could find out about people who might trade Vernese kilili. He was so bloody far away from anywhere, though. Maybe Krike was having better luck finding kilili at Filia Tartula's pig farm. Tali said the Tartula estate was on the outskirts of Silveraine, so if Krike was allowed to roam, he might be able to track down information in town, or the Dross.

"Still here, eh? If I were you, I would've grabbed a horse from the stables and been galloping my way north by now."

Vivica's wry voice drifted to him through the darkness. She reclined with her arm flung along the back of a garden bench beside the house. Moonlight danced on her collarbones, highlighting the slope of those sensational breasts.

Eulo swallowed as she lifted her chin to him, pouted lips apart, her gaze smouldering.

Shades. What was a man supposed to do? He smiled, his veins warming, ignoring the bird of common sense fluttering in his mind. "Vivica. I didn't see you there."

How could he have missed her, though, in a dress the colour of hot coals, with a neckline slashing deep between her knockers? She'd pinned the gauzy sleeves down at the wrist, and the hemline skimmed her knees, short enough to lift up and reveal the treasures underneath.

"Looking is so boring." She ran her red-nailed fingers along the bulge in his crotch. "Wouldn't you agree?" She snared hold of his waistband, pulling his hips towards her.

He sucked in a gasp as he opened his mouth to reply.

"How dare you defile the Sarsega estate and your mother's name by bringing that sand-grubbing filth into this house?" Ranson's outrage echoed off the stone walls in the great room.

Eulo closed the front door with a click. He edged his way to the library where they'd first met Ranson, on legs weak from his encounter with Vivica. His heart galloped, spurred on by the argument he was about to interrupt. He balked in the hallway, listening.

"Don't insult me, Father," Tali said. "You're just mad I didn't humour your scheme. Do you really think Loy bloody Myrtis would let you live here in lazy splendour? If we gave his mother half the chance to get a claim on our estate, she'd sell it out from under us and kick us out on our arses."

Eulo glimpsed her through the doorway, nose to nose with her father, throwing her hands up in frustration. She had a spine of iron Eulo hadn't expected when he'd agreed to the binding, and he liked it.

"Why do you think the thug tied a binding with you, Tali? Cove Vasker would love nothing better than to invade Vernesia from within, and you're helping him. Those men come here to take our women, our money. Our land."

"That's funny; Mema used to say exactly the same thing about you."

"I loved your mother." Ranson thumped his fist against a wooden sideboard.

Eulo narrowed his eyes. Surely the gutless old fart wouldn't dare.

"She didn't love you though, did she? Which is why I couldn't let you blackmail me into binding with Myrtis. Not for all those same, sorry reasons. Mema and Mother built our estate; I won't let you trade it away to try to save your own arse."

Ranson laughed, throwing his head back. "And look at it now. Your mother didn't even want to stay here, and now your grandmother spends her miserable life shitting her pants, while you parade about pretending all of this still means something." He shook his hands at the room. "How are you going to run this place, Tali? You're deluded about making an income off your horses. Do you think your husband hasn't noticed the rot and decay setting in here? You think he'll stick around when he realises the Sarsegas haven't got two gold coins to rub together?"

She laughed. "Is the gossip true about you having an affair with Shilya?"

He swung his fist at her. Caught by surprise, Tali staggered away from his wild haymaker, falling over a footstool and out of his reach. She sprawled on her arse on the rug, gaping wide-eyed at her father swaying over her. Apparently Eulo wasn't the only one who'd been swilling down good Vernesian wine over dinner.

"I'm ashamed to call you daughter," Ranson spat, raising his arm again.

Eulo crossed the room in three strides. He locked his fingers around the Vernese's wrist, reefing Ranson's arm back at the shoulder. "I wouldn't do that if I were you," he said in his hunter's menacing whisper. Ranson struggled, so Eulo wrenched his arm far enough to make the gristle scream. The colour bled from Ranson's face.

"Raise a hand to my wife again, old man, and I'll shatter every fucking bone in it," Eulo snarled. He swatted him aside like an annoying blowfly.

Tali scrambled to her feet. "That'll do!" She glared at Ranson. "If Mema could, she'd revoke her vow to let you stay here after Mother left, just like she did with my grandfather. Start thinking about how you're going to earn your keep, Father." She held out her hand to Eulo, her ring catching a gleam of lamplight.

He sneered at Ranson as they walked out. The older man shrank back against an armchair, clutching his arm, his eyes rolling white.

Out in the great room, Vivica sat halfway up the staircase, her dress pooling around her. She pouted at Tali's hand in Eulo's, although a smirk played across her lips.

"Shut up, Vivica," Tali said, walking out the front door without stopping.

Eulo held her hand all the way to the cottage, connected by the warmth of skin against skin, binding ring to binding ring, dwarfed by the star-spilt darkness above. Colours winked in the sky, grey-green and mauve, so fast Eulo must've imagined it. He swallowed, his belly crawling as Vivica's mocking tone chased him up the path: *What do you think Tali will do, if she gets the idea you've been screwing her sister?*

Tali hadn't spoken since leaving the house, her mouth slashed into a thin line across her face. Eulo reckoned the Sarsega's earlier argument would've been fiercer if he hadn't been there. Tali had handled her family like a duty-bound Iskarlian soldier. He studied her for a long moment. Shades knew, he was no expert on fixing broken families, so he let her be, drowning in her thoughts.

Her boots rattled against the wooden planks of her verandah. She let go of Eulo to push open the cottage door. The dying firelight inside caught her silhouette, casting a glow on her loose hair, in the sunset hue of her dress. An aura, a butterfly he couldn't catch.

"Eulo." She faced him in the low light, her voice heavy with emotion.

"Don't," he mumbled. Don't apologise, don't say thanks, don't feed the serpent twisting in his guts.

Tali silenced his protest with her lips. She dug her fingers into his upper arms. His hands rose in surprise, lost between pulling her into him, carrying her across to the bed, or the couch, or the rug. Or table, or whatever bloody bit of furniture they struck first. Mako's teeth, he'd lusted after this woman for days, and now he had her.

Right after he'd threatened her father for naming Eulo for exactly what he was—an opportunistic bastard without morals.

"Stop," Eulo growled, at himself. "I won't...I can't do this—"

Tali cut him off by shoving herself back from him. Not even surprised, just resigned. She composed herself quickly. "Well, I suppose that tells me what I needed to know." As though he'd failed a trial.

Eulo's mouth went dry. If she thought he was messing around with her sister, she'd send him on his way with no money, no contacts. Truth was, he needed Tali; needed time to learn how Vernesia worked, who he should ally himself with, and where to get kilili. So he shrugged, nonchalant, although it wasn't what she deserved. Eulo's guts writhed. It made it so much worse knowing he was going to hurt her before their agreement was up.

# Chapter 12

Typical, how the more you looked at something, the less it added up. Tali pulled a face at the neat row of calculations in her ledger, as thought it would magic them into the right numbers. Even when she included the coin she'd earnt selling her kilili blades in Port Garnet, the Glimmers Gap outgoings exceeded incomings.

"Well," she said to Chance, "I guess it'll never add up while Ranson and Vivica are dipping their hands into the jar for wine and new clothes." The cat stared at her through yellow eyes, not helpful in the slightest.

Early sunshine spilt over their seat on the front steps of her cottage. The overnight chill wouldn't relinquish its grip on the air for hours yet. She gathered a mug of kaif from beside her boot, blowing away the steam rising from the black liquid. Chance blinked, twitching an ear at the sudden sound of crashing inside, followed by Eulo yelping out a curse.

Tali shook her head. "So, for all his flirting, it seems my husband is fickle about women." She sighed. Not to mention Vivica's complete disregard for her. Again. Toying with Tali's partners seemed to be Vivi's way of rebelling against being at Glimmers instead of the Academy. Tali oughtn't have been surprised, so why was she so bloody disappointed?

Eulo stepped out to join her, his bare feet slapping on the lopsided verandah. "Mornin'. What'cha looking at?"

She angled her head to block the sun from her eyes. "They're the Glimmers Gap ledgers, for counting all the money we don't have." After the problem with their debts at Kylas's store and Ranson's tantrum last night, there was no point dancing around that fact anymore.

"Uh," Eulo shrugged, disinterested.

"I can teach you. Being able to read and write would help you a lot when you leave here."

"It ain't the sort o' thing for me." He leant over the handrail and spat into the grass.

"That's right, I remember now: mercenary, enjoys sticking things into people," Tali said. She sipped her kaif, drowning her curt disenchantment with him.

Beside her on the step, Chance's eyes grew big and black. Almost like he knew. He extended his open paw to Eulo's foot, swiping his big toe.

"Gah." The big Iskarlian jumped in the air.

Chance narrowed his eyes. He lifted his leg and licked his arse.

"It's fine, Eulo. The cows won't care whether you're illiterate or not. I suppose you'll need breakfast before we go?"

"Go where?" For the first time, Eulo noticed the pair of horses at the hitching rail. "That ain't my horse."

"Well, you rode Flame so well I thought I'd put you to work on the youngsters." She stretched her legs out straight along the splitting grey planks. She tapped her toes together, reining in her temper. It'd be pointless getting sour at Eulo when he'd only just gotten here.

Still, Tali smarted at his rejection last night. After dealing with her family, she'd just wanted the comfort of losing herself in someone fit, good-looking and removed from the tedium of the Sarsega estate and upper-class Vernese politics. She couldn't even do that right. She rubbed her scabbing shoulder, trying to ease the pulling, itching wound. At least it was healing now she'd returned to Glimmers, in time for her to smith more kilili.

Eulo shuffled inside, swearing as he stubbed his toe on the threshold. How in blazes did he fight in battle—by falling on people?

He returned with his breakfast in one hand and a mug of kaif in the other, sweetened so heavily Tali could smell the sugar before he sat down. On his lap he balanced the pan she'd left with two fat sausages in it, which were now joined by three fried eggs.

"Did you sleep alright?" he said, through a mouthful of food.

"Fine," Tali said, as though the incident with Ranson had passed her by like a summer breeze. Inside, she churned at the knowledge she'd enraged her father enough to want to punch her. He never raised his voice at Vivica, who'd gained all his affection and approval growing up. The best Tali could do was remind him how she'd failed to stop his wife from leaving them.

"I'll tear both his fucking arms off if he tries it again."

Tali shivered. This was the man she'd bound with. "I'm paying you to be my husband, not to kill people. I can sort out my own family problems."

He bit off a mouthful of sausage. "Is that why you got a fancy knife? That's a blade what ought to be in the hands of a fighting man, not a rich pastoralist girl who's got no clue how to handle a blade."

She pressed her tongue into the corner of her mouth. If only he knew. "Is that what you were doing when you carved a chunk out of my table?"

He grinned at her, "I'm surprised you noticed it under all the mess."

Oh, she'd noticed. Same as his boots askew in the doorway, when she'd woken this morning, and his clothes scattered across the bedroom floor, along with a knife and woollen hat, coins and a whetstone. His naked, sculpted back and tousled hair, where he'd sprawled asleep in her bed. Those little bits of Eulo Juke's life suddenly peppered through her own. After not even a whole day.

"It's a good knife."

"I know." Of course she did. She'd made it, after all. She'd recognised her talent for kililismithing from the very first time she'd enticed the motes of magic free from their physical self and melded them into red-hot iron.

"One of them," Eulo waved his fork around, searching for the right word, finding it and mangling it in his thick twang, "kaleeli blades."

"Kilili," Tali corrected, unsurprised an Iskarlian warrior would know about flickerblades. The red island was their biggest market for kilili; the very reason she'd been in Port Garnet in the first place. Eulo wasn't going to find out about that, though. Singing the kilili was a Sarsega secret; how Tali and her aunt Cyska were the only ones left in the family with the silver tattoos lacing their skins, and the talent to coax the magic aura out into beautiful and often lethal forms of silveriron.

"Silveriron makes the best weapons I've ever used. All the Covesmen and Scabmen like 'em, if they can manage to buy or steal one," Eulo said. "Where'd you get it from?"

"Oh, you know. Here and there."

"A man always take a bit more care when he realises you're coming at him with a flickerblade in your hand. It makes you lighter, quieter. Deadlier."

"Weapons for a strong militia." Tali thought of Ranson's words. Was he being hysterical, or were she and Cyska really arming a potential Vernese enemy with their enchanted weapons? Her back prickled. She shifted to rub her troublesome shoulder against the wooden post behind her. Eulo didn't notice, being too busy teasing Chance with a wedge of sausage.

The cat peered at him, his purr crackling loud in the still morning. He lifted one ginger paw, reaching out to bat Eulo's fingers, which pincered the morsel. When Eulo dropped the sausage on the step, Chance fell on it with the same unrestrained pleasure as the Iskarlian devouring his own breakfast. Eulo mopped up a trail of grease and egg yolk with his last chunk of bread, then pushed the empty pan aside, grinning at Chance as the cat rushed over to investigate it. He stretched out, resting on one elbow.

"What does Ranson do?"

"Blazes," hissed Tali, scooping the cat up with one hand under his belly. She deposited him away from the pan, in the sweetgrass gone wild around the side of the stairs. Chance's eyes grew wide and black. Lured to Eulo's alliance with food, the fluffy ginger traitor licked his lips.

Eulo studied Tali over the top of his mug, his blue gaze sharp. He lifted a sandy eyebrow, waiting for her reply.

"Ranson does the dirty work. Business meetings, finding markets for our produce, paying our taxes to the Kestrine, dealing with the money house. And," she grimaced, "managing estate relations."

"Like the Myrtises?"

"Yes." Tali eased her fingers through a tangle in her hair. "Ranson turned my mother's idea for me to bind with Loy into an idiotic scheme to fund his retirement. The Myrtises would sell our land if they could, ruining everything my mother and Mema worked so hard for, and her mother and grandmother before her. Shame Ranson doesn't understand the concept of spending less than you earn." She broke off without mentioning how much her father and sister criticised her hopes to expand the Glimmers horse enterprise.

Her intimate family politics weren't of Eulo's concern. He shouldn't be of her concern, either, if she'd followed her plan to sell Flame and the binding rings to build up the estate's coffers. All she could do now was hope their temporary arrangement would eventually benefit everyone.

Tali felt no triumph in avoiding being chained to the Myrtis family. With her bound out of the market of eligible Vernese dignitines, everyone else who wanted to get their hands on the Sarsega's supposed wealth would turn their focus to Vivica.

Seven flickerblades. Twenty cows. Ten Flames. One urn of Lolani in the Silveraine shrine. The price she had to pay for Vivica to audition at the artists' Academy to become a lyricene. Blazes, the idiots there would beg her to enrol if they'd just let her sing without seven thousand kistars in her hand. But the Sarsegas had more chance of pulling down the sun than getting a Silveraine official to waver from the rules.

Almost without noticing, Tali rubbed her wound again. Five more blades? She was only just recovering from making her binding rings and the flickerblades she'd sold in Port Garnet. She let go of her shoulder, splaying her left hand in front of her. A fresh wash of green almost completely covered the silver of her binding ring, renewed by contact with her kilili tattoo, even through her bandage and linen shirt.

The Myrtis family's binding endowment to her would've covered the Academy fee, and more. Shilya Myrtis would've embraced the chance to send the temptress Vivica to Silveraine, removing her from the southern high society's impressionable sons and daughters. Breaking the Sarsega family into pieces while she took their estate. Not that Vivica would care.

There was no room to worry about it. Tali's decision had been made, bound in a smattering of vows and a pair of silveriron rings.

She straightened up and turned to Eulo. "We should get going before the rest of the morning disappears."

The black gelding scrambled up the creek bank, tossing his head as he reached level ground. Tali scratched his withers, murmuring to him as they settled beside Eulo's mare. Huon would be taking the pair to Rithisak Tath next week.

She chewed her lip. Now that he'd be over the shock of finding out about Eulo, Rith might refuse to buy her horses. If word spread that the Kestrine didn't want Sarsega horses, it wouldn't take long for others to create more rumours to twist the situation to their advantage. Tali rubbed a strand of the gelding's mane between her fingers. Rith was the gentlest person she'd ever met, but love and lust could bring out the worst in people, sometimes from those you thought you knew best.

"Hey, mercenary," she said to Eulo, clicking her horse faster, "race you to the top?" The drumbeat of hooves pounded her worries into the dirt. Skua parrots darted through a tangle of old gums and clamouring undergrowth, banking to head beyond the canopy of silver-green leaves. Their screeches were coarse enough to shred holes in the sky. Pretty animals with jagged voices, like some people Tali knew.

Eulo's mare plunged ahead, reaching the crest first. He reined in, open-mouthed at the sight of cows trailing down the pasture like spots of ink on an emerald scarf, to browse ribbons of bull kelp on the beach. For a moment, the steel in his eyes and the bluster of his grin softened into unguarded wonder.

He twisted to look at her, resting one hand on his thigh. "This is all yours?"

She nodded, struck by how little she knew about him. "This, dear husband, is where you'll be checking our livestock, earning your wage for the month."

"This'd be the sort of place for smuggling. You could moor a ship here and get ashore, not like them cliffs up north."

A finger of tension tugged at Tali's spine. "No one would be landing ships here. There's a reef about three hundred paces offshore, waiting to tear the belly out of any vessel. If the tides didn't toss you onto the rocks first."

Eulo shaded his eyes, squinting out over set after set of waves.

"Did you come here to spy for smuggling routes?" An edge cut into her tone.

He turned his horse to face her. "What do you know of it?"

Their knees brushed together as the horses fidgeted. Tali shifted her leg back on the gelding's flank, cueing him to step aside. The Iskarlian's fierce gaze clung to her like a three-corner jack. Whatever impelled his interest in boats sneaking into Vernesia, it burnt in him with the might of a bushfire.

"I trade in livestock, not people," she said. "I'd sooner die than help exploit anyone."

"Me too."

Eulo spun his horse around, spurring the mare down the track. Tali's gelding bounced after them, unbalanced on the slope. Thoughts jumbled in her mind, pushed by the itching curiosity to know more about her husband. She'd been so quick to assume he'd been escaping Iskarlia, she hadn't considered that he might've been hunting something. Or someone.

Eulo's mare crossed the breach from soft pasture to coarse sand and cantered away. Tali's gelding wheeled and bucked, running sideways, wanting to follow. The horse settled as they drifted through the herd of cattle making sure her assets were all healthy and well. The job Eulo should've been learning. She chewed her lip, frustrated by her spiralling lack of control over everything: her family, their debts, the kilili, and now the husband she'd dragged here in defiance. Loneliness spiked at her, prodding awake an overwhelming sense of self-doubt.

She sighed, letting the sun soak into her bones. This was where she healed, in the breath of parrots on newly unfurled leaves, the kiss of saltwater tides on millions of grains of sand, under a sky painted by cloud and sun, moon and stars. Boulders clustered here like marbles rolled down the hillside by a giant hand, coming to eternal rest at the water's edge, gathering a coat of fire-orange algae.

Tali dropped a slender knife out of its sheath in her left sleeve. A mauve shadow rippled along the blade, catching the glare of the sunlight and ocean. No wider than her thumb, the silveriron held the same keen edge as any other kilili weapon. She ran one finger along the flat of the blade. A deep resonance hummed through her veins, striking harmony with the higher-pitched greensilver in her half-healed tattoo.

She blinked back sudden tears. Mauve was Mema's colour, a variation from Aunt Cyska's brilliant violet. Tali's green deviated from the Sarsega spectrum, probably affected by the paternal lines over each generation, which happened more than anyone cared to admit. Not that anyone admitted to bearing kilili, though, unless it was to a trusted confidante. The secrecy fostered the appeal of the enchanted silver goods and, of course, self-preservation of those who carried and smithed it. Swallowing hard, she secured the blade in her sleeve again.

"People ask me why I don't live in Silveraine, you know," Tali said to Eulo, when he rode back to her. "As though I'd want to be in a stinking muckheap where everyone gets all crabbed about living on top of everyone else." She rolled her eyes. "They don't know what to do with themselves out here. Like Vivi. She doesn't believe me, but the cows are happier when she sings. Fat cows make better meat, and better meat makes better money."

"We always reckon something else is better than what we got." Eulo twisted the end of the reins in his big hands.

"It's alright if you don't want to tell me about yourself," she said, even though it rankled her.

"There's things about me, Tali, what you're better off not knowing. People I know who you don't ever want to meet."

# Chapter 13

He blew out a deep breath. "I'll be gone in a few weeks, and you can keep doing what you're doing like I was never here. It's the only way I can protect you."

"Protect me?" Tali laughed. If only he knew about the knife in her sleeve or the death she whispered into blades so men could maim and murder each other. "I need you out here, Eulo, protecting my herd."

"Protecting cows?"

"Protecting my assets, my income, the Sarsega estate, and my ability to pay the month's wage I promised you." There, now she had his attention. She'd never met a soldier who didn't think in coin.

"What'll you be doing?"

"Training the horses, keeping the books, fighting with my family, smoothing over upsets with every man and their dog."

*Kililismithing.*

"Sounds busy."

"Don't doubt it," Tali said.

Eulo nodded. Good. His readiness to act was a nice change from her father and sister.

"What's that?" He pointed out over the ribboning aqua water to an isolated expanse of pasture and trees.

"Glassrock Island, where we graze the cattle sometimes."

"Over there? Across the water?"

She nodded. "We take them over at low tide."

"Isn't it dangerous?"

"It's what we quarrelled about the day my mother left," Tali blurted, like a dam wall cracking open in a flood. "We made the crossing late, and her horse panicked. She'd ridden that stretch of water regularly for thirty years. It was an accident, but afterwards she…she was so angry.

She rode out the front gate and we never saw her again." Life in their house had never been the same since. A familiar ball of remorse and sadness choked her words.

"That must've been rough."

"Ranson changed overnight like all his happiness was gone forever. He had these furious arguments with my aunt Cyska, blaming her. Blaming me." She swallowed. "Cyska's refused to set foot in the house ever since."

"He must've really loved your mother."

"He's empty without her." Tali blinked back tears, surprised by Eulo's gentle response. She steeled herself. "I didn't employ you to have to hear this."

"Maybe you ought to talk to someone about it. Your aunt, or Vivica."

"Maybe." Cyska avoided discussing it and Vivi, too young to remember much, stuck steadfast to her father's side, holding Tali and Cyska responsible.

Eulo reached across to take her hand. Maybe she'd underestimated him. Tali ran her tongue over her dry lips. "Tonight, I'm going to the Bintau pub with Huon and Cyska. We go for a drink every week or two. You're welcome to come."

"Looking for someone to carry you home, eh?"

"Well, and I thought I might show off my exotic husband to all the gossips,"

"Maybe I ought to get those fancy pants back off your stockman." He squeezed her fingers. Their rings chimed together, a song which hummed through Tali's tattoo. "We could have some fun, eh, wife of much beautiful." Mischief gleamed in his eyes.

Tali's pulse quickened. She ducked her head as a huge wave crashed onto the rocks nearby, stinging their faces with salt spray. Scraping hair out of her eyes, she said, "I'm in for trouble with you, aren't I?"

He grinned. "It's what I do best."

"Tell me Tali, how did you choose which husband to buy?" Cyska Sarsega slouched on the leather lounge, turning her boots to and fro in front of the famed Bintau pub fireplace. The warmest spot in the south, they called it. She tilted her head at Tali, raising an eyebrow.

"I picked the best-looking man with bucketloads of ego and a talent for bullshit." Tali winked over the top of her mug.

Cyska laughed. "Don't s'pose any of them were looking for a nice quiet librarian to settle down with?"

"I'm pretty sure none of them was looking to settle down," Tali said, debating whether to admit what she was really doing with the big Iskarlian on the other side of the room.

"I don't know about that. Your bloke's had eyes on you the whole time we've been here."

"Eulo?" Tali sat upright. Her tattoo prickled. She squashed the urge to turn around and glimpse him standing at the bar with Huon.

"Like he owns you." Cyska shrugged, waving her drink around.

"What?" Tali spun, glaring past tables of drinkers. Eulo watched her openly. His knowing smile loosed a flutter in her belly.

Cyska's deep chuckle should've come from a burly blacksmith, not a middle-aged woman. "You idiot. He's admiring you." She pushed her glasses up on her nose.

Tali pressed her lips together. "Great. Dealing with a drunken, possessive Iskarlian isn't in my plans."

"No, not jealous. More...like he can't take his eyes off you."

She smacked Cyska on the arm. "Stop it."

"You surprised us. No wonder Ranson is in such a filthy mood. Huon said he was stomping around the stables this afternoon, muttering something about a binding in Oyster Bay."

"Oh, I forgot," Tali said. Eulo's imposing presence slipped right into the raucous, warm pub, but a dignitine's binding was another crowd altogether—and nothing like their own ceremony. "He might insist me and Eulo don't go."

"And lose face? Ha! You know the rules—Mr Sarsega must be presented to the world." Cyska tucked a lock of hair behind her ear. "How did the rest of your business go in Iskarlia?"

"Good," Tali nodded. "He was happy. Paid a good price. Wants more."

"Mmm. Those Iskarlians can't get enough silveriron. The Scabmen are frothing for the stuff that's been smithed well. Not everyone has the knack for it." Cyska played with one dangling earring. "Besides, what Iskarlian man doesn't want a good flickerblade on his belt?"

Tali's gaze strayed to her husband's languid figure where he leant on the bar, laughing with Huon and Aidene, the publican. Aidene pointed to the unattended snarlsboard. Five lilac snarls spiked the centre of each target, while the blue snarls were stuck in the board's dead-land. One had jammed in the plaster above the board, thrown by a player with brute strength and no aim. The trio laughed again.

Tali rolled up the sleeves of her green shirt, an old favourite with the wool soft against her skin.

"Going to challenge him to a game, eh? The poor bastard." Cyska cocked her head, smirking. "Imagine the smugness being slapped off the Myrtis's jowls when they find out you've tied a binding to an Iskarlian. I hope I get to see Loy's face when he meets him in person." She sipped her cider, bouncing one leg across the other. "Did you banish Eulo to babysit the beach cows to keep him away from other women?"

"*Cyska.*" Tali thumped her empty mug on the table.

"Shit. I'm sorry." Cyska patted her knee. "Huon's happy to have another Iskarlian at Glimmers, at any rate"—her tone sobered—"but only if Eulo treats you well."

Tali stood up, brushing her off. "You know me, disappointing everyone again."

"That's crap, girl. I bet right now, Eulo Juke counts himself the luckiest man alive."

Cyska's words bounced in Tali's mind as she sauntered over to the bar. The grog sent an extra swing into her hips. Fuck 'em all, every one of them watching her and whispering behind their hands. She'd save her property and get Vivica into the Academy, no matter what. Then, and only then, would she have made amends for their mother leaving, for Vivi growing up without a mother's love and kindness.

"Hey." Eulo shot her a crooked grin. He slid an arm around her waist, playing his role with glee.

"We were explaining to your man here how to throw a snarl, geeing him up for a game," Aidene said, eyes shining in her square face. She nodded to Eulo. "The snarlsboard has pride o' place in all the best Vernese pubs. It's been part of Vernesia's history, our heritage, for thousands of years."

"Oh, I could show you—" Tali began.

Trailing in her wake, Cyska cut her off, saying, "Tali can't play to save her life. You'd beat her easy, Eulo."

Tali said, "In that case, you and I can play while he watches. I wouldn't want anyone getting hurt." She stamped on Cyska's toes on her way to pick the snarls out of the board. It was kililismith tradition to make a set to leave at any pub in any town, as a blessing of good fortune. Legend said anyone who tried to steal snarls would be cursed by the goddess, and in time it had become something people dare not do in Vernesia. Years ago, Tali had left her set on the bar in a pub west of Silveraine, somewhere she hadn't visited since and couldn't easily be traced to.

"Anyone care to lay a bet?" Aidene clapped her hands, eliciting a snicker from her patrons.

"A splinter on Cyska," someone hooted.

"Ten splinters on Tali," Eulo said. He hunted in his pockets, then dropped a handful of coins on the bar, beaming at her.

Blazes, he thought he was being kind to her. Tali relished the chance to show off a little. She held her hands out to Cyska, revealing blue snarls in the left, violet in the right. "Show us how it's done, snarlsmaster."

Her aunt leant close to hiss, "Look, Tali, I'm sorry, alright. Is this really necessary"—she glanced sideways at a trio of men—"in front of the drovers?"

"They're too busy gawping at Aidene's tits to care what you're doing. So choose your colour."

Cyska took a handful of kilili silveriron, each snarl twisted like a fencing knot. Violet—her own work, but the magic wouldn't save her now. Her first shot went wide, landing in the blue felt on the upper right-hand side of the board. The crowd let out a collective "ah" of sympathy. Tali took position seven paces back from the wall where the snarlsboard hung, toeing a floorboard worn smooth by years of contender's boots. She held one prong of her first bluesilver snarl, sizing up the seven circles of varying sizes and colours on the board. The small black circle was worth the most in points, coin and respect.

To one side, she glimpsed Cyska standing with hands stuffed in her trouser pockets. Tali relented a little, aimed to the left, and loosed the snarl with a flick of the wrist. It landed true, at right angles to the red two target. The crowd offered polite applause. Eulo raised an eyebrow at Tali and nodded his approval. She spread her hands wide, pleased to have surprised him.

"Going to toy with me, are you?" Cyska muttered to her as they swapped places. She managed to score a four, which Tali knocked out with her next turn, and the two after it, to the crowd's delight. Letting her aunt keep the one she narrowly skimmed on her last shot, Tali opted to land her final bluesilver snarl dead centre in the black ten. The onlookers clapped and cheered.

"Shades, don't let this get out or the Cove will have you fighting in his army," Eulo said, tossing his arm around Tali and squeezing her body into his.

Her lips tasted sweet from his kisses, having fallen easily into the charade of playing newly-bounds with a strong attraction to each other. It hadn't been hard to make each other laugh or play up the connection they had. No, the hard part was going home drunk to share a bed without crossing the tenuous line they'd both drawn.

Blazes. Tali puffed out her exasperation. Of her already long list of problems, she really didn't need the added complication of letting

Eulo get under her skin. She'd chosen him because he'd been funny and approachable straight up. It'd never occurred to her she might actually start to fancy him.

"Here, handsome, it's your turn." Aidene stretched across the bar to Eulo, offering him a handful of smoke-tinged snarls. She winked at Tali, as though bringing the Iskarlian here was the best decision she'd ever made. At Aidene's age, there probably wasn't much she hadn't seen, and she treated all her patrons with the same courtesy, no matter what their background.

Eulo collected the pieces, considering one between his fingers. He trailed behind Tali to the marked floorboard. "What's the trick, beautiful wife of much luck?"

"Luck and skill are different talents, big husband of much cheek." Tali plucked the snarl out of his grip, rolling it between the tip of her thumb and forefinger so she could take hold of the longest prong. "Start with the big one if you want to stick it in"—she held it a handspan from her eyes, lining up the target—"find your mark and throw." She snapped her wrist down without letting go of the piece. Smiling, she passed it to Eulo. "Easy, eh?"

"Easier than hitting moving prey with a starfire dart, at any rate." He toed the pitch-line, ghosting his shot. Fluid and easy, barely measuring the weight of the snarl before flicking it in one deliberate motion. The snarl thudded into the ten, lodging deep into the felt beside Tali's bluesilver. A few people in the crowd whooped over resounding applause.

Her mouth went dry at the thought of a bundle of metal spikes hurled into someone's back, then the marionette jerk of their body being drawn in on a starfire leash. No Sarsega had made such a weapon or ever would, even though just one could've paid Vivi's fees at the Academy twice over. And Eulo had just admitted to using one.

Tali swooned at a sudden surge of dizziness, throwing out a hand to steady herself against the thick ashwood bar. Her fingers met sticky, stale alcohol on the wood, waiting to trap the unwary. No one noticed her. Not when the tall Iskarlian had just sunk five snarls into the ten-point target with quiet assurance, making himself even more conspicuous in the crowded pub. Patrons had crowded over to watch, grinning and clapping at the Iskarlian's fortuitous game. Huon slapped him on the back, while Cyska offered prim applause.

"Now we know why Tali picked you, eh?" Aidene called to Eulo. "For a bit of competition. She deserves someone whose skills are nearly as good as her own."

"Is that right?" Eulo strutted over to Tali, hitching one corner of his mouth. "*Nearly?*"

"I didn't learn my skills by spiking people in the back."

"Criminals, not people." He sobered. "Rapists, murderers, rebels." He placed his hand over hers, rubbing his thumb over her knuckles, his voice low, hoarse. "It ain't no use a man regretting a past he can't change."

"He could make himself a better man," Tali said, thinking of Ranson moping about the house, refusing to go out, just wallowing in the never-fading misery of losing his wife. Deluding himself into thinking the Myrtis family would happily pay for him to keep doing it.

Eulo flashed a sad smile. "Maybe he don't know how." He let go of her hand and went to retrieve the snarls, his deep voice resonating in the crowded room. "Any takers on another game? How 'bout some real bets this time?"

# Chapter 14

Flame stumbled, his forehand dropping away beneath Eulo for a heart-jolting moment. The Iskarlian let the reins slide through his hands, easing the gelding back into a canter, both of them keen to be heading home after a busy day drifting through the hills. He also wanted time to wash the stink of sweat off his carcass before his wife saw him.

Despite his gnawing impatience, he brought Flame back to a walk. Tali would be angry if her best horse broke down. He ran a hand over his mouth. It was easy to make her laugh, but he was pretty good at frustrating her too, and she didn't deserve that.

The disappointment of being stuck out on a wind-battered hill instead of finding kilili had eased after visiting the pub with Tali. People respected her, so most of 'em had accepted him too. When the carry-on about him faded, he'd dig for leads on who might sell kilili, maybe from canny old Huon, or in Oyster Point, where they were heading tomorrow for some fancy party.

The trees stretched long shadow fingers to brush at Flame's hooves. A chill swept down Eulo's spine. Tali would've laughed if she knew how much this massive forest plucked at his nerves. There were too many shapes and silhouettes to hide behind, under the cloud-scratching trees which bobbed their branches together to block out the Vernese goddess-loving sky. He shivered in his oilskin coat, not just from the sunless air along this track. Nowhere in Iskarlia made him this jumpy.

"I must be going soft, eh, Flame-boy, getting homesick for that lump of sand over the ocean." He rubbed his palm along the horse's warm neck. It'd be good to sit down tonight with Tali over a mug of kaif. He'd gotten a taste for the stuff, and he liked the way she brewed it up with a good slosh of rum to share with him.

He ran into her coming out of the cottage as he lumped his saddlebags up the steps. Caught in the tight space, Eulo pulled away from her. Her eyebrows dipped for a moment, then she covered her confusion with a frown. Mako's teeth, he'd messed up here.

She hesitated at the bottom of the stairs. "Long day?"

"Mmm." He'd explored as much of the property as he'd dared, but only finding pasture, mountains and ocean in any direction. "You going out?"

"For a walk." She raised one hand in a dismissive farewell. A ginger ball exploded out of the shrubs at the corner of the cottage. Chance, tailing his mistress into the gloaming. Tali's lean figure disappeared through the trees edging the track up to the back hills.

What the fuck was she doing, anyway, wandering off at this time almost every night?

Eulo ought to call her back, tell her it wasn't safe to go off in the dark alone. He wasn't the type to get jealous, but something yellow and ugly clawed at him. Maybe his wife was going to a place where she wouldn't be alone.

He dug into his saddlebags, pulling out the salt beef he'd put aside from his lunch, and a handful of splinters he'd collected. Keeping an eye on the path Tali had taken, he strode around the cottage, heading for a big old tree beyond the horse yard. Placing one palm on the dead wood, he reached inside the hollow, groping around until his fingers touched leather. He retrieved the pack he'd hung there, crouching over it as he unlaced the ties.

The wash of his heartbeat raced in his ears. He shoved aside clothes, hiding the coins and parcel of food under them. His fingers brushed against a purple kilili necklace he'd found down the back of Tali's armchair, one she must've already given up on finding. He stuffed the clothes back and tied the pack firmly to keep vermin out. Tali owned so much already, she'd hardly miss a few belongings. He reached into the tree, stashing the pack and its contents out of view. He'd need them when it came time to return to the Scabmen.

The tightness pressing on Eulo's throat gave him the sense of being in a nightmare where he was choking, except here he was dreaming awake. He tugged at his collar, clearing his throat.

"You sound like Chance coughing up hairballs," Tali said. Amusement lit her face, although not even carefully applied eyepaint and carmine red lip stain could hide the black hollows under her eyes.

No wonder, when she'd come crawling into bed around midnight, drawing her cold limbs away from Eulo, hoarding the scent of whoever she'd gone to meet. He swallowed, running a finger around his collar again. He'd picked the black shirt out of the bundle of clothes Huon gave him when he'd arrived at Glimmers Gap, without bothering to try it on first.

"Here." Tali stopped him with a hand flattened on his chest, above his thundering heartbeat. She popped open the top shirt-button. "That suits you better, eh. A good Iskarlian should never be fastened up to the chin."

Eulo shared her smile, now the pressure had lifted from his throat. Bloody arse he was, all edgy as if he were trooping into a skirmish beside the Cove's legion, instead of arriving at some party full of prissed-up Vernese with too much money. Not just a party, either, but a binding. A formal one, between the daughter and son of some high influence dignitines. Exactly the sort of people Vasker would go after if he ever got reckless enough to try overthrowing Vernesia, not that anyone around Eulo right now seemed too worried at the prospect of Iskarlian militants appearing on their doorstep.

The Sarsegas trod a raked white shell path, following the other guests to a stone mansion. The Ces family had pruned and smoothed their estate into perfection, from its spotless stables to the rows of fruit trees parting the hillside and animal-shaped shrubs along the driveway. No scrubcats though, Eulo smirked. The mansion echoed the straight lines of the Sarsega homestead, except it was much bigger and had painted doors and verandahs. Glimmers Gap must've once been this well-kept.

He noticed a smatter of ginger hair clinging to the velvet over Tali's left breast and decided he ought not try to brush it off. She looked down and swiped at it herself, muttering curses at Chance.

"Look at us, eh," Vivica's venomous tone rose beside them, "the Sarsegas pretending to be a happy family." Her gaze sharpened over Tali and Eulo, as though they stained her immaculate presence.

"Everyone here is pretending, some just do it better than others." Ranson flattened his greying hair with one hand, without having even looked at Eulo once the entire ride there. "Some of them even enjoy it." He climbed the stairs with Vivica holding on to his elbow.

"So did he, when my mother was still around," Tali said, so soft Eulo wasn't sure if she'd meant him to hear. She ran an appraising look over him, from his shaven cheeks to Huon's good pants. "You scrub up alright."

"What sort of husband do you want tonight?"

"You do as you please. I'll stay in the shadows."

Having missed his chance to tell Tali she was beautiful in her blood red dress, Eulo reached for her hand. He'd do his best to make them an enviable couple. They emerged into the bright bustle of a room big enough to fit four whole troops of Covesmen. If this was the Cove's stronghold back in Port Jarrison, it'd have four troops just to guard it, but here the only people Eulo saw who might be half-ready to fight were the Iskarlians like him.

Tali spoke to everyone with her usual calm assuredness, quick to laugh with some, not others. Their reactions to Eulo varied from flaring nostrils to smarmy greetings. He was polite to anyone who spoke to and looked at him with half a scrap of respect, including Kardia Riole; Tali's friend from the wifeship. The guests stood about the whole time, stuffing their gobs with petite finger-food and drinks ferried about by a tribe of silent, white-jacketed staff who startled whenever Eulo thanked them for their offerings. It gave him the chance to look each one in the eye, but he didn't see any hints they'd be interested in sharing gossip about Scabmen or kilili with him.

Eulo craned his neck to see acrobats spinning and swinging overhead, like spiders in orange and blue silk. He sucked in a breath as one acrobat spiralled twelve feet down her ribbon. The crowd around him gasped, but she caught herself, flipping around to scissor the ribbon between her legs. She let go with her hands, spreading her arms wide to the audience below, smiling. All part of the act.

He rubbed a thumb across his knuckles, staring at the way skeins of silver glittered through the silk, the sky-defying way the acrobats twisted and twirled in it. Glimpses of kilili spiked his veins: hanging from the guests' ears, across their collarbones, banding their wrists and fingers, threading a silveriron blade hanging on the wall nearby.

The guests eyeballed each other's bright silk dresses, frowning at the silver-shot stole draped around Tali's shoulders. Covering her injury, Eulo reckoned. They eyeballed him too, from the open neck on his shirt of strangulation to his overlong hair and scuffed boots. When their stares strayed into his, he shark-grinned, showing his teeth; the hunter finding his target.

He steeled himself against the noise, the people, his galloping heart. No one among all these people would notice if he slipped away to see what was in the other rooms. There would be rooms full of keepsakes made from kilili. He just had to find them.

"This is worse than I expected," Tali grimaced. "Let's go find a dark corner to hide in."

Eulo wrapped her fingers in his. "There's one good way to stop people from pestering you." He kissed her hand, smouldering a deep gaze at her, the one women couldn't usually resist.

Of course, as he'd realised, Tali was no usual woman.

"Shit." She frowned at an approaching dignitine, her hand straying past her right collarbone.

Her shoulder bothered Eulo, too, in a way he couldn't quite be clear about. He didn't know the dignitine; an older woman who'd scraped her greying hair back tight enough to strain her face against her cheekbones.

"Tali Sarsega. We need to talk." Her mouth wrinkled into a cat's-bum shape.

Tali crossed her arms, edging around so Cat's-bum ended up looking away from Eulo. Like two desert dogs circling each other, ready to fight.

Before he could hear Cat's-bum speak, another woman ambushed him from the side. "Sweet goddess, I almost missed all the excitement."

Eulo swung around. A woman grinned up at him with a mouth full of horse-teeth, knowing she'd caught him speechless. He couldn't escape her hazel stare, magnified by a pair of silver-rimmed spectacles. Cyska Sarsega; the aunt.

"Good to see you again." She offered him her hand. "Are you enjoying yourself?"

"Hmmm…" He shook her long, callused fingers. A worker, like Tali—and his mother. She was about the same age as Shandy Juke too, somewhere in her late forties.

"There are worse things," she said. "But if you didn't know that you'd still be in sunny Iskarlia instead of rubbing shoulders with this lot."

"Who's the beauty talking to Tali, there?"

Cyska clapped her hands together. "That's Shilya Myrtis, Tali's new mother-in-law, and stealer of the Sarsega estate. Almost, anyway, until you appeared." Her eyes sparkled with mischief.

Eulo bristled. When they'd been introduced earlier, Loy Myrtis had sneered at his offer to shake hands. No wonder Tali put a stop to any plans of getting tangled up with the Myrtis family. "You don't reckon she ought've bound with the sour little tosser, do you?"

"So Shilya could sell Glimmers Gap? I've lived there my whole life too, you know."

"No, I don't know. Tali ain't said much."

"No surprise. I'm not often home, I'm usually off carting a library around the countryside. Besides, I'm hardly the most interesting member of the family." She cocked an eyebrow at Vivica, who nuzzled into a round-faced girl on the other side of the room. They kissed openly, without a care for the crowd around them. "Audra, Vivi's friend there, is very good at spreading secrets."

Eulo's mind raced, gabbling over the top of Cyska's chatter. Sweat sprang up on his palms. He'd never considered that the aunt also lived at Glimmers Gap. And if Vivica and her gossipy friend started rumours about Eulo, like she'd threatened…

"This will be very different from your binding ceremony with Tali." Cyska gave a wry smile. "It'll be a glorification."

Eulo recalled muttering his own vows in Iskarlia—something about love and serving his wife. Mostly he remembered the incredible ring she'd presented to him, and their kiss.

Tali returned with the Myrtis woman a step behind her. Seeing as the granite-faced bitch was still watching, Eulo bent to press his lips against Tali's. She squeezed his arm as she pulled back from him. Anticipation shivered down his spine.

"Shilya, this is my husband, Eulo," she said, with a broad, sly smile.

Eulo didn't offer his hand. "Afternoon."

Cat's-bum grimaced. "Oh sweet goddess. I should hardly be surprised that Tali's too insecure to bind herself to a thinking man."

He shrugged. "I like a woman as fierce and beautiful as her estate. Guess she likes having a man with some balls around."

"Keep believing it while you can. You never know when the unexpected might happen." Shilya's eyes glittered.

"Maybe not, but you can strike back harder and faster than your enemies."

"Enemies? What an Iskarlian concept." Shilya laughed, turning her back on him so she faced Tali. "By unexpected things I meant more like your family members suddenly walking off the estate. Imagine what it's like to shirk one's duty as a dignitine, Tali?"

"Don't waste your breath asking Tali because she never will," Cyska cut in, her voice cold. "Besides, you never know when and where you'll find allies to support you. Or tell you when you've overstepped the line. Which is why I must excuse you from our conversation." She extended a hand, dismissing Cat's-bum.

Eulo was pretty sure both women were on the knife-edge separating Vernese respect and rudeness, but Myrtis was the one scowling as she stalked away.

Tali kissed her aunt on the cheeks, right, left, right, the tension on her face melting. "You said you weren't coming."

"I could hardly miss the chance to witness Eulo in action," Cyska hooted with glee. "He's superb. Shilya just turned so red her head might rupture."

"We can dream." Tali rolled her eyes.

Cyska gestured to a vacant bench behind them. Tali sat without argument. Just when Eulo reckoned she looked better, she wasn't. If the aunt noticed, she didn't say so.

"Eulo and I were talking about the binding ceremony," Cyska said. "At least this one should be short. The Ces's are always to the point. Blazes, some of the ceremonies I've attended went for hours." She pulled a face as she dragged her finger across her throat, and added, "Nonetheless, it's good to see Ranson out again, and Vivi never changes, eh?"

"She's so miserable at Glimmers," Tali sighed. "I'm putting all the money I can aside for her."

She'd given Eulo extra money, too, at the Bintau pub so he could gamble and buy people drinks to earn their shaky acquaintance. He drummed his fingers against his thighs. Even here, he couldn't escape the demon appeal of making a bet.

Tali kept talking. "I've got no doubts Vivi will pass an audition. She *was* invited to perform tonight, after all."

Eulo said, "Well, that'll help pay the audition fee."

"Actually, it doesn't. She can't command payment until she's titled Lyricene. So she's performing for goodwill and reputation."

"And no doubt good favour with the Ces family and their many sons. The eligible ones, at least."

Cyska punched Eulo's arm. "These are the games we Vernese like to play."

He shrugged. He didn't understand—or *want* to understand—their games. The women's conversation parted and floated around him. A hook-nosed old man scowled out from a portrait on the wall beside them. No one in these dusty Vernese pictures smiled, as though life on their glorious estates was hard and unhappy.

"Alright, I'll let you two get back to whatever it is the newly-bound get up to in dark corners at parties," Cyska said, winking at Eulo. She hugged them both in turn, then disappeared into the crowd, raising her chin the same way Tali did.

"I'm just going to sit here a little longer." Tali pinched the bridge of her nose.

"You need help for that shoulder," Eulo said. He should've mentioned it to Cyska, in case she knew how to help, or had more sway in getting Tali to consult a physic.

"I'm tired, is all."

"All? More like always, don't you mean?"

Eulo wrapped an arm around her, taking her hand in his free one, liking the way their binding rings hummed together, wondering how he could make her feel better. He touched the silver earring dangling against the long slope of her neck. Without quite looking elegant, she shot him a crooked grin. He smiled. She didn't need to be beautiful to stir his heart. Being reachable was enough.

"I'll get us a drink," he said, leaping up to chase a young part-Iskarlian woman who'd just carried a tray past. She stopped, holding the tray between them, her expression bland as she spoke in a low voice.

"Your brother Remmy is spending some time with the Cutters. In case you started thinking you'd rather stay in Vernesia with your wife instead of doing what you came here to do."

Ice gripped his chest. "What the fuck are you talking about?"

"It makes more sense to you than me. I'm just a messenger. When you've paid in full, you get him back."

"Remmy? What have they done to him?" Eulo stepped in front of the girl, blocking her from walking away.

She frowned. "She said to tell you not even hunters can hide."

"Lilla? Is *she* here?"

"And who would Lilla be?" A smoky voice joined them, Vivica, brushing Eulo with long curls and perfume as she reached past him to pluck a drink off the girl's tray.

"No one you need to worry about." Eulo growled, his heart thudding. Around them, a calamity of bells started ringing.

"Probably not, but the question is more whether she's someone Tali needs to worry about." Vivica raised her chin, a smirk pulling her lips tight. Gleeful at Eulo's stumble, she added, "Off you go to find her then, hmm? The binding is starting and you don't want to make her late."

Open-mouthed, Eulo turned back, but the messenger was gone.

# Chapter 15

"What d'you mean the binding is outside? At this time of year?" Tali laughed at Eulo's wide-eyed expression as she slid her fingers through his. The Iskarlian seemed startled by the whole event. "We're people of the sky. The Goddess must bear witness." As unfussed as she was about pandering to protocol, even she and Eulo had upheld that tradition.

Rows of chairs arced around a podium on the lawn, the whole area enclosed by a hedge peppered in white flowers. Women and girls sat in the chairs, with their husband, father or son standing behind. There was a hushed moment as the leftover men hurried to find an unaccompanied woman, a feat carried out with Vernese efficiency.

Tali chose a seat at the end of one row. Eulo rested his hands on her shoulders, rubbing his thumbs along the flesh at the base of her neck. She rolled her head, savouring the pressure of his fingers working the tightness out of her muscles. Pointing out a group walking a path through the guests, she said, "They're the most important women in both families." Mothers, grandmothers and sisters, draped in fine silk dresses with full sleeves and skirts, the women dressed in orange outnumbered the blue by about three to one. "The Ces family are wearing blue."

They were all elders, too, except for the girl leading the whole procession, holding her chin high. The bride-to-be, in a flowing blue skirt and bodice. Tiny kilili bands gleamed in her hair, haloing her in shards of rainbow light that danced and flickered as she moved. Pale blue motes of kilili sparkled and disappeared above her head, although Tali knew from experience she was the only one who could see it, and only then in certain circumstances.

Eulo leant close, keeping his voice low. "Where's the rest of the Ces women?"

"There aren't any. The last few generations keep throwing sons. Young Nerida there will be under a lot of pressure to produce a horde of daughters to carry on the family name."

The procession arranged themselves on the podium behind Nerida and a grey-haired woman in a white dress, the celebrant. Everyone fell silent, their attention on a slender youth navigating the path to the podium. He carried a cushion with one orange and one blue ribbon draped across it, and a feather balanced in the middle. Was he holding his breath, hoping the goddess didn't blow the feather away? No one wanted that sort of omen at their binding.

Tali knew that, before her own binding, the agency had told Eulo to choose a feather from a bird he thought reflected his wife-to-be's strengths. She'd accepted the brown goshawk's feather from him, holding it while the celebrant bound their ring hands together. Her prevailing memory of their ceremony was the blazing sun, the striped feather, and a mauve ribbon rippling in the Iskarlian breeze, while a horde of blowflies witnessed her and Eulo clasp hands and repeat vows neither of them meant.

Now, Nerida plucked the long black feather from the cushion. The celebrant asked the pair to face each other, with Nerida's left hand pressing the feather against the man's right hand. The celebrant tied the orange ribbon around their wrists as the man promised to cherish and honour his wife until death. She tied the blue ribbon as Nerida spoke of love and duty to her family, of doing her best in the name of the goddess. Vows the bride and groom made in earnest, with the expectations of both families heavy on their shoulders. Knotting their ties with a kiss, the couple raised their entwined hands to the guests, who cheered and clapped.

Tali twirled the silveriron ring on her own finger, grasping the enormity of what she'd chosen to forego by binding with Eulo, instead of a man who offered financial security and loyalty. Across the lawn, Cyska twisted around in her chair, laughing with Lenix Ces, the handsome young Vernese man who'd chosen to accompany her for the ceremony. Tali narrowed her gaze. The Ces family were evidently taking steps to secure their own family legacy and security—by offering one of their sons to the Sarsegas.

Tali's stomach dropped. Given Skylani Ces and her husband were both involved in running the Academy, she doubted Vivi would successfully audition without escaping discussion about the benefits of accepting a binding with Lenix.

With the present binding tied, however, the Ces's staff ushered the guests inside to dine. Acrobats performed around the room, some of whom used silveriron in their acts. One girl spun a hoop that left aqua motes of kilili glittering in its wake. She tossed the hoop high in the air, twirling it around, under and over her, her body slipping like liquid through the middle each time it passed her by.

"How'd they stop people taking more than their fair share?" Eulo asked, gaping at the banquet tables piled high with food.

"They don't. There's plenty for everyone."

He shook his head in disbelief. "If this were back home, you'd have an uprising, with everyone grabbing as much as he could carry. There's almost always at least one fight during an Iskarlian binding party."

After dinner, people got up to dance in front of the stage where Vivica performed. A band of musicians accompanied her, their strings and woodworked notes making a fine complement to her strong, clear voice. She turned from beautiful to breathtaking on stage, when all her arrogance vanished in the purity of her performance. Her talents deserved a bigger stage, a more appreciative audience, and the recognition and income both would offer.

Even though Vivi hid her nerves well, Tali noticed her sister's hands trembling when she'd gone to warm up her vocal cords, and how she'd refused to eat anything. This was the biggest and most important performance of her life so far. Being asked to perform at a Ces family party was an enormous opportunity to be seen by some influential people, including Skylani Ces.

It wouldn't pay Vivi's formal audition fee, though. The Ces family must've been watching Vivica far more than she or Tali had realised, long before Lenix's open declaration of interest in the Sarsega family.

At least the flickerblade Tali smithed last night would add a good pile into her savings and, with a couple more, she'd soon have enough to cover the audition costs. With Vivica's future secured, Tali could refocus her efforts on the estate, restoring the main house and expanding her horse stud. Then she'd stop drawing down the kilili, the source of her self-imposed problems. Eulo, the goose, had no idea how strength flowed from his kilili ring into hers, helping to replenish the depleted silver tattoo on her back. What she needed to complete the replenishment, though, she sought in the Glimmers hills.

Fatigue tugged inside Tali's skull, threatening to bloom into a blinding headache. She nursed a cup between her hands, staring at the water in it. Half full or half empty? Eulo had gone out to get some air after dancing her footsore. Maybe also to clear away whatever thoughts had been consuming him since the binding ceremony. She couldn't ignore his restlessness, or how he'd withdrawn from much conversation.

At least, she mused, glancing over at her singing sister, he wasn't off somewhere with Vivica. Tali sipped the water. It didn't matter, not when Eulo assumed her flirting kisses and cuddles were simply an act for everyone around them. When their agreement was over, she'd be her own woman again.

So she kept telling herself, anyway.

She liked him more than she'd intended, his uncomplicated, willing manner and the way he made her laugh. Her cottage would be empty without his clumsiness and jokes, and the ambushes her little cat subjected him to. At some stage she'd have to consider a real binding, and start her own family with a husband she didn't have to buy, who cared as much for her as she did for him. A man she could allow herself to fall for, who wasn't using her as a way into Vernesia, or to climb into money or prominence.

"She's quite something, isn't she?" The woman several seats from Tali gestured at Vivi, illuminated on stage. "As ethereal as one of Lolani's feathers."

Tali glanced across, realising who'd addressed her.

"Filia Tartula, what a surprise," she said, meaning it. The older dignitine was renowned for her reluctance to socialise far from her beloved piggery south of Silveraine. Granted, the binding of a Ces daughter was a prominent event in Vernesia's social circles, so everyone who'd been invited would've come along to fill their evening with gossip and scandals.

"A good surprise, I hope." Filia rearranged her scarf, one with a pale-yellow pattern on the light blue silk. No, not patterns—symbols; like the ones tattooed on Eulo's chest. She smiled at Tali. "Do you like the wrap? Darley gave it to me as a binding present. We made good use of it when we first knotted our ties on the wifeship." Her wink confirmed the innuendo.

Envy seeped through Tali. So Filia got a pretty scarf and all the coin it'd cost to pay Eulo's way out of his boneheaded fight with Krike.

Filia continued, "You're like me: smart enough to wrap up and keep warm. These younger ones enjoy getting about bare-shouldered. They're all vying for Lenix Ces's attention tonight."

Tali's smile thinned. She'd be bare-shouldered too if she wasn't hiding the bandage wadded over the ragged flesh on her back. Even if the kilili were fully replenished, unblemished, the way it'd been yesterday morning, she couldn't risk exposing her magic, either. When she had enough spare coin, she'd buy some new dresses, ones cut to hide her tattoo.

"Everyone is talking about how Lenix chose to chaperon your aunt during the binding, and whose attention he's vying for."

"Maybe he likes older women." Tali snorted, although she was still thrown by the Ces's bold statement of interest in her family and the implications it would have for Vivi's future.

Filia laughed. "All the young men like Cyska because she's cheeky. And related to one of the most desirable women in the room."

"Given Lenix's reputation for debauchery, he should ask Vivi's permission before he starts aligning himself with her," Tali said, knowing full well Lenix Ces was merely a puppet for his family's aspirations. She'd been pleased to see Cyska shoo Loy Myrtis away though, when he'd tried to claim the position behind her seat during the binding.

Vivi started a lively new song. She shimmied across the stage, waving her arms to encourage the crowd to sing and dance along. They cheered and clapped in adulation.

"She looks so much like your mother; as beautiful as a sculpture," Filia said. "Whereas you're your grandmother, for sure."

"What would you know of it?" Tali slumped against the wall. She was too exhausted to care about talking so rudely to an older woman—something considered a huge insult in Vernese culture. Coral Sarsega—her Mema—had the reputation of a fearsome woman who didn't tolerate nonsense. Shilya Myrtis would never have dared speak to Mema the way she did Tali: *You Sarsegas are ruining your estate all by yourselves. All we have to do is sit back and wait for it to fall into our hands.*

"Ah." Filia nodded. "We got off on the wrong foot, didn't we?" She crossed and uncrossed her legs, drawing her skirt tight over her knees. "You were impressive, you know, arguing your case on the *Seadancer*. Keep it up and you'll have greatness ahead of you, just like your grandmother once did." She stared Tali in the eye. "I hope your fist-flinging husband went above and beyond to show you his gratitude for keeping him out of the cells."

"Um…" Tali scratched her ear.

"I danced at the Academy, you know, about fifteen years behind your grandmother. It's hard to believe, looking at me now." Filia tapped her fingers against one meaty thigh. "Coral was a fabulous woman. She worked hard, with the tenacity of a heeler, and she talked a young man or two out of trouble." Her eyes clouded behind the remoteness of her memories. "How is she?"

Tali spoke slowly, unsure how much to reveal about her grandmother's deteriorating health. "Mema can't talk or walk anymore, and she"—*is as vacant as the summer sky*—"she's not very good." She studied her fingers, picking at the fringe on her stole.

"I'm sorry. It mustn't be easy for you, especially without your mother." Filia clasped Tali's hand, seeming genuine enough. "I'd love to see Coral if you'll have me come visit."

"I suppose we can arrange it," Tali said, pushing aside her reservations to bring Eulo and Krike together under her own roof, and for inviting anyone into the crumbling heap of sorrow that held up the Sarsega name. It would be for Mema, not her, or Vivi or Ranson.

"Good, I'm free after next week."

"Certainly." Tali caught herself smiling. Women of her grandmother's generation didn't offer choices.

Filia tucked a strand of dyed black hair behind her ear. "I'll have Darley on his chain, of course. It's amazing how compliant people are when they think you'll feed them to the boars." She giggled.

"I can't imagine why."

"Well, it's a gruesome reputation, but it's mine," Filia said. "I'll tell you a secret though, Tali. Four times I've helped Iskarlia men become someone new in Vernesia. I get bored with them, you see. I haven't met one yet I'd keep, except maybe Darley. He *is* very good." She tapped one finger to the side of her nose.

They sat for a long while in silence, listening to Vivica's smoky melody weave through the room. Tali fiddled with her ring. She'd been as quick as everyone else to disregard Filia Tartula. Perhaps not for very good reasons.

"They have history, you know," Filia said.

"What?"

"Darley and your Juke. Darley told me. Juke courted his sister, madly in love, until she disappeared. Gone one day, never to be seen again. They say he lost his temper and killed her."

Everything spun white in Tali's head.

"I'm sorry." Filia patted her hand again. "You two looked lovely dancing, and so happy. Still, I thought you should know."

A band pressed around Tali's ribcage. Her chest rose and fell too fast, fuelling her rushing heartbeat. She stood up. "I need some air." Eulo could've told her the truth. All his questions about the Dross and sneaking people onshore. Filia was wrong about one thing, though: Eulo hadn't killed his love—he was here in Vernesia looking for her.

"Look after yourself, Tali. And be careful outside"—Filia's smile arced from ear to ear—"Loy Myrtis fell down the stairs out there a little while ago and broke his perfect nose."

# Chapter 16

The best part of a Vernese dignitine's party, Eulo decided, was not being at it. Going out into the garden to relieve himself of the last three beers he'd drunk had been pleasant, while tapping his fist into the Myrtis maggot's nose had made his stroll even better.

Myrtis had appeared on the lamp-lit step outside the door, ranting about how Glimmers Gap would become the Myrtises' no matter who Tali spread her legs for. Already pissed off by the Cat's-bum bitch upsetting his wife and the servant's garbled message about Remmy, Eulo grabbed the chance to unleash. He'd pinned Myrtis to the wall with a squeal-crushing hand against his throat. Eulo could've kept pressing, harder and harder, or drawn a knife and slipped it through Myrtis's ribs, satisfying the fury boiling in his blood. In the end, he'd snotted the pathetic grub and left him there.

He was Eulo Juke, and no one threatened his woman. Or was he Eulo Sarsega? He grinned as he drifted back into the hall. Next, he'd knock Krike off his list, or his feet. He spotted his target to one side of the stage, nursing a mug against his chest.

"How're the pigs, you big bastard?" Eulo thumped a hand onto an unsuspecting Krike's back, sending him staggering. The goon lurched around to blink at Eulo through bloodshot eyes. Shame—it wasn't much chop hitting a man who could barely stand up.

"Juke." Krike grinned, wrestling an arm around Eulo's head. Startled Vernese drew away from the lumbering pair, their lips pursed in disapproval.

"I've done it, I'm in love." Krike jabbed a thumb into his chest, where his stained shirt revealed evidence of a battle with his beer.

"In love with the big sow what wanted me locked up for murdering you?"

"Pfft, idiot." Krike shook his head, stumbling. He'd always been a silly drunk. "With the Sarsega girl."

*Vivica.*

"I'm sure your wife will be pleased to hear it. Her pigs, too."

"Sarsega." Krike beamed, as though Vivica were singing just for him.

Un-bloody-likely, when he was grabbing another man as big, dumb and spoony-drunk as he was. Eulo disentangled himself from the goon's long arms. "I'd pay to see how many little pieces her sister would shred you into if you went near her."

"She as good as she looks?"

"Leaves me so weak in the knees I can hardly walk."

"Shades, out of all of us looking for a ride on that wifeship, and she picked *you*, you lucky fucker."

Eulo glanced over at Tali, who floated across the hall towards him with her chin raised.

"Cracked, ain't it?" Krike swayed. "Two weeks ago, I were ready to crawl into the soldiers' station at the Grinders and beg 'em to let me back in." He clapped his hands. "Then Speer talks me into selling meself to a Vernese wife. You ever heard anything so screwy?"

Eulo had. He'd heard the exact same thing, from the exact same mouth. "Speer said that?" His bowels turned heavy. Had Speer known the Scabmen would snatch Remmy as soon as Eulo left Iskarlia? Did Krike know—had they sent him here to keep an eye on Eulo? He itched to know why the goon was here in Vernesia, or whether Krike even knew himself. What else could Eulo bluff out of him?

He stretched and said, "You find out anything about kilili smugglers?"

Krike laughed. "Reckon you're a hunter, do ya? And you're here, askin' me?"

"Bit hard to ask questions when you're on a bloody isolated cattle farm, ain't it?"

"I been looking around when I go to the Silveraine market. Keep me ears open, but no-one much talks about kilili, not like the Scabmen do. They reckon one of them women from our boat buys up blokes so she can put 'em to work in her brothels. Says the Vernese birds can't get enough of a nice big soldier."

Eulo didn't want to think Remmy might suffer the same fate. Had the Scabmen brought his little brother here, to become a plaything for rich pervs, or was he caged somewhere back home? Lilla, the conniving bitch, must be part of it all. Rage churned in his belly. "What about in the Dross?"

"Nah, it ain't safe in there, not even for Iskarlians. I tried askin' a few people, who reckoned heading thatways would be the quickest way for a stranger to get hisself vanished. Ain't no laws in the Dross, they reckon."

Eulo scratched his neck. Mako's teeth, this shirt bothered him something severe. "There'll be someone running the smugglers though, keeping their own law." For the amount of silveriron that turned up in the Scabmen's hands, he doubted the Kestrine would be letting the Iskarlians arm themselves so easily. The idea of his countrymen invading Vernesia suddenly didn't seem as far-fetched as he'd first thought.

Krike stumbled over his own feet, slopping grog down his sleeve. "Ah, shit." He shook his arm, spattering droplets in an arc across Eulo's cheek. He turned his attention to the woman who'd arrived beside them, greeting her with a mush-mouthed smile. "Tali Sarsega, ain't you beautiful tonight?"

"I'm surprised you could get your hands off Eulo for long enough to notice. And here I was thinking you were trying to kill each other on that boat trip," she said dryly.

Eulo blew a deep sigh out through his nose at her shitty timing. He couldn't grab hold of the warning fluttering in his mind.

"Don't let me interrupt the fun," Tali said. "I came to tell Eulo I'm going to bed."

He let out his breath. Good. He could still ask Krike about the back-stabbing bastard Speer, and try to figure out what the fuck the Scabmen were up to.

"Ah," Krike hooted, slapping Eulo's back, "go on, mate. I ain't gonna stand in the way of you and your woman." He swayed, not doing much of a job to stand at all.

Tali flashed Eulo a tight smile, shaking her head in the slightest indication he didn't have to leave. A good Vernese husband would follow though, wouldn't they, Eulo reflected. He snugged Tali into his side. Her body went rigid against his.

He laughed, "You're right, Krike. Luckiest man on the wifeship, that's me."

Krike grinned stupidly, mumbling a goodnight before staggering off into the crowd.

"No more," Tali said. "I'm tired of the acting."

"Who says I'm acting?" Eulo murmured behind her ear, close enough to brush his lips against her skin. The whiff of perfume sent his pulse rushing.

She pushed him off with a hand against his chest. "You broke Loy Myrtis's nose."

Shit.

"Eulo?"

"Nah, nah, yeah. It's possible."

Her gaze narrowed. "It's possible?"

He spread his hands wide. "I ran into the maggot out in the garden. Didn't like what he said to me, so I gave him some advice. The Iskarlian way." He shrugged. "Turns out he ain't the big man he thought he was."

"And you are, obviously. What happened?"

"Your would-be husband pissed himself and slipped over in it when he tried to run away. Face first, down four stairs." A rebellious grin tugged at Eulo's mouth. "Ain't that the story he's telling everyone?"

She readjusted the wrap around her shoulders, sending silvery light through the folds of silk. "Blazes." She let out a heavy sigh.

"You hired me to keep the Myrtises off your land, yeah?" Eulo's drunkenness danced away on the tail-end of Vivica's song.

"That's not quite the truth of it, and you bloody well know it." Tali rested her hands on her hips, her gaze silver-green. "Stay away from the Myrtis family. You don't know what they're capable of."

The grog in Eulo's veins caught fire. "Yeah? Well, you don't know what I'm capable of." Killing a man, for the right cause, or the right price, letting the Cove wield him as a weapon of civil war. Putting his hands around a woman's head and twisting 'til her neck broke. Making those Scabmen fucks regret ever laying their hands on his brother. Eulo belonged in chaos, not in Vernesia. He cracked his knuckles, curling his lip off his teeth.

Tali's chest rose and fell too quick. She didn't shrink from his anger. The crowd erupted around them, applauding Vivica's flawless performance. Whose bed would the temptress grace tonight?

"I meant it when I said you didn't have to come to bed with me, Eulo."

"You want everyone to see us arguing before you storm out alone?" Shades, he couldn't make sense of this woman.

"I didn't quite plan for that, no." She gazed through her eyelashes, her eyes dark green again.

"Then I'll do the job I been paid for, and leave with my wife of much beautiful," Eulo said hoarsely, stepping back from the razor edge he'd lumbered onto. This time, when he slid his arm around Tali, she didn't protest.

Vivica remained on stage, above a crush of male and female fans. She beamed, bathing in adulation, glancing up in time to see Eulo and Tali pass, laughing at a stupid joke he'd made about a chunder-smeared man staggering around near the bar. Eulo wouldn't let her catch his eye. It was bad enough she'd caught a few of his secrets. Sand-skulled arse, he was, blundering into all sorts of trouble.

When he got Remmy away from the Scabmen, he'd be a better man, find an honest job, keep his nose clean, pay his debts and take better care of his assets. What a shame Tali Sarsega wouldn't be around to see him do it.

They said nothing burnt hotter or brighter than the Iskarlian sun, but the clear Vernese morning scalded Eulo's drink-dried eyes well enough. He raised a hand to shade out the glare, but not before tripping down the steps of the guest room he'd shared with Tali. She'd left him snoring in grog-fuelled bliss, slipping out ghost-quiet sometime earlier, an ember that never quit growing, waiting for her chance to burn his fingers.

There was no guessing where she'd be now, not with the elegant sandstone building ahead and the smell of horses strong in the air. The stables were grander than most Iskarlian estates, the stone bullied into straight lines and archways its guests would never appreciate. Like any soldier, once a horse had food and company, it didn't care where it shit. Eulo snorted. If only he'd worked that lesson out a little quicker himself.

He trampled along the crushed shell path, under the tallest archway into the stable yard. Sure enough, fifty paces along, Tali stood on tiptoes peering over a half-door, clad in black pants and jacket, her hair cascading loose. The elder beside her spread his hands as he talked, tracing shapes in the air. Tali shook her head, pointing into the stable, gesturing. An age-old language—the talk of horseflesh. Eulo had quickly learned the futility of trying to change Tali's mind about a horse. Still, the stableman was having a bloody good crack at it.

Happy to stay out of the discussion, Eulo fetched his own horse from her stable. He hitched the mare to a ring in the stone wall, whistling as he brushed her down. Tali had been surprised when he suggested not taking Flame. She'd agreed it would be useful training for the mare, without realising Eulo wanted to make himself less distinctive by not always riding the same horse.

"Whoa, whoa there." A thin voice rose over the sudden clatter of hooves.

A sleek grey horse skidded across the yard, dragging a young Vernese with it. Stupid tall, too, throwing its head up in the air, wild-eyed and snorting. The grey spun in a tangle of legs and tail, knocking the youth off balance. It screamed out a neigh, prancing over to Eulo's mare. Even as Eulo's hand closed on the grey's rein, his mare squealed, jabbing out a hind-leg in warning.

"C'mon you goose, you're the sort of horse who breaks a little too easy for my liking." Eulo frowned at the grey's slender build and fine legs. It jogged beside him all stir-crazy and ignorant as he led it back to the youth. He'd clambered to his feet, although he doubled over with hands on his knees, gasping for breath.

"You right?" Eulo said.

A swathe of fringe, knocked loose from the rest of his slicked-down hair, dropped across the boy's face when he looked up. "I'm fine." His eyes clouded. He dropped his focus to a streak of dirt on his otherwise spotless, bone-coloured pants.

"Fiery horse, eh," Eulo said, "and it's got no bloody manners." The grey stopped beside him. Stopped jogging, anyway. Its body tensed as it pulled away, snorting at a blanket hanging over a stable door.

"A horse to turn heads." The boy's defiance wavered.

"Yeah, I reckon he'd turn your head 'round so far it'd snap off, don't you?" Eulo peered at the spotty-faced youth, guessing he was about Remmy's age; maybe fourteen or fifteen years old. He could never quite tell with someone as skinny as a dripweed. He offered him the reins.

The youth stared at Eulo's outstretched hand, without moving to take the horse.

"S'pose he might settle once you work him down." Eulo half-turned to study the grey. The gelding flinched, blasting offended air through its flared nostrils. Shades, what an animal.

"I don't know how," the youth muttered, unable to look Eulo in the eye. He swiped at his loose fringe, trying to smooth it out of the way. It bounced straight back into his face.

"Because of you, or the horse?"

"I can ride." The youth snatched the reins, sending the horse skittering backwards. Its hooves crunched a panicky tempo into the gravel. Tali and the stableman glanced over at the ruckus, then resumed their conversation without pause.

"How 'bout you show me on my little Sarsega mare here?" Eulo nodded at his mount, which dozed in the sun with a cocked hind-leg.

"You? Riding a Sarsega horse?" The youth raised his eyebrows. Half-interested.

"I'll saddle her up. See what you can do on a horse with half a brain in its skull."

"You're trying to trick me."

"If you ride as good as you reckon, you got nothing to lose, do you?" Eulo said, and the lad's pride caught him neat as a beetle in a sand trap.

The mare won him over with her gentle curiosity, nuzzling him while Eulo tacked her up. Beside them, the grey pawed restlessly at its tether on the hitching rail. "Good idea," Eulo said. "Let him get used to everything going on in the yard before you hop on him."

The youth opened his mouth as if to admit it hadn't been his idea at all, then closed it. A quick learner.

The mare worked nice and quiet in hand for Eulo, circling around him, soft and responsive. He smiled. Tali did a bloody good job starting her horses. When he called the youth over to get on, the lad swallowed hard, the bluster in his stance betrayed by wide-eyed fear.

"Be kind to her, and she'll be kind to you." Eulo held the rein while the youth climbed into the saddle. He winked. "Same as you would a woman, eh."

The youth cracked a tight smile, forming a tiny bridge between them. He clicked the horse into a walk, using the same cue Eulo had. Nerves pulled him tight in the saddle, tipping his shoulders forward instead of sitting his weight solid on his arse. The mare forgave his heavy hands on the reins, but the grey wouldn't be so obliging. The lad sorted himself out as he rode around the yard, relaxing and softening, realising he didn't have a four-legged lunatic beneath him.

Eulo fetched the grey, ignoring the gelding's snorting opinion about walking the perimeter of the stables. He picked up one rein, asking the horse to work now, to pay attention, same as he'd done with the mare, so it could realise nothing would eat it. The grey gelding moved quick, all muscles tense, his concentration as scattered as a regiment of new recruits. Not a mean horse, just worried and not knowing any better. Eulo watched the animal carefully, softening his hand when the horse quit fighting the rein, sharing a pat and a murmur when the horse showed some try.

"You there." A woman interrupted Eulo's concentration, snapping the horse's fine thread of attention. She stormed across the yard, her loosely belted shirt billowing out behind her, stabbing a forefinger at the grey. "That's my son's horse. You've put him on someone else's nag, you imbecile." She stopped a ten-pace away, at least sensing it might not be clever to bring her flappy outfit close to the bug-eyed horse. She crossed her thin arms, frowning at Eulo. "Blazes, you can't even understand Vernese, can you?"

"I hear you fine. I figured the lad ought to try riding a horse that don't make him worry it's going to kill him."

"Are you threatening him?" Her nostrils flared wide.

"Nah, whoever gave him this half-broke horse is."

The woman stomped closer, braver with anger. She was about Ranson's age, smaller than Tali even with a dark purple scarf wrapped around her head. Her hooked nose matched her son's, and the old man whose portrait Eulo noticed in the mansion last night.

"I'll assume that's a comment of ignorance rather than insult, Iskarlian. I won't do it a second time."

Eulo rubbed the grey's head, coaxing it lower, asking the horse to listen to him instead of the huffed-up woman spitting fire at them. Behind her, the lad trotted the mare in circles, doing a fair job of it.

"The Sarsega girl owns you, doesn't she?" The woman's voice was as jagged as Mako's teeth.

Eulo shrugged, amused. "You mustn't know her too well if you put it like that."

"She bought you the same as a slave or horse, or any other of the Iskarlian husbands who were here last night. I don't think there are too many ways to put it, do you?"

He stared at the uppity bitch. The way she spoke and stood, unyielding, warned him to hold his tongue. He wasn't often let down by a warning twist in his gut.

The youth whooped as he pressed the mare into a canter, drawing his mother's attention. She watched for a moment, the tip of her tongue darting over her pale lips. "He does seem happy."

"The mare's for sale."

"How convenient. I suppose you'll tell me she's perfect for Tipan, too."

"Why don't you ask him?"

The grey jerked its head up as Tali approached. Eulo applied a smidgen of pressure to the rein, rubbing the gelding's neck when it focused back on him, even though it champed on the bit.

"Good morning, Loress Skylani," Tali greeted the angry little woman. "You've met my husband, Eulo Juke?"

*Loress.* That explained a bit, including Tali's sudden appearance. Eulo sniffed, a big, mucky snort in the back of his nose. The grey stared at him without spooking. Progress.

"Mmm." Skylani half-shrugged. Both women ignored Eulo's rudeness. "How much do you want for the mare, then?"

# Chapter 17

Tali arched her eyebrow. "Eulo?"

He scratched his elbow, pleased she trusted him to make the negotiation. "Six hundred kistars." It was a good chunk more than the five hundred kistars she'd suggested during their ride to the estate, before the Loress and her beloved son had crossed their path.

The older woman studied Eulo, her gaunt face stern. "That's more than I paid for this gelding. It's one of Bhitar Jikah's, you know."

His lips twitched. "It don't mean nothing to me. If you're asking, I reckon he's too long in the back, short in the neck, and short on training. And he can't carry any foals."

"I wasn't asking." Skylani moved smoothly around Eulo, gesturing to her son. The silveriron bangles on her wrists chimed together. "Tipan, come here."

Startled, the lad trotted over. He slid straight down, tossing a betrayed glance at Eulo. "Mother, I'm sorry. I was only having a look." He studied the dirt between his shuffling feet.

"So I see. Do you like the mare?"

Tipan glanced at his mother, his eyes sparking with interest. He nodded quickly. She cast her painted gaze on Tali. "Fine. Have your man unsaddle her so she's ready to come with us."

"Well, the thing is, we didn't bring a spare horse," Tali chewed her lip, "and Eulo has to get home to Glimmers Gap with me."

Skylani groaned. "Surely one of you can manage the grey, hmm?" She scorched Eulo with a sneer. "Oh dear. You're not scared to get on him, are you?"

"I'll assume that's a comment of ignorance rather than insult." He stretched his lips into a grin. "No, Loress, it's more about upholding the Sarsega reputation. I don't reckon I'd feel right about myself, onselling this sort o' horse." He jerked a thumb at the grey.

"An Iskarlian with a conscience, won't that send the gossips into a spin." She arched an eyebrow. She could've been a painting; all fine bones and immaculate makeup with the bright scarf wound around her head.

"I don't care for gossips." Tali edged closer to Eulo. "We'll take the grey, train him up and return him for you to keep or sell as you see fit."

"For a fee, no doubt?"

"No, for goodwill," Eulo jumped in. Tali's lips parted at his interruption, although she didn't argue.

"How generous of you, considering the coin I'll be paying for this mare," Skylani said to Tali.

Eulo would've liked to see her face the Cove. She'd bite Vasker's head off and spit it out without even smudging her lip stain. He slung an arm around Tali. "She ain't the best woman in the south for nothing." He smiled at his wife, not having to dig far to find genuine warmth for her.

The Loress smiled too, a cold smile which didn't meet her eyes. "Least of all the cost of a boat ride to Vernesia, I'm sure. We'll take the mare, then, and you take the grey, to be delivered back to me in one month."

"Thank you." Tipan, the sullen son, surprised Eulo by stepping forward with an outstretched hand. "Thank you," he repeated in Iskarlian, his face lighting with a grin.

Eulo shook his hand, muttering something about having fun and being kind to his new horse. Skylani watched on, an unreadable jumble of pride, wariness and steel. Eulo pressed his lips to Tali's forehead. Her crooked smile made his belly lurch. He'd done good.

Eulo led the grey to the hitching rail with Tipan and the mare alongside him. The crunch of their footsteps on the path filled the silence until Tipan said, "I thought you were making fun of me, but you were helping me."

"Yeah."

"I tried telling Mother that Cloud was crazy. She won't listen because she broke him in herself. She can't accept she didn't do a good job of it."

Shit. "I reckon she knows now."

Tipan smiled. "You're brave. I don't think women like being told that sort of stuff. Especially not Loresses."

Eulo rubbed Cloud's neck after tying him up. No wonder he was nervy, after putting up with the woman. "What does your mother do?"

"She's a Ces. This is our family estate, where my aunt lives. It was my cousin who tied the binding last night." The lad squinted at him.

"We're from Silveraine though. My mother is Loress of Culture. My father manages the Academy, where people come to study dancing, or singing, or theatre, or any of the arts. It houses the Library of Scholars, too."

"Skollars?" Eulo rolled the strange word over his tongue. "What's that?"

"Don't you have schools in Iskarlia? The Library is where clever men and women study the world and its history. One whole section is about Lolani, can you imagine?" Tipan played with a horse brush, folding the bristles down with his fingers. "Were you a warrior in Iskarlia?"

"Yeah." Eulo swung the grey's saddle over the nearest rail. Skylani wouldn't be happy if she found all her fine tack had gone to Glimmers Gap on her not-so-fine grey horse.

"Did you kill anyone?" Tipan's earlier scowl had been replaced by a cleanskin's adulation. When Eulo nodded, he said, "What was it like?"

"Hard." It'd gotten easier though, hadn't it? All the earlier remorse ended up being smothered by necessity, sooner or later. Eulo lay the grey's bridle over the saddle, pulling his hands away to hide how they were trembling.

"It sounds exciting, fighting in war. Some say the Iskarlian men here are dumb, opportunistic thugs. I don't think you are. Not now." Tipan's eyes shone as he spoke, betraying his idealistic youth. "My parents say I have to study painting because my father did. My older brother's a musician, and my mother was a dancer until she became sick."

Eulo untacked the mare. He'd been idealistic at Tipan's age too, except his parents hadn't talked him out of it. Six months later, someone put a blade in his hand, shoved his warrior pack out into battle, and Eulo Juke was blooded, crossing the abyss from cleanskin to manhood.

Tipan watched his mother, still talking to Tali. "Are you really bound to her? My brother says you're her drudge."

"She's my wife. Tali."

"I know. Well, I mean, I know Vivica." The lad's cheeks burnt red. "Everyone does."

"No doubt." Stunningly beautiful, parading on stage, enchanting the crowds with her voice, who wouldn't have known her?

"Mother says she's one of the best singers in the country. It's a shame her family can't afford to send her to the Academy."

"Is that what they say?" Eulo paused. Pieces of the Sarsega puzzle slid into place. Tali's preoccupation with money, Vivica's contempt of their estate, their unpaid accounts.

"It's obvious, isn't it?" Tipan shrugged his narrow shoulders, emulating his mother. "My brother says he won't be a drudge."

Eulo rested his hand on the mare's rump, tilting his head to glance at Tali. Unusually reserved, she still stood with Skylani, listening to her talking. Yet she'd trusted Eulo to talk to the Loress alone and negotiate the sale of her horse. Now she was probably promoting her sister to the Loress, while Vivica lazed in bed, resentful and sour.

"Get your saddle, I'll make sure it fits the mare properly," he growled at Tipan, wanting to tell the lad his parents were sand-skulled not to take Vivica on her abilities alone, without payment. He exhaled. It wasn't worth his while getting tangled in the Sarsega's problems, not when he had enough of his own to worry about. None of this was any help to Remmy. He needed to find something to grip onto, to find the trail that would lead back to his brother.

Any relief Eulo had at arriving back at Glimmers Gap faded when Tali took a track leading off to the beach pastures instead of the one to the stables. His arse-cheeks ached from two days in the saddle, though not as badly as the chafed skin on his inner thigh where his pants and saddle had met and conspired for half the ride home, despite his constant efforts to readjust it all.

He kept his complaints to himself though, and by the time the gloaming came, they were riding into the top paddocks.

The sun relinquished its golden glow as they broached the last hill, looking down to where jagged teeth of coastline bit into the pastures. They stopped in a tree-lined cleft, tucked away from the easterlies blustering off the ocean. The copse of trees shivered overhead as Eulo lit a fire, bent on one knee to blow hope into a single flame, cursing it to spark alive the eucalypt kindling he'd collected.

Rising, he pressed his hands into the small of his back. He breathed in deep lungfuls of burning wood, salt-encrusted pastures, and endless cool skies. The sharp, wild scent of Glimmers Gap.

When the fire roared into life, licking along the tinder he'd collected, Eulo swivelled to pick up the closest saddlebag. He froze, bent over with his hand outstretched, his eyes growing wide at the sight across the beach. A chill traced his spine. He spun to Tali with one hand on his flickerblade.

"Mako's teeth, what the fuck is that?"

Colours danced across the star-flecked sky, as though Mako himself had knocked a bucket of rainbow paint over the night. The pink and green glow blossomed, feathering to white, its edges smudging into blackness.

"They call it Lolani's Song," Tali said, her face upturned. "As astonishing as a kiss from the goddess, the warmth of her touch, and the sweetness of her breath."

Eulo swung her around, pulling her into his chest. "Kisses like a warm, sweet goddess, you say?" They twirled, dancing to an invisible song in the knee-sweeping grass.

"How many goddesses have you kissed?" Tali smiled, wry, lifting her chin to let him nuzzle her throat.

"Only you." He pressed his lips under her jaw, working his way along the fine bone.

"Only one? A man like you? Go on," she teased, playful.

Eulo pulled back, staring at her. The jibe drove deeper than it ought've. "A man like what?"

A mercenary who'd fought ruthlessly in the Cove's army, who'd hunted people and gambled away everything he'd had—even his own brother. A man whose hands would never be clean of blood.

It took one pounding heartbeat for Tali to disappear from his embrace. She set her mouth into a straight line as she squatted down, reaching down to take their bundles of food from the pack Eulo had dropped on the grass. She moved upwind of the fire, settling cross-legged in the grass, drinking in the sky while she ate.

Desire flapped through Eulo. Stranded, hopeful. He'd do better if he kept his gob shut and didn't talk anymore. He grabbed the food she'd left for him, and took it over to her, his steps tentative. Tali glanced at him, using her teeth to tear a mouthful of salt beef off the strip in her fist, then stared up at the dancing night sky. He sucked in a breath as he sprawled beside her. Out here, she ate like a soldier, though she could walk into any mansion and know what to do with a tableful of cutlery. Eulo ate like a soldier no matter where he sat.

They chewed in silence. Owls hooted in the surrounding trees, and the cows murmured and bellowed across the hillside, calling their calves closer for the night. When he'd finished eating, Eulo stretched out to watch the magic unfolding overhead. Tali edged between his outstretched legs, slumping against his chest without saying a word.

He closed his eyes, his heart stuttering from the rush of the *something other* flowing between him and his wife-who-wasn't. He slid his arms around her slender, strong body. A month ago, if anyone had told Eulo Juke he'd end up sitting in a cow pasture holding his wife close, watching wild colour streak the skies, he'd have laughed and told them they were sand-skulled.

Then Tali was on her feet again, tugging his hand to urge him up. 'It's time. Come on.'

He stumbled down the slope after her, turning his ankles in the ditches she danced over. Hungry waves tore at the beach below, shimmering silver in the moonlight. Once their boots landed in the sand, Tali ran headlong towards the water like she was addled. Alarmed, Eulo sprinted after her.

She stopped so suddenly he collided into her, knocking her face first into the sand. Unbalanced, he fell on top of her.

"Sorry," he muttered, trying to find somewhere to put his hands. She laughed, propping herself onto her elbows, and slid one hand along the damp sand.

Green sparks flared in her finger's wake.

Eulo pushed himself onto his hands and knees beside her. He swept his hand the way she had. Two pinpricks winked green at him.

"There's more, closer to the tide." Tali moved beyond the water's reach.

Eulo brushed white grains of hard-packed wet sand. Masses of tiny green specks twinkled for a heartbeat. The exact shade of greensilver that patterned their binding rings. The night reeled around him.

"What's this?"

"This," Tali smiled, "is Glimmers Gap." The moonlight sharpened her cheekbones, glowing in her eyes and smile.

Eulo stared, awed by the way she knelt with arms raised to the mystic, strong as ironwood, at one with the night. Flecks of greensilver spiralled and floated above her. Now he understood why she'd made him part of the charade to keep her grip on this goddess-blessed lump of southland; where the sky merged with the earth and came together in every breath entering her body.

He stood unmoving under the immense sky, a speck of a man surrounded by endless green forest and aqua ocean. Once this strange twist in his story was over he'd have no more excuses about why he didn't have enough kilili to save Remmy.

# Chapter 18

A bittersweet song of craving and loathing thrummed into Tali's veins as she planted her boots in the dirt on the escarpment, gazing at the lean-to. She willed herself to move across the clearing, not stopping until she'd turned the corner to the workspace. Smoke twirled above the rust-speckled roof, tainting her tongue with its molten-iron taste.

"About time you got here," Cyska said, without looking up from the pendant she was polishing, her smudged spectacles magnifying her eyes.

Tali plonked herself onto a nearby stool. She pulled a poker off the hook beside the forge, dragging its charred tip through the dirt between her boots. "I know. We need this money."

"For Glimmers or the Academy?"

"For Vivi. She was born to be there, not here, where her talents are wasted. Goddess knows the cows don't appreciate my caterwauling." Tali smiled wryly. "I didn't get a scrap of her lyrical ability."

"You have your own talents." Cyska squinted past the pendant. She handed it to Tali.

The silveriron teardrop sat light and flawless in her brown palm. The sunless afternoon couldn't mute the violet shades sweeping from the top down, darkening in increments like high tide colouring a beach. She passed it back. "It's beautiful."

"I'm playing around with a new technique, blowing across the kilili as it settles, to get the graded tone." Cyska undulated her hand through the air. "I want to fill another trunk before the next wifeship sails. Are you in shape to help?"

"I couldn't be better," Tali said. At Cyska's insistence, she slipped her right arm out of its sleeve, pulling her shirt aside to reveal the swirling, ever-changing silver tattoo on her shoulder. Each time she coaxed the tattoo to release motes of its kilili gift for her to smith into silveriron, it left her skin open and raw. Last night with Eulo in the darkness of the new moon, watching the aurora of Lolani's Song play across the sky, had completely healed her tattoo. Her kilili was replenished, ready to harvest again, before it grew too big for her to control.

"It looks good. Such a beautiful shade of green."

Tali nodded, pulling her shirt back on. "I can smith more flickerblades when I need to. No more trips to Iskarlia for me, though."

"Yes. We go there to sell things, not bring them home." Cyska's hazel eyes lit up.

"Maybe next time I'll bring home a husband for you."

"I doubt Ranson could handle another foreigner in the family." Cyska pushed away from the bench, unfolding her long limbs like a grasshopper. "We'd better get to work, or we'll end up scrambling down the escarpment in the dark, trying not to break our necks. What are you going to make today?"

Tali shrugged, staring at her scratchings in the dirt: spirals and waves, an echo of Eulo's tattoos. Inspired, she nodded, her mind made up. "I'll do jewellery."

"For the Iskarlians? Blazes, Tali, I thought you wanted to make money."

"Jewellery," Tali said, digging the stick deeper into the dirt, tracing symbols, "that represents beliefs. We'll make smaller pieces the middle-class men and women can afford. I'll smoke-sing them to set. It'll be much faster than making even just one knife."

"How many Iskarlians would rather buy a flashy earring than put food on their table?" Cyska folded her arms, unconvinced.

"Eulo told me most of their remote settlements don't have any money, so they trade whatever they can. It's much easier to barter a small pendant or necklace than an expensive blade when you're out on the plains, right?"

"I suppose, if they weren't in need of practical goods. There's always someone who thinks they can buy love."

"Or buy themselves out of a loveless binding," Tali said, unsure if Cyska was needling her. No one except Eulo knew the truth about their pact. She cleared her throat. "In that case, what about symbolised kilili discs that could be hung from a necklace, or seated in a blade or a piece of leather, or carried in a purse or pocket? A kind of talisman."

"They could be different sizes and values."

"Or tradeable," Tali persisted.

"The Cove won't appreciate someone introducing a new currency into his country, especially if he doesn't have control over it." Cyska clapped her hands together, the sharp snap bursting Tali's enthusiasm. She grinned. "Oh, come on, don't go sour on me. It's a good idea, and one the Iskarlians will like, but we need to be clever about this. We don't want the Covesmen sniffing around to find out who smiths in silvergreen and violet."

"Yes, but we're safe here." Tali hated the hopeful naivety in her voice. Conversations rattled through her mind. *Lyselle's Iskarlian cutthroat left her flayed body on her dining table and fled with all her coin. They say he lost his temper and killed her.*

She blinked, fighting for focus, to push away the nausea rising in her belly. "We *are* safe, aren't we?"

Cyska spidered her long fingers over her elbows. "As long as the truth of our kililismithing is secret, our anonymity keeps us safe."

Tali nodded, although her aunt's words did nothing to ease the sense of dread yawning inside her. When she'd first come into her skills, Cyska scared her stupid with horrific tales about smiths enslaved to fuel the old empire, a practice the first Kestrine outlawed immediately. There were other stories, too, of Vernese smiths being captured by tyrants who sold them into similar slavery in Iskarlia, for a different master. Maybe smiths had hidden their talent ever since because they were ashamed to freely practice something so many women had died for.

"What would happen if kililismithing wasn't secret anymore?"

"If enough women revealed their abilities, it could force a change from myth to freedom," Cyska said. "But if kililismithing became a common trade, the value of our work would drop, and our income with it. The secrecy of what we do ensures its success."

"How much do you trust your contact in Iskarlia?" Tali weighed a hammer in her hand. The broken-nosed man who'd bought her blades in Port Garnet had seemed decent enough...

The corners of Cyska's mouth curled like paper catching a flame. "I trust him with my life, which is why I trusted him with yours."

Tali considered asking at what point enough coin outweighed trust, the way it had with her own bought husband. Instead, she pulled the leather tie from her hair, reknotting the wind-tangled mass to keep it out of her way while she worked. She set out her tools while Cyska stoked the fire, melting a silver bar in the crucible. Once she'd stirred off impurities in the slag, both women broke into song.

Tali's kilili stirred, prickling her shoulder where it pulled free of her body. This part was never painful, more like hot wax plucking hair off her skin. The kilili sifted through her shirt into the air, loose in star-twinkles overhead, although still linked to Tali's body on invisible chains, a binding no smith could ever fully untie until death.

Tali prepared a mould for the discs, creating rows of circular indentations in the clay and sand mixture. On the workbench beside it, she arranged a series of cuttlefish moulds for jewellery. Above her, shimmers of her green kilili mingled with Cyska's violet, each colour dancing mid-air to a different song. Thrill spiked through Tali's chest at the wonder of her magic misting with another. The kilili had no end of secrets in what it could do, or how.

Cyska lifted the crucible in a pair of tongs and poured a series of molten puddles into the disc mould. When she nodded, Tali stopped crooning and waited for the kilili to drift down. She puffed air out of her cheeks into the eddying magic, blowing it across the liquid silver. The blended colours spun and spiralled, laying themselves over the metal and sinking into its surface. A hint of lilac and eucalyptus sweetened the odour in the lean-to.

Cyska's soft song didn't end until she'd chased every mote of kilili into the rest of the molten metal, coercing a deep intensity in the hues and tinges, before pouring it into the jewellery moulds. Tali let out a deep exhalation, locking her stare on the span of their creations. The discs glowed red around the edges, yet to be quenched.

"It worked," she said, too loud in the sudden quiet. This was the moment she loved the most: when she could appreciate her inspiration and handiwork coming together.

"It's brilliant." Cyska said, squeezing Tali's hand. "Better than I could've imagined." She used the tongs to quench each piece in a water bucket, cooling and hardening the metal. Kilili smudged the discs, their colour concentrated into the Iskarlian symbols and patterns the two women had sketched into their songs.

"It's some of my best work," Tali admitted, peering over her aunt's arm at the pieces shimmering in the bucket. Impatient to pull the cuttlefish moulds out so they could start polishing and tidying the pieces. She resisted the urge to rub the twinge in her right shoulder. Not even a twinge, really, more the habit of pain she'd become accustomed to during her smithing. Today she'd restrained her harvest, taking her cue from Cyska's controlled approach, but she couldn't help wondering how the pieces would've looked if she'd drawn more kilili out.

"How come we've never thought to do this before?" she asked.

"You weren't ready. You didn't have the ideas in your head or heart yet, or maybe not the knowledge of how to create them." Cyska picked out a disc enamelled with a fishhook, running her thumb over the swirl of colour. "Maybe I didn't either. The most important lesson I know about kililismithing is that you never stop learning about it. The drive to keep pushing and challenging your skills is what makes it so addictive."

Tali's hand strayed to her tattoo. Cyska would throttle her if she knew how much kilili she'd been drawing out. Blazes knew Tali put up with enough of Eulo's unspoken disapproval, and he didn't even know about her tattoo, let alone the grief it caused her.

Cyska tidied away the hammers and tongs, handling each one as gently as if it were a kitten. She peered out from under her blunt fringe. 'You should tell Vivica what you're doing, you know. It'd take a lot of the strain out of your relationship.'

Tali unwrapped one of the cuttlefish moulds, revealing the head of a desert dog coloured into a heavy cuff. The kilili had melded beautifully, sinking evenly all the way around the piece. She stacked it with the discs, on a wonky plank serving as a shelf along the lean-to wall, grouping them by symbol, although no two pieces were the same. "After this shipment, I can pay the Academy's fees. Vivi will find out as soon as they offer her an audition. Until then, I can't face disappointing her if something goes wrong." Enduring her sister's volatility for another month or two would be nothing compared with the risk of blabbing this secret too soon.

"And then what?"

"Then," Tali said, frowning at the disc in her hand, "I don't know. I suppose we'll be busy placating her about Skylani Ces coercing her to bind with Lenix. She doesn't even like men."

Ever the calm voice of reason, Cyska said, "The Sarsegas will sail through, my girl. We always do."

Creeping fingers of night-shadow followed Tali home. She kicked her boots off outside the doorway without bothering to stand them straight. Warmth embraced her when she burst inside to find the fire roaring and dinner cooking.

"Mrrw?" Chance looked up from his bed near the fireplace. He yawned, stretching, already purring when Tali scooped him into her arms.

"Hey, it's good coming home to you, eh." She cuddled the cat into her arms, wriggling her back in the fire's blissful warmth.

Eulo slouched against the table, quirking one corner of his mouth upward. "Everything alright, darl?"

"Hmm." She studied her grime-lined fingernails, half-buried in ginger fur.

"I reckon you might want this, eh? It's bloody cold outside." He offered her a mug of steaming kaif.

"Thank you. There's snow up on the mountains, the last fall before winter is really over." Tali relinquished Chance for the mug. Her fingers brushed against Eulo's.

"Cold hands."

"I'm freezing. I'd have been home earlier but I ran into trouble with a fence."

"There's hot water there for you to wash up. The stew's almost ready."

"I never knew mercenaries could keep house, too."

He winked. "I've got lots of talents."

After dinner, Tali set out her pen, ink and ledgers on the table. She flicked past the pages of Ranson's neat handwriting, wondering if she could convince him to take up the books again. She'd be much happier not having to tackle them. Filling the pen with black ink, she paused, aware of Eulo loitering at the edge of her senses. He stared at the books in front of her, looking as uncertain as Eulo Juke might ever look.

"Are you alright there, big husband?"

He twitched, as though she'd caught him picking his nose. "Fine. Nothing." He ambled over to the window, craning his neck at her bookshelf. When he realised she was still watching him, he shifted away near the fireplace. Leaning one hand against the wall, he rubbed the other down his jaw.

"Are you going to keep drifting around like a fart in a bottle, or will you tell me what's bothering you?" Tali asked. She waited. For what— an apology? A confession?

"Ah," he cleared his throat, "would you teach me my letters? So I can write my name."

"'Course I will," she said. Most of her life she'd heard dignitines calling the Iskarlians stupid, even to their faces. Just because Vasker was a ruthless tyrant who didn't see the value in schooling his people didn't mean they weren't smart.

She set Eulo to work with another pen and paper, practising how to get the right pressure to coax the ink to flow. He twisted his mouth into grim severity, his usual teasing smile and jokes gone, even shooing away Chance when the cat tried to sit on his lap.

She squeezed her hand over his rough fingers, guiding his hold on the pen, drawing squiggles across the paper. "It takes some practice to get a feel for it. Sometimes you need to press soft and gentle, other times you need to push harder."

"I reckon I can do that. As much as you want," he said in a molasses drawl.

Tali's ears flamed. Sitting so close to him, touching his hand, made her realise how long it'd been since anyone had touched *her*. She was turning crack-headed from lying awake each night beside his sculpted body, trying to smother the lust he stirred in her. Even though he'd knocked her back the one time she'd tried to seduce him. She sighed, chewing her bottom lip.

"That bad, am I?"

Tali realised her hand was clamped tight on Eulo's. Black cobwebs of ink seeped into the cracked skin on his fingers.

"No." She let go and folded her hands into her lap. "Sorry, I was thinking of something else." Her nostrils flared.

"Other people's burdens, eh?" Eulo slid a sideways glance at her, his pupils wide in the lamplight. "You carry a lot of 'em."

She stared at him, lips parted, wanting to spill out the weight of everything crushing against her. Then, out of nowhere, she pictured him straining and grunting into Vivica's naked body. Tali shoved her chair back, trampling Chance's tail as she went. The cat screeched, flying across the room in a blur of ginger. He stopped by the door, glaring at her with big, accusing eyes. Tali sucked in a breath, wrestling a surging wave of emotions. She dug her fingertips into the flesh above her knees, fighting to keep herself under control.

"I reckon he'll be scheming to shit in your boots while you're asleep, eh." Eulo raised a lazy finger towards the cat.

"Let him try," she said, retreating to bed with the maw of loneliness stretching wide over her soul.

She was still awake when Eulo padded in a little while later, too aware of him undressing in the darkness, of his weight sinking into the bed, limbs jumbled alongside hers.

"So, I talked to a woman at the Ces binding," he said, his voice thick with sleep, "and she tells me how she was on a ship once, feelin' all hopeless and stuck, drowning under other people's burdens, and her own. She went up on deck, late at night, and stared into the water for so long she reckoned she'd best fall over the rail into the blackness 'cause no one would care if she was gone. Especially not the other passengers."

He paused for a heartbeat. "She had one foot up, ready to climb the rail, when someone appeared out of nowhere, talking like they were best friends. And this other young woman wanted her to look at the sky," he said. "So she did, and all the stars were sparklin' around the full moon, and this colour streaked through the sky, all silver and green, the most beautiful thing she'd ever seen."

He rolled over, his bare skin hot against hers, curling against her back and wrapping his arm around her. Warmth flooded from her tattoo down her back, around to her hips and belly. Lower. Deeper.

"Kardia said you stopped her throwing herself into the ocean. You were the one person who told her to stop looking into the blackness because she had the whole sky wide above her." His words dropped into a murmur. "Don't forget you got that big sky too, Tali."

She stared at the window, her heart thumping.

"Loress Skylani knows it, too, eh, otherwise she wouldn't have bought your mare."

"I hope she also thinks my sister does, because Skylani leads the lyricene's audition panel." And, of course, the family whose son was now vying for an alliance by binding with the Sarsegas.

Eulo shifted, said, "How many other wives would let their husbands negotiate with a Loress?"

Tali laughed, surprised. "Not many." Then, "You made a good sale. Better than what I would've made selling that mare to Rith as amends for Flame."

"Why go to him at all? Why don't you go straight to the Kestrine?"

"Rith is her Stablemaster. He buys the horses, not her."

"Then what about selling more horses to the dignitines? And training 'em."

"I could." A pinprick of excitement lit inside her. "Although I've been thinking how the Vernese horses are too small for Iskarlians. I can breed mine taller using Duskari bloodlines." She fell silent. It'd be a risk to buy Duskari horses, to gamble money she might not earn back.

"You're somethin' different, Tali. You and your horses."

She blushed. "There's no point trying to butter me up for more money, 'cause you know I don't have any."

"Yeah, I know." He pressed his cheek against a strip of exposed skin where her neck met her shoulders. "I still reckon you prob'ly got an angry little cat shit in your boots by now."

"Oh, you bastard." She jabbed her elbow into his ribs. He squeezed even tighter against her, chuckling, and a big sky appeared through her darkness.

For a little while, anyway.

# Chapter 19

Eulo turned his cheek against the collar of his coat, using the stiff oilskin to cut out the wind's bite. All bloody day he'd been buffeted by gusts straight off the frozen mountains. He grimaced. Tali reckoned it sometimes snowed down as low as Glimmers Gap. With any luck that wouldn't happen before he left, not now they'd slid into spring. The pastures and damp, thick-scented rainforest still smothered him with their strange lushness, and the treetops closing out the sky way overhead.

His grimace twisted into a half-grin. Stupid bastard he was, hunched in his saddle fretting for the vast plains of home. Most days, when he was sure no one else was around, he sat on a boulder near the kelp-eating cattle, gazing out at the sea, the closest he could get to flat land and open skies.

Not today though. No, today he'd ridden out with Tali to muster the steers off Bald Hill into a paddock near the house, ready to go to market. Taking Tali's mare out with Skylani's grey gelding was the quickest way to getting Eulo's skull broke, so he'd asked her to ride Flame 'cause the chestnut would be a calmer lead.

"What's wrong, scared you'll come off?" she'd teased, but she rode Flame like he asked.

He tugged his wool cap tighter over his ears. Mako's teeth, it'd be a miracle if he ever thawed out. While he huddled miserably in the chill, Tali rode tall and proud, seeming not to notice it. At least they were almost back at the stables.

Cloud pricked his ears, knowing they were going home. The gelding settled well enough once he'd done some work, although he still got high-strung about little issues. Eulo stared at Tali's waist, picturing her naked with the greensilver chain slung low on her hips. The image warmed him up nicely.

"What's that?" She reined Flame in, cocking her head to listen.

"Birds?" Eulo shrugged. There were plenty of 'em here, hawks and parrots and larks. Strange how all those different types of birds shared the sky just fine, but if you put two groups of people together, one always wanted to better the other.

"Oh." Tali's cry wrenched the air.

The unfamiliar sound sent Eulo's heart racing. Cloud danced beneath him, sensing his sudden tension.

"What's Huon doing?" She stood in her stirrups, peering down the slope to where the stockman stood beside a boulder in the stable paddock.

Except, with heaviness sickening his guts, Eulo knew it wasn't a boulder. Tali must've too, because she shouted out, urging tired Flame into action. Cloud spun sideways, hauling on the bit, leaping after Flame at a speed Eulo wasn't so keen on—way too fast for heading home down a hill. Eulo braced into his stirrups, leaning his weight back in the saddle where he was better balanced. He'd be happy to just stay on, now. The horse's endurance lasted all day, which would've been good if he wasn't so bloody nervous.

Tali galloped Flame to the stable paddock, her hair streaming out behind her. For a heart-strangling moment, Eulo expected her to set the chestnut over the wooden gate. Instead, she brought him into a sliding stop in the mud. She flipped the latch open and spurred the horse through. By the time Eulo got there, danced the grey back and forth for long enough to close the gate and jam the latch shut, Tali had flung herself off Flame and run to Huon and the horse beside him.

Eulo abandoned Cloud with Flame, their flanks heaving and ears pricked towards the fuss nearby. He chased Tali, gritting his teeth against the twinge in his right knee. She sank into the pasture beside the beast at Huon's feet. Sweat dulled Sepher's once gleaming brown coat. She thrashed, groaning from the effort of trying to get her legs under her, then sank back down with a snort. Tali lay her hands on the mare's neck, frantically trying to calm her. Huon clutched his head in both hands, looking from the wretched horse to Eulo, the usual ruddiness of his face now turned to ash.

Sepher fought to stand again, unable to get her left foreleg into place. White shards of bone pierced ribbons of skin where a solid cannon bone should've linked her knee to fetlock. The mare fell, landing with a thud, groaning out pain and resignation.

"Oh no, oh no," Tali said, over and over, choking on the words.

Sepher rolled flat onto her side, her eyes glassy. Eulo closed his own eyes. He knew death intimately, had held it in his hands, called its name in the night. This time, with his wife's horror distorting her face, fate's black claw tore deep into his heart.

"She's hurting, Huon," Tali shouted, hair sticking to her tear-streaked cheeks. "You ought've helped her, instead of being so bloody weak." She shoved the tail of her shirt aside, fingers scrambling over the slender pouch hanging from her belt.

"I'll do it." Eulo touched Tali's shoulder. "It'll be quick, I promise." He'd stained his hands with enough blood over the years, both human and animal. The expert killer.

"No." She sprang to her feet and shoved him in the chest with both palms, catching him off guard, making him stumble. "How dare you. You think I don't know how to put my animals out of their misery?" Her scowl burnt through the strings of black hair hanging over her eyes.

Eulo raised his hands in surrender, taking another step back. Tali whipped her greensilver knife out of its pouch, holding the blade downturned. Sepher's breathing shallowed, her fight gone, almost motionless.

"My bird without wings, now you can fly," Tali whispered. "Lolani forgive me, I'm so sorry." She wielded mercy in one quick motion, arcing her hand under and up. She knelt, stroking the fine bones of Sepher's head, murmuring. *Safe home, friend.*

After the horse gasped her last, agonising breath, Tali glared up at Eulo and Huon. Both men waited, useless in the wave of her distress.

"What are you two standing around for? Go unsaddle those geldings, then get back here to cover Sepher." She turned to hunch over the dead mare again.

Sweating despite the cool air, Eulo gripped Huon's bicep. "Come on, leave her be." He steered the slack-jawed stockman away, letting Tali grieve in peace even though all he wanted was to pull her into his arms.

A defiant glow of late afternoon sun turned the paddock gold, softening the valley's wild beauty. The ranges didn't have Iskarlia's starkness, although they were desolate and harsh in their own way. Eulo thought of Tali's rawness, her emotions breaking free while her hands smoothed the mare's face and neck. A lump balled in his chest. Once they'd watched their own children starve or die of flummox, with their noses and mouths clogged full of foam, people on the plains sometimes said things like "it's just a horse". When you'd worked with an animal though, and come to know its quirks, it became so much more.

Rubbing the heel of his hand against his jaw, Eulo trudged after Huon in search of a shovel.

An owl took to the sky, hooting its departure, wings slashing rents in the dark. Like a blade through skin. Eulo blew out an exhalation, knocking the mud off his boots into the bushes at the foot of Tali's cottage. He plodded up the stairs, his gritty soles abrading the timbers with Glimmers dirt that stuck and clung. The same black loam streaked his skin and clothes, marking the rites he'd finished. He shrugged out of his oilskin coat, leaving it on the hook beside Tali's, then tossed his blood and dirt-sodden shirt into the corner of the verandah. The frigid wind across his chest whipped his breath away.

He padded inside in his socks, glad to be somewhere warm at last, where the ice might shift from his bones. Tali stood silhouetted against the hearth, the firelight dancing gold against her hair. Her lips parted as she scanned Eulo's bare torso and filthy pants. The whiff of honeyspiral followed her across the room to him.

Entwining her fingers with his, she led him over to the fire and pushed him into a chair. She squeezed out a washcloth into a steaming basin on the stone mantle. His belly twisted as she stared at him with lines of grief etched deep in her forehead. He couldn't speak. If he hadn't insisted she ride Flame, her beloved mare wouldn't have broken her leg.

Tali pressed the cloth against Eulo's forehead, working its fibres against his skin. He couldn't look away from her, but she wouldn't meet his eye as she washed the guilt off him. Back and forth from the basin, cleaning and rinsing. First his face, then his neck, and grime-smeared chest.

"Tell me about your tattoos," she said, using one finger to trace the artwork fanning across his torso.

Eulo opened his mouth, mute. All he could think about was her butterfly touch on his skin and the heat in his groin. In a voice coarsened by the collision of life and death, and his fascination with this woman, he said, "They're Iskarlia." He sucked in a breath as her fingertip found his nipple. He didn't dare move, in case he broke the unexpected intimacy.

"What do they mean?"

Smoke laced her words, weighted the glance she gave him from under her long lashes, weaving around his body, engulfing him in burning desire.

"This one," Tali pressed. Her finger sketched the black lines from his throat, across his collarbone from the left to right.

"The eagle's wings. Vigilant and unrivalled."

Her hand wandered down to the ridge of muscle above his navel. "And this?"

"The fish hook. For prosperity and luck."

"A sun?" She circled her finger in a slow, deliberate motion.

Eulo gasped, gripping the sides of his chair. "The circle of life. Eternity."

She skimmed his left ribcage. "A hunter?"

Shades, his dishonest prick strained at his pants. As obvious as a tree on the plains. "The desert dog. Loyalty and friendship."

"And?" She brushed her fingertips along his belly, sketching the spiralling black snake above his waistband.

"Copperhead, the loner." Eulo's chest surged, but he could hardly breathe through his anticipation.

Her teasing touch moved over to the double twine of wire and barbs on his right ribcage. "I know this one is Mako."

"Of course. To hunt off evil spirits and bring greatness and strength."

"Indeed." Tali sighed through just-parted lips. Still without meeting his eyes, she ran her hand over the bulge in his pants, dragging a groan through his lips.

Eulo rested his thumb along her fine jawbone.

"I'm sorry—" he began, for being so bloody lust-crazed while she was blackened by sorrow, but Tali didn't let him finish. She straddled him, her gentle tongue probing his open mouth, silencing his confession and spinning his mind out of the way of his body.

He pushed up her shirt without stripping it off, hands around her waist, drowning in her. He slid his fingers under the fine greensilver chain looped there, resting his knuckles on her spine. "What's this for?"

"Keeping out nasties, like diseases and babies," she panted, "but not husbands." Her lips found his again.

Without breaking their kiss, she stripped off his pants, shrugging her slim hips free of her own as he tugged them down. He pulled her back onto his lap, sliding into her, far too excited, far too fast. Like an inexperienced cleanskin, he gasped his climax out with his face in her breasts. She rested her cheek on his head, arching her body against him, their chests surging.

Eulo ran his hand up her spine, shocked to realise her shoulder was unbandaged. Still, he shied away from touching it. When he drew back to look at her, her gaze darted away. He clamped his teeth together, suddenly aware of his prick wilting inside her.

A flush coloured his ears. "It...um...that wasn't what I intended."

"I didn't want pleasure." Now she scrutinised him straight-on, her eyes silvered by steel.

Not shy, then, just evasive. She climbed off the sticky mess in Eulo's lap, discarding him with an odd hollowness in his chest while she went to refill the wash tub with hot water.

Later in bed, she wriggled over into his welcoming embrace, meeting him in a light, exploring kiss that went for a long time and left his belly dancing. She climbed on top of him, easing down onto his hard prick. Their bellies slapped together as she rocked her hips into his, guiding his hands onto her breasts. He savoured her lips, her nipples, unable to contain his own pleasure when she moaned out her climax.

Without once looking him in the eye.

He moved in an aura of golden bliss, shuffling barefoot out of the bedroom into the empty cottage. Tali had rolled out of the blankets earlier, away from Eulo's clumsy goon hands. The corner of his mouth turned up. All the other women he'd lain with wanted to stay in his arms, mooning at him with eyes full of hope and affection he didn't share.

Not Tali.

Nudging the front door open, he followed Tali's laughter out to her usual spot on the top step. Head tipped aside, she incited Chance to chase a piece of blue yarn. Disinterested, the cat padded over to Eulo and tangled around his legs, purring. Tali glanced at him through red-rimmed eyes.

"Morning."

"Mornin'." He loosed his most charming smile on her, then faltered. "Listen, Tali, about the horses—"

"When you first arrived, you made me think you hated them."

He nodded slowly, remembering his blunt comments on the Silveraine escarpment. "Tambo Tarch taught me to be a mercenary. He had a stable of mares we'd use to go hunting. They were fast and nasty, so nobody much bothered to try stealing them." He snorted. "The few goons who did got about a mile down the road before getting chucked off and left in the dirt with broken bones. Those mares were crazy— they'd bolt and buck, scrape you off under tree branches, roll on you in the creeks. But they'd always go back to Tambo's, sooner or later."

"That's why you can ride so well," Tali said, resting her chin on her hand, gazing at him as he sat beside her.

"One mare gave Tambo a real hard time, but her and me got on well. She never tried to throw me off, not once." Eulo swallowed, struck harder by recollection of the black mare than he'd expected. "Tambo was jealous, but it was also the reason he kept me around. That mare had a go at everyone who went near her, except when I took her home, showing off like she was the best horse in the country. My brother Remmy ran out to meet us and he was so excited to see me sittin' in the saddle with a flickerblade on my belt." It'd fed his pride, seeing the awe and envy in Rem's eyes, the way his mare rested her chin on the boy's shoulder. "Rem loved the horses. He'd be gobsmacked to see what you got here."

"Did you keep her, the mare?"

Eulo let out a long breath, steadying himself. "Nah. I got back one day from a job with a different horse. Tambo had taken my mare instead of his own, rode her real hard after some fucker who attacked 'em both with a blade." He stopped, stumbling over the memory.

Tali slipped her fingers between his hands, breaking apart his compulsion to rub the web of scars there. "He killed her?"

"Fuck no. He rode her home with a gash above one hock. She was three-legged lame by the time I found her, standing in a cloud of blowflies. Ain't no coming back from a wound like that." He clenched both hands, one around Tali's fingers. "Tambo said he knew I'd want to say goodbye, so he left her there 'til I got back to stop her suffering. I reckon he was jealous enough to do it to punish me. And he did." He ground his jaw.

Tali lay her free hand against his cheek, her breath short and sharp, punctured by sorrow. "I would've hated him for that."

"I do." Eulo opened his hand, playing her fingers between his. "That's why I'm sorry I asked you not to ride Sepher yesterday."

She held up her palm, stopping him. "It doesn't matter. She might've broken her leg in the hills, or today, or straight after being put back in the paddock last night." A tremor ran through her words. She sniffed, her eyes wet. "Death is just a part of my life."

"I know what that's like." Eulo wrapped his arms around her, holding her close.

After a long moment, Tali moved back. She rose to her feet, reaching for a canvas pack and water flask on the rail.

"Off already?" he said. Mako's teeth, she didn't muck about. She'd dressed in tan pants, buttoning a thick vest over her shirt. Work clothes. Eulo stretched, showing off his chest in the hope she'd come touch it.

"Off already."

A ripple of disappointment killed Eulo's firing lust. He rested his forearm on one of the posts holding the verandah up. "Wait up and I'll come with you." He'd pull some clothes on, grab some cheese and fruit to eat in the saddle.

"No." Tali ducked her head and jogged down the stairs.

"Where are you going?"

"I have something to do." She flicked a dark glance at him. "Go see to the cows, Eulo. I'll be home later." She turned on her heel and marched up the path to the southern escarpment, skirting the edge of the trees until she came to a fallen log. Resting her hand on the wood, she vaulted over, neat as a scrubcat.

Eulo folded his arms, staring at the green and brown mottle of undergrowth his wife had disappeared into. Odd bloody behaviour. Sneaky, like she had something to hide. And he knew that well, considering he did it himself. He went inside, kicking the door shut behind him.

A little while later, light footsteps landed on the porch. "Changed your mind, eh?" Eulo called out. Abandoning his breakfast, he got up to push the door open.

The triumph slid off his face.

"What the fuck are you doing here?"

# Chapter 20

"My wild Iskarlian," Vivica said, batting her thickly lined eyes at Eulo, trailing a finger down the dried blackvine hanging beside the door. Tali reckoned it kept the bad spirits out, but it didn't seem to be working this morning.

"What do you want?"

"I came to visit my big sister. About her horse."

Tali entered Eulo's mind, kneeling in pristine grass, her blade gleaming. Copper coated his gums and the scent of blood sat thick in his nose.

"Is she here?" Vivica raised both plucked eyebrows.

"Nah. She's gone off up the forest."

"Oh." Leaning against the doorframe, she stretched both arms above her head, watching Eulo with a coy smile. "Maybe you should sneak off with a secret lover, too."

Jealousy slammed into him, merging with the simmer from Tali's snub this morning. Vivica, the voice of his suspicions, lifted her leg in a ripple of blue silk. She dropped her knee to the side, with her lips and legs parted.

"You could take me right now," she said, fluttering her eyelashes at him, drawing him closer, "if you were brave enough." She patted him on the arse as he turned away to go back to his breakfast, her laughter tinkling in the crisp morning.

"Get the fuck out, Vivica. I ain't doing this," Eulo grunted. Here he was, with his mind full of Tali, and his hands full with her sister.

Vivica stuck her tongue out as she followed him inside. She combed her hair out with her fingers, spilling a trail of black curls down her cheek. Tali's angular profile hid the kindness inside her, while Vivica's radiance masked her hard, sharp nature. She peered at a sheaf of papers cluttering the ashwood table.

"What's this? Is Tali trying to tame you?"

He cringed, realising what she was looking at. "She's teaching me my letters," he said slowly. He practised when he could, trying not to drop crumbs from his breakfast into the wet ink.

"What for? No one keeps an Iskarlian around for his brains."

"Except Tali, and she's the smartest Vernese I ever met."

"Especially when she's lining your pockets with kistars. Come on, you and I both know she's dreaming. She'll make all sorts of promises she can't keep—saving Glimmers Gap, for one. Replacing all the cattle with horses? Pah." She tossed her head. "Money is the real power, and none of us has it. Tali still hasn't worked that out yet."

Eulo might've defended his wife if he wasn't still crabbed about her sneakiness this morning. The Sarsegas weren't his bloody problem, anyway. He'd walk away from all this like he'd walked away from Lilla, three months before sailing off beside Tali on the wifeship.

Lilla, who'd persisted for month after month, welcoming him with a smile and affection, especially when he rode into town with his pockets full of coin. They'd been convenient for each other, Eulo happy to share her bed in between hunting jobs. Then, after a year, his money wasn't convenient enough, or his work, and she'd cry and scream, wanting more. For him to love her as much as she loved him. A binding. A baby. A commitment to always go back to her. Clinging tighter when he tried to prise her away, insisting she needed money for indulgences when he was trying to pay his Scabman debts.

"See," Vivica said, revelling in his silence. "The faster we talk Tali into selling this place, the better."

"Where would you go?"

"Silveraine, so it wouldn't matter to me where everyone else was. Maybe Tali can do the housekeeping for once; washing all Mema's messed clothes and bedsheets. Let her work it out—she's always telling us how good she is at solving problems." Vivica brushed off her skirts. Long, deliberate motions down her backside, her thighs.

Eulo bristled, focusing his gaze squarely back on hers. "She's trying to. She–"

"She tied a binding with you so she could have a man at her beck and call, and when she gets sick of you..." Vivica raised her fist, opening it as though she was throwing something away. "See, that's the thing about us dignitines—we always have men running around behind us, falling over themselves to be the drudge for our dirty work. Except you're already running around after someone, aren't you? Who's Lilla,

Eulo? You're not already married, are you?"

"Fuck no," he said, too quickly. Lilla had defied the advances of everyone except Eulo Juke, but the flattery of her attention turned sour, controlling. When he walked away, he told her he'd never be back. She'd cried, again, and screamed, again. She swore she'd do whatever she could to help Sif Cutter and his Scabs teach Eulo a lesson.

Now they had Rem, and Rem needed him. Eulo would buy more kilili as soon as he could, but this week's pay was already late. He needed more time, more money. Tali's money.

Vivi went on, "I know you're trouble, Eulo, so I want you off Glimmers before you hurt my sister. You don't even need to lay a hand on me for her to believe you did." She feigned sadness, let a quiver into her voice, "I swear, Tali, I didn't want to, but he pushed me down and forced himself on me. He's a bad man. You have to make him leave." She touched her tongue to her top lip, smirking. "And if she doesn't, I promise I will." She sashayed out in a fluster of perfume and skirts, leaving Eulo trapped between his past and her triumph in realising she had something to hold over him.

He flattened his palm on the tabletop, on the scraps of paper he'd laboured over, using all his concentration to shape the little letters Tali had showed him. *Eulo Juke*, he'd written, but instead of Tali's elegant handwriting, all he saw was squiggles and smudges. No better than a toddler scratching with a stick in the dirt. Ashamed, he crushed the paper into a ball. He flung it into the unlit fireplace.

He imagined Rem resting his chin on his fist, laughing when he heard what Eulo had done to get to Vernesia, and the story of Tali. *You tied a binding? You?* They'd always been there for each other as kids, while their parents were off working. Wherever Remmy was now, pretty letters were no help to him. If Eulo meant to find his little brother and rescue him, he had to remember who he was.

A soldier, a man of blood and dirt, a hunter who brought death. Not some useless cow-herder pissing about on a hillside pretending to be a learned man and grouching about his wife and the secrets she didn't trust him with.

At Tali's beck and call, was he? Just her drudge, a hired man to do a job for her, exactly the sand-skulled Iskarlian Vivica said he was?

Eulo bolted down the rest of his breakfast, barely tasting it. A dirty brown fizz of jealousy and bruised pride washed through him. Curse Tali for being cagey about where she'd gone. Having a secret lover made sense, especially if she was meeting with a bound man. Or woman.

He slunk out to the porch to pull his boots on. He didn't care, anyways.

Did he?

He paused with his oilskin in one hand and saddlebag hanging from the other. Chance perched on the handrail, blinking at him through trancelike yellow eyes. Witness and judge.

"Reckoned I was scratching an itch last night, I did," Eulo said to the cat. "Seems in all the fun my wife has edged herself under my skin." Or else he'd never noticed her there 'til now.

Chance yawned, showing off fangs white against his little pink mouth.

"Ah fuck it." Eulo jammed the oilskin and saddlebag back on their hook. He strode into the forest, leaping over the fallen log before he could change his mind. He barged through the encroaching scrub, weaving through tallwoods and tree-ferns, their bright green leaves unfurling tiny hands towards him.

His heavy boots trod over her smaller prints in the mud. A job. This was just a job. Tracking someone, the way he did in Iskarlia. Tali mustn't have gone far on foot, heading up this incline. He spat a gob of slime into the ferns. Back home, he'd never gotten too involved, never asked questions that were none of his business to have answers to. Mako's teeth, he was more than halfway done here with Tali; two weeks short of freedom, from going after Remmy. Why get so bull-headed now?

He grunted, knowing full well why. After last night, he couldn't keep denying how much he wanted to find out what made Tali Sarsega do what she did, and why she'd become so bloody irresistible to him.

Eulo picked at a splinter in his palm. He'd already made it halfway up the slope, so he might as well keep going. The steepening hillside forced him to lean into his steps, his boots slipping on the damp earth. At the top, he stopped where the path turned across the escarpment, gulping in breaths of fresh air. Stands of trees unfolded below, all the way across the paddocks to the Sarsega homestead.

His eyes fluttered shut, blocking out the forest's browns and greens, its streaked sunshine, the sounds of birds twittering and chirping, and dry leaves sighing over one another. Breathing in loam and soft eucalypt and breathing out all his weaknesses.

He shifted to face west, catching the faintest whiff of smoke, mingled with a hardness like biting down on a fork. It was all he needed to lead him on. Moving slowly, he picked his way over boulders in the clamouring scrub, leaving the escarpment behind. At least the undergrowth would break his fall if he tripped and lost his balance. All of a sudden, something scrambled away from him, leaving the bushes agitating in its wake. It must've been about the size of a desert dog, going by the ruckus it made.

Eulo scanned the forest ahead until he picked out a solid span of timber, mostly obscured by undergrowth and shadows. His pulse throbbed in his neck. Whatever Tali was doing here, she didn't want him knowing about it. A lean-to took shape as he crept closer, its drop-slab walls cleverly mimicking the stand of trees around it. Whoever had propped the rough-hewn planks into place had left thumb-wide gaps between the chunks of wood.

He paused at the corner, straining his ears. Inside, Tali murmured in her low, throaty voice. Her sudden giggle jarred with the woman Eulo thought he knew. He frowned.

"Oh yes, yes," she crooned, "yes, in here. You'll like it there."

Eulo Juke didn't scare easy, but what he saw after storming around to confront his wife lanced a needle of fear into his chest.

A steel sliver glowed red on an anvil in front of Tali. Sweat soaked the back of her white singlet and greased her arms. She flicked her head, trying to shift rogue hairs that had escaped the messy knot there. Gold dust shimmered in the sunlight bathing her work area, twinkling as it fell. No, Eulo realised, his mouth turning dry, not falling. *Dancing.* In spiralling eddies, bouncing sideways, massing into streams which exploded out in starbursts. The dust wasn't gold at all, either, but a familiar greensilver.

"What are you doing here?" Tali demanded, shattering Eulo's astonishment. She glared at him over her shoulder. The glittering dust burst outward, scattering, panicking.

"What are *you* doing here?" he said, shocked by her fury.

"You have to go, Eulo. It's too dangerous. You can't see this." Tali grimaced, as though she battled with a heavy burden. She peered at the shimmer cavorting above her head. "Come on, my pretty ones," she sang, stretching a palm out to them. The dust regrouped, fluttering to her, chittering like the busy, bossy crimson parrots in Iskarlia. Tali sing-songed back in rapid Vernese. She glanced at Eulo. "They like you. Because they're as stubborn and bloody-minded as you are."

"What are they?" The skin on Eulo's arms tingled. "Is this magic?" The word sounded stupid, out loud. Only little tackers and the sand-skulled believed in magic. "Come on, you reckoned you'd answer any question I asked."

Tali winced, closing her eyes for a moment. "Not about this."

He glanced at the flattened steel on the anvil, and the hammer beside her, and suddenly he understood. "Please, Tali, I'll keep out of your way. Let me stay and watch."

"No. Go, now. It's too dangerous. You've seen too much already." She flapped her hand like she was shooing blowflies. "Go!"

Eulo stumbled away, his skin turning hot and clammy. Of all the situations he'd reckoned he might've found, this hadn't been one of them. The world had its order, and in Mako's world there was no place for magic.

Was there?

Rain-spattered wind chased Eulo on his ride home in the evening, tangling Cloud's mane as they navigated the downhill slopes. The horse scrambled in the mud, throwing his head high as he fought to stay upright. Least it gave him something else to think about instead of spooking or trying to scrape Eulo off on the trees. Tali had agreed for him to ride Cloud to drove a mob of steers to Gullwing market in a few days, even though she still frowned in disappointment any time Eulo picked the long-barrelled grey over her youngstock. She said it'd be a day's ride to the coastal town, where they'd stay overnight. Eulo chafed for the chance to look around and find out who was selling or smuggling kilili.

Then, he'd have to suffer through a dinner Tali had arranged with Krike and his wife. At least the big goon might have some news to share. Allying himself with Krike didn't sit easy with Eulo, but his options were pretty thin. He spat onto the grass. He'd worked alongside men he didn't trust plenty of times in the past, and would again, too.

Cloud crested the last hill, giving Eulo a clear view of Tali's cottage in the valley below. He peered through the raindrops fringing his hat-brim. Not a hint of smoke rose from the chimney. The gelding jig-jogged down the slope, slipping and sliding on the soft ground. He'd been ratty all day, picking up on Eulo's dirty mood, testing him out. Eulo scowled. No grimy, hungry man wanted to come home to a cold house, especially not when he had a furious woman to face, and a filthy conscience to hide.

Once he'd put Cloud away, Eulo trudged through twilight to the cottage, swinging his water flask by the strap. He landed one foot on the bottom step and stopped. The hair prickled on his nape. He knew he'd shut the door when he'd left in the morning. Now it gaped open, sucking frigid air into its hungry mouth.

"Tali?"

Eulo edged into the darkness. He tripped over something near the door, barking his shin on the edge of the wood box as he fell. "What the fuck?" He sprawled along the floorboards, his shin throbbing. Squinting, he rolled over to find out what lay across the doorway. A boot. Attached to a leg. And another beside it.

Steel gripped Eulo's guts. "Tali?" He scrambled onto his hands and knees, crawling to her.

"Mreow." Chance wailed. The cat squatted on Tali's back, fur fluffed against the chill, eyes black and accusing.

"What the fuck is going on, you ginger goon?" Eulo's voice sounded strange, distant to his own ears.

The cat howled again.

"Tali." Eulo brushed hair off her cheek, the tresses greasy in his fingers, her skin ice-cold under his touch. Panic flooded his veins. She'd gone down face-first and not moved again.

# Chapter 21

"Get out." He shoved the cat away so he could turn his wife over. The acrid reek of vomit rose from the dark floor below her. She rolled bonelessly, like a corpse. No, not quite. Not stiff. Not dead. Eulo flattened his ear to her chest, listening until he heard the thump of a heartbeat and felt the press of her breasts rising in a breath. Weak with relief, he kicked the door shut. If he didn't get her warm, he might really end up with a corpse on his hands. He tugged a wool blanket off the armchair, sweeping it over her where she lay.

Shadows whispered around him as he fumbled to coax flames through kindling in the fireplace. The wind whipping through the open door had tossed burnt-out ashes over the floor. Fuck knew how the cottage hadn't been razed to the ground and Tali with it. Eulo made a half-arsed attempt to sweep the mess out of the way so he could place her beside the fluttering heat.

He nestled beside her on the rug, tucking the blanket closer, begging her limbs to warm up. Firelight glistened off a snail-trail of saliva and crusted bile in her hair. Eulo lunged for a cloth draped over the nearby washtub, to dab the muck off her face and tresses. He reached back up to fling the cloth over the tub.

"What the fuck?"

Bright blood streaked his hand. He sat back, pushing the blanket aside to find red smears across his pants. Tali's back was drenched. Eulo swore, tearing her shirt to expose a blood-soaked bandage. His breath whistled through his nostrils. Last night, her shoulder had been bare, although he'd been too preoccupied to look at it. 'So much for it being better,' he muttered, tugging at the knot on the bandage, determined to see the injury beneath.

The bandage came free, peeling back from rents of raw flesh where

Tali's skin gaped open.

Without warning, she flailed into motion, wild as a cornered scrubcat. She struck the washtub with one swinging hand, sending it clanging against the wall. Her other hand cracked Eulo across the face. Stunned, he let go of her. She writhed off his lap, twisting up onto her hands and knees, snarling at him through tangles of black hair. Her chest heaved.

"Shades, woman, you need a physic," Eulo growled. His mind raced. He'd grab Flame out of the horse paddock behind the cottage, ride to the stables and send Huon to Bintau for help. He didn't want to leave Tali but he had no other choice.

"No physic." Her eyes shone greensilver.

"Then let me stitch it so it's not pissing blood everywhere." Eulo stared her down. "I've done it plenty of times on the war field. I got bone needles in my pack—"

"No."

"But—"

"Don't touch it, Eulo."

He folded his arms. "Right, so you'll just lay about in the doorway 'til the bleeding stops, will you? Or until that fuckin' stubborn little heart of yours gives out? How much longer d'you reckon you can go without getting bloodsick?"

Tali drew a hand across her eyes. Her teeth chattered, echoing a tremble throughout her body. She sank onto her haunches, hanging her head. "Would you," she said, in barely a whisper, "trust me and just put another dressing on it, over the top?"

Eulo rubbed his jaw, shocked to see her so vulnerable. "Righto." He shoved his misgivings aside to help her into a chair. Mako knew when she'd last eaten, so he swung a pot of broth over the fire to heat while he worked.

She straddled the chair, sagging over the back with her spine outward. Eulo pulled a seat up behind her, tucking a bundle of clean rags into his lap after he sat down. He pressed a wad of the rags against the bloodstained bandage marring her naked torso, holding them in place with his right hand, doubtful about the whole bloody mess.

"How long you bin lying there?"

"I came home for lunch."

While Eulo had been over at the beach, festering sour with her. Shame spiked his heart. "What were you doing up the escarpment this morning?" Thinking of it now was like remembering a dream. All that shimmer in the air, the blade in the forge. He wanted to see it again, to know what it was.

"You shouldn't have followed me, Eulo."

"I wanted to know if you were meeting someone."

"Like who?"

"Dunno. A lover, maybe."

She surprised him by laughing. "Lover? You're an idiot."

"Oh," he said, clenching his fist.

"What you saw this morning, I'm trusting you not to speak of it. To anyone. Ever."

"Huh?"

"Not even Ranson knows. Or Vivica." Tali gripped the wooden chair so tight the colour fled her knuckles.

Eulo pressed his fingers against her bandages. His greensilver binding ring turned luminous against the rust-coloured stains.

"Eulo?"

"Oh. Righto," he said, not understanding why she was so protective about it all, and not sure how to convince her to tell him.

The wad of rags grew warm under his palm, drawing blood out of whatever mess Tali hid under the old bandage. He blinked at the kilili band on his finger. Must be he was imagining a tingle in his bones. Tali folded her arms along the chair. She rested her cheek on one forearm, closing her eyes with a sigh. Eulo pulled the wool blanket around her, covering the smooth brown curve of her naked side. Sharing themselves last night seemed unreal now, after what he'd seen and done since.

"Keep warm, darl. The last body I touched what was as cold as you, was a corpse."

Tali shivered. "I can't believe Sepher's gone."

Eulo recoiled from his bad choice of words. "I wasn't meaning your horse," he said. "I've seen how people bond with animals. I know soldiers what've broke down over losing a dog, or a horse, when they didn't even cry about their own family dying."

She didn't speak for so long, he thought she'd fallen asleep, or unconscious. Then, she said, "Is your family alive?"

Eulo tossed the stained wad of rags beside her feet. "You need a good wash." She might've offered to answer any question he asked, but that didn't mean he would. Not then, on the wifeship. Not now. Knowledge gave a man power over others, made 'em weak. Tali Sarsega already threatened to weaken him, and he couldn't afford to give her that. Not when Remmy needed him.

"I have to rest." She braced the muscles through her upper body. "If you don't want to share a bed with me, you can sleep with the cat."

Eulo folded fresh rags into a wad, which he fastened over the old bandage, crabbed that she wouldn't let him take the whole lot off to clean it up properly. "I shared barracks and campsites with scores of soldiers for five years. You'll have to try harder than that to put me off." He tied the new bandage, then wrapped the blanket around her, with a motion as delicate as handling a scrubcat likely to explode in enraged claws and teeth at any moment.

Tali's green gaze tracked him across the room, from washing his hands to finding her a clean shirt near the bed. He paused on his way back, tucking the shirt under one elbow so he could lift the simmering pot of broth off the fire.

"I'm not hungry."

"Swallow it anyway." Eulo scooped a mug into the pot. He sat it on the table beside her. "Even the stupidest Iskarlian soldier knows better than to let themselves get weak 'cause they didn't eat." He rapped his knuckles on the wood. "And who's going to run this place if you're sick or dead?" The tension coursing through him yanked his light-hearted tone askew, leaving his words cruel.

She gave in enough to sip the broth, although she slapped him away when he tried to help her into the bedroom. "I don't need to be carried around like an old woman."

He snorted, raising his hands in defeat. "Mako help the poor bastard what ends up dealing with you when you *are* an old woman. You're stubborn as a fencepost already."

Her mouth curled in one corner. "Haven't you noticed yet—it's the Sarsega way."

The Iskarlians would've cried with happiness to know a season where dampness sat thick in the air, beading in perfect rows on their horses' manes, soaking into rich soil and green vegetation. Eulo swept a hand over the seat of his saddle, flicking droplets off the leather.

"Give me sun and heat any day." He ducked under the gelding's belly to grab the girth. His frozen fingers refused to thread the straps onto the buckles. Cloud went taut, raising his head, ears pricked, staring into the fog. He snorted once, a sharp, rude noise in the still morning. Or what was left of it, anyway. Eulo had woken late, alone, and just as foggy in his bloody head as outside it.

"And you're a woolly-headed bastard too," he told Cloud, "lookin' for ghosts out there." He peered at the rolling white gloom.

"It must be in his breeding," Tali said, clear and wry, her dark-clad figure emerging on the path.

Eulo poked a finger under his wool cap to scratch his ear. He'd spent most of the night lying awake beside her, listening to her breathing, too edgy to sleep in case he woke up to find her cold and rigid beside him. "Are you well?"

She leant against the hitching rail, her cheeks brushed pink from the chill air. "I'm better than I was."

"Good," he muttered. Even with black shadows lining her eyes, she looked a fair few steps farther away from death than she had last night. She'd bundled herself into layers of clothes, burying her shoulder. Eulo squinted, noticing a sheath the length of his forearm hanging from a leather strap across her chest. She pulled it over her head and threw it into the grass at his feet.

He bent to pick it up, slowly straightening, turning the plain leather case over in his hands, admiring the hilt's swirled wood. He slid the blade free from its cover, sucking in a deep breath. Mako's teeth—he was holding a highly-polished, perfectly straight, and lethally sharp flickerblade.

"I take it you approve?" Tali lifted her chin.

Eulo ran a thumb over green swirls in the silveriron. A fish hook. Eagle. Snake. Mako and the desert dog. A thrill gripped his chest. "It'd sell for three thousand kistars in Iskarlia." At least.

"It might if it was perfect."

"Are you sand-skulled? It's amazing."

She leant in to lift the knife out of his hands. Her soft scent drifted to his nostrils, her fresh-washed hair glossy again. He glanced at her shoulder, wondering about the wound. Last night, wrapped around her, his hand had strayed to rest on the bandage, even when he'd consciously moved it away.

"If you hadn't interrupted me and disturbed the kilili, it wouldn't sound wrong." She lunged forward, wielding the knife in a broad arc.

A shriek ripped into the air, setting Eulo's teeth on edge. Cloud milled at the hitching rail, spinning as far as the lead would let him.

Tali held the blade point-down. She took a step, shifting into a defensive pose with her knife hand across her throat, turning the blade's tip out.

Eulo whistled, impressed. "And why does a horse breeder know how to fight with a blade?"

She straightened into her normal stance. "I don't fight, but I need to know how a fighter would use my blades."

"Your blades?"

She licked her lips. "There are two people alive who know I can make kilili silveriron. I meant it when I asked you not to tell anyone."

He nodded, taking the knife from her, speechless. Kilili silveriron and flickerblades had always been around, but they were in high demand and hard to come by unless you happened to be a Covesman, thug, or one of the Kestrine's Goshawks, who were all armed with it. Eulo weighed the knife in his hand again. He had to have it. There was the small problem of not having three thousand kistars, though.

"How much will you sell it for?"

"You don't sell a flawed silveriron blade," she snorted.

Eulo tested it in a series of quick moves. The blade sang as it cut through the mist, a triumphant, discordant tone. It fit his hand better than any other blade he'd held. "A flawed blade for a flawed man," he said, grinning at Tali. "I want to buy it." For himself though, not the Scabmen.

She cupped her hands over her elbows. "I didn't make it to sell, Eulo. It's a gift."

Shocked, he ran his thumb over the greensilver symbols. The same symbols Tali traced on his chest two nights ago. Shades, she'd made this—*made* this—half-killing herself by opening the bloody wound on her back, and ended up senseless in a puddle of her own vomit while her bastard husband plotted ways to steal a ransom of kilili for the Scabmen. Bile rose into Eulo's mouth.

He sheathed the knife and offered it to Tali. "I can't take it."

"You will, because I can't afford to pay you." Her eyes gleamed in the fog. "I'll have money after we get those steers to market." She kicked at a spur of clumpweed in the mud, avoiding his gaze.

"Shades, woman," Eulo blurted. "You reckon it was clever climbing the escarpment again to get this, after what happened to you yesterday? Why didn't you ask me for help? You need to rest."

"I have to check the steers I'm selling."

"Fuck the steers." Eulo's heart kicked against his ribs. She made silveriron. *His* silveriron, clutched in his hand like the tool of a lunatic spouting Mako's return. *I just want to get my brother back.* He wanted Tali now too, though, and the chance for a new life. He shook his head, trying to shoo the spinning disbelief and clamour away.

In a steadier voice, he said, "I'll check the steers and calves."

"My cranky cow will drop in this foul weather. She does it every year."

"Lucky I've gotten Cloud acquainted with her, eh." Eulo slid a hand around Tali's waist, angling his face so he could kiss her soft lips. "Thanks for the blade. I don't deserve it." He didn't deserve any of this. She'd boot him out on his arse with nothing if she knew what he was and what he'd done.

She lay her palm against his cheek, her touch warm against the too-long bristles. Lust and longing tangled with Eulo's restless guilt. His emotions were hobbling him in this binding, whether he liked it or not.

"Best get your horse out before he digs his way back to Skylani's."

Eulo spun around, having been too fixated on Tali to notice Cloud gouging a hole in the loam below the hitching rail. He untied the gelding and looked up to say goodbye, but she'd already vanished into the mist. Her silveriron was too valuable—too special—to sell or give to the Scabmen. He had to find out where she got the kilili from, though, and how he could get more, before his time ran out.

"Aren't you going to practise your letters? You didn't do them last night,"

Tali's words struck Eulo between the shoulder blades, freezing him on his chair beside the fire, dangling a strop from one hand. He selected a blade from the pile beside his feet. "I got to finish sharpening my knives."

"You have a flickerblade. You don't need the others anymore." She peered at him over the ledgers lying on the table in front of her. "Eulo?"

"What I don't need is letters." He stared at the flames licking the logs in the fireplace. "I got all the power I need here." He raised the fist with the blade in it.

Tali propped one elbow on the table, leaning in to rest her chin on her hand. "Don't you believe there's power in words, too? To be able to read an agreement? Or write one? Or sign your name to one, instead of scrawling a mark?"

The wooden legs of Eulo's chair screamed against the stone floor as he shoved himself back from the too-hot fire. Chance glanced up from his position at Eulo's feet, licking his lips in disapproval at being woken up.

"Bit hard to sign an agreement in Iskarlia when no bastard can write one."

"Can't anyone in your village read?"

"Slue Tearle does."

"What does it do for him?"

Eulo chewed a hangnail on his thumb. "People ask him to read and write things for 'em. Most often they ask him for advice."

"Oh." Tali smoothed the tip of her plait. "They think he's wise because he can read?"

"S'pose so." Eulo wrapped and unwrapped the strop around his hand. Of all the symbols inked on his skin, wisdom wasn't one of them.

"And it gave him power, no?"

He nodded, mulling over the idea of it. "He once told Humf Greyler it'd be a poor season for stripleaf, then charged a fortune when he planted a crop of it and Grey didn't."

Tali twitched a smile. She returned to her books without saying anything. The lopsided grin curling up her face told Eulo what she was thinking well enough. He chewed at the hangnail again. In a handful of words, Vivica had kicked his feet out from under him. A handful more and Tali held him out a gem. She was right—words held power, for sure.

He lay the strop over his fingers, pulled the leather back 'til the tendons in his hand screamed out in protest. In the hills today he'd ridden hard, giving Cloud no excuse to play up, so he could get home faster. It weighed on his mind whether to tell Tali her sister had come looking for her yesterday. In the end, shame drove him to silence. Over these last few days, the lines marked between him and Tali had shifted, merging into a bond he couldn't name or define.

"Why'd you do it?" he said, finally letting the strop hang loose. "Give me a horse, a silver fucking iron knife, teach me letters? You could push me out the door empty-handed at the end of this and be all the richer for it."

"Because you're in my employ like any other stockman here, and it's the right thing to do." She turned a page in her book. "You and I don't exactly sit around talking about our families and lives, so we may as well do something in the evenings."

Eulo bunched his fists on his knees. "Y' understand I can't trade you anything for it though, don't you?" Not when his whole life fit into a pack and a pair of saddlebags.

"I never thought of it like that, because I didn't expect to be repaid for any of this." Tali tapped the pen against her chin, contemplating. "If it makes you feel better, why don't you teach me something?"

"Ain't nothing I can do except hunt people, and you already know how to handle horses," he said. He stared at his fists, let them open. "I could show you how to move your feet properly when you got a knife in your hand. Most people don't understand how much footwork matters in hand-to-hand fighting."

"Good. We'll start when we get back from Gullwing." Tali nodded, pleased.

Her approval made Eulo grin. He pointed one of the knives towards her. "I better finish these." When he picked up the third knife, festering over her comment that they didn't talk about their families, he relented on his vow not to open up to her.

"You asked if my parents are alive." His slow words broke the muted scratch of Tali's pen on paper, and the rhythmic swish of metal on leather.

She shut the ledger and pushed it to one side. "Tell me while I brew us some kaif."

"They are. My old lady is a gem hunter. She has a good eye, good hands, and shitloads of patience. My old man was a soldier, a real hard bastard; Ruckus Juke. Folk know his name, even if they don't know him." A legend that had grown way past reality.

"Is that good or bad for you?" Tali hung the kettle. She came to stand by the fire, stroking Chance with her foot. The cat stretched out a foreleg, opening and closing his paw, claws pricking into the rug.

"Not everyone likes him. Not everyone is game to pick a fight with him. They were happy to pick 'em with me, though. I proved myself over and over." Eulo tested the edge of the blade against his thumb. Memories of fists and fury clamoured at him. "It ain't easy to please an Iskarlian soldier. Especially my father."

She cried out, startling him. Tired of his mistress's attention, Chance had rolled over and attacked her foot with his sharp teeth and claws. He kicked with his back feet, swishing his tail from side to side. Tali extracted herself from the savage beast's clutches and retreated to sit on the table next to Eulo.

"His basket's too close to the fire, you know. He overheats. It makes him cranky."

"If I move it any further away, he'll squat on the floor there whingeing until I put it back," she said, tapping Eulo's thigh with her toe. "What does the infamous Ruckus Juke do now?"

He stared at her leg. "He got blinded in a skirmish, defending the Cove's convoy. Some firedust blew up in his face and no one could do anything about it. The Cove barely noticed him leave, even after twenty-nine years of service." Eulo couldn't avoid his bitter tone. He tidied away the strop and knives. "There ain't no pay for has-been warriors in Iskarlia, so Ruckus went home to the gemfields and started growing vegetables." And an exceptionally bad temper.

"Being blind mustn't be easy."

"'Specially not on that overbaked lump of sand. But he grumbles through and him and me mum get by. It takes more than a bit of crow-peck to slow a Juke down, he reckons."

"I don't doubt it." Tali hesitated. "Is it just you and your parents?"

He chewed the inside of his cheek for a moment. "I got a brother. Remmy's the baby of the family, the best one out o' the lot of us." Eulo cut himself off before admitting he'd let his family down by sacrificing Rem for his bad debts.

Unable to ignore the temptation any longer, he caught Tali's foot. He slid his hand up her smooth calf. "All the work's done for the night."

"Good. You can start on your letters while I pour the kaif." She pushed herself off the table, out of reach.

Smoke through his fingers.

# Chapter 22

Tali settled into the saddle, its familiar leather worn smooth. Hurt stained the excitement thundering under her ribs, blurring the horse's thin brown neck. This was her first run without Sepher in over five years of droving. She shoved the sorrow aside as fast as it had risen. There wasn't time to dwell on it, not when her mob of cattle was disappearing up the driveway without her. She sat easily when the filly sprang forward, ears pricked in the direction of the mob.

Barking dogs darted in the beasts' wake, pushing them along the fence beside the driveway, past the house and beyond. The crack of Huon's stockwhip cut through the morning now and then, heading off the boldest steers from any idea of rebellion. The cattle would settle into their rhythm soon enough, marking out the beat of the road with their hooves. Huon's gelding meandered loose with Flame in the midst of the mob. If she managed to sell the two fillies they were riding, as she hoped, Tali and Huon would ride home from Gullwing on the geldings.

She wriggled her right shoulder against her cotton shirt, pleased it was healing. She'd over-stripped her tattoo in the rush to make Eulo's blade, and during the daze of his interruption while she'd been singing the kilili. He didn't ask the questions that clouded his eyes when he looked at his blades or at her shoulder. Questions she wouldn't answer. She had to trust he'd keep her kililismithing to himself—the bit he'd seen, anyway.

Tali shortened her reins, clucking her filly into a long-striding trot. She loved all the horses she bred, but some more than others, and this one less so. People were usually happy to part with their money for a flash little pony, though, even when it didn't have a lick of sense between its ears. These youngsters lacked polish, which Tali had neglected because of her travel to Iskarlia and her slow, frustrated recovery from singing the kilili.

She edged over to eavesdrop on Huon and Eulo's conversation.

"We gotta tail 'em all gentle-like." Huon motioned with his calloused hands. "They're tough beasts, growing up on these southern hills and beaches, but the boss lady here won't be happy if we push 'em too hard and don't get 'em all to market."

"Those beasts," Tali said, waving at the steers, "are money on legs, Huon."

"So says some. Some says they're sweet little fellows with soft eyes and brains like a horse. Some people even says both, eh?"

"Soft alright." Tali rolled her eyes. The stockman knew her too well.

"And the fillies?" Eulo said.

He'd done a good job getting some sense into the grey gelding. Shame it wouldn't make them any money, but it would boost Glimmers Gap's reputation, irritate her rival breeder; Jikah, and refine Skylani Ces's favour of the Sarsega sisters. She grinned at Eulo. "The fillies are spares for when your grey breaks down."

"Look at the fire in her eyes." Huon tugged at his wild beard. "She gets it whenever we go droving, ever since she was six years old."

"You've known her for a long time." Eulo's expression betrayed nothing.

"For sure. The Sarsega women have always looked after me. Tali's like my own daughter."

*To Ranson's disgust.* Tali blew out a breath, letting the irritation at her father fade. She wouldn't let her family problems wreck the joy of droving, not when she'd been looking forward to this morning for weeks. The weight on her heart lifted a little in anticipation of visiting Gullwing again, with all its colours and characters.

The cattle ambled along the roadways ribboning the lush southern countryside. Each of their sixty gleaming rumps bore an interlaced GG. The Sarsega brand was known for calm beasts and sweet, tender meat, buoying Tali's optimism they'd reach good prices in the saleyards.

The midday sun smouldered in a cloudless sky, raising perspiration in the small of her back. She'd have the chance to shed some clothes now they'd reached Lark's Waterhole, where they were stopping for lunch. The cattle trooped down an incline through the trees, keen to reach the creek. Tali's filly picked her way after them, dropping her head to drink.

"It seems you kept the better horse for yourself," Huon shouted across to her. His horse pawed torrents of water up against herself.

Tali laughed, amused even more when her own filly joined in.

"I'm tickled pink to have another man around to talk to." He lifted his hat away from his damp hair. "It's almost like I handpicked Eulo for you myself."

"At least someone approves," Tali said. The men had been deep in conversation for the last hour.

"Don't be so tough on yourself, or your family," Huon said, "considering Cailene told me how she hears Vivica sobbing when she thinks no one's around." His eyes widened in alarm. "Ah, sorry. Didn't mean to gossip. You know we all reckon you're a good egg."

*Oh, Vivi.* Tali swallowed a lump in her throat. "I'm trying my hardest." She faltered, shocked by the tremor in her voice. Blazes, she'd staked so much on getting a good price at market for the mob of animals around them. What if she couldn't?

Huon shot her a gentle smile. "I know. I didn't mean to make you feel bad."

She played with the filly's mane, flicking it to the right, then the left side of her neck. "I do. Feel bad, I mean. They're all so miserable and I don't know how to make them happy again."

"So don't."

"What?"

"Don't. Maybe you can't. Maybe they have to do it. They're the only ones who can control how they feel."

Tali chewed her lip.

"See, there you go overthinking things again." Huon leant back in his saddle, stretching his legs out past his filly's shoulders. "As Cyska says—just *be.* You should be enjoying this glorious blue-sky day, the beasts that'll line your pockets at market, and"—his eyes lit with mischief—"that Iskarlian who spends a lot more time staring at you than you do noticing."

Did he? Unable to stop herself, Tali sought out Eulo. His gelding splashed through the creek on the far side of a dozen steers, while he waved his hat up and down to shoo the mob through the water.

Laughter crackled behind Tali again. Huon said, "Goes both ways, eh?" He collected his reins, parting ways from her with a lazy wink. "Just be, Tali." He mimicked Cyska's droll tone perfectly.

Her aunt would've come along if she hadn't been across the ocean delivering their latest lot of kilili works to her secret trader in Port Garnet. The way her eyes gleamed when she mentioned him hinted at more to their relationship than financial transactions. To Tali's irritation, Cyska wouldn't reveal much about her Iskarlian arrangements because she insisted it kept Tali safe from the dangers associated with kilili trading.

Nevertheless, Cyska usually returned to her little cabin on the northern boundary of Glimmers Gap with colour in her cheeks, the hint of makeup on her lashes and the tang of perfume and satisfaction clinging to her. Let alone the purse full of coin and whiff of danger Tali had found so irresistible since she was a little girl.

Eulo's smile and sharp gaze oozed the same hint of danger. He left his sweat-streaked horse grazing the verge, cocking his head at Tali's approach. She returned his grin. They might as well have fun in their last week together.

She dismounted, rolling her shoulders. The filly might make a good horse with a bit more work and could've even been worth keeping as a broodmare. Tali dug her fingers into soft bridle leather, having let the filly loose to graze in a pair of hobbles. They needed money now, though; she didn't have time to wait until the filly matured enough to carry a foal.

Eulo snared Tali from behind, tucking his strong arm around her waist, pulling her close into the tang of fresh mint on his breath.

"How goes it?" he growled into her neck.

"Thirsty and hungry. You?"

"Mmm." His lips grazed her throat, leaving her fluttering like some half-cut dignitine at her first estate dinner.

Tali edged away in the guise of unbuckling the water flask from her saddle. She took a long drink, then offered it to Eulo. Closing her eyes for a moment, she inhaled the whiff of horse sweat, cow shit and damp earth. Huon would be squatting beside the campfire, crumbling tea into his billy can to make a brew, with his dogs nearby.

Mint filled her nostrils again.

"What are you smiling at?" Eulo said, his tone low and husky.

She opened her eyes. "Does it feel the same when you're out on the roads in Iskarlia?"

"In a way, except the cattle smell better than the soldiers,"

Laughing, she pointed out a flurry of white in the rich blue sky. "They say it's a good sign—Lolani's wake, the trail of the goddess."

He shaded his eyes, squinting. "Them clouds there? We call 'em mares' tails."

"The goddess doesn't need horses when she has wings."

"She obviously ain't never ridden a Sarsega horse."

Slow pleasure warmed Tali as they passed the two grazing fillies.

Horses fit for the goddess. She loved the sound of it. With any luck, the buyers in the Gullwing marketplace would feel the same.

Contentment hung over the group during lunch. Eulo stretched out on his side behind Tali, propping himself onto one elbow. She leant back into the hard, flat curve of his torso. Their bodies fitted together too well, like kilili and steel melding once they'd become part of the same song. He walked the fingers of his free hand up her spine, then rubbed his palm down in a long, slow stroke. She kept nibbling at the heel of bread on her plate, pretending lust wasn't surging through her blood. The sensation prickling her nape lingered even after Eulo took his hand away.

He stretched and shifted his hips a little, making Tali acutely aware of a bulge bumping against the small of her back. She glanced at him to gauge if he'd done it deliberately, but sheepishness edged his smile, not arrogance.

Eulo cleared his throat. "So, Huon, tell me about this market town we're heading for."

"Gullwing?" The old stockman's blue eyes lit up. He rested an elbow on his knee, relishing the chance to share his knowledge. He'd taught Tali more about the world than Ranson ever could.

She wriggled her waist to find a better position against Eulo, moving off the hard hipbone poking into her. Onto the bulge again. Eulo's breath hitched. Was he embarrassed how his body reacted to her? A prickle of hotness settled over her chest. He slid his blunt fingers over her hand, where it rested on her thigh. His features darkened, cautious, maybe mirroring her uncertainty. She entwined her fingers in his, making him smile.

Huon scratched a crude map of Vernesia into the dirt with a stick. He stuck a couple of stones into it and tapped the stick against one. "This is Silveraine." Another tap. "Oyster Point, Glimmers Gap." He tapped the southernmost stone, then one on the coast. "Gullwing. The star o' the south, they call it. Gateway for trade with the Threes, who're happy to offload their goods to a lucrative market without having to sail through Cracktooth Reef to get to Silveraine." His teeth shone yellow through his grin. "They fill their ships with our cattle and horses, eh, Tali?"

"Do the ships from Iskarlia come this far south?" Eulo let go of Tali's hand. The abyss grew between them again, despite his body still nudging against hers.

"Why, you looking to catch a ride home?" Huon laughed.

Tali wound a strand of long grass between her hands. Eulo wasn't interested in ships from the Threes, or the outgoing ships. He wanted to know about the ones coming in, which might've carried Darley Krike's sister here, Eulo's love. Tali wound the grass so tight the tip of her finger turned dark red. In a sprinkling of days, he'd be gone. Then, if these sales went to plan, the Academy would call Vivi north, to Silveraine.

Tali studied Huon's weathered face, beneath what was left of his greying hair. He'd see out whatever remained of his life at Glimmers Gap. Mema's years grew sparser, and skies knew what Ranson would do when Vivi moved to Silveraine. Cyska's eternal adventuring would leave Tali alone on an estate she couldn't manage by herself, with no money to pay for help. Loneliness seeped into her bones. Maybe she'd made a mistake tying the rash binding to Eulo. The heat in her chest spread, becoming suffocating. None of the other estates wanted her now—not the ones she'd consider, anyway.

"Fuck 'em," Eulo said, slapping an open hand against his thigh, shocking Tali out of her maudlin.

Her heartbeat drummed in her ears. Had she blurted out her private thoughts without realising?

Huon said, "That's what I told them, and they were none too keen to hear it, but they couldn't do much about it." He prattled on with his story. Nothing to do with her.

The effort of getting to her feet made Tali's head spin. She concentrated on walking away without stumbling, overwhelmed by panic flooding her veins. No one paid her any notice as she pushed through the bushes off the track, probably thinking she'd gone to squat. Retching, she fell to her knees in brown dirt which spun and blurred under her hands. She clutched at gravel and twigs, trying to keep herself upright, choking down a greasy roiling in her stomach.

*Alone.*

After a few moments, the nausea passed, leaving Tali on her hands and knees, gasping into the hair hanging over her face. Grass parrots twittered in the branches overhead, flighty and suspicious. Using a sapling for leverage, she struggled to her feet, her boots scuffling in the grit and leaves. Shrubs and low-hanging branches snared her, stifling her efforts to get back onto the road.

When she did, she was startled to find Eulo waiting nearby, resting one foot on a log, stretching his long body. His smile vanished. "What happened? You're pale as a cleanskin." He drew out his flickerblade, instantly on alert, scanning the scrub she'd emerged from.

"I'm alright. It's just the grog from last night catching up with me."

The lie fell from her tongue. She wanted to offload her worries, just not to a man who she'd had to pay to be with her.

"Is it your shoulder?"

She resisted the urge to scratch at the bandage. "No, it's almost healed." More lies.

"Are you up the duff?"

"Up the what?"

Eulo raised an eyebrow at her midriff. She clapped a hand to it. "No, I'm not pregnant." Not while she wore a kilili chain. Babies, at least, were one complication she could control.

He scratched his neck like he was getting ready to say something difficult.

"Come on, we need to get these cows moving again." She pushed past him, hardening her resolve.

# Chapter 23

Eulo couldn't tire of the road or colourful characters travelling alongside Tali's mob. Bullockies and hay carts rattled past families on foot and, closer to Gullwing, dignitines in polished sulkies pulled by high-stepping horses. A legion of the Kestrine's Goshawks passed; sober-faced men and women wearing the pale purple tunics assigned to guards-in-training. Eulo and Tali bought cakes from a baker's cart on the outskirts of town. Children stopped and pointed, their mouths falling open at the sight of a handful of riders and dogs keeping the chain of black cattle marching together.

Brilliant late afternoon sunshine filtered through the roughbarks siding the road, stretching the cattle into long-legged silhouettes. Huon whooped, whistling his dogs to push the mob together. A tumbling breeze carried the tang of brine and smoke to Eulo's nostrils. The road cleaved orchard-lined hills, leading towards an arc of white sand and aqua water.

Eulo rested a hand on the back of his saddle, twisting to both sides to stretch his muscles. He ran his tongue over the road grime clinging to his teeth, more of which dulled the sheen of sweat on his face. Huon worked his dogs, keeping the cows flowing off along the stock route and away from rows of timber houses. People moving along the streets acknowledged Tali's group with a nod or raised finger.

"Gullwing is the biggest market town in the south." Tali rode up alongside him on Flame, having swapped horses earlier to let her filly arrive in better shape for sale. "They put the saleyards north of town, so the buyers can load new stock straight onto their ships for the voyage home."

Horses, cattle and sheep filled the post-and-rail grid which stretched away from the port, their calls drowning out any other noise. Men and women edged through the chaos, shifting animals here and there, or surveying what was on offer. Tali's beasts poured through a gateway, clogging when three steers refused to follow their herd-mates.

"Ah, look at those rascals there." Tali spurred Flame away, waving her hat at the rogue cattle. Huon's heelers sprinted behind her, eyes shining in their square heads, barking some extra encouragement to push the cattle into their holding yard. A stockwoman shut the gate behind the last steer.

Tali dismounted to greet the woman and her offsider, who were supervising the incoming stock. She still smiled, even after all the miles they'd done in the saddle and her odd turn at lunchtime. The offsider rested one hand on a rail and the other on his hip, leaning towards Tali in the stance typical of cocky young men talking to pretty young women. She turned her back on him to talk to the stockwoman. Probably a mother and son, if their protruding ears were anything to go by. Eulo grinned, nodding his approval at how Tali managed her business without fluttering eyelids and innuendo.

"Your Jikah donkey made it?" Huon interrupted his thoughts.

"He's alright." Eulo patted Cloud's neck. He'd grown to like the grey, not that he'd admit it to Tali.

"He'd bloody well want to be. Lolani knows how Tali will explain to potential buyers why her own husband's arse is on her rival's horse."

"It's not my horse." The protest died on Eulo's lips. Huon was right, of course, and for whatever reason Tali hadn't said anything, just shrugged and let Eulo do what he wanted. He snorted back, the dust clogging his nose. She ought've told him if it worried her, rather than have her stupid husband prance into town on the Jikah gelding.

"Still," Huon said, "you must be doing something right for her, 'cause she's happier today than I've seen her in months."

Eulo nodded. Tali was happier than he'd seen her before, too. Now the cattle were yarded up, he'd be free to wander the markets, with his ears open and his flickerblade on his belt. A few more kistars in his purse would've been sweet. What excuse would Tali give him this time, when he asked for his pay?

He hoped she'd get top price for her cattle tomorrow, for both their sakes. Eulo shuddered at a sudden crawl of unease up his spine. He needed to buy as much kilili as he could when he left Glimmers Gap, and have enough money left to pay his passage back home to Iskarlia.

Having settled arrangements with the stockwoman, Tali joined Eulo and Huon.

"What'd they reckon? They're the best-looking cattle in the lot."

Huon slapped his thigh, grinning.

"The overseer says there's a good group of buyers in town already. They'll all be at the markets tonight, ready for the stock sale in the morning." Tali put her foot in Flame's stirrup and swung into the saddle.

"Not leaving the fillies here?" Huon said.

"No, I'll stable them with our horses tonight, where I can keep an eye on them." She shortened her reins. "Let's go to the Albatross for a wash, then find ourselves a drink and dinner at the markets."

The men muttered their agreement, happy to leave the cloying stench of shit behind.

The town mushroomed out from the port in receding rows of slab-walled cottages with shingle roofs. Seagulls spun and wheeled in the distance, above what must be the waterfront. Gullwing's tidy streets and houses shattered Eulo's expectation of the town being a colder version of Port Garnet.

He was glad to drop his pack in a corner of the room they'd hired in the Albatross, a pub looming between the saleyards and market square. He'd left Tali downstairs talking to the publican, who apparently lodged the Sarsegas whenever they were in town.

"Blazes, look at him, eh." The wiry older woman had eyeballed Eulo the moment he'd excused himself from their company at the bar. "Lolani herself would lift her skirts for a go with that." Her voice drifted after him. "Don't know why you went all the way to Iskarlia to get a husband though, Tali, there's plenty o' handsome men round here who'd be happy to oblige you."

Eulo missed Tali's answer, but he reckoned the publican wasn't telling her anything she didn't already know.

Alone in their room upstairs, he peeled off his shirt and pants, dropping them in a dust-smeared heap in the corner. He stood in his undershorts, scratching idly at his chest, staring out the window. Traffic streamed up the laneway outside the pub, speckled through with Vernese soldiers in their purple uniforms, some riding on horseback. Smatterings of Iskarlians stuck out, their skin pale beside the tall ebony-skinned Kizans, gold-skinned Duskari, and Jalassi women wrapped in rainbow colours. All traders, Tali said, here to buy and sell. They'd barely given Eulo a passing glance, not like the down-the-nose sneers he copped in Silveraine and Oyster Point. Were there Scabmen, too, shadowing him? Maybe even there buying silveriron and other weapons to take back home.

Did Tali come here looking for her mother's face somewhere in that crowd, wondering if she'd ever see her again, always hoping, even after all these years?

He jumped, startled by the door slamming open into the wall behind him.

"I didn't think I'd ever get away from Kittia." Tali tramped in all rumpled and red-cheeked. "She's having a bath run for us, and even offered to attend to you personally. I told her it wasn't necessary." She slung her bag in the corner and finally looked at him. Her scrutiny travelled over his bare chest, her green eyes smouldering. "Oh."

Heat stirred in Eulo's groin. All of a sudden Tali was in his arms, her hands on his chest and tongue flickering between his lips. He slid his hands under her arse, spinning her around to sit her on the windowsill. He fought to unlace her pants with his grime-lined fingers, groaning when he slid the cloth off her smooth thighs. Kissing her neck, nuzzling into the collar of her shirt. She rested her hands on his shoulders, pushing him down, away from where her nipples pressed against her shirt. His lips grazed her belly, moving lower. Lifting her parted knees, she rested her feet on either side of his neck, pushing her hips forward.

Tali Sarsega was the only one who'd ever made him question his ability to please a woman. It'd be paralysing to disappoint her again. He spread his hands over her belly muscles, gripping the kilili chain against her waist as he licked into the curls between her legs. Deeper. Rewarded by her sharp breath in and moan of pleasure, the press of her fingertips against his scalp and, eventually, the sweetness of her climax.

Tali guided him up with one finger under his chin, panting as she kissed him. Leaving him on his knees, she stood to pull her pants on. She skipped out the door with her clean clothes in one hand, only pausing for long enough to say, "I'll be back from the bath in time for you to go wash before the water goes cold."

Eulo inhaled the tang of roasting meat and the faint hint of rot that drifted through all towns and cities. Fingers of sunset burnt through the clouds, searing their reflection into the ocean. He looked at Tali for the umpteenth time, striding along with her hair loose and bouncing down her back with each step, dressed in a dark red shirt and black pants. Other men stared too, openly admiring her. They glanced at Eulo with eyes full of envy.

He brushed a hand down his blue shirt. He'd quibbled with Tali about wearing it, telling her men who blended into the shadows didn't wear bright colours. She wouldn't back down.

"I don't care. You look handsome in it," she'd told him, slapping away his wandering hand when she leant in to straighten the shirt across his shoulders.

"I look handsome without it, too." He winked at her, hoping she'd fool around more with him. Instead, she kicked his boots across the room, telling him to hurry up.

Of course she was right, and Eulo's new shirt blended in with the others on the street. A man in dark clothes would've stuck out like a sore thumb, while bright blue Eulo hid in plain view. He looked up in time to dodge a pair of Kizans coming the other way. The couple's teeth shone white when they smiled at him and Tali. He had to crane his neck to return their greeting.

"I doubt you have to look up at women often," Tali said, still wearing the half-smile he'd put on her face in the hotel room.

"She was tall, eh?"

"All the Kizan women are. They're beautiful."

"So are you."

She glanced away, shrugging off Eulo's compliment. Did she reckon he didn't mean it? Or she just didn't want to hear it. He rubbed his jaw. Even after weeks under Tali's roof, he was just as clueless about reading her now as he was when he'd first clapped eyes on her in Iskarlia.

"Are we meeting Huon?"

She grinned. "I'm pretty sure he's visiting a woman tonight."

Eulo didn't blame him. Glimmers Gap was a long way from anywhere, and Bintau was small enough to have too many noses stuck into other people's business. It suited him just fine to keep Tali to himself tonight.

"Look." She stopped so quick he collided with her.

"Sorry," he muttered, although he didn't regret the chance to stand close enough to smell the mint and tea-tree soap from the Albatross's washroom on her skin. Mako's teeth, didn't she notice how she sent him as giddy as a cleanskin?

The crowd around them oohed and aahed at a trio of Duskari fire dancers performing in the square. Their firesticks twirled red-gold blurs into the final traces of gloaming. Silver armlets circled the women's biceps, their long hair bound into tight plaits, hooded eyes and lips painted in black liner. They twisted and folded like water around the flames reflecting off their oiled gold skin.

The male dancer released an ear-piercing cry. He loped between the women, running up the wall to propel himself into a backflip. With a flourish for the audience, he arched skywards, bringing his flaming torch almost to his lips, and blew a gout of blue and silver flame six feet into the air. People burst into applause.

Eulo's scalp prickled all over. Something about how the flames danced in the darkness was familiar. The sensation on his skin intensified as the Duskari man blew out another plume of fire. He plunged his fist into the wavering flames. The crowd gasped, some of them crying out in horror. The Duskari drew his hand out, displaying a glove of silver-blue smoke over his fingers.

*Kilili.*

Eulo sucked a breath through the tightness in his chest. Did they bring the magic here, for people like Tali to buy and bend into weapons? The more he watched, though, the more he wondered if it was all a clever illusion.

The Duskari planted his feet wide on the stage. He raised his shimmering fist high above his head, together with the firestick in his other hand. The women twirled and undulated on either side of him, their semi-naked bodies slick with sweat. The three bowed in perfect unison. The firestick threw flickering light over the crowd's rapt faces.

Tali squeezed Eulo's hand. Exhilaration shone in her eyes when she turned to shout over the applause to him, "Let's go get a drink, eh?"

He nodded. "A bite of food wouldn't go astray, either." The yawning pit in his belly had grown ever since they'd reached the Albatross.

Despite his protesting gut, Eulo kept stopping to gawp at different market stalls along the laneway. Leather goods and spices nestled between bright-feathered parrots from Jalassi, opposite men haggling the price of kaif from Kiza. Through it all wove people who sold and people who bought, those who smiled when they reckoned they'd made a bargain or had avoided selling one. Children darted through the mass of bodies and tables, probably picking pockets. Not those of the big Iskarlian though, or his woman, when they stopped to buy dinner. The people around them smiled, relaxed, like a respectable version of the Jarrison Bay emporium in Iskarlia.

Armed with a mug of ale and a pancake oozing spinach and cheese, Eulo followed Tali to a row of tables set out near the food stalls. The Jalassan men sitting there promptly moved over for her, although their gazes came up short when they landed on Eulo. He grinned, enjoying his Iskarlian bulk and reputation, letting fierceness narrow his eyes. The Jalassi smiled and laughed, holding their long-fingered hands out to show they meant no harm.

Eulo squeezed onto the end of the bench beside Tali, pressing close to her to keep his arse from falling off the wooden slats. A thrill ran through his limbs when she didn't move away. He relished a long sip of ale, the perfect end to their long day on the road.

"How'd he do it, the firebreather? With the kilili?"

"They were amazing, weren't they?" Tali said, through a mouthful of pancake.

"Was it real, though, or just an illusion?"

She shrugged.

He bit into his own pancake. Juices ran a tasty, rich trail over his tongue.

"That Jalassan bird lady really wanted you to pat her parrot." Tali's eyes gleamed, betraying her straight face.

Eulo snorted. "I'd choose an eagle over a gaudy parrot any day."

The bird lady had fawned over him, batting her eyelids while assuring him how beautiful the goods in her stall were. She'd hooked a finger into the collar of her dress, pulling it lower and lower down in the cleft between her breasts, while Tali laughed at Eulo's awkward exit from the shop.

Two performers sang to the diners, in perfect harmony. "Should've brought Vivica," he said, licking his fingers.

"Should we?" Tali narrowed her gaze.

Eulo choked down a too-big mouthful of unchewed food. Shades. She knew about him and Vivica, she must do. He swilled a mouthful of ale, trying to dislodge the lump in his throat. The ale tickled, forcing him to splutter. "I mean, these crowds would love her. Imagine the money she'd earn singing here."

"If my sister ever actually got off her arse for long enough to earn some money, she'd never demean herself by performing to a bunch of roughnecks, beggars and working class." Tali strangled her half-eaten pancake in one hand. She tossed back a draught of her drink with the other. "There's only prestige if you're swanning around on the great stages of Silveraine, in front of the dignitines, the Loresses and the Kestrine."

Eulo stared at her, surprised to hear her talk so bluntly about her sister.

"They hate Gullwing, you know, all of them up there in the capital." Her mouth twisted into a savage smile. "And the rest of us uncouth southerners, who welcome the dirty Threes with open arms."

"You don't agree with them though, do you?"

"You know I don't. Look at this." Tali swept her arm at the colour and noise around them. "This is one of the things I love about Vernesia.

Gullwing is where magic happens, Eulo. People don't look down their nose at each other, they just get on with it." She tilted her head in contemplation. "Trade is so important here. It brings all these people together and lets us buy treasures we wouldn't see otherwise. I could never sell my cattle for such a good price in Silveraine."

A wave of black hair swept over her forehead, trailing a handful of loose strands into her glimmering eyes. When he'd first met her, Eulo reckoned she might've been a tad naive. Now, she seemed so worldly, and far from common. She stared at him for a long moment, then nudged her elbow into his ribs.

"Get up, Juke. I have things to do."

From a clearing beyond the dining area, the two singers belted out a new tune. Their voices attracted enthusiastic dancers, a thousand miles away from the rigid formality of the dignitine's parties. Here, old danced with young, whiteskin Iskarlians with blackskin Kizans, men with other men, and they all laughed.

A Duskari man stepped in front of Tali. He bowed low, smooth as liquid gold, holding his hand outstretched. The fire-breather, tilting his face to her, revealing black-painted eyes. Eulo reached for his blade as the Duskari opened his mouth to speak.

# Chapter 24

Tali considered the fire-dancer's invitation. "Alright." She turned to Eulo, smiling. "Go wander. I'll meet you at the keg stand in a while." With her hand on his arm, she stood on her toes, touching her cheek to his as she murmured, "It's only dancing, big husband. There's nothing to worry about." She kissed him, letting her lips linger on his in a show of ownership.

For his sake or hers, he didn't know. He stepped back with the same off-kilter sense of control he'd had—or not—on the wifeship a few weeks ago.

The Duskari dipped his chin to Eulo. "Just to dance," he said in Iskarlian, his accent rolling over the words. "I would not want to upset a big man like you. Especially one with such a fine blade." His amber eyes sparkled, knowing.

Eulo narrowed his gaze. The flickerblade hanging on his hip was sheathed in leather, so it looked like any old knife. His skin tingled. For all he knew the Scabs might've made allies in the Threes, even if they'd always refused to in the past.

"If you misbehave," Tali said to the man, also speaking Iskarlian, "I'm the one you need to be worried about."

The Duskari laughed, holding a fist over his heart; the symbol of honesty. "I would not dream of it."

"If you say so." Tali slipped into the crowd of dancers, leaving the Duskari to rush after her.

Eulo shook his head. Maybe he'd cracked. If they'd been sitting in a pub in Iskarlia, the Duskari would've ended up on the ground, sooking through a broken nose. Maybe he still would, if Tali didn't come back. He didn't know whether to be angry or impressed with her.

"Lost his girl to the magic man, won't get 'er back now, no one can," a deep voice recited the old children's rhyme into Eulo's ear.

He spun around, coming face-to-face with an Iskarlian twice his width and a head shorter. The man laughed, clapping him on the shoulder like a long-lost friend.

"Let 'er go, son, there's plenty more lovelies to be had in Gullwing." He threw his head back, booming out more laughter. A leather vest strained across his torso, leaving his hairy arms bare. Duskari-coloured, with pale blue eyes set deep in the creases of middle age.

Eulo glimpsed a marlin tattoo on the man's bicep. A seaman, then. His blood fizzed with the thrill of sniffing out a trail. "Are you in port long?"

"Two days. Long enough to offload and pick up stock to take home. Yourself?"

"Ah." Eulo stuffed his hand into a pocket and slipped off his binding ring. Guilt trickled like a Scabman's slash from his throat to his guts. "Not sure. I might stay awhile."

"This place gets into your blood, don't it? While them at home says we're sand-skulled sailing down here through the reefs. It's bloody worth it, though." The seaman flexed his knuckles. "Especially when there's just two ships from Iskarlia what can do it, and Daf Korin only knows 'cause he learnt off me." His bulldog face screwed up. "I'd have bloody pushed him overboard at sea if I'd known he were planning to edge in on me business later."

"Righto," Eulo said, aiming to fill the pause with the right balance of curiosity. Whatever it took to keep the man talking.

The Iskarlian narrowed his eyes. "You ain't on his crew, are you?" He laughed again. "You don't look like no sailor if you don't mind me sayin'. And too fuckin' bad if you do mind, eh."

Eulo held out his hand. "I'm Dogger."

"They call me Whitey. Some joker in Jalassi City started it, so me crew picked it up, and now every bastard in every port from here to Tiglia reckons it's the most hilarious fuckin' thing in the Opalline." He clapped Eulo's hand into his crushing grip. "Now how 'bout we leave them tiptoeing twiddlers to it. I'm thirsty and we got to find you a nice woman."

After buying Whitey and himself each a tall mug of beer, Eulo manoeuvred the seaman to the edge of the drinking crowd, away from flapping ears. They stood at an upturned barrel, its top stained with the rings of countless drinks. The throng of dancers swept aside Eulo's intention of keeping an eye out for Tali. It'd actually be better if she didn't appear too quick, really, now he'd found someone cluey about shipping between Iskarlia and Vernesia.

"So, what's your business here?" Whitey sipped his beer. A layer of froth stuck to the yellow bristles on his top lip.

Eulo hesitated, unprepared. After all his years walking into towns and pubs with vague stories about who he was and what he was doing, it threw him not to have a lie ready.

When he didn't reply, Whitey said, "You're a quiet one, eh, Dogger. What say I have a guess, and you tell me if I'm right?"

"Fair enough." A span of tension eased out of Eulo's muscles. Rather than make something up, he'd just go along with one of the seaman's tales.

Whitey rubbed his hands together, grinning. "So, I see the way you're watchin' the crowd, pickin' out those you might worry. Or them what might worry you. A man what moves like the shadows you glimpse out of the corner of your eye. When you turn to see him better, he's gone."

The seaman wasn't as dumb as he seemed. Eulo covered his surprise behind a long draught of ale. He held his breath as Whitey whispered, "You're lookin'. Hunting. Ain't you, Juke?"

Eulo leapt back in alarm, rocking the barrel. His mug rattled on the pocked wood, sloshing beer everywhere. He snatched his flickerblade into his hand, resting it flat along the inside of his arm.

"What the fuck?" he snarled. His heart thundered against his ribs. "Who's paying you?" The seaman had to be one of Cutter's men, keeping an eye on the port, moving things in and out.

Whitey took another sip from his mug. His bushy eyebrows knitted in amusement. "I ought've guessed you'd be a hothead same as Ruckus." He leant his elbows on the still-rocking barrel, squinting at Eulo. "Settle down, you fuckin' young goon. I doubt you want more attention than what you've already got." All of a sudden, he guffawed, pointing over towards the stage. "Have a go of that, eh."

Eulo didn't turn around. Most of the people staring at him did, though, quickly forgetting about the two Iskarlians.

"You look just like your old man. You got the Juke fire in your eyes."

Rage seared through Eulo's limbs. It'd been too long since he'd spilt blood. "Blind or not, he'd still cut your fuckin' plums off and stuff 'em down your shit-dribbling throat."

"Nah, he wouldn't. Not to an old mate what stood beside him when we fought the Saltspitters off from Jarrison. We kept each other alive."

"He's never said your name once." Eulo knew all the stories; when he was a boy, he'd made Ruckus tell them over and over.

"And I never said it here, now, did I?" The seaman sneered. "Back then, I were called the Madman and I would've mashed your silly little arse into the dirt if you'd done what you just done now. So settle the fuck down and drink your fucking drink."

Eulo rolled his head from one side to the other, cracking his neck. The soldiers talked about his father and the Madman with wide-eyed awe. Ruckus, however, gave the Madman the same passing indifference as most of the other old, infamous warriors he'd fought with. Especially when Shandy, Eulo's mother, was around. He raised his mug, slow and cautious. For now, he'd keep the flickerblade ready, hidden from view beside his leg.

Just in case.

"You obviously ain't here on the Cove's business."

Eulo shook his head. "Nah. I gave up on fighting for what I didn't believe in a while ago." At least he'd thought he had.

"I bet your old man weren't happy 'bout that. He ain't spoken to me since I gave it up, either, after I ran out of patience with the Cove and his fuckin' Scabmen. I grew up on ships though, and the sea were callin' for me. Ain't no time for regrets."

Eulo wouldn't forget Ruckus losing his temper and hurling a chair at him. He'd sidestepped it, letting it smash the window behind him, then walked out leaving the old man ranting at the empty room. Shades, his mother and Rem tore strips off him for it later, as if Ruckus was faultless now he couldn't see anymore.

He glanced around, unsuccessfully scanning the crowds for Tali. He didn't have much time. Forcing a light tone, he said, "So if no one from Iskarlia can sail this coast, where do the darkships end up?" He couldn't avoid being so blunt, so obvious. It'd be a good start if he could understand the smugglers' routes and where they'd land or load kilili.

Whitey's face sagged into a frown. He leant over the barrel, keeping his voice low. "Take my advice, young Juke, and stay the fuck away from 'em. Me and you have met a lot of shitty people running in the Cove's army, but darkships? Lemme tell you, it ain't worth getting mixed up in them affairs."

"It's not the ships I'm after, more what's on 'em. Do they come through here?"

"Gullwing? Shit no. The Kestrine's Goshawks check the boats here from top to bottom before they let anyone or anything on or off the waterfront. They keep it closed up tighter than the Cove's arsehole."

"What are the darkships carrying, then? Contraband rotgut? Wool?

Gemstones?" Evading the port taxes? "People?"

Sucking his teeth, Whitey nodded once. Eulo held the older man's gaze. He needed more. "Where do they land?"

Whitey shook his head, all his bluster disappearing. "Mako's teeth, you Jukes are trouble, through and through. You reckon the Scabs ain't got eyes and ears here? I'll not get mixed up in this. I won't."

"Righto." Eulo sighed. He stood, not wanting Tali to find him in this conversation. "Guess I'll go talk to Daf Korin then."

"Like fuck." Whitey thumped a fist on the barrel. He screwed his eyes shut for a long moment. "Blackrock Cove. Skramos." Two names hissed out in a breath of frustration. "N' if you ever tell anyone I said so, I'll be dropping pieces of your good body out to the sharks, you get me?"

"Then Cutter's definitely got men here. Who?"

The seaman's face contorted, his eyes bulging. "I don't fuckin' know. They're crazy, murderous bastards and I don't want nothing to do with 'em. And I don't want nothing to do with you no more, neither."

"Safe home, Captain." Eulo rapped his knuckles twice on the barrel and dumped a handful of coins beside Whitey's empty mug.

He shoved his way over to the line for another drink. When he glanced back at the barrel, Whitey was gone. Eulo threw his next beer down in one go, slamming the mug onto the bar and calling for more. A hand pressed into the small of his back, moving with him even when he shifted away.

"I thought you'd gone." Tali beamed, her cheeks flushed. "That was fun. I'm thirsty as hell now." She cocked her head at him, noticing the tension in his jaw. "You aren't jealous, are you?"

"A little." Eulo shrugged. It'd be easier to go with a shade of the truth than admit he'd gotten riled about his drink with the seaman. Getting answers was like floating back and forth on the tide. At least now he had a trail of names to follow. He waved the barman over to bring Tali a drink. Then, mugs in hand, they moved away from the bar.

"Ozar wouldn't risk his reputation by offending me, or you. He knew about our binding rings, same as your flickerblade." Tali grabbed Eulo's hand, holding it up to demonstrate. "Oh."

She let go of him, her playful smile fading because Eulo's fucking ring was still hidden in his fucking pocket. Frantic excuses swam in his mind, eclipsing his question about how the Duskari knew about the kilili. There was no good explanation for why a husband would go off drinking without his binding ring, while his wife danced with some gold-skinned shyster. He opened and closed his mouth, drowning.

"I need to visit someone, so you're free to do as you please, Eulo. I just"—Tali jutted her jaw—"can't pay you the rest of what I owe until the cattle are sold." She wrapped her arms around herself.

He rested his hand on her shoulder, clumsy and awkward. "You ain't getting rid of me just yet, darl." Shades, did she notice the emotion burring his voice? He snorted, cowed by regret and an unfamiliar rawness chafing under his ribs.

"Were you a good man in Iskarlia?"

Now he did look at her, startled by her low, smoky words. All this time she'd given him free rein, trusted him to do right by her without demanding anything of him, or asking about his past in Iskarlia. Their gazes locked, intense, like standing in the ocean with the waves pushing one way and the undertow pulling the other. His nostrils flared.

"I was a shit, Tali. A no-good maggot. You wouldn't have wasted a second glance at me." He cared what she thought of him now, didn't he? And he was still a shit.

She dug in her pockets, bringing out a handful of splinters. She dumped the coins in Eulo's hand. "Go get us both another beer, and one extra. I'll meet you here." The rainbow current of the marketplace swallowed her again, leaving him to line up for the drinks.

When she returned, carrying another stuffed pancake, she nodded in the direction of the south road. "Head over there."

"I'll clear the way." Eulo bulled into the crowd with Tali in his wake as he breached the wall of bodies. A few times people turned to rouse at him, their arguments fading from their lips when they saw the broad-shouldered, no-good maggot eyeballing them.

"D'you know of a place called Blackrock Cove?" Eulo asked Tali once they'd left the crowd behind. "A fella who goes by the name Skramos?"

"I've never heard of either. I can ask around."

"Nah, it's better if you don't. I'd reckon he's earnt a reputation for a reason." Whoever Skramos was, it'd do no good if Tali caught his attention, and especially not if the Scabmen were around.

Eulo's footsteps fell more softly on a downward slope where the mud and muck collected. Oil lamps flickered in the fading daylight, deepening the town's mystique. These back-alley stalls sagged like a row of drunks at dawn, their canopies faded and torn. A woman standing beside one tent-flap leered at Eulo. Her hair blended into the dirty yellow canvas behind her. She pulled her dress open, juggling her huge titties in both hands, her grin a crimson smear. "'Ere we go, handsome. How 'bout you bring us one of them beers? I'll give you an extra special good time."

"He's spoken for, darling. The beers and his prick," Tali called out. She jabbed an elbow against Eulo's side, urging him on as if he needed to be pushed away.

"Shame. I bet he's got a bloody huge one, too." The woman's cackles chased them down the laneway.

Tali laughed. "Oh, go on, Eulo, tell me you've never been propositioned before."

"Yeah nah, not when I've been with my wife. Or had her talk that way."

She bowed her lips, amused. "Here we are."

He paused a half-step behind her, outside the second-last stall, screwing his nose up against the reek of shit and faded dreams. Inside, a man sat hunched over something on his lap, rocking back and forth like a simpleton. Rows of brooms lined the canvas walls, wooden soldiers each standing tall on their single brush foot.

"Hello there, Leisik," Tali greeted him. "We brought your dinner."

The man squinted at her, his mouth slack, his gnarled shoulders barely moving. Recognition dawned. "Blazes, is that you, girlie?" He put down the switch he'd been binding, doddering upright to embrace her. He peered at Eulo through pupils dulled grey in the lamplight, his lips pulling together in distaste. "Who's this brute? Following you round like a stray dog, is he?" His accent rolled with what Eulo now recognised as the southern dialect. Leisik flapped his crippled hands at him. "Go on. Go find someone else to bother or we'll set the Goshawks after you."

"Stop it," Tali told the old fart, "else I'll take my brute off to do something far more enjoyable than listen to your rot."

"Pfft. First Cyska gets herself some secret lover, now you got a bloody Iskarlian rummaging around in your purse. She's a bad influence on you."

"She's your daughter, and she's the reason you're not scavenging a living off scraps in the boneyard," Tali said, without a hint of whether she knew about the secret lover or not.

Cyska was Leisik's daughter? Eulo made out the same horse face, stretched and sunken across the old man's skull, with far less teeth. This broom-man had to be Tali's grandfather—the one evicted from Glimmers Gap.

She waved the pancake, flinging a spatter of sauce across the dirt between Leisik's boots. "We brought you dinner."

"Same as her, you are." He mock-scowled at her, sinking onto the stool, smacking his lips together as Tali handed him the pancake and mug of beer.

"Except if you were *my* father, I wouldn't let you get away with being so rude." Tali wiped her hands on a nearby scrap of cloth. She retrieved her own mug out of Eulo's hands and took a long sip.

"You don't let *anyone* get away with being rude."

"You're an ungrateful old goat."

"Bit rich coming from you lot when you're all swanning around in your homestead out there at Glimmers Gap." Leisik sniffed, gazing at his pancake. He dropped his chin. "How is she?"

Tali watched him over the top of her mug. "Mema is just as ill as last time I saw you, and she's getting worse. The others don't change."

Leisik rolled his clouded gaze at Eulo. "What does she do with you, then? Banish you to the stables? It wouldn't be the Sarsega way to tarnish things by letting a grub like you inside their fine old house. Trust me, I know from experience."

Tali held up her left hand to show the binding ring. Leisik laughed into his mug of beer, hard enough to fill his worn-out eyes with tears as he coughed and spluttered.

"So here you are in person," he said to Eulo, "the scourge of every man and woman with their greedy eyes on the Sarsega estate."

# Chapter 25

He waved a finger in the air while another set of coughing wracked his body. "Why'd she pick you, soldier boy?"

"'Cause she likes me." Eulo flashed his desert dog smile.

"That would be our Tali, wouldn't it?" Leisik bit into the pancake. Oily brown juice soaked his bristled chin.

Eulo shifted, uncomfortable with the stale air in the tent. Especially the way it reminded him of Ruckus.

"It says a lot about a man if Tali Sarsega overlooks him. The one she picks is worth admiring. Even if he's Iskarlian." Leisik grunted.

Tali rolled her eyes at him. "The older you get, the more nonsense you talk." She wandered along the row of brooms, picking out one here and there to scrutinise more closely.

"I bet Glimmers Gap shines even more now you have another Iskarlian there. S'pose you're still letting the other mongrel hang about too, are you?" Leisik talked with his mouth full.

"Huon is in town with us. He's gone to ask the market guards to arrange a stall for you near the square tomorrow, where the prime buyers will be."

"Ah." Leisik swiped a greasy paw over his brow. He might've hidden his tears if his bottom lip didn't tremble. "You needn't have, girlie."

"Just think, you'll earn so much money I won't have to come here listening to your tripe every time I'm in town."

Leisik pressed his knuckles into his eye sockets. Collecting himself, he turned his bluster to Eulo. "I suppose she chose you because you can't talk?"

"'S'pose." Eulo shrugged.

"Choose a broom, Eulo," Tali said in Iskarlian. When he raised his eyebrows at her, she tilted her head in the direction of Leisik's wares, her expression hard.

"Don't start," Leisik said. "You're as bad as Cyska, coming in here fussing, swearing at me in Duskari 'cause she don't know I know what it means. She learnt it off the man she meets."

"What man?"

"The fellow she's nobbing. The lover." Leisik waved a thick-fingered hand at her. "How would I know anyway, I'm just her father. Isn't it the sort of stuff you women are always blabbing about to each other?"

"Yes, women have nothing to talk about except for men." Tali's expression could've withered stone. She softened. "Cyska hasn't mentioned him to me." Disappointed?

"Then he must be a shady, no-good grub."

Keeping one ear on the conversation, Eulo sifted through the cluster of brooms like he'd been asked, finally picking one out at random. Those, at least, were mostly well made. He passed it to Tali.

"Here, Leisik, how much for this one?" she said.

He grinned, showing the few lonely teeth studding his gums. "For you, fifteen splinters. For your Iskarlian, it'll be twenty." He rubbed his hands together with the rasp of callus against callus.

"I'll give you eight because I'm in a good mood." Tali toed a bundle of rags in the corner. "Please don't tell me this is your bed."

He held his brown paw out so she could count the coins into it. "I won't tell you."

Tali frowned into her purse. She gave her grandfather a thoughtful look. "I'll be back in a moment."

Eulo shifted his weight from one foot to the other, edgy at being left with the old goat, despite suddenly becoming the keeper of a new broom. He wrapped his hand around the wooden handle, all the while staring at Leisik's petulant sneer

"Look at you there, measuring it up without hardly thinking about it," the old man said. "The weight, how it feels in your hand, how it might feel to belt a man with it. How much force you could use before it broke."

"I ain't exactly the type to sweep the fucking floor with it, am I?"

"No. I know your type; arrogant, bold, with no cares, and won't take advice. I'll tell you now, even though you won't listen, you ought to grab onto Tali with both hands." Leisik raised his gnarled fingers in the direction of the laneway. He squinted at Eulo. "I can see in your face, the way you've hulked around in here like some big lump of meat, that you're not clever enough to see what's in front of you."

Eulo rolled his shoulders. He closed his fingers tighter on the broom handle, confirming the old man's accusation without even having to say a word. His disgust shifted off Leisik onto himself.

"Tali's smart though," Leisik went on. "You'll find out she don't muck around, and she'll be rid of you soon enough. You'll realise it then, when you lie awake at night aching for the woman you let slip through your fingers like stardust. When it'll be too late."

"You don't know me, old man."

Leisik's laugh startled him.

"I know, all right, because I was you, once. Too smart-mouthed and cocky for my own good. I had a woman as beautiful and strong as silveriron, and she threw me away the moment she saw she'd get hurt. She gave me my daughters, kicked me off her estate, and never talked to me again." His face crumpled, sad and sorry.

Eulo looked away, embarrassed.

"You only know what you got when you don't got it no more. Coral Sarsega was my silveriron, and Tali is yours."

"Why are you so fucking rude to her?"

"I have my pride. Not much of it, but I pretend as best I can." Leisik threaded his fingers into his beard. "She'll cope with an awful lot of bullshit, but she's a desert spinny. When you push her too far, you'll find yourself running for your life with a set of fangs sunk in your arse."

Eulo wanted to choke the smugness out of him. Not because of Leisik's contempt—because he was right. Tali saved him by bursting in with her arms full of folded red cloth.

"Here." She sat the bundle on the old man's handcart. "New blankets, so you can burn that flea-ridden mess in the corner."

"Well aren't you just even sweeter than my own mother."

"I doubt it. What do you know of Skramos? Blackrock Cove?"

Leisik froze. He eyeballed her. "Now why would you be asking about him?"

"Just curious."

Eulo gripped the broom handle, hardly daring to breathe.

"Skramos the Saltspitter. The smuggler, the uncatchable, the bane of Vernesia's border guard." Leisik wove his hands in the air as he spoke. "Bringing in all the contraband he can without paying a single splinter of the Kestrine's taxes."

"Contraband? Including people?"

Leisik's gaze slid from Tali to Eulo. "I doubt it. There's no call for border-hoppers here. Most of 'em go from Iskarlia to the Threes. It's easier to get 'em there and get 'em in, and they have more chance of staying there." He scratched his chest. "No sense coming to Vernesia when you're just going to end up in the Dross."

Eulo blinked at the switch on his broom. He'd been so sure the Scabmen had kept Remmy at home. They could've taken him to the Threes, or the Saltspit Islands, while Eulo was fucking around chasing cows. Rem might've even chosen to leave Iskarlia himself.

His mind spun at the possibilities. Could he really have gotten it all so wrong?

Tali scraped her boot against the dirt, drawing circles with her toe. "Huon will be here at sun-up to help you move your stall."

"She got plans for you too, I expect," Leisik said, tossing his wry comment in Eulo's direction.

"Same as any other wife does for her husband in the early hours," Tali said, straight-faced.

Leisik cackled at the burn scalding Eulo's ears. Him, embarrassed by a woman? Not possible. He stood trapped, captivated by the tip of her tongue tugging on her bottom lip. Heat rushed to other parts of his body, making the tent stifling as Tali said goodbye to the broom-maker. She caught Eulo's hand and tugged him out into the mild evening.

The stinking laneway almost smelt fresh after Leisik's stall. Nearby, a man grunted along with the slap, slap, slap of meat against meat, the woman responding with emotionless moaning. Without meaning to, Eulo glimpsed them through a gap in the whore's tent. She lay splayed across a bench, her sagging breasts swinging as the customer ploughed into her. Her expression was as blank as the slack-jawed baker's son from Eulo's village.

Tali bumped their entwined hands against Eulo's thigh, reminding him she was waiting, watching him watching the whore. She let go of him, continuing on her way. Shamed, he ambled after her, clutching their new broom, crabbed for ruining the moment when he'd intended to pull her close and growl his intention of ravishing her at the Albatross. Now he'd have to stare at the fall of her hair and the swing of her hips, with Leisik's accusing voice niggling at his conscience, telling him a truth he already knew but didn't know what to do with.

Two Iskarlians stumbled down the laneway, hanging onto each other for support. The short one faltered to a stop, pointing at Eulo. He doubled over with his hands on his knees, spraying out snorts of laughter. It wasn't all he'd sprayed out tonight, judging by the stains down the front of his shirt and the sour reek of vomit clouding around him.

"Looks like the hired help lost his boss," his mate wheezed.

Eulo glared at the broom in his fist. First Leisik's shit, now this. His temper burst alive. "D'you reckon I look like hired help, you fuckin' fish-kissing idiot?" Scrawny bloody sailors, they were, who must've had an absolute skinful to've been bold enough to stir Eulo. Not many other people were so ballsy.

"Naw, you look like the sort of sand-skulled thug a Vernese buys when none of her own sort will have her. So, you're hired help either way." Shorty laughed. He cried out, surprised when Eulo slapped him across the face with the broom.

Eulo squared up to the sailors, gripping the broomstick in both hands across his body. Fuck knew how well it'd sweep the floor, but it'd make a good enough weapon tonight. The sailors gaped, realising they faced a fighting man. If they were spying for the Scabmen, they were about to regret it.

"It were a joke, ya thin-skinned woman," Shorty said, giving Eulo a hurt frown.

"I don't give a fuck what it was, you wet-nosed pissdrip," Eulo snarled, letting out the menace he'd kept subdued since leaving Iskarlia. Darkness rejoiced in him. Out of the corner of his eye, he glimpsed a flash of something flailing towards him. He reacted without needing to think, thrusting the broom handle into his assailant. The wood cracked solid against the second man's skull, knocking him clean off his feet and into a groaning heap in the gutter. Eulo thundered past, ramming his shoulder into Shorty, driving him back a half-dozen paces. He left the pair rolling in the mud behind him.

Tali waited twenty paces along the laneway, her face framed by a tumble of glossy hair. Instead of tongue-lashing Eulo like he'd expected, she said, "If you break our broom, you can go buy another one."

"Not bloody likely."

Tali chortled, filling him with a rush of warmth even though she was laughing at him. He said, "I can't believe he's your grandfather."

"No one can, especially not him. He's from the far south." As though that explained it. She caught his hand. "Come on, I want to look at one of the stalls along the way."

"What are they peddling? Cooking pots?"

"It's something much better than that, I promise you."

The jeweller's glare pierced Eulo and Tali when they stepped into the stall, her cheeks hollowed into a permanent scowl. Eulo held back, awestruck by rows of jewellery pinned to the black velvet curtains. To his left, a range of silver-clad opals hung at eye level. Here in this colourful market town, thousands of miles away from the Iskarlian mines where his mother destroyed her lungs breathing in dust and decay, they were all polished and prettied up for rich Vernese and Threes to buy. The amount on each price tag was a far cry from the pittance Shandy Juke and her fellow miners earnt for digging the uncut gems out of the ground, before the Scabmen took the lot and sold them, lining Vasker's—and their own—pockets.

"Ooh, look at the kilili," Tali squealed, her uncharacteristic shrillness jerking Eulo out of his daze. Beaming, she dragged him over to look at a display case on the table in front of the jeweller.

Eulo scratched his ear. Of the necklaces, earrings and bracelets arranged in rows on the velvet, none was what he recognised as silveriron. Tali clutched his arm, bouncing with excitement.

"How pretty is the pink necklace?"

He peered at it, bemused by his wife's reaction to the dull metal filling the case. It was like comparing coal to the sun. "It's, um, pink." His eyebrows knitted together. Nothing in Tali's house was pink.

"They call it soft kilili," the jeweller said in nasal Vernese. "The colours are muted so they don't outclass the wearer and their outfit." She eyed Tali from head to toe, frowning at her unfussy clothes.

"There's more than one type of kilili?" Eulo said. Tali had never mentioned that.

The jeweller fixed her mouth into a pained smile. "Of course. The dark kilili is rarer, which is reflected in the price."

"Righto. We'll look at the dark ones," Eulo pressed. He smiled at Tali, playing the role of a husband desperate to indulge his wife. Not a hard act.

The jeweller sniffed. "If you must." She shifted boxes behind the table, finally bringing out a much smaller display case. The burly Jalassan who'd been loitering outside came to block the stall entrance, scowling at Eulo and Tali. Security to protect the Scabmen's wares. Holding the case up, the jeweller gave her would-be customers a far-away look at the jewellery inside.

Eulo's breath snagged at the sight of the shimmering, exceptional pieces. This, now, was real kilili, shot through with red, orange, yellow or pink.

Tali clapped a hand over her mouth. "I could try one on," she said to Eulo, then again to the gaunt woman, adding, "How about the grey earrings?"

"Those *silver* earrings cost four thousand kistars. You can try them on once you've paid for them. *If* you can pay for them." The woman snapped the lid shut and pushed the case out of sight.

Eulo took Tali's hand, wrapping his fingers over her binding ring. His own ring still sat in his pocket. "Ah well, the pink necklace?"

"The pink is normally eight hundred kistars. I could drop it to seven-nine for a nice couple like you," the jeweller said, without a pinch of sincerity.

Eulo gulped. More than the price of a good horse for fake kilili?

Tali stared at him, her chest rising and falling in an exaggerated sigh. "I didn't know they cost so much. They're so pretty…" She smiled, girlish and hopeful. Anyone who didn't know her would've missed the gleam in her eye.

"We don't have that sort of money," he said. Her smile faded.

"Then you'll never own kilili. Only I have a licence to sell it in Gullwing, and only I have the sources for it. It's not cheap to mine, you know." The jeweller crimped her mouth into a pout with more wrinkles than a cat's arse. "You have to leave. My real customers need me."

Eulo and Tali squeezed out past a well-fed Jalassi couple who'd just entered the stall. They walked some ways in silence towards the Albatross.

She glanced at Eulo. "Tell me what you saw there."

"A heap of overpriced gems and fake shit." He spat away into the gutter.

"But what did you see?"

"A Vernese woman who don't eat selling very expensive jewellery made from Iskarlian gemstones, while her Jalassan lover watches from outside to make sure no one tries robbing her. He carried a kilili nail down the side of his boot, prob'ly for dealing with any would-be robbers. She sold a heap of junk she claimed was kilili, and a bit of real kilili, which was also very expensive. And my wife stood in the middle of it all, acting like her head was full of empty."

Tali grinned at him. "Oh, you're good. Definitely worth every kistar I paid for you."

"What were you doing in there?"

"Looking at my competition."

"She was a fraud," Eulo said, shocked Tali would compare her skills and creations with such a shyster.

"I know, but it's the fake kilili these merchants peddle that keeps real kilili so highly valued. It's safer for me if people have no idea I know what real kilili is."

He blinked at her, confused. "Where does she get it from? She talked about mines."

"She's a liar." Tali's eyebrow twitched, but she'd say no more about it.

After dropping the broom off in their room at the Albatross, they edged into an elbow-jabbing smother of drinkers in the public bar. It took Eulo a long wait to buy drinks from a damp-faced bartender, his dislike of crowds increasing with each heartbeat. He passed one beer mug through to Tali, who was huddled deep in discussion with an older couple. He hung back, waiting for them to leave. As soon as they did, someone else stepped in to take their place, just one more in the line of people wanting a moment of Tali Sarsega's time.

Bored, Eulo drifted away, opening his ears to the conversations around him. People talked about the price of wool, the weevil-ridden wheat someone was selling, the colours of the most recent shipment of Jalassi silk, and the latest women's hairstyles in Silveraine. He paused near a pair of Iskarlians in the hope they'd gossip about kilili smuggling. After wasting his time listening to them slurring about the tits of various women in the bar, Eulo moved on, knowing he'd lose his temper if they mentioned Tali.

He didn't really have the right to get offended on her behalf, not when she would've just ignored their sand-skulled comments. He'd grown a tad protective of her though, an iron-clad sliver sitting right in his guts, same as it did for Rem. Maybe what he reckoned he felt for Tali was more about making amends for his lost brother.

Heat enveloped his body, cloying and smothering in his face and lungs. He couldn't breathe in this airless box of a room, full of drunken hot wind. With his big hands outstretched, Eulo shoved people aside, hunting for a way to escape the packed bodies and their stinking sweat. He burst onto the front verandah, lurching through a line of people waiting to get in. They stared at him, probably reckoning he couldn't hold his drink.

The Duskari firebreather stood near the stairs, draped around one of his stunning gold-skinned dancers. He caught Eulo in his kohl-lined gaze and tipped his chin once in greeting. With his heart still pounding from the need to escape the crowd, Eulo turned away without responding. He shambled off to check the horses. He'd sit for a while with the smell of beast and leather in his nostrils, until the tremor left his limbs.

The shadows beyond the hotel shifted. Two figures came apart, then pressed together again, and again. Their rhythmic moaning left no secret about what they were up to. The clouds shifted past the moon, exposing the couple. Eulo recoiled at the sight of the Albatross's stableman bent over bare-arsed behind a swarthy Iskarlian.

He continued to the stables. Maybe no one in Vernesia cared much if men took intimacies with other men, but in Iskarlia it often ended in someone's death. As far as Eulo was concerned, his interests were with women, and women only.

Straightaway, the recollection of Vivica kissing her friend Audra rose into Eulo's mind. He shook his head, trying to get rid of the image. It wasn't like he'd done anything with the pair, even if a part of him had wanted to. Scraps of conversation tumbled through his thoughts, of greasy Leisik's warning, of Tali's touch around his hand.

And his heart.

He paused in the stable doorway.

A sense of wrongness set the hair rising on his nape. Horses snuffled in their stalls, browsing their hay in contentment, the straw bedding rustling as they shifted to rest a hind leg, with a blown-out breath here, a rattle on the door latch there. Cloud looked out over his stable door, his neck muscles bulging. He pricked his ears across the breezeway, to where Flame was stabled.

Eulo edged through the gloom, placing one boot carefully after the next. He strained, listening for any out-of-place noises, or the sensation of a breeze over his skin when there should've been none.

The door to Flame's stable stood ajar.

His heart hammering, Eulo craned his neck to glimpse inside. A dark-haired man huddled at Flame's shoulder, muttering in Vernese. Holding the gelding's hoof between his knees, he stretched one arm high above his head. The blade in his hand flickered silver-gold in the lamplight as he drove it toward Flame's sole.

# Chapter 26

Eulo unwound, bursting through the door in a streak of muscles and rage. Flame shied away, unbalancing his attacker. Launching into the air, Eulo knocked the maggot into the straw. Rat-fast, the man squirmed beneath him, undersized and overpowered.

Eulo caught his flailing knife-hand by the wrist and slammed it against the wall, knocking the blade out of his fingers. He dragged the maggot up by the shirtfront. A cloud of stale garlic hit Eulo as he pinched his elbow around the man's throat. Flame backed into the corner with his head high.

"Who sent you?" Eulo hissed. It had to've been the Scabmen, who'd somehow seen him arrive and decided to send him a message. Or Skramos, the man he'd been warned off asking about. His heart drummed.

"Where's my brother?"

"Only kilili will stop them," the man gasped.

*Kilili.*

The Scabmen then, knowing Eulo was here, come to remind him time was running out.

An odd noise burbled out of the man's mouth. The fucker was laughing. Pain speared into Eulo's upper leg. He growled, wrapping his arms tight around the Vernese, and sweeping his right foot sideways, kicking the man's feet out from under him. Eulo's thigh screamed as they tumbled into the straw. He pressed the man down with both hands on his chest and knees on his biceps. A patch of blood darkened his pants where the fucker had cut him. For a heartbeat, he scrabbled for a hold on the man's oily neck. Relief flooded through him when his fingers crushed the rigid band of windpipe.

The Vernese gargled, thrashing. His eyes bulged bloodshot out of his purpling face, awash with the terror of knowing he was going to die. Eulo sat calm, like riding a bucking horse, squeezing, squeezing. Even when his own harsh breath became the only noise in the stall.

The man sagged in his hands.

"I reckon you might want to stop before you kill him, don't you?" someone said in mild Iskarlian, from outside the stall.

Eulo sprang off the Vernese man, spinning into a crouch to face the newcomer, gripping his knife. Once a warrior, ever a warrior. He unfolded slowly, straightening to his full height. Huon stood motionless in the doorway, a frown deep in his wild beard.

"Mako's fucking teeth," Eulo said, fighting to catch his breath. "You might've stepped in to lend a hand."

"You had it under control." Huon edged closer. He rested his hands on his knees, bending over to inspect the man sprawled in the bedding. "Who is he?"

"I don't know." Eulo glowered. Tambo Tarch, his mercenary mentor, would've skinned him alive for killing someone without learning their identity first.

"Well, it's too late to ask him now." Huon eyed Eulo from head to toe. "I'll make myself scarce when you go tell Tali what you've done."

Eulo picked at a flap of his ruined blue shirt, torn and bloodied from the fight, and the slash in his right thigh. Shit. "No. It's better if she don't know."

"That'll make her angrier than just telling her outright."

"This isn't about Tali. I've upset a man over something, is all. I'm sorting it."

"I hope so. I've known the Sarsegas a long time, and they've been good to me. I know she's been bloody generous to you, too, so if you do anything to harm her, I'll kill you."

The two men stared at each other. Huon's scowl left no doubt he meant every word he'd said. The tang of fresh shit wafted to Eulo's nostrils, calling his attention back to the body lying between them. The Vernese must've crapped himself as he'd died.

"I got work to do, old man." Eulo crouched to retrieve the Vernese's gold flickerblade from beside the brick wall, a plain piece aside from the warmth of colour shot through the silver. He tossed it beside the attacker's other blade, still smeared in blood from his thigh. More kilili pieces to give the Scabmen, at any rate.

Huon helped him search the dead man. All they found was a handful of kistars which Eulo took without hesitation.

"You know the penalty for murder in Vernesia is beheading, don't you?" Huon rubbed a hand over his beard. "Who's seen you here tonight?"

"No one," Eulo said. Like it or not, it'd be easier to finish this with Huon's help.

They wrapped the corpse in some hessian feed sacks Huon found, and carried it through the laneways, pressing into the cover of doorways and alcoves any time someone approached. Once they'd stuffed rocks under the hessian layers, Eulo shoved the bundle into a full inlet for the tide to take. The water parted like black silk around the corpse, swallowing its prize whole. Eulo stood up, panting. Exhilaration sang in his veins.

Huon stooped, pushing a hand against his lower back. He glanced at Eulo, mirroring the hunter's guilty thrill. "Never to be known again, righto?"

They each spat on their palm and shook hands, sealing the agreement the Iskarlian way.

"Thanks," Eulo said, grateful for the older man's help. He winced as they skulked away, forced to limp from the ache in his thigh. The bandage he'd tied around it had held so far, but the wound needed proper cleaning and dressing. If his bad knee also seized up, he'd barely be able to walk.

He licked his lips. "I'll sleep in the stables, to keep an eye on the horses." He wouldn't risk drawing the bastards into Tali's room.

"What about your wife?"

"I'll talk to her, make sure she locks her door." With Eulo on the wrong side of it. "You'll look out for her?"

"I always do."

Eulo bristled at the stockman's barbed insinuation he wasn't keeping an eye on Tali himself.

They devised their lie on the way back to the Albatross, agreeing it'd cause havoc if anyone saw Eulo's bloodstained clothes.

"You really ought to disappear yourself, Eulo."

"Where *do* people go to disappear in Vernesia?"

Huon sniffed. "Fucked if I know. When you get there, say hello to my wife for me."

"You have a wife?"

"She walked out on me with my son, two days after Adeline Sarsega left, would you believe it." The stockman pinched the bridge of his nose and refused to say anything else until they returned to the Albatross.

Eulo waited in the stables while Huon stomped off to fetch Tali, muttering about how he still had to bloody-well move Leisik's stall, and how sick he was of cleaning up after everyone else's messes. If only he could clean up Eulo's questions about what the fuck was going on.

It felt like eternity passed before Tali appeared, greeting Eulo beside the horses.

"I assume you're not intending to seduce me in the stables, then?" she said, eyeballing his ruined outfit. "And you seem to have a spot of blood on your new clothes."

He smelled honey mead on her breath—a fair bit of it, judging by the way she'd swaggered across the Albatross's stable yard with enough colour in her cheeks to stir the fire in his veins. He frowned down at himself.

"I got in a fight. It's my blood."

"Huon told me."

"I'll sleep in the stables tonight. I don't want trouble around you." Skirting the truth without telling any lies.

Yet.

"Ah." She brushed spider-light fingertips over his cheek. "I suppose I need to get used to sleeping in an empty bed again, don't I?"

Eulo's heart tore. He squashed the feeling, fast. Letting himself fall for this girl absolutely *would* bring her trouble. He opened his mouth to speak as Tali tilted her head, blinking slowly at him with her long black lashes. All sane thought galloped out of his mind. Tali caught him around the back of the neck, pulling his head down so she could kiss him.

For a heartbeat, he hung suspended in the honey on her tongue, craving her desire. In it formed a sweet, exquisite bliss, bittersweet in its fate.

"No," he said, fracturing the moment. Not here, not like this. Not clandestine fucking behind a shitheap close to where an Iskarlian goon had throttled a man under the feet of a renowned breeder's horse.

Hurt swam in Tali's eyes, simmering into a frown.

Iskarlians were honest without finesse, so Eulo couldn't find the words to say he didn't want to remember Tali as a half-drunken screw against a barn wall. Not this girl, not his wife, who mattered to him.

Which was why he couldn't admit to killing someone tonight.

He took her hand, wrapping his naked fingers around her binding ring. Pressing her knuckles to his lips, he said, "Tomorrow, I'm yours. I'll do whatever you want." He stared her in the eye, willing her to have faith in him, the closest he'd ever been to begging.

She half-smiled and looked away the way a shy girl would, or one who knew better than to trust Iskarlian thugs.

Years of slogging his guts out in the Cove's army had refined Eulo's ability to sleep with a dirty conscience. Tired men were soft, sloppy and made bad decisions—weaknesses a hunter couldn't risk.

He rested well enough in the stable, even with his raw-nerved worry the darkness would reveal another knife-wielding Vernese, or Goshawks who'd found his attacker's corpse in the bay. No one came, though, and he woke under a dawn sky blushing pink then yellow.

Harsh daylight stripped away the previous night's mystique, leaving the crowds sidestepping puddles of muck on their way back to the marketplace. The scent of stale alcohol and regret mingled with smoke from the cooking fires, tangling in the hair of women buying silk and fish, skimming over canvas tents, bouncing off the bluestone warehouses on its way up to wide-open skies.

Eulo sagged against a post on the front step of the Albatross. He folded his arms across his chest, frowning at the ache in his right thigh. Luckily the maggot's knife had sliced in on an awkward angle, nicking a few blood vessels without causing any real damage. He'd dropped a pinch of Kizan pepperdust into the wound while stitching and bandaging it last night. It burnt like hell when he woke, but he'd rather a few days of pain over getting bloodsick.

Pairs of Goshawks sauntered through the laneways, quick to dispatch anyone still drunk and disorderly enough to upset the sellers and buyers. Eulo had spent plenty of time in both situations on the streets of Mako-knew how many Iskarlian towns. The Vernese soldiers weren't brutal like the Iskarlian ones, though. He shifted, needing to piss.

Where in shades was Tali? Huon hadn't appeared either.

With any luck, one Vernese man wouldn't appear today. Were last night's tides big enough to carry away the maggot's corpse, or had he washed onto the rocks or a beach nearby, bloated by death and saltwater?

Eulo's nape prickled. Someone was watching him from the laneway at the front of the pub. He spun around, sending a jolt through his bad leg.

"Good morning, husband." Gravel lined Tali's voice.

He eased off the step to meet her, surprised when she grabbed the front of his shirt, pulling herself in close to him, sunshine to his dark mood.

"I do appreciate a man who saddles the horses before breakfast," she murmured into his neck, full of sweet promise and drifts of honey-spiral.

He slid his arm around her waist, resting his hand on the curve of her backside. "Who says I didn't have breakfast?"

She laughed. "I forgot you Iskarlian soldiers rise early. Huon drank himself stupid and kept me awake snoring through the wall all night."

"Did he now?" Eulo raised his eyebrows. So much for his promise to keep Tali safe. While Eulo had been guarding a horse.

"What stirs your anger so much I can taste it, Eulo Juke?"

"Taste my anger?" he snorted, clenching his jaw, unable to meet her silver gaze.

She ran her thumb down his cheekbone. "Havoc clings to you like embers in a bushfire. Today, you're a conflagration." She turned away, squaring her shoulders. "Come with me? I want something to eat."

When they returned to the Albatross, Huon was waiting in the sunshine outside the cold, dark pub. He stared at Eulo through sullen, bloodshot eyes. Could Tali taste his anger too? His probably tasted like an old boot, while Eulo's would be as sweet and dangerous as Iskarlian rum.

When they rode out, Huon slowed his horse beside Eulo, letting Tali lead the way to the stockyards. The stockman hunched in the saddle, scowling at Eulo. "So you managed not to get yourself arrested?"

"I make a point not to."

Huon considered him for a moment. "Until last night, I liked you, because Tali does. Now, I want you to collect your gear and leave after we get back to Glimmers Gap. Tell Tali whatever you have to so she don't waste her time fretting after you."

Huon was a decent fellow, so Eulo couldn't blame him for wanting to protect Tali, but the stockman didn't intimidate him. In less than a week, they'd all have what they wanted, and Huon would be glad to find out Tali wasn't keeping Eulo around at all.

"You're a true bastard, eh Juke, no doubt about it. Y'might know it all in Iskarlia, but you don't here, not in Tali Sarsega's house."

Eulo's grin stretched wider. "You don't know a scrap about what's going on with me and Tali." He stared ahead, through Cloud's pricked ears, in a fair bloody ungrateful way towards the man who'd helped him dispose of a corpse.

"What do you reckon she'd say if she knew you'd killed someone last night?"

"What do you reckon she'd say if she knew you'd stood back to let it happen? I was defending myself—what's your excuse?"

Huon shook his head, grimacing as he broke away from Eulo. They were in this together now, and neither could risk himself by causing trouble for the other.

The Glimmers Gap cattle sold in the mid-morning lots, raising a good price, judging by Tali's huge smile after she'd collected her earnings. The fillies sold too, with Ozar the fire-dancer taking ownership of the better horse. Maybe because Tali danced with him last night, or as a result of it, although she'd bought a pregnant Duskari mare and filly off him in return.

"It's all part of my plan," she told Eulo. "This deal will secure the future of the Glimmers Gap stud."

"You sold your fillies to buy more fillies?"

"Not quite." She licked her lips. "Ozar paid coin for mine, but I traded him for the two I got."

"Traded what?" Eulo's hackles rose.

"Not what you're thinking." Tali lifted one shoulder. "He swapped them in return for silveriron."

"Kilili?" Eulo covered his surprise. "You ought've asked more for your filly. He would've paid it."

"I know. Next time, though, he'll come back wanting more, for the right price."

"You sure?"

"We've already agreed on it." She grinned, full of confidence.

Yellowness bubbled inside Eulo. He didn't want the sly Duskari appearing in Tali's life again. Fancy old Ranson hearing *that* news. "It sounds like a complicated business."

"It's business," she said. "Now, this fight you had last night wasn't with Huon by any chance, was it?"

"You reckon he stabbed me with a pitchfork?"

"I have no idea. I can see your egos bumping, is all." She hung on the top rail of the yards, resting one heel up on the wood, waiting for Eulo to give her a reply. When he didn't, she sighed. "He's upset with you."

"They're all itchin' for you to boot me out the door. I s'pose they act the same with every man you bring home, eh?"

"Not at all," she laughed, easing off the fence and brushing her hands off on her thighs. "Except I've never brought home a man quite like you before."

# Chapter 27

Eulo whistled as he rode from paddock to paddock, checking Tali's cows. Sure enough, the big old girl Tali worried about was nursing a new calf. She spun to eyeball Cloud, stamping her foot when the grey got too close. The calf was feeding alright, nuzzling up to her mother's swollen udder.

When he couldn't ignore his hunger anymore, Eulo headed for the shack, lured by the temptation of a few mugs of hot kaif. His hand strayed to the handle of his new knife again. In the last few weeks, Tali's surprises had shifted the world under him, from the image of her kneeling beside her injured horse with the air ringing from the throat-slitting chime of her flickerblade, to her seductive passion, and the kilili blade she'd made for Eulo. What he'd seen of her, crooning to the shimmering cloud of green in the lean-to atop the escarpment, seemed unreal. Tali Sarsega was drawing him in like a cod hooked on her line.

Cloud whinnied, pricking his ears towards the shack. Vivica's liver chestnut mare called out, followed by a deeper, different whinny. Eulo frowned. He wasn't keen on facing Vivica as it was, especially if she wasn't alone. He snuck up with his hunter's stealth, even though anyone in earshot would've noticed his horse greeting the others. Pausing with his fingertips on the rough wooden door, he heard women murmuring inside. Vivica's shit had to end. Eulo rolled his shoulders and went in.

She lay along the table without a scrap of clothing on, propped on her elbows, her black hair cascading from her flung-back head. Her nipples were tight, hardened by the caress of a naked girl sitting on a chair with her face buried between Vivica's thighs. Long hair draped the second girl's face, hiding her identity.

Eulo's prick tingled.

Vivica's playmate half stood, kissing her way up the singer's belly to her nipples. She worked one hand between Vivica's legs, stroking the other over her breasts and neck.

"About time you arrived," Vivica said, deep and breathy, looking at Eulo as she arched and strained against her friend. "I brought Audra for us to enjoy." She tipped her head back again. Audra licked her neck, finding Vivica's lips, whimpering as they kissed.

Audra, the wide-eyed girl who'd been all over Vivica at the dignitine's binding in Oyster Point. The gossipy one, everyone had said. Eulo glowered.

Vivica hissed in pleasure, smirking. "Oh, come now, it's too late to worry about Tali. I'll always be her sister, so she'll forgive me. You, though? You're no one special. There's plenty more where you came from."

Mako's teeth, what the fuck was he thinking? He stepped back. "This ain't right."

"Does it matter when it feels so good," she purred, locking her long, smooth legs around Audra's hips. "You know she'll find out about Lilla, don't you?" She rolled the name over her tongue. "And when she does, she'll kick you out on your arse before you can draw another breath."

"D'you reckon you got nothing to lose, either?" Eulo barked out a laugh. "Stay the fuck away from me. You're done."

He withdrew, slamming the door shut on Vivica's ugly expression, her friend's moans and sighs, and his plans to have a break out of the cold wind. He'd be fucked if she convinced Tali he was messing around, especially now he was finally accumulating some kilili to pay the Scabmen.

He rode away, braced with the certainty he'd made the right decision, even if Vivica was going to make him pay for it later.

"Of all people to invite here, Tali," Vivica said, "why did it have to be Filia Tartula and her brainless husband?"

Eulo resisted the urge to tug his collar away from his throat. How had he ended up standing like a lump of sandstone between two stunning gems on the front porch of the Sarsega homestead, with the air bleeding from their barbed exchange while the Tartula's carriage crawled along the road towards them?

Tali levelled a stare at Vivica. "I invited her for Mema. Not you. And I didn't invite her brainless husband here for you, either."

Vivica smoothed wrinkles out of her yellow pants. She smiled, crimson-lipped and friendly as a snake. "Cailene's rustling up some burnt offerings, is she?"

"If you don't like her cooking, get off your arse and do it yourself." Tali rolled her head from one side to the other, stopping abruptly. "I don't suppose you thought to bring Mema downstairs?"

"I was busy getting ready. Didn't you and your oaf here bring her down?"

"I'll do it." Eulo took the opportunity to escape before Tali could protest. He put his hand down to vault the long clay flowerpots at the end of the porch. Green plants brushed at his fingers, replacing the neglected mess that'd been withering in the pots the first time he'd stood on this porch. Over the last week or so, he'd seen Ranson working in the gardens, turning his glare away from Eulo to hunch over the rambling shrubs or hoe the beds in the vegetable patch. Twice Vivica had been beside him, close as a conspirator, in a way Eulo hadn't seen either act with Tali. Ranson was the only one Vivica didn't sharpen her claws on.

Each day that passed strengthened his determination to keep good on his word of avoiding her. He and Tali had spent the last few nights with their limbs tangled around each other in bed. Uncertain, he'd curbed his craving to share more intimacy with her.

He climbed the staircase two at a time, up to the top floor where shadows stretched across the stone walls. Mema huddled in her chair, nothing more than wisps of white hair above a blanket. Abandoned. She could've been dead, for all anyone knew.

Eulo pushed away the unsettling thought. "Evenin'," he said to the old woman. She moved her head to peer up at him through crepe-thin eyelids. He blew out a breath. "Bit cold up here, ain't it? I'll get you downstairs in a moment, 'cause the party's about to start."

Eulo blinked at the two tiny kilili studs in her earlobes. He glanced around the room, his mind racing. Mema's eyes rolled shut, like she'd faded from consciousness, not responding when he waved a hand in front of her face. He edged back, his chest surging in the effort to keep quiet. Her dresser drawers opened with a whisper, revealing her hairbrush and personals, and sachets of dried flowers tucked among folded clothes.

A tangle of silver and red glass stuck in the back corner of the last drawer caught Eulo's eye. He snatched up the necklace, pushing the drawer shut. They wouldn't miss it, would they—a tiny chain lost in an old woman's muddle? Guilt and desperation roiled deep, like two snakes fighting inside his belly.

"You picked the wrong one."

Eulo's nape prickled. The voice was so faint he could've imagined it. But he hadn't. He straightened slowly, staring at the old woman. "What did you say?"

Mema blinked at him, lizard-slow, her lips slack with disuse.

Wrong what? He closed his hand around the chain. Wrong kilili? Wrong woman? Grasping the armrests of her chair, he leant over her. "You sit there listening, don't you? Tell me what you said. What did you mean?"

"What are you doing to her?" Tali barked from behind him. Her boot-heels clicked on the floorboards as she ran over to them, her skirt and bell-sleeves drifting behind her.

He sprang back, startled.

"What's wrong with you? Threatening an old woman?" Tali crossed her arms, leaning towards him, a storm in blue velvet. Angrier, even, than the night he'd fought with Krike on the wifeship.

"I wasn't. She said—"

"Said?" Tali spat. "Mema doesn't talk. She hasn't spoken for five years. Why would you even suggest it?" She kicked a cushion that had fallen on the floor. "Blazes, I'm regretting this party already."

"Tali—" Eulo spread his palms, realising too late he was still holding the necklace. Behind his wife, he glimpsed Mema's smug smile.

"Alright. What did she say?"

He opened his mouth. Closed it. He couldn't tell her without admitting to his deceit. His chest rose, fell. Caught in his own trap. "Guess I did imagine it."

"For Lolani's sake, this doesn't even match her dress but it will have to do," Tali snapped, plucking the kilili chain out of Eulo's hand. She turned her back on him to bend down and fasten it around Mema's neck.

He stepped around her to take the handles of Mema's chair. Tali's scowl bored into him, but he didn't back down, holding the smooth handles of the chair with the shrunken elder between them both. He cocked an eyebrow at Tali. "Oh what, you gonna do it, are you? And split open the fucking wound on your shoulder again?"

Her pupils dilated, blacker than Mako's soul. "How dare you. And in front of my grandmother!"

His jaw dropped. "No one else knows you're injured, do they? Shades, woman, there ain't no harm in asking for help when you need it."

"Stop it, Eulo."

"Why? You worried she'll repeat it? You said it yourself—she can't talk. Can she?" He paused for a heartbeat, hating the pain swimming in Tali's eyes. "Pfft. Even if she could, she'd be too busy telling you lot to value what you got instead of fighting with each other all the time." He wheeled Mema past his wife and into the passageway. There wasn't time for regrets, for wanting there to be no reason for Tali to doubt him when instead she had plenty. From the little bits he'd learnt about Vernese culture, he knew insulting the matriarch of the family was one of the stupidest mistakes a man could make.

Tali stalked downstairs behind him, her heels a drumbeat of disapproval. She bit her lip as she helped Eulo resettle Mema, checking the old woman's clothes when he lifted her out of the chair. She rearranged the cushions, without saying a word the whole time. Her silverviolet earrings bounced on her neck, right over the smooth skin Eulo had kissed earlier, tasting salt and fire.

"It's not your issue if people ain't happy with the best you can do, Tali," he said. "You ain't the only one in this family. Stop trying to carry their problems on top of your own."

Mema farted in his arms. Giggled.

"You know what's going on alright, don't you, old girl?" He placed her in the chair and stood back so Tali could tuck a woollen blanket over her. He lowered his tone. "I'd never hurt her, or you."

"Just because we're sleeping together, it doesn't mean I trust you." Tali lifted her chin. She considered Eulo for a long moment. "Now, can you get through the evening without insulting the Tartulas as well?"

"If you want, darl," he rasped. The great Eulo Juke, being yanked up short on his chain.

"What I want?" Tali scoffed. The iron in her posture faltered. Huskiness burred her words. "Just be the man you think you should be. I have to go to meet our guests." She pushed the wheelchair away, leaving Eulo alone to stumble over what both women had said to him.

He stretched his right hand out. The binding ring gleamed, offering no explanation of Tali's secrets. He cracked his knuckles, right hand then left. The hunger to ride north, hunting again, without worrying about anyone else, burnt in his belly. A greensilver flame flickered there too now, though; Tali and her kilili secrets. He took a deep breath and went to face the palaver on the front doorstep again.

Tali stood rigid as a soldier bracing for trouble, waiting for Krike and his wife to climb the steps to the house. Eulo entwined his fingers in hers, kept squeezing 'til she raised an eyebrow at him. Trouble might sway the night into fun. She smiled, all grit and honesty.

Filia Tartula greeted them in the formal Vernese style, bowing her head and raising her left hand. She'd retrained Krike so well he hesitated before catching Eulo's handshake. For someone who'd mostly spent his time running around a battlefield with his lunatic grin speckled in blood, Darley Krike was apparently a changed man. No, Eulo corrected himself; not Krike, not anymore. He was a Tartula now, with his hair and beard washed and trimmed, dressed in a suit as good as any the Cove'd ever worn, prancing about beside his sturdy wife, proud as if she were as beautiful as Vivica Sarsega. Even his moustache had been oiled down on his top lip.

Filia acknowledged Vivica and Eulo with bland courtesy, yet gushed over Mema. The old woman stared at her visitor, suddenly as sharp-eyed as Tali.

"How lovely to be here," Filia said to Tali. "Is Cyska around, too?"

"Not tonight. She's travelling again."

"She's a wanderer, isn't she? Even as a little one she'd always be off looking for adventures." Filia smiled at Ranson. "I knew your mother well too. We spent many afternoons chatting over mugs of kaif while you played at her feet. Such a quiet, reflective boy. It seems not much has changed, eh?" She drew him inside the house, woven into the conversation, pushing Mema ahead of them.

"She's good, isn't she?" Tali glanced from the men to Vivica.

"She's amazing," Krike said, flashing his teeth in a wide grin. He trailed after his wife.

Eulo stared at his back. The man seemed too content for someone who might've been there working for the Scabmen. He squeezed Tali's hip, holding her back a moment after Vivica went inside too. The cool evening air buzzed with the cicadas' chorus. Birds cawed their night song, heading for the safety of their nests.

"Guess you'll just have to enjoy yourself, huh?"

"Oh, I know I will," she murmured in a smoky tone. "I've even convinced Ranson to open up my mother's snarlsboard." She grinned as she half-spun out of his grasp.

"Wait a moment." He lumbered after her, catching her hand. "What are we playing for tonight?"

"Playing for? You mean a bet?" Her grin turned wicked. She ran her finger over his collarbone and chest. "Let's say if I win, I get to do whatever I want to you."

Heat pulsed in his groin, roughening his voice. "And if I win, the same."

She nuzzled into him, brushing her lips against his throat. "Alright. If you win, I still get to do whatever I want to you. How much you'll like it will depend on whether we get through dinner without any kerfuffles."

Eulo turned his head, hunting for her lips so he could kiss her. She slipped away from him in a shimmer of blue.

"After dinner, I want you to take Krike to check his horses. It'll give Ranson some space to relax with Filia."

Eulo might've taken a smidgen of offence at the snub if it didn't offer him a chance to question Krike. Hopefully, the big man had found out some useful information since they'd last spoken. He bowed, extending one hand out to the side.

"Anything for you, wife of much beautiful."

Eulo sank into his elegant chair beside Tali at the dark wooden table, facing a painting of cattle grazing on a beachside slope. Never in his life could he have imagined sitting in a Vernese house with a fire crackling in the hearth, breathing in the scent of roast meat and vegetables, stopping to sip at blood-red wine, then carrying on the clink of serving spoons and cutlery. No wonder his countrymen kept lining up to get on the wifeships.

After swapping from wine to ale, he found himself telling a ridiculous story about a scouting party he and Krike went on as freshly recruited soldiers. Even Ranson smiled when the story ended with the cleanskins falling into a swamp. Tali leant back in her chair to loose a belly laugh, the best chuckle Eulo had ever heard from a woman. He reached for her hand under the table. Tonight, she sat strong and attentive to everyone in the room, even the housemaid Cailene. The Sarsega matriarch had emerged, even if her husband was an imposter in this world.

With his free hand, Eulo gripped his ale mug, swirling it a little to agitate its white-frothed head. Froth-headed alright, for reckoning he'd suffer through Ranson and Filia's disapproving stares any night, and Krike's sand-skulled banter, if it meant he could make Tali laugh that way again.

Vivica turned her smirk on Eulo. She closed her mouth, keeping in her lies. For now. Eulo twitched, suddenly aware he'd been rubbing his thumb along Tali's binding ring, over and over. He pulled his hand away. Vivica sniggered. The bitch knew the power she might force over him and her sister, and he'd given it to her, racing in with his ego waving about. She was right—he was a stupid fuckin' puppet. He threw down the dregs of his ale, keen to scramble for the jug to pour himself another one. Might as well.

"I'm so pleased we were able to visit." Filia scraped the last trace of cream off her empty dessert plate. She patted Mema's hand, the old woman's eyes sharper than Eulo had ever seen them. He swallowed, looking away from the silveriron chain at the old woman's throat.

"You're always welcome, Mrs Tartula," Ranson said. The mood of the house had shifted, rebalanced, finding purpose again by having guests there. A reason for the sour man to get out working in the garden, to refill the planter boxes with life and colour.

Krike, meanwhile, banged on at Tali about pig farming. She listened, nodding, asking questions about the price of salt pork, who they sold it to, and when.

"Fil's clever, eh? She built herself a market through Silveraine. Them Iskarlian ships can't get enough of it."

"I wonder if they'd feel the same way about Glimmers Gap salt beef," Tali mused, toying a dessert fork between her hands.

"I'd say the Iskarlians would love some tender Vernese meat," Vivica said across the table to Eulo, her voice low.

Something bumped his knee, then his inner thigh. He shoved her stockinged foot away before it could nestle in his crotch. The gleam in her eye hardened. Eulo swallowed the nasty taste filling his mouth. Her spite troubled him, worse now she'd brought her friend into her games. Mako's teeth, it'd be a miracle if Tali didn't question his motives, and when she did, he didn't reckon she'd offer him a pinch of mercy.

# Chapter 28

Ranson prowled down the side of the table, wielding a tall silver pot. "Anyone for kaif?"

"Not for me, thanks," Krike said. "I can't get the taste for it."

Thank Mako he still had a taste for ale, though. He'd kept up with Eulo drink for drink. Under all his fancy new manners and clothes, the man was still just a grubby soldier. Hopefully one with a tongue loosened enough to blab a few secrets.

Having ended up as half-cut as Krike, Eulo nodded to Ranson. "I'll have one, thanks mate." The Vernese poured him a mug, then moved on to Mema. The aromatic drink steamed between Eulo's hands, a bitter version everyone except Tali usually drank with milk. She made hers stronger, with honey or sugar, the way the underclass drank it out of a billy can over a campfire.

Vivica snorted as Eulo reached for the milk jug. "Too dark for you?"

"I prefer Tali's, it's much sweeter," he drawled, casting a sly glance at his wife.

"She's a good trainer, isn't she? She's turned you into her dog faster than I thought," Vivica said, wrinkling her nose.

Tali leant away over the table, listening intently to Krike dribbling about his glory days in the Cove's forces, as though he'd single-handedly won entire battles. Never once looking at Eulo, she dropped her hand to rest on his thigh. Had she noticed Vivica's foot there too, a heartbeat ago? His stomach flipped over.

"Did you see the smoked meat the Tartulas brought?" Vivica said to Eulo. "How much do you want to bet it's made from Filia's last husband?"

He glanced at the big woman, who lumbered over as though she'd heard her name mentioned.

"So, Vivica," she said, sitting down, "your father tells me you dream of auditioning for the Academy?"

"As a lyricene, yes, once I pay the fees. I have the talent," Vivica pouted.

"Indeed. The cost to train an artist isn't cheap, and there's no guaranteed success afterwards. When I danced there with your Mema, we saw many dreams crushed. One year alone, four girls threw themselves off Lolani's Bridge."

Eulo hissed as he spilt hot kaif over his hand. Tartula—a dancer?

Vivica rolled her eyes. "I'm not weak enough to kill myself, even if I did fail to get in. Which I won't."

Filia's pink lips arced into a knowing smile. "If you say so. Can I give you some advice?"

"It's not like I can stop you."

Eulo tipped down another scalding mouthful of kaif. He ought've stuck to drinking ale. He slouched in his chair, waiting for the women to continue.

Filia rested an elbow on the table. She was solid, like the women who hauled potch out of the mines at home, her gaze stonier than quartz.

"I know you're wondering how an old bitch like me could ever have set one of her fat feet through the Academy gate. Well, I did, and I can tell you from experience; it takes skies more than talent and money to succeed there." The two women stared at each other long enough for Eulo to wonder if he'd need to throw the water jug over them. Filia's tone softened. "You have to work hard, and I know what that's like because I did it too. And I know how it feels to have it all taken away from you."

Vivica crimped her mouth. "I'm nothing like you."

"Neither was I, at your age, but things happen that you never could've imagined, changing your life in a heartbeat." Filia leant closer, her gaze unwavering. "Cherish the people who believe in you, and treat them well, because one day they might be all you have. If you still have them at all."

The Sarsega homestead's endless hallways and doors led to a sitting room Eulo had never been in. He edged between sofas and armchairs, shrinking his arms against his sides so he didn't bump any knick-knacks off the cabinets lining the side wall. Stale air tickled his nostrils, as though they'd cracked open a crypt. Stopping beside the fireplace, he stifled a sneeze. A painting hung above the crackling flames; Vivica sitting on a bench with her arm resting on one knee. The feathered smears of black ink made her face thinner, the nose hooked, the mouth kinder.

"It's my mother," Tali said softly. Her arm brushed against Eulo's elbow. "This was her favourite place in the house."

"It's different from how they paint back home, how only a few lines make the whole picture." With no bold Iskarlian colours.

"Ranson painted it, and most of the others on this wall." Tali pointed out horses and landscapes of trees and coastline, her finger wavering at the suggestion of two girls with long hair, facing each other, smiling. Two sisters, young and innocent, showing a closeness either imagined or eroded.

A brief melody made Eulo look around, to where Vivica had perched on a stool below a corner window. Standing a wooden instrument between her legs, she strummed gently at the long strings that ran from top to bottom. She fiddled with the tuning pegs, then tested the strings again, until each reverberating note met her approval. Her mask of stone slipped, exposing a softer, vulnerable side she hadn't shown until now. She played without singing, her music soft in the background. Not, for once, demanding to be the centre of attention.

Ranson, the old goat, slouched on a couch beside Filia Tartula, deep in discussion. They'd wedged Mema's chair between a side-table and candelabra, another odd display in this room full of dusty memories and forgotten hopes.

"Well, darl," Eulo said to Tali, "you ought to get those snarls out before Krike starts gawping at your sister again." The lie slid off his tongue. Krike's attention stuck to Tali like shit on silk.

"You're keen to lose." Her lips curled into a half-smile.

"No, but I'm thirsty, and you can't play games like this without a drink, eh?"

"A drunken loser? Blazes, I'm going to have fun with you." She tapped a finger on his chest. "Go pour us something, would you?"

Eulo served them all rum while Tali placed a big snarls box on the side table. The box's honey-coloured wood matched the rest of the furniture in the room, which she'd said was her father's work.

Krike edged close to Tali, whistling in appreciation when she lifted the box's carved lid. Eulo tapped a finger against his glass, smug again about the prize wife choosing him out of the line at the binding agency. He snorted at the irony of two Covesmen being all dressed up in Vernesia, quaffing white rum with their wives.

"True craftsmanship," Krike said, peering into the box with the excitement of a little tacker picking sweets.

Tali spun it away from him, offering it to Eulo. "Pick wisely."

He held his breath. A kaleidoscope of snarls winked at him, each colour nestled in an individual compartment. This set put the one at the Bintau pub to shame, for sure. One hand gleamed red, another yellow, while others matched the silveriron he'd seen in Tali's cottage. He picked out the greensilver hand, trying not to prick his fingers. Had she made these, too? Balancing the snarls in his palm, Eulo glanced at her, unsure if it was rude to take her colour but she smiled, dipping her chin in a single nod of approval.

"Darley, your turn." She held the box out to him.

"No thanks. I brought me own." The tall man slapped a hand to his chest pocket. With a flourish, he produced a small leather pouch, tipping out a hand of snarls as dark as the sunset sky, unlike any other in Tali's set.

"Very nice." She plucked a hand of violet spikes out of the box. The same colour swirled through her earrings and one of her knives.

The box intrigued Eulo. Who'd made the snarls sitting in each of the twelve compartments? Tali? Did she control the colours, too? These were different to Krike's snarls, though, and the silveriron blades Eulo had seen in the hands of men and merchants in Iskarlia. This secret no one wanted to talk about bothered him more than a sand tick between the toes. Where had this kilili come from? Another question to ask Krike.

Tali glided over to open a cabinet on the opposite wall, revealing the coloured snarlsboard. A slit in her skirt parted as she turned to the two men, revealing one long, tantalising golden leg. She caught Eulo staring at it. "Why don't you start us off, husband?"

She fetched her drink from the table beside Krike, propping one hand on the smooth wood. All grace and poise.

Eulo lined himself up on the edge of the rug, where the burgundy wool bled into black. He tilted his head, straining to hear Tali's conversation with Krike.

"So, Darley, you've known Eulo for a while, haven't you?"

"We fought for the Cove, for a long time, 'til Eulo became a hunter."

Eulo clenched his jaw, willing Krike not to spill his guts telling stories Tali didn't need to know. The big goon must've already been spreading rumours, judging by Filia's frowns any time she looked Eulo's way.

He flicked his first snarl. It spun wide, lodging into the edge of the board's dead zone. He cursed out loud. Ranson glared at him. Mako's teeth, he must've broken some golden rule by swearing in this shrine to the Vernese's dead wife.

"Shades, Juke, your eyes are as bad as your old man's." Krike smirked a little, stepping up for his turn. He glanced at Tali. "He were always the one with the best aim."

"I'm going easy on you, is all," Eulo scraped out.

"What'd they say back home if they knew you lost your touch?" Krike grinned, twirling a single blue snarl between his thumb and forefinger.

Eulo frowned. They already knew in Iskarlia, didn't they, otherwise he wouldn't have gotten into this whole sorry mess. "Take your shot, Krike." He'd been stupid to reckon the past would stay hidden. Shades, all he'd wanted was to get through this one month without collecting more problems.

Krike readied, squinting past his outstretched hand at the board. He threw a crap shot, although he'd bettered Eulo enough to gloat on his way to the table. "Juke were famous. If he were on your tail, you knew you was in real trouble."

"Really?" Tali said.

"Ain't never seen a man throw starfire as good as him," Krike said, too loud.

Tali flung her snarl almost carelessly. It thudded into the middle target; perfect.

She trapped Eulo in her cool gaze again. "I'd almost started believing he was a half-decent man."

He cracked his knuckles, remembering her reaction last time they'd talked about starfire. Krike deserved a fist in the nose for coming here and tearing down the fragile web Eulo had built. His snarl hit Krike's with a click and fell, hanging by one spike from a wisp of felt.

"Too bad, eh," Tali murmured when he hulked beside her. "Even the great hunter should know which target he's aiming for." She stepped around him to wait her turn.

Eulo stared at the hourglass curve of velvet over her waist and arse, seeing and not seeing. He had no idea how many backs he'd stared at in his life, focusing on the span between the shoulder blades where his blackmetal fire would land and spring its hooks open into his target's flesh, yanking them out of flight. His eyes refocused on Tali's spine.

Nausea swirled in his guts.

"It's not the barbs themselves what stops a wanted man, it's the pain what brings him to his knees," Krike told Tali, clawing his hand down in a grabbing motion.

Did the maggot have conversations like this with his own wife?

Eulo snorted, "Tali don't want to hear about how kilili weapons hurt men, Krike." Even if hers bloody did, too. Plenty of men had died with Eulo's flickerblade in their chest, or across their throats, 'til the Scabmen came to collect on his debts and all he'd had left to sell was his fine set of weapons. It'd been a lot harder catching his targets alive without the starfire.

"I can speak for myself, Eulo." Tali cast a flat look at him. Neither backed down from their locked stare.

He hulked over his drink. It was better to settle issues the way a soldier did, with fists and finality, than to play these games of shifting smoke, and be talked down to by a woman in front of this audience. Then, Tali's lips softened into the faintest of smiles—one just for him. He scratched his ear. He still had lots to learn about Vernese women.

"Maybe no one else here understands it, but a man does what he has to, to put food in his belly and look after his family," Eulo said. Like the good job he'd done taking care of Remmy. His attention drifted off Tali. He'd bet money the Sarsegas never had to sit at an empty table, listening to their father turn his hovel of a house upside down in a drunken rage, even when he couldn't see what he was doing. Or hear their mother cough up the lungfuls of dust she'd breathed in after hours of chipping away in the opal pits.

Tongues of flame licked around the logs in the fireplace, hungry and ruthless, firing the grog in his veins. The greensilver snarls stung his palm as he bunched his fist around them. It didn't matter what these people thought of him, because he'd be out of the dignitine's world and into the shadows again in just a handful of days.

Butterfly soft fingertips landed on his fist. He let Tali open his hand, filling his nostrils with honeyspiral, exposing him without even knowing she was doing it. Reminding him why he was there. She drew in a sharp breath as she uncurled his fingers.

"It's your shot," she said, plucking the last snarls out of his hand and pressing his palm to her lips. "For luck." Her eyes smouldered as she dropped the snarls back into his blood-smeared palm. Suddenly he was a moth tangled in her fragile web, tearing holes in the gossamer strands with his big, clumsy being.

It'd all be so much easier if she wasn't so bloody decent. Eulo sidestepped her, sidestepping his shame. She'd be rid of him soon, and the pain he was going to cause her. Vivica wouldn't keep his secret for long, not when it filled her hand with such a solid stone to throw at Tali. He ought to tell her himself except, deep down, he didn't want to face her disappointment.

He didn't even see her take her second shot. The snarl missed the red centre panel, lodging beyond it in a blue square. He focused on the red felt. One more target in a warrior's life. His mind cleared, muting out a stupid joke Krike told Tali, the fast-paced tune Vivica played, and laughter coming from Ranson and Filia Tartula.

Laughter?

His snarl clinked against Tali's, its prongs straddling hers, pinning it into the centre target. Always a warrior…

She slipped close to him, laying her hand against his clean-shaven jaw and left a lingering kiss on his lips. "Nice try."

"You win."

Mischief gleamed in her eyes. "I was never going to lose." She drew back from him, smiling. "Now we're done here, Eulo, how 'bout you help Darley check the horses?"

The Glimmers Gap evening wrapped itself around Eulo, rich as velvet, cold as a dagger in a stranger's hand. His breath puffed white into air heavy with the scent of damp earth. Cattle lowed and shifted in the holding paddock beyond the stables, waiting for tomorrow's saltwater muster.

He licked his lips, willing saliva into his tacky mouth. He'd better bloody-well drink some water soon, so he didn't end up doing a long day in the saddle with a filthy hangover. Beside him, Krike whistled an old soldier's drinking song, "The Ballad of the Butcher", clomping his boots on the gravel driveway in time to the tune. How anyone could've written a ballad about a Cove who'd slaughtered his countrymen was beyond Eulo, but the first lesson every Iskarlian warrior learnt was to get stonkered spoony drunk while singing this song. Some of 'em even dreamt of becoming as notorious as the bloodthirsty Cove who'd died hundreds of years ago. Vasker was giving it a red-hot go, at any rate.

"She's magnificent, Eulo. What'd you reckon they'd say if you took her home to Iskarlia?" Krike slurred, in their native tongue.

Eulo lifted his chin. Stars studded the black sky like handfuls of silver snarls thrown wild. He'd never considered taking Tali back home. She wouldn't be interested in Iskarlia, anyway, not with all the opportunity her own country offered her.

"You reckon she don't know you're in trouble back home? How long d'you reckon she'll put up with it? She'll be long rid o' you before you work it out, Jukey boy."

Eulo *had* worked it out, though. He'd known it the whole fucking time. Tonight, the moon hung pale in the crisp night, hiding a sliver of its perfection. When it came full in a whisper of days, pregnant and round, his binding with Tali would be untied, ending their pact. His voice slowed by drink, he said, "Maybe y'ought worry about your own wife, Krike."

"Ha, I ain't got no worries at all. She's teaching me letters and numbers, and how to be a gentleman." Krike smoothed his moustache. "Fuck, Juke, don't tell me you believe the crap about her feeding men to the pigs?" He laughed. "Then again, you're kinda stupid, so maybe you do."

Eulo clenched his fists, rippling frustration all the way up into his neck.

"Filia helps men start a better life, and she knows how to please a man, too. Some o' her tricks, I ain't never felt nothing so good."

A muscle ticked in Eulo's jaw. He didn't give a shit about what Krike's wife did to him in bed, or that their binding was happy. He wanted information. Seeing as he had nothing to trade for it, he needed Krike on an even keel. He batted away a trickle of jealousy. "Is the mighty Darley Krike falling in love?"

"I could be. When I find Pirin, she'll come live with us, too. We got nothing back home."

Krike really seemed to believe what he said. Not the words of a man working for the Scabmen.

Eulo shook the flask in his hand. The rum swirling inside it sent a shudder into his fingers. To someone with no parents, Filia Tartula must've been like the mother Krike never had. Ten years had passed since Pirin disappeared, though. Krike was sand-skulled if he reckoned he'd ever see his sister again. Blackness bored a little deeper into Eulo's heart. Would Eulo be like Darley Krike in another ten years, hanging onto the useless hope he could still rescue Remmy? If old Ruckus Juke didn't live up to his reputation first and kill Eulo for losing his baby brother.

He fumbled the lid off the flask, taking a swig of liquid fire to scour away the dark thoughts of his father and all his ignored advice.

"Always a killer," he muttered. The bane of having been a Covesman.

Too aware of Krike's newfound strut and posh clothes, Eulo hunched in his shabby coat. It didn't matter—under it all, they were still the same shitty men, who'd spent their young lives doing shitty things to other shitty people.

# Chapter 29

"Whassat?" Krike burped, gesturing for the flask.

"Nothing." Eulo passed it over, cursing him for being such a big bastard who could handle his grog so well. Still, Krike was pretty spoony off the household grog, so almost pickled enough to be useful.

Lantern light glowed around the stables, its warmth easing some tension out of Eulo's shoulders. No one but Tali understood the calm reassurance of resting animals and the scent of leather and horse.

"It stinks, eh?" Krike wiped his mouth with the back of one hand.

"Says the man running a piggery," Eulo replied.

"They're smart animals. Smarter than your cows, and worth their weight in gold."

Eulo rested his hand on the worn wood of the stable door. It swung open on fresh-oiled hinges. Huon had run around like a chook with its head cut off, getting ready for the Tartulas' arrival, almost more excited than anyone to have guests on the Sarsega estate again. Tali had invited him to share dinner in the house kitchen with Cailene and the Tartula's horseman. With any luck, they were still there. Huon's shrewd ears would start flapping if he spotted the two Iskarlians together.

"Your woman breeds a good type of horse, for sure," Krike said, peering at a handful of animals in for the muster.

"You'd know about it, would you?"

"Nah, I never liked 'em. Grumpy, dangerous and always hurtin' themselves at the wrong time." Krike screwed up his nose as they lurched on.

The pair of Tartula bays dozed size-by-side in their stalls, both resting hindlegs far thicker than those of any of Tali's horses. Where hers were agile and slender, the Tartulas' were solid and sturdy for pulling carts and carriages. Hay poked out of their feeders, so no one would be hanging around after having just fed them, or likely to return anytime soon.

"They say them Myrtis folk got the wind up 'em. Reckoned they already had their hands on this place, 'til your woman made other plans. That lot ain't putting no wings on your back, mate. Just hexes."

"Fuck 'em," Eulo said, meaning it. Tali refused to bend for the Myrtises, no matter what threats they made. He stroked the nose of the nearest bay horse, running his fingers over hard bone and velvet nostrils. All it took was a horse to swing its head the wrong way to knock a man senseless. Krike was right to be scared of them.

The tall man frowned at a smudge of dirt on his dark blue sleeve. He brushed at it, his brow furrowing when it didn't budge. Eulo smirked. Maybe wearing his plain workman's clothes wasn't so bad after all, instead of being pomped up and taught letters, the way Filia was doing to Krike. His veins warmed with the slow, familiar burn of the hunter. He was no woman's man. Eulo Juke rode the wind alone, and he had work to do.

He rested a hip against the wall and squinted at Krike. "D'you get into the Dross yet?"

Krike rubbed his neck. "It's hard. People know I'm Filia Tartula's husband. They don't trust easily."

Eulo unscrewed the flask, threw back a gobful of rum. When his agreement with Tali ended, he'd head north to find a way into the Dross himself and have a little chat to its tenants about getting hold of a few thousand kistars worth of kilili. A warning flutter in the back of his mind stopped him asking about Skramos.

Krike took the flask from Eulo. He tipped his chin, beard glowing red in the lamplight. "It's a strange feelin' coming here to become a man with no name."

"You got a name. You're Tartula's latest man." Eulo punched him on the shoulder.

Krike lurched forward, spluttering. He wiped rum off his chin, grinning. "No one cares about Filia's husbands anymore. Not when they can gossip about Tali Sarsega's."

Did they? Eulo shrugged to hide his surprise. "There ain't nothing clean about my skin." He stared at his blunt hands, the skin that told a story in ink and scars, now immortalised in a blade of greensilver. A surge of excitement tore through his chest, mingling with strength and nerves. All given to him by one woman.

"Mako's teeth, it's fuckin' cold down here." Krike dragged a pile of horse rugs off a nearby rack and dumped them in a heap on the floor.

Eulo dropped beside him, huddling into his coat, glad for the warmth of his cap. He dug a pair of gloves out of his coat pockets. More hand-me-downs from Huon. "I never owned gloves," he said, turning them over in his hands. "Never needed 'em." Not even when he'd gone deep into the Scarlands, where the Iskarlian desert baked during the day and froze at night. He liked the feeling of steel on skin, not the clumsiness of wearing gloves.

"Missin' home, eh?" Krike rubbed his hands together.

"I'd take wide open plains over another dinner party any day."

"Yep, you got it real hard here. What'd your old man say when you told him what you were doing?"

"I didn't," Eulo said. He'd just disappeared, same as Rem did. Too much of a coward to face his parents' reaction.

"Ruckus woulda been real happy to hear about it from Speer."

"Maybe Speer ought to keep his fucking mouth shut." Eulo bristled at the mention of the traitorous bastard. When he next saw him, Speer'd be lucky to walk away.

Krike nodded, or maybe he was too drunk to hold his head up anymore. "Everyone talks about Ruckus, y'know, like he's one o' Mako's best. Your Da's a legend."

He was a mean drunk who'd never watch the sun rise or see his wife's face again. Eulo pressed his fist into the stone floor. "I don't reckon the Cove has thought of him once since kicking him out of the troops."

"It weren't right. It made a lot of us stop and wonder why we were still there."

"And youse all stayed anyway, 'cause none of the cockies want fighting men round their sheep stations." Eulo knew well enough what a good mercenary he'd had to be so others wouldn't take his work.

"I don't give a shit about 'em anymore," Krike said. "I'm here now in the goddess land. Ain't never going back to Iskarlia."

Eulo glanced at him. "Who's lining Speer's pockets?"

"Speer?" Krike's eyes opened wide. "Why you asking me? He's *your* best mate."

"I reckoned so, too, 'til I found out he gee'd you up to get on the wifeship. He did the exact same to me."

"So what, someone wants the two of us out of Iskarlia? Or here in Vernesia for some reason? Maybe both." Krike furrowed his brows, mulling it over.

The same question Eulo kept asking himself. He'd still only thought of one answer. "Have you pissed the Scabmen off too?"

Krike tipped his head against the stable door, looking at the roof. "I ain't dumb enough to have any debts to those fuckin' bastards, but I did get in a scuffle with Navin last summer. The little maggot reckoned I rooted his girl."

Eulo gave a humourless laugh. Navin Cutter, Sif's youngest son, stirred up shit with people so he could claim they'd wronged the Scabmen and owed the gang a favour or money in return. He flexed his fingers. He'd be happy to sink starfire into young Cutter's back if he ever had the chance.

"You really reckon Speer would work for them?"

"Maybe he didn't have a choice." Eulo shrugged. It wasn't like a man did when one of his hands was forever folded in at the wrist, his fingers mangled and useless. Speer had been laughed out of the Grinders when he'd tried to enlist as a Covesman. With Eulo's help, he'd set himself up catching vermin with a pair of trained terriers. Maybe now he'd chosen or been forced into activities with bigger, nastier vermin.

"Where'd your girl get all her kilili snarls from?" Krike asked, off-hand.

"Fucked if I know," Eulo said, without lying. Until tonight, he'd had no idea about the room where they'd played snarls. Tali still hadn't let on where she got the kilili she smithed, either. "What about yours?"

"Gift from me wife. Kilili is its own currency, huh."

"Yeah." Eulo's flickerblade sat on top of his pack up in the cottage, ready to take mustering. In Iskarlia, the right weapon gave a man a name, notoriety. Just like his starfire had.

"You ever seen Sif Cutter's knife?" Krike asked. He dragged his finger through the air. "All blackmetal, hard as nails and sharp as billy-o."

Eulo hissed. The Scabmen chief had pressed the tip of that fuckin' knife into his throat, while Rylen Cutter, Sif's eldest son, stood his boot on Eulo's chest, demanding to know where their money was. It'd taken their whole gang four weeks to catch Eulo.

And one night to snatch Remmy.

No thanks to Lilla. Eulo cracked his knuckles. One day, the Scabmen would taste his revenge. They were elite warriors who roamed under the Cove's protection, armed with silveriron, supposedly keeping order in the south. Rylen had hooted his madman's laugh the day he'd forced Eulo to give up his starfire, lying on the ground with red sand stuck to the blood inside his mouth while the Cutters stood over him.

"Imagine the irony when I come to collect from you, Juke," Rylen had said, "by hooking you in the back with your own weapon." He'd draped the barbs of blackmetal over his palm. No one in their right mind mentioned the copper skin Ry Cutter had inherited from his Jalassan mother, because he'd just as soon slice your hand off with his goldsilver scimitar. The weapon matched the hue of his skin, like a savage extension of his arm.

Huddling a little deeper into the Vernese night, Eulo stared at the hay-strewn bricks under his boots. Krike's casual questions about the kilili in Tali's house made Eulo wonder if he knew more than he was admitting. He froze, with right fist against left palm, the kilili ring pressing against skin and bone. Maybe it wasn't a coincidence Krike ended up on the wifeship, spiralling in and out of the Sarsegas' life where he could keep watch on Eulo.

He snatched the cap off his head, twisting it in his hands. "Yeah, the Scabmen love kilili, don't they?" The fuckers valued it almost as much as their position and power in Iskarlia. He glanced at Krike from the corner of his eye.

The tall man fiddled one fingernail under another, digging at a line of dirt buried there. "Sometimes when I butcher the pigs, I see me hands all washed in blood. Hot, red blood, like what came out of all them people I hurt and killed."

"It's a soldier's lot. There ain't no secrets about that," Eulo said. A tic pulsed under his left eye. They all paid the price—kill or be killed. That's why most of 'em had signed up to become Covesmen in the first place. What would Tali say if she knew how many lives he'd stolen? All the deathfields he'd trod, the tracks he'd followed, the throats he'd slit. He rubbed his jaw. He'd sleep in the stables from now on, so people didn't ask so many questions after he'd gone. Tali didn't need to know who she'd tied her binding with, and when he left there'd be no more need to pretend.

An hour later, Eulo sprawled on the floor, beating the empty flask on the dirt beside Krike's newly scuffed and marked boot, in time to their raucous song. He threw his head back to bellow the next line. Shock rippled through his chest.

A silhouette blended with the shadows beyond the closest glow of lamplight. Eulo peered at the suggestion of long hair and the curve of a hip. How long had she stood there, listening to the men's drunken dribbling about their former lives? The flask dropped out of Eulo's hand with a clatter. Krike fell silent mid-chorus, confusion clouding his eyes.

"The horses might appreciate it, but don't stop for my sake." Tali's voice drifted like smoke from the silhouette.

Eulo wanted to wrap his arms around her, squeeze her tight against him and fu—

"—ck d'you come from?" Krike slurred.

Tali didn't reply.

Eulo beamed at her. He leant against the half-door, too boneless to rise. Behind him, someone ruffled his hair, their exhalation warm on his neck. Whiskers tickled his cheek, followed by breath as sweet as hay. He raised a hand, grinning as the Tartula carriage horse sniffed his fingers.

Krike rolled onto his hands and knees, clambering to his feet in a mess of long limbs. He wavered like a sapling in the wind, then staggered into a bucket. It clanged down the breezeway, drowned out by a thud as he face-planted onto the stone floor.

"Filia's asking for you," Tali said to the motionless figure. "She wants to go to bed."

Krike giggled, spidering his way upright. He stumbled towards the double doors, reaching out a hand to steady himself on the wall.

"Stay on the driveway, and follow the house lights," Tali called after him.

Eulo stared at her bare ankle, wanting to run his hand up her calf. And higher. His prick tingled. Then it sank faster than a scuttled ship. Useless.

Mako's teeth.

Tali's face smoothed in that expression he couldn't read. She burst out laughing, her chuckles cascading into rich, doubled-over hysterics. Squatting beside Eulo, she rested her hand on his arm.

"Looks like you get to ride home in the wheelbarrow," she said.

He laughed, too. He told this woman he could fall in love with her, in a mush-mouthed, spoony-drunk sort of way.

"Blazes, Eulo, you've had an absolute skinful. I can't understand a word you're saying."

"Sleep here tonight?" He remembered some far-off plan about doing that, for a reason he wasn't so sure of anymore. A yawn caught him, stretching his jaws wide. What he wouldn't give for a bed just now, draped in this woman's warmth.

"Good idea. I'll bring the blankets while you get yourself into the empty stall over the way." She kissed him on the lips. Honey bliss.

Sprawled in the sweetness of fresh-laid bedding, Eulo grinned as Tali settled a blanket over him. The edges of his vision blurred. He pitched into blackness.

# Chapter 30

Spluttering snores emanated over the stall door, breaking the early morning tranquillity and dashing Tali's hopes that Eulo was already up and ready for a long day of mustering. She nudged the door aside with her foot. Her husband remained spread-eagled under a mountain of horse blankets, more or less where she'd left him. He wasn't alone, either, with one arm flung over his bitch visitor.

She looked up at Tali from Eulo's embrace, her lips peeling open in a huge grin. Tali raised her hands in a gesture somewhere between amused and annoyed.

"Huon," she called, "I found your missing dog."

The stockman limped beside her to peer over the half-door. He shook his head at the red-speckled heeler, who thumped her tail against the floor. "So that's where y'are, you sneak." The bitch twisted around to lick Eulo's face with her long, pink tongue.

"Farkin' Mako." The big Iskarlian shot backwards in a rustle of hay, his torso writhing under the blankets. The bitch wiggled after him, wagging her tail even harder, enjoying the game.

"Enough, Blue," Huon growled. "C'mon, it's work time. We got cows to chase." A smile tugged at his mouth when he turned around to leave, the dog at his heels.

Still askew on his arse in the straw, Eulo peered through bloodshot eyes at Tali. He blinked. Squinted. Blinked again. "Looks like I got a new bed."

She chewed her lip, hiding a grin. He thought he was in trouble with her. "Well, dear husband, you weren't in a state to've been of any use in mine." His ears flushed red under the Iskarlian tan.

"I don't remember much after me n' Krike came down here," Eulo admitted in disbelief. He coughed, clearing the squeak out of his throat.

"Spoony drunk singing Iskarlian pub songs probably sums it up quite well."

"Ah. That'd explain why I ain't feeling the freshest." He rubbed his eyes.

Tali stepped closer to swing a water flask to him. "Huon is cooking breakfast on the fire outside." She paused, wrinkling her nose against the stench of stale alcohol bleeding off his skin. "He might spare you some hot water for a wash if you hurry up."

Leaving Eulo in his bed of straw, she strode off down the chill, sunless breezeway.

To his credit, he shambled out into the yard close behind her, squinting like a newborn calf in the dawn sunlight. Shirtless, he bent over the trough, plunging his whole head into the water. Rivulets streamed off his hair, tracing silver down the smooth muscles lining his torso.

"Close your gob, you don't want him to catch you dribbling, do you?"

Tali spun around, ready to flame Huon. He smirked, patting her arm.

"Don't panic, he's not going anywhere. Yet."

Her belly flipped. If only he knew the truth of his words. Words that snagged in her mind as she helped herself to a plateful of eggs and bread. Eulo ate with his usual enthusiasm.

She couldn't decide if she was happy having him along for the day, or because it meant he wasn't home alone near Mema. The warm pleasure in Tali's chest turned hollow. She didn't know what to make of the strange incident with Eulo and her grandmother last night. Suspicion swirled in her thoughts, although she didn't want to believe he'd hurt the old woman. Still, hurting people was what he did. She'd known that when she tied the binding with him.

After sending Eulo and Krike to the stables, she'd stayed at the house for longer. They'd finished the evening with the Tartulas after playing cards with Ranson and Filia, who'd been genuinely kind and decent. A possible ally, should she ever need one. Vivi even managed to lose some of her usual scorn when Tali convinced her to play a few games of snarls. It'd be back quick enough once Tali had to address Lenix Ces's interest in Vivi. She hadn't quite worked out how to do that, and she hoped approaching it once she'd been able to pay the Academy's audition fees would ease the discussion.

Now, though, excitement bubbled through Tali's veins. Thank Lolani to be heading out on the road again, with spring warm and happy in the air.

The household clustered on the front steps of the house to watch them leave, joined by the distinctive figures of Filia and Darley Tartula. Another man stood on the grass beside the path, holding the reins of his lean grey horse.

Tali's frown deepened with each hoofbeat. Annoyance with Eulo. Or herself, for not ever being sure what his intentions were. When she reached the house, though, surprise swept the anger right out of her. Someone had sat Mema in her chair on the gravel below the first step, cocooned in a yellow wool blanket. Eulo stood beside her, hitching one hip up in his at-ease stance. The grey gelding Cloud stretched his neck out to sniff Mema's knees, though he tilted back on his bunched hindquarters, ready to spin away.

Cloud flung his head up to look at Tali's approaching filly. The sharp rebuke vanished off her tongue as her own mount shied sideways. Familiarising the horses with a wheelchair wasn't something she usually included on her training schedule.

Gentle laughter drifted to her on the breeze. Apparently, everyone except Tali found her horse amusing. Biting her lip, she set the filly into spiralling circles to recapture her attention. She reined in her pride and the filly a safe distance away.

Eulo, meanwhile, regained Cloud's focus with a touch on the rein, quick and calm. Mema stretched out a trembling hand to the grey's face. The group watched, silent in anticipation. Filia's smile gave Tali the certainty she couldn't see herself—confirming her grandmother's pleasure in meeting the horse. Hot tears pricked her eyes. Poor Mema, locked inside all these years, away from the horses she loved so much. It'd taken Eulo Juke, of all people, to be the one to do something about it.

Tali pressed her tears away with a knuckle. What reason would he have to do this, after threatening the old woman last night? She struggled to make sense of what she'd seen, and Eulo's protest otherwise. Even if he didn't owe the family any loyalty, she didn't want to believe he'd lie to her.

Her husband glanced over his broad shoulder, catching her in his intense stare. He touched his hat-brim in a farewell to the group. They waved goodbye, except Ranson, who didn't raise his hand to Tali until after the others extended their well-wishes and "home safe"s to her.

Eulo and Tali trotted after the tail end of the mob, their horses floating across the rich expanse of grass to the dirt road.

"Great morning, eh?" He flashed a wide, white smile. The tan might've returned to his cheeks, but a hangover clouded his eyes and clung in the acrid tang of alcohol-sweat.

"You've certainly come a long way with my grandmother. Last night you were shaking her like a terrier with a rat, yet here you are this morning charming her and everyone with your blasted Jikah horse."

Eulo wheeled the gelding in a tidy rollback Tali would've admired if she hadn't been so stung with him. He sidled Cloud right up to Tali's filly, head to tail, grabbing the rein when the filly tried to startle away.

"How dare you." Tali kicked him in the leg, upsetting the filly even more. Her breath hissed through bared teeth.

He hung on to the rein, heedless of the jostling horses. "I've got no reason to hurt the old duck, even if I wanted. I took the horse to her because the pig wife asked me to." It wasn't anger in the gaze angling out from under his broad-brimmed hat. More…offence.

"You've just insulted two women. Are you going to try for a third?" Tali chopped the edge of her hand down on Eulo's forearm, trying to break his hold on her rein. Blazes, the man was hard as stone. "Let go of my horse and don't ever grab my reins again." She could handle a squabble. Upsetting her animals, however, bordered on unforgivable.

Eulo took a deep breath, as though fighting to settle his temper. A storm rippled across his face. He let go of the rein, leaving his dark blue gaze boring into Tali.

She threw her hands up in exasperation. She wasn't going to beg him to stay when their agreement lapsed, no matter how much she wanted to.

Their horses still stood close enough for Eulo to wrap his calloused fingers over hers, strong yet gentle.

It ate away at her to think Mema had spoken to him. She would've given her right arm to receive her grandmother's sharp wisdom again. Mema hadn't spoken in years. She couldn't, could she? And to an Iskarlian, rather than one of her own family. Maybe Ranson was right and she did disapprove of Tali's ways in running the estate. Except the old ways had changed, and so had the prosperous times from before Tali's birth.

"What did she say to you?" she asked.

"I can't tell you." Eulo fixed his gaze on his horse's ears. "I'm sorry, I can't say."

Her leg pressed against Eulo's as the horses sidled together. The filly squealed, snaking her neck out to bite Cloud on the neck, pushing him away.

Eulo's eyes darkened in a way Tali couldn't read. More irritating secrets and intriguing mystery. She touched her right shoulder, silently asking the kilili to stop the buzzing it started every time this man came close. She'd half-killed herself singing the mystic for someone who was a very good actor or hiding something from her—maybe both.

"Twenty-seven."

"What?" she stared at him.

"Twenty-seven Vernese women inspected me at the binding agency in Port Garnet." He looked away across the paddocks, mimicking their voices, "Open your mouth. Take your clothes off. Put your face between my legs. Have you worked in a brothel before? Turn around so I can whip you. Whiteskin. Beast. Insolent." He worked his jaw.

"I heard you were one of the rudest men they've ever had through the agency."

"I had to be, so none of those women insisted on taking me." Bitterness injected his words.

Tali's eyebrow twitched. "By swearing at them?"

He snorted. "'Come here, fuck me,' one said. So I told her to go fuck herself." His gaze swung back to Tali. "I'd just about decided to walk out of the place, when you strutted through the door and stared me down with that gleam in your eye. The only one who spoke Iskarlian to me. The only one I wanted to bind with, even before you made me the perfect offer."

"You'd already relinquished your right to leave," Tali said. Her hair lifted in the breeze, arranging itself wild around her neck. "I saw the contract they made you sign. If you'd been rude enough for every woman to reject you, you would've been offered up at a discount price to Mila Jei. She's madam of Silveraine's biggest man-fair. A man for every taste. Especially if you're partial to Iskarlians whacked off their heads on Strange."

Eulo's face stretched into a grimace. He rubbed his jaw, distracted, then managed an unsure smile. "D'you know that from experience?"

"Don't be stupid. I prefer mine seasick with a touch of bilah root."

He smiled, all lust and fire and rough edges. "Good."

# Chapter 31

The moon sat fat and round behind the hills, edging above the trees and into the sky, lighting Eulo's way home one final time. Like Lolani watching to make sure he knew the time had come. Earlier, he'd helped Huon and Tali muster the biggest mob of cattle across to graze the rich pastures on Glassrock Island, then drawn in his last views of the Glimmers pastures, pretending not to feel the burr in his heart. This might've been the closest he'd ever come to true contentment.

He frowned the thought away. What the fuck was contentment anyway?

Not something a man could have while his brother was missing because he'd upset the wrong moneylenders in Iskarlia. It wasn't something Tali Sarsega wouldn't get from a murderous goon, either.

Eulo groaned at the pinch in his muscles. His stabbed thigh flamed its complaint, too, but the stitches were holding, together with his thin story about getting hurt in a Gullwing alleyway scuffle rather than a death tussle.

Tomorrow he'd be back in the saddle, watching the full moon from a different view, through the eyes of a hunter. A thrill bucked in his chest, fading into hollowness for the feelings he'd grown for the woman who wasn't his wife. No matter what he'd tried to believe earlier, he'd allowed himself this stupid bloody weakness, even if Tali wouldn't look him in the eye when they made love. Her life would be quiet again once he left, drawing his would-be attackers after him and away from her.

Hunger nipping at his belly, he washed in the fast-cooling twilight air. Tali must've heard Cloud call out to the mare in the yards there, because she hefted a bucket of hot water and a towel out to the front doorstep as Eulo climbed the stairs. His heart twitched at the sight of her smiling from the door, leaning on the wooden frame with her hair loose.

Tali shut the door in his face, leaving him tired, sore and filthy beside the steaming bucket. Eulo peeled off his shirt, shaking his head in amusement. He could've fallen in love with her if Mako had handed him a different fate. The realisation shocked him more than the crisp Vernese evening on his bare skin.

When he went inside, Tali looked up from whatever she'd been reading on the table. The corner of her mouth quirked up.

"I didn't have any clean clothes." Eulo gestured to the towel he'd wrapped around his hips.

"You don't need them." Tali crossed the room in five swift steps. She slid one hand around Eulo's arm, kicking the door shut behind him.

His fatigue slid sideways, eclipsed by lust. She drew him over to the fireplace and turned her back on him as she skinned off her shirt. Naked from the waist up, she eyed him over her unbandaged right shoulder.

Eulo froze where he stood, caught in disbelief.

"Well," she drawled, deep and molasses-rich. Her gaze skewered him, dark with intensity. "What do you think?"

"It's a tattoo," he breathed. Not a wound, or even a scar.

A silver fucking tattoo.

Its lines and colour swirled from her shoulder to hip, catching the firelight in a kilili shimmer of silver shot with green.

All this time, Tali had been making herself a tattoo like nothing Eulo had ever seen. He reached out, his open palm trembling above her body without touching it, as though he was about to cross a line he wouldn't come back from. He let his hand fall to stroke the intricate patterns. Tali watched him, her skin warm and soft under his thumb.

"You made this, the desert dog?" he asked, tracing the symbol the way she'd traced his before she'd sung it into the metal of his flickerblade. A tremor rippled through his chest.

"Is it?" Her brow furrowed.

She guided his hands over her body, sliding one onto her breasts and the other past her unbuttoned waistband. His fingers slipped through the black curls into the silky depths between her thighs. After pushing her pants down, Tali twitched away Eulo's towel so her fingers could find his erection. She started to turn away from him, parting her legs.

"No," he groaned, catching her by the hips. He spun her around so her mouth was a handspan away from his. "I want to look at you. I want you to see me."

Tali caught him in a gaze as strong as spider's silk. She rested her backside on the armchair behind her, then swung her legs around his hips, her eyes burning into his. His heart sang in the certainty she knew how he felt about her. She nipped his bottom lip, hissing out a sigh of pleasure when he entered her.

"I saw you, Eulo Juke. I've seen you this whole time."

Eulo woke in bedsheets tousled by energetic sex, wrapped in the warmth of intimacy, of long deep kisses, and the green gaze he'd basked in the whole time.

He rolled over. A few strands of black hair lay on the empty pillow beside him. His chest tightened a hitch. Rain drummed on the roof, an impatient reminder that today was the first morning after the new moon.

The last morning.

Unless Tali had changed her mind. Eulo tumbled out of bed, scrabbling for clean clothes and socks. They could make another agreement and he could come back after he found Rem. He could be good to Tali. Him and Remmy could help her train the horses and restore the Sarsega homestead. How else was she going to manage it? Now was the time to stop denying he'd f–

"Fuck!"

In his rush to leave the bedroom, Eulo stubbed his bare toe on the door jamb. He hopped into the main room with his socks dangling from one hand. His wife sat so quietly at the table he didn't even notice her at first. A ring shining silver-green sat on the sheet of paper in front of her. Eulo's belly twisted hard enough to send a burn spiralling under his ribs.

Tali scrutinised him, so impassive he almost couldn't believe she'd ravaged him a few hours ago. He swallowed, facing the level-headed young woman who'd bought his services for her business one month ago. Not a wife, or lover.

"Fuck," Eulo cried out again, launching skyward at the sudden prick of needles into his other foot. He crashed against the wall. A ginger fluffball shot away in a scrambling escape across an armchair and behind the wooden chest.

Chance, the demon in a cat-skin.

"Righto." Eulo dropped into the chair opposite Tali, who hadn't even cracked a smile. After scanning the room to be sure Chance wasn't preparing another ambush, he bent to pull both socks onto his feet. When he straightened, she pushed the piece of paper across to him, followed by a pen and inkwell. He drew in a breath.

"This is it, eh?"

"This is the agreement to untie our binding. It spells out the terms under which you leave, being with Flame and—" She broke off as he dipped the pen and scratched his name beside her looping signature. "Don't you want to know what it says? I can read it to you if you can't—"

"I trust you." Eulo shrugged. He pressed the nib to the paper, shaping his letters how she'd shown him.

Tali waited a moment to let the ink dry. She folded the paper in half and slid it across to him with her ring on top. "It's best if you leave today. You can lodge the paper with the registry scribe in Oyster Point." Her relentless stare faltered, dropping to where her hands rested on the table. She cleared her throat. "I don't have enough coin to pay you as we'd agreed, but you'll be able to sell the rings for more than enough to cover it."

Regret gripped Eulo as he took his own ring off. He folded both bands in the agreement paper, tucking the lot into his shirt pocket with the identity papers Tali had finally given him. On impulse, he offered his upturned hand across the table to her. "Pleasure doing business with you, Miss Sarsega."

Smiling, she shook his hand, firm and brief like the first time they'd met. "Same." She rose, scraping her chair across the floorboards. "Huon isn't well so I'm helping with the horse work. I'll leave you to pack your belongings."

Eulo nodded, staying seated while she left the cottage. She appeared briefly through the window, pausing on the front porch to yank on her boots and oilskin, then strode down the muddy path to the stables without looking back.

"I'm going to miss you," Eulo said, reaching out his hand. Chance sniffed his dirt-ingrained knuckle with irrational suspicion before preening both ginger cheeks against it. He stared at Eulo and licked his lips.

"Yep." Eulo hefted his pack onto his shoulders, carrying a fair bit more than when he left Port Garnet. "You'll miss me too, cat, when you figure out you got no one to torment. You reckon Tali's going to put up with your shit?"

Chance licked his lips again, looking pointedly at the cottage's closed front door, then at Eulo.

"Nope. Both me and you got kicked out. Look after her, huh?" Eulo stepped out onto the path. His boots squelched past mist-blurred eucalypts. The rain hung in the air more than it fell, as bleak and resigned as his mood.

A trickle of guilt touched him as he reached into the hollow tree behind the horse yard, retrieving his stash of items for Remmy. Clothes, food, money and kilili. Tali hadn't asked him where any of it was. He stuffed the lot into his saddlebag, hoping no one would question why his pack was so full it strained against its buckles.

Down at the stables, he stopped under the eaves to flick water off the brim of his hat. Flame and Cloud were hitched in the breezeway, their coats spotless. Eulo leant his pack against the wall. He rubbed Cloud's neck in satisfaction when the gelding stood quietly to be tacked up. "At least one of us has learned some sense."

"I was about to say the same to you," Huon called out, hobbling over. "You made the right decision." Deep lines crossed his face, etching worry straight down to the bone.

"Decision?"

"To go, and let Tali get on with her life. Whatever trouble you're in, she don't need it here."

"Oh." Eulo scratched his elbow. So, Tali still hadn't come clean about the real reason for their binding. He blew a long breath out through his nose. It didn't matter anymore. He glimpsed her sauntering their way, with two cattle dogs jogging at her heels.

Huon glanced at him. "Do her a favour, and keep away from her, and from here."

"Blazes, even with the two of you the horses still aren't ready," Tali teased, her tone mismatched with the shadows in her gaze.

"I'll leave youse to it. Ride safe," Huon said.

After shaking his hand, Eulo continued tacking up the horses, working over leather straps worn soft and smooth. Tali watched in silence, her fingers light over the head of the blue dog sitting on her feet. She didn't ask where Eulo was headed, or what he'd do next, like she'd only come here to be sure he left. When he'd led both horses out into the yard, she held a calico bundle out to him.

"I raided the kitchen."

Eulo took it, surprised. "Thanks." His smile carved a slash from his cheeks to his heart. Before he could falter, he blurted, "You traded kilili for your Duskari horses. Would you do the same for me and take Flame back?"

"You're after kilili?" Tali's tone flattened. She squeezed the bridge of her nose. "Of course you are. It's the whole reason you're here, isn't it?"

He looked her in the eye. He wouldn't lie to her. "Yes."

Her eyelashes fluttered on her cheeks. "I have nothing else to offer you. Please go."

He didn't know how to say goodbye to someone who'd linked herself to him with a strange mystique he couldn't begin to fathom. Impulsively, he pulled her into his arms for one last embrace. Tali arched away from his hold, as unhappy as he'd ever seen her. He let her go, his heart sinking. She didn't want him, or his fumbling fuckups.

"Safe home, Eulo Juke."

Home, wherever that was now. Without a farewell kiss or last-moment confession of his weakness for her, Eulo closed his mouth and tugged the brim of his hat down in farewell. He led his horses out into the overcast day and the road away from Glimmers Gap.

A hunter free from binding or obligation, ready to finish what he'd come here to do.

# Chapter 32

A gust of wind hit the campfire, rolling over the coloured stones piled on a slab of granite between Tali's boots. Resting her forearms on her knees, she buried her face into one sleeve to avoid the disarray of smoke. When the wind backed off, letting the smoke curl beachward, away from her, Tali looked up. She let out a long, resigned breath, frowning at the liver chestnut mare trotting down the slope.

So much for coming here to be away from her family, where she could plan for the estate's future without interruption.

"Thank the skies you lit a fire, otherwise I'd have been riding around all afternoon trying to find you," Vivica called out as she halted her mare, Sonata, beside Tali's hobbled horse. She dismounted, her red shirt bright in the sunless day.

"She's stunning, Vivi," Tali said, raising a finger to Sonata, "I wish you'd agree to breed from her." Especially because the mare was Sepher's full sister, and she'd sold the only foal she'd ever bred out of Sepher to the Kestrine's stables.

"Honestly, this again?" Vivica's voice prickled. She lifted the lid on the billy can over the flames, squinting at the water inside. Settling on the grass, she waved at the stones Tali had been moving around. "How do the pebbles fall today?"

Tali chewed her lip, hesitant. Blazes, she had to give Vivi the benefit of the doubt at some stage. Pointing to the haematite on the far right, she said, "That's the old cows, who're in the top paddocks with Hammer." She slid a lump of quartz over the pile. "Whatever he doesn't get pregnant will go to the markets." She cut a half-dozen haematite stones out into a separate pile. "The young heifers are running with Bale, who'll give them smaller calves for an easier season, and the steers are on Glassrock." Her fingers walked over one pile then another.

She'd made sure they moved the steers across the channel while Eulo was still around. The problem would be having enough hands to bring them home after they'd fattened up over spring. Ranson and Vivi always refused to help with the saltwater musters. Whether it was a bad omen, or some kind of punishment for her mother leaving, Tali never knew.

"Here's me, Father and Mema, same as we've always been." Vivica tapped a long fingernail on the pyrite, agate and lapis lazuli, which lay together. Their mother's amethyst remained in the velvet bag she'd always kept the stones in until Tali inherited them. Vivi picked up a lone green aventurine. "And you, over here, all by yourself."

Close to a group of chalcedony—one each for the Glimmers Gap stallion, riding horses, broodmares and youngstock.

Tali nodded. She'd returned Eulo's opal to the bag with her mother's stone and the others she didn't need for now.

Vivi gently placed Tali's stone beside her own; the pyrite. In a careful voice, she said, "Did Eulo really leave you yesterday?"

"I suppose that's one way to perceive it."

Vivica glanced at Tali, her gaze softer than expected. "Oh."

Tali braced herself for a cutting, blunt criticism. It never came.

"I thought you'd be upset."

"I'm not."

Except she was, deep down. But why bother telling Eulo she cared about him, when he didn't want to stay anyway? She'd contemplated it, right up until the very last moment when he'd admitted he was only there for kilili, not her.

Vivi narrowed her eyes, perhaps wondering if Tali was lying. "Is he so stupid it took him a whole month to work out we don't have any money?" She sucked in a breath, her pupils dilating. "Sweet Lolani. I see, now. One month—just long enough to wreck Loy Myrtis's plans to solicit you. His mother could never damage her reputation by letting him bind with a woman who'd already broken bindings with someone else, let alone an Iskarlian."

Tali clapped, nodding. "No matter how much she wants to get her hands on Glimmers." She rose to her feet, stretching. From her pack, she produced two cups and a tin of dried tea leaves. Luckily, she hadn't emptied out the extra supplies she'd been carrying during Eulo's employ with her. She took the water off the fire and poured the tea.

"I saw Jikah the other week," Vivi said. "He's been telling people your horses are so bad your own husband won't ride one. So, I told a few of the girls a rumour that Jikah had pink scab, same as his horses." A devilish gleam lit her eyes.

"He's not my husband," Tali said, although she smiled, surprised by Vivi's sudden move of solidarity. When had they grown so far apart from each other? The smile faded because she knew the answer all too well. Everything had changed the day their mother walked out.

Vivica cradled a mug between both hands. "I know you think I don't know what's happening here because you won't let me look at the estate ledgers. It's obvious whatever money you're making from selling the horses and cows can't keep Glimmers Gap going."

"It will." Once Tali paid Vivi's fees at the Academy, she'd invest all their income into the estate and towards expanding her horse enterprise. More plans she wasn't ready to disclose.

"You're being ridiculous. Would binding with Loy really be so bad?"

"Why don't you try it and find out, then?" Tali pictured the idiot slipping over in his own urine outside the Ces binding in Oyster Point. Didn't Vivi realise how often Ranson met with Shilya Myrtis, trying to salvage the broken pieces of his scheme? She wrinkled one nostril. "If Myrtis doesn't take your fancy, Lenix Ces is ready and waiting for you."

"Mother never intended for me to tie a binding." Vivica waved her arms in protest, spilling tea out of her mug.

Tali chipped her boot-heel into the soft loam. Her sister's nostrils had flared at the mention of Lenix. "Mother's not the one who has to make decisions for our estate now though, is she?" She couldn't mask the bile rising on the back of her tongue.

"So, sell it!" Vivi swept up a handful of the coloured stones and shook her fist at Tali. "Sell the lot to the Myrtis bitch for three times what it's worth, so we can all move to Silveraine and get on with our lives."

"Glimmers Gap is our home. I'll never sell it."

Vivica laughed, high-pitched and verging on hysterical. "Blazes, Tali. One day I'll be as far away from here as I can get, Father, Huon and Mema will be long gone, and you'll still be sitting here in the paddock dreaming about your fucking horses, as cracked as Cyska, with that house crumbling into dust along with all your hopes for this place, and no one left in your life who gives a shit about you."

She flung the stones carelessly across the granite. Their mother's stones.

Tali dug her fingernails into her palms, forcing herself not to bite, forcing tears back from her eyes. Soon, she'd be the one juggling Ranson and Mema, as well as fighting to earn enough money to rebuild her stock and employ another stockman now Eulo was gone. All with the Myrtis's stinking breath on the back of her neck and Skylani Ces vying to manipulate her own arrangement with the Sarsega family. She closed her eyes. Those problems would have to wait until she'd sorted out the more urgent ones.

"You know, Eulo might've stayed if you weren't such a selfish fucking bitch."

"What?" Tali flinched at the venom in Vivica's words. Then the fire in her belly exploded. "That's ironic coming from someone who's been trying her hardest to chase him off."

Vivica lurched back. She pulled at one ear, her nostrils flaring. Tali levelled her in a flat stare, undecided whether the tears brimming in her eyes were genuine or not.

"He told you?" Vivi said at last, looking at the stones still lying where she'd strewn them. The aventurine winked beside the other stones. Her pyrite sat at a distance, alone. Dull without the sun.

Tali snorted. "He didn't need to. The difference with Eulo is I didn't bring him here to be loyal. I expected more from my own sister, though." She let a smidgen of Vivica's betrayal harden her gaze. "If you've come here to gloat, get on with it and get out of my way. I'm busy." Her kilili had grown full and strong again, ready for singing into more flickerblades. Maybe some snarls, too, and another set of binding rings, if she had enough strength left over.

"Yes, that's right. You're *always* busy."

"Well, maybe you and Ranson could lift a finger once in a while and help." Tali rounded on her. She gestured in the direction of the homestead. "But you'd both rather sit and mope in the house, complaining about how unfair life is instead of doing anything about it."

Vivi gasped. "That's what you're really angry about, isn't it? Not because your husband walked out of this mess, just like our mother did." She swiped a stray hair off her forehead. "Who do you think does everything for Mema, Tali? Dressing her, cleaning her, feeding her. Do you know how she used to pick on me when I was little? How she'd pinch and poke me, comparing all my weaknesses to all your strengths?"

A flush darkened her cheeks as words kept spilling out. "And who do you think gets our father out of bed every morning? You have no idea how much his grief for Mother cripples him because you're never around to see it."

Emotions tore inside Tali, slamming into the walls she'd been constructing ever since Adeline left and Ranson turned his back on her. "Then where does he find the energy to keep blaming me for Mother leaving? I was thirteen years old, Vivi. I was a child, same as you, but he's hated me every day since for something I couldn't stop. Nothing I do will ever be good enough for him, because I can never bring her back."

She turned away from Vivica's beautiful, furious face, throwing the dregs of her tea onto the fire, then kicking dirt over its spitting, sputtering flames.

"Did Eulo tell you about Lilla, too?" Vivica hissed. "He didn't touch me once, but I'm sure he got exactly what he wanted out of you. The question is if you got your money's worth out of him." She dropped her cup with a clatter and stalked off to her horse.

Tali bit her lip, watching her sister canter away in a fluster of long mane and tail, the two perfectly matched in beauty and elegance. Eulo would never have stayed with her. She'd opened herself up wide to him, trying to show who she really was, and he'd left without saying one word about it. Whoever the fuck Lilla was, let alone why Vivi knew about her.

While Tali's revelation of the sham binding must've thwarted Vivi's satisfaction in toying with her big sister's husband, her fleeting smugness was obscured by sorrow at the constant conflict with her sister and father, and the crushing weight of her remorse and responsibility.

She squatted to pick the stones out of the grass, unsure whether she'd ever been more alone in her life.

"Is this what you call early afternoon?" Cyska peered over the top of her spectacles at Tali as she arrived home.

Tali managed a brittle smile, pleased to find her aunt waiting on the front doorstep. "I was moving some cows and arguing with Vivi."

"Ah." Cyska raised both eyebrows. Although she didn't spend time with Vivica, she never fuelled the unease between the two sisters.

Tali swallowed. Now she'd confronted Vivi, she could put the last month behind her. "I'm glad to see you. Let me go make some kaif."

Once she'd boiled the pot, Tali carried their drinks out to the step, where Cyska sat stretching her arms in the sun. She reached for one of the mugs, inclining her head.

"Your wild hunter brought you a present."

Tali frowned at a lifeless bundle of hair on the worn planks beside the doorway. She picked the bush rat up by the tail, its fist-sized body swinging from her finger and thumb. "Chance is punishing me because Eulo's not here to torture anymore." Last night's present had been a turd next to the bed.

Perched on the railing, the ginger cat watched her fling the rat away into the scrub. He swished his tail. Tali sat on the top stair, wiping her fingers on her thigh.

Cyska snatched her hand, turning it over. Her mouth fell open. "Where's your ring?"

"With Eulo, wherever he is. We untied our binding."

"Giving those carping cows enough to gossip about for months at their dinner dances, eh? More Sarsega scandals."

"More?" Tali drew away from her aunt's grasp and searching concern. Her family lived so far away from Silveraine and the bigger towns they usually didn't provide much fodder for the gossip-mongers. She tucked her hands between her knees. People always loved to talk about frayed bindings, though. How one person had become disloyal to another.

How ironic that loyalty was symbolised by the Iskarlian desert dog, now shaped into her own skin by the kilili. The magic's doing, not hers. She hadn't even known it was there until Eulo told her—bemused how it matched his own Covesman inkings. Tali's throat tightened. Now she knew how the Cove's warriors stole into her country: right on the arm of rich Vernese wives just like her, and straight into their beds where their kilili tattoos were revealed. Lyselle probably thought she was safe too, until her Iskarlian husband killed her.

The forest blurred around her. She'd been so careful about hiding her tattoo, until her stupid ego pushed her to strip bare for the Iskarlian mercenary who'd walked away from her without looking back. She coughed, trying—and failing—to dislodge her unease. What would Eulo tell people when they asked where his flickerblade had come from? His face had filled with so much awe the first time he'd seen it. Unguarded, impressed.

The thrill she'd felt at the time was clouded now, her pride over-shadowed by the hindsight of bad judgement. All his questions about where to get kilili, and she'd never stopped to ask why. Never stopped to wonder if there was truth in Filia Tartula's accusations that Eulo had murdered Krike's sister.

"It's different, isn't it, when you make a piece for someone, rather than anyone?" Tali said, running her fingernail along a groove in the stair. "It's a hard secret to keep sometimes." Startled by Cyska's frown, she added, "I visited Grandfather in Gullwing. He never mentions

Mother, but he asked about you, and the rest of our family. I don't have the heart to tell him how much his granddaughters fight."

Cyska smiled, blowing wisps of steam off her mug. "Your mother and I were like you and Vivica, especially because Mema was always whisking me away to sing the kilili," she said. "Adeline loved you girls more than anything though, and she had such big plans for Glimmers Gap."

"By having me bound to Loy Myrtis and surrounded by cows?" Tali blurted. What would her mother say now, knowing her eldest daughter had shattered those long-held plans? Her mother, who'd had so many plans but left anyway. Her hackles rose when Cyska laughed.

"Oh please. Don't tell me you've still got it all back-to-front?" Cyska said. "Everyone assumed you tying a binding with Loy would've put Glimmers Gap into his mother's hands, when my dear big sister actually saw it as a way to expand the Sarsega boundaries. Adeline was plotting to take the Myrtises' land—not give them ours."

Blood rushed in Tali's ears. Ever since her mother's departure, all she could remember was the risk such a binding posed to the Sarsega's estate—a risk that wouldn't exist if her mother was still there. She stared into her kaif. In reality, her family were a threat to the Myrtis estate. It was so obvious, why hadn't she seen it?

"So that's why Shilya was so keen to push the binding through after Mother disappeared," she said slowly. When the solid foundations under the Sarsega family had begun to crumble, and Shilya Myrtis saw the opportunity to flip the situation. Tali lifted her chin, shedding relief like rain off her shoulders. "Thank the goddess I put an end to it, then." Now, at least, she could settle her constant doubts about impulsively binding to Eulo. They didn't have the Myrtises' land, but nor would Shilya have Glimmers. She might never find out where or why her mother had gone, but it helped to understand a little bit of Adeline's thinking.

"What are you going to do now? Go back to the dinners and dances? Skylani Ces remains desperately keen to send her eldest son our way. He's very eligible."

Tali jabbed an elbow into her ribs. "Lenix? Hardly." She tugged her earlobe, wondering how much to say. "I bought two Duskari mares."

"What?" Cyska's eyebrows disappeared under her fringe.

"A Duskari at the Gullwing sale bought one of my fillies. He wants a Glimmers Gap mare, too," Tali said. Ozar had presented her with a card inscribed with each mare's bloodlines in swirling handwriting. "The fillies are pregnant to different stallions. Eulo and Huon agree they're good types. I need new blood in our lines before anyone else in Vernesia thinks of it."

"No one else will do it, because the Duskari horses are too big for our people."

"I'm not just breeding them for the Vernese. There's interest in Iskarlia for good horses. I talked to Eulo about it, and your broken-nosed friend in Port Garnet."

Cyska threw the dregs of her kaif onto the dirt. "You were a busy girl over there, weren't you?"

"Talking about horses is what I do." Tali kicked her heel against the step. Those conversations in Port Garnet had only sprouted to life after Eulo told her stories about his homeland and encouraged her to follow her dreams. "Even if shipping horses over the Straits is too hard, plenty of Iskarlians here would be happy to ride something bigger than our local horses."

She backed down a little, reluctant to cause someone else she cared about to turn and walk away from her. "Please come to have dinner at the homestead tonight." The answer never changed, but she asked all the same.

Cyska rubbed the heel of one palm across her forehead. "Last time I tried, Ranson made it very clear I'm not welcome there."

"It's not his house!" Tali banged her mug down on the wooden step. "It's Mema's, and yours, and Mother's."

"No, it's *your* house now. The fact your mother walked away from us doesn't matter anymore. Ranson's been so blinded by bitterness all these years, he'll never stop blaming someone."

"She was ours, too."

"We can't change his selfishness in taking all the sorrow. What happened to Adeline wasn't your fault or mine. She chose to leave without any prompting. Our argument about doing the saltwater muster that day was bullshit—she knew that stretch of water better than anyone. She was just looking for an excuse." Cyska pulled Tali into a hug. "Her fate was what it was, my girl. Your father may not be able to move on from it, but we can. We have to."

Tali closed her eyes against a wall of tears. Only Cyska would talk to her about it and understand exactly how it felt to be blamed for causing someone so close to abandon her entire family. Her hands trembled, fuelled by disgust for her father's bullheadedness, and how he'd done everything in his power to banish Cyska from the family. He'd probably do the same to Tali, too, if he didn't need her so much. Deep down, she mourned the loss of both parents. How could a man blame his child for her mother's failures, and poison her sister against her?

"Let it go on the wind, my girl," Cyska murmured close to her ear.

Tali did, exhaling the storm inside her out with force. She opened her eyes in alarm as her aunt stood up.

"I have to go. I promised one of the drovers I'd have dinner with him tonight."

"Please tell me you're joking."

Cyska shrugged, grinning. "He's paying. I couldn't say no."

Tali's suspicions rose. "You didn't cut your hair for him though, did you?"

"What?" She parted her lips, ruining the fib by reaching up to smooth her feathered tresses.

"Don't think I don't notice how you have it styled each time you go to Iskarlia. Who's the secret lover?"

"Well, if I told you all my secrets, they wouldn't be secrets, would they?"

Tali cocked an eyebrow, the surge of curiosity rippling through her. Cyska the adventurer, with a spark of the wild unknown always gleaming in her eyes. It reminded Tali one of her own secrets needed attention. "Listen, Cyska, when you're in Silveraine, there's something I need you to do for me."

# Chapter 33

A dull mist shrouded the ocean, its brine-stung dampness clinging to the gelding's grey mane. Eulo shrugged the sleeves of his coat over his fingers, trying to coax some warmth into them. The weather echoed his gloom, shadowing him down the slope into Gullwing, where he hoped to find some silveriron and a way to get home.

After two unsuccessful days trawling for kilili up North, and another week lost since leaving Tali, he'd decided the southern port offered a better chance of finding what he needed. His horses plodded through muddy streets stripped of the festive colour of market-time. Thank Mako he didn't encounter familiar faces and their inevitable questions, although the empty streets left him exposed and notable.

He bypassed the main street, ignoring the instinct to head for the Albatross's familiar settings. The proprietors and guests in the smaller, quieter boarding houses were more likely to remember him, so he checked into Lolani's Anchor, the busiest, rowdiest hotel near the waterfront. The idea of Vernesia's sky-loving goddess being anchored was ridiculous, but the Iskarlian proprietors had stuck with their homeland's way of naming pubs. It hadn't hurt the establishment's popularity, at any rate.

Leaving the horses in the stables, Eulo pulled his hat low over his eyes and headed out. He passed a few permanent stalls in the main marketplace, continuing on to the ramshackle huts and lean-tos of the far alleys. Two dirty white dogs circled each other in the corner where he'd first met Leisik, their mange-thinned hackles raised. Fighting was part of their instinct, their nature. Eulo rubbed the cobweb of scars on his left hand. Not so different from the dogs, really.

"The old man ain't there," a woman called out, her voice harder than the splitting timbers on the shack walls.

Eulo recognised the big-breasted whore who'd propositioned him last time.

"D'you know where he is?"

"Need a new broom, do ya?" She winked, pushing a lock of greying hair behind one ear. She shrugged. "I haven't seen him for days."

"Thanks anyway."

"You'd be better off coming when the markets are on. He never misses them," she said. "It's pretty quiet 'round here otherwise, 'less you already got business." She laughed, a spark of warmth in the late morning. "And I've always got business in a port town. You'd be surprised how many men off the ships just want a woman to listen to 'em talk while she lies with her arms around 'em. No matter how big and tough they act, I never met a man who doesn't want a good woman to love him." She fixed him in a knowing stare.

Eulo rubbed his jaw, caught off guard by a flash of how much he'd laughed with Tali, how much he'd wanted her to like him. He traipsed back the way he'd come. First, he'd find Daf Korin, the other seaman who sailed between this stretch of Vernesia and Iskarlia. Then he'd look for Skramos, the darkship captain who must be working with the Scabs. Someone had to know about covert movement of people and kilili in and out of Iskarlia.

Evening shadows ran long through Gullwing's alleyways, the incoming sea breeze carrying traces of saltvine. Eulo stretched his arms until his joints popped and loosened, keeping watch on the dilapidated pub. Workers drifted in and out without rhythm, their bodies bowed by a day of hauling cargo or tailoring clothes for rich and fashionable Vernese.

The pub would've fit straight into Iskarlia, where acceptance was earned by the glint in someone's eye or the pride bracing their spine, no matter what the colour of their skin. Men and women gripped mugs in hands ingrained with as much dirt as their faded shirts and pants, their creased skin and thick arms hinting at the hard, cheap labour they'd be employed to do. The women's bare faces and scraped-back hair were a long way from the extravagant dignitine's clothes and makeup Eulo encountered during his time with the Sarsegas.

A dog barked somewhere to the east, where the sun melted behind the horizon. Eulo's guts rumbled at the scent of roasting meat. He hadn't found out much from Daf Korin's first mate, aside from him swearing black and blue Skramos was in that pub right now.

"Hey, friend." A youth strutted out in front of him, wearing a gap-toothed smirk. "Don't s'pose you could spare a coupla splinters so I can get some eggs for me Ma?"

"Ain't no such thing as spare money," Eulo growled, sidestepping the lad in one smooth movement.

"Ah, come on, surely you can help a brother out?" The youth skipped after him, ducking into his path again.

Eulo bared his teeth. "You ain't my brother, and I got better things to do than help out smart-arsed scabs in the gutter. You got to help to be helped." He extended his arm, sweeping the youth aside like he was swatting flies.

"I can help you. My sister's a real looker."

"Fuck off."

"I'll help you. Help you get your smart mouth reshaped by the Scab-men."

Eulo spun on his heel, stalking back to the startled youth. "Yeah? Then go tell Cutter I'll see him as soon as I'm ready." He tipped his head from left to right, cracking the tendons in his neck. "Wouldn't want to keep him waiting."

Quick as silver, the youth flung a handful of sand into Eulo's eyes. By the time he'd scrabbled his vision clear, the youth had scarpered.

Picking up his pace, Eulo shouldered through people muddled along the way. At home, he was skilled at blending into his surroundings. Here, his size and impatience stuck out. He bowled along, swinging around the corner. He didn't see the woman until he was lurching sideways to stop himself colliding with her. The mutter of an apology died on his lips.

The woman barring Eulo's way held a wooden pole in both hands, her blue gaze dark under a sweep of pale hair. A tic flickered under her left eye. The breeze rippled through her pants, the same homespun linen her bodyguards wore.

"I reckon you've come far enough, handsome, don't you?"

She adjusted her grip on the pole, tension from her biceps running through the sinews in her forearms. Feet braced in the mud, reinforcing her intent to stop Eulo from going any further. A pair of thugs lurked to either side of her, lifting their chins in open challenge, like scrubcats readying to fight. One Iskarlian, and a Vernese with a long black plait down his back. Neither was familiar.

"Lilla?" Eulo raised the palms of both hands. "What the fuck?"

The woman's eyes rolled white, weighing him up the same way he did her. Her guards shifted and fidgeted, ready for action. If Eulo wanted to scuffle, they'd kill him on the spot.

"Dear deluded Eulo." She parted her lips in a *pah!* of contempt.

"You reckon you're any different to the other Iskarlians who gammon some hopeless bitch to get onto a wifeship, thinking they're on a ride to the honeyed land? You're all the same—men who get stir crazy when they're not out killing other men for the name of war, hunting a satisfaction they'll never find." She shifted the pole, keeping it between her and Eulo. "Doesn't your pretty little wife mind you leaving her at home, all alone?"

He cracked his knuckles. Lilla must've seen him somewhere with Tali, seen how much he cared about her. "I want my brother back."

"Maybe he doesn't want you to find him. Maybe he's still alive, for now, waiting for you to pay your fucking debts to my father. Time's run out, Eulo. What you got for me?"

Eulo's nape prickled. It was too soon for the Cutters to be chasing him. Not 'less they'd decided to change the rules again. "Sixty days, your Pa said. I'm getting the kilili."

"More hollow promises, and more reason not to trust you."

"Remmy ain't done nothing wrong by you, or your family. He don't deserve this."

She laughed. "I know that. It's a shame you didn't work it out yourself, before you decided not to pay back what you owe. If anyone's to blame for his situation, it's you." The shifting wind caught her shirt, pressing it against her swollen abdomen.

Shock spiked Eulo in the chest. "Got yourself up the duff at last, eh Lil? Who's the lucky father?"

She cupped one hand over her belly, smiling with pride. "Not you, thank Mako. You were right about Speer though. He's a good man."

"Speer?" Eulo's eyebrows rose. His old friend had been busy. "What'd old Sif say about that?"

"Who cares? He's too busy making stupid plans with my stupid brothers," Lilla said. "Messed up as the Vernese are, they're smart to give women all the power. Shame we don't live here, where Ma and I would be in charge of the Scabs with an extra forty thousand kistars-worth of kilili in our pockets."

"You already got my weapons from back home," Eulo pointed out. "The starfire alone is worth seven thousand, at least." He stared her down, his lip curled and blood rushing.

"You're in a society run by women," Lilla said, like she hadn't heard him. "Women who have money, power and independence to do what they want. Who walk like your wife, talk to people like she does. The Vernese men hunger for those women and their status and security." She sighed. "And if they prefer to lust for an Iskarlian lad as pretty as

Remmy Juke, there are people who will cater to them."

Her biting words reminded Eulo of the young Drosswoman offering herself to him in the roadway, the day he'd arrived with Tali, and the Vernese whoremonger from the wifeship. He squeezed his forehead, trying to press away his clamouring thoughts. His blood ran cold at the idea of his brother being violated by men.

"No one would smuggle Remmy here, not if it risks putting their neck on the Kestrine's chopping block," he said at last, not really believing it.

"Don't you understand that it's not really Remmy we want? He's just the bait." Lilla relaxed her grip on the pole, reaching up to flick her hair back.

In that heartbeat, Eulo launched himself at the Iskarlian thug, driving him into the wall. The Scabman's breath whooshed out of his lungs. Eulo rammed him again, this time grabbing a handful of brown hair to crack the Scab's head against the stone.

Once, twice, moving fast before the Scabman could land a blow on him. The bastard opened his mouth but couldn't say much through a gaping maw of broken teeth. At last he crumpled, his face painted in blood. Darkness and fire surged in Eulo's chest. He leapt over the Scabman's body, going for the plaited Vernese. They both grunted, flailing against each other.

Eulo pulled the sheathed flickerblade loose from his belt. He launched into the air, using the Vernese's left shoulder to push himself up high. He slammed the knife hilt down into the back of the thug's skull with the full force of his body behind it. He didn't have to kill this fucker to beat him. The Vernese roared as he pitched over, catching Eulo's left hand on his way to the ground. They rolled through a puddle of muck, its stench stinging Eulo's eyes as he clobbered the man again.

The Vernese shifted.

Eulo's blow bounced off his bicep. Grunting as the thug struck his cheek, he fought to dig his heels into the ground and flip the wiry bastard off him. In the chaos of arms and legs, he drove his right hand down, still with the blade in it, gasping out relief when the hilt sank into the persistent fucker's abdomen. The Vernese was lucky he didn't fall with his guts full of silveriron.

Eulo hammered down, again and again, forcing the man back. He spun, firing the palm of his left hand into the thug's nose. A crunch and cry pierced the sound of their panting. Eulo's pulse thundered as he stumbled and fell backwards, losing his footing with the Vernese on top of him. He booted the keening man away and flipped over onto his hands and knees in the muck, sucking air into his heaving chest. He grovelled in the dirt, scrambling to find his blade.

A shadow fell over him.

"You got one last chance, handsome, if Krike don't beat you to it first," Lilla crooned. "I met him earlier at the Albatross. He reckons he's got a good source of kilili, and he'll take it with or without your help."

"What the fuck did you promise him?" Eulo said. "That you got his sister, too?"

Lilla's tongue darted over her lips. "Pirin Krike saved up every splinter she had to get on a ship to Duskari. She never told you or Krike because you would've forced her to stay in a country that offered her nothing."

Stunned, Eulo wiped the back of his mouth with one hand. Pirin, leaving without telling anyone? And Lilla, the bitch, had kept it a secret all this time, letting Krike suffer in the black unknown. Letting everyone blame Eulo for somehow being responsible.

"I wonder what your rich little wife would say if she knew about the mess you're in. How many pairs of kilili earrings does she own? How many necklaces?" Lilla asked. "Does she look at you the way you look at her?" She turned Eulo's flickerblade back and forth in her hand, ignoring its squeal of discord. "Maybe I'll go ask her myself, eh?"

"I hope she cuts your shrivelled black heart out." Eulo spat venom and blood across the ground.

He glanced up right as Lilla's boot drove heel-first into his face.

F**uck.**
*Fuck.*

Eulo sprayed red drool into the darkness beside his boots. He swiped a hand across his mouth as he staggered on, his steps echoing off the dog-eared fences lining the laneway. Fire lit his right knee when he moved, the old injury angry, awakened after being caught under the weight of two falling fighters. None of it helped the still-healing knife wound in his thigh. Even the horse-piss soaking his clothes didn't made him as angry as the boot print on his jaw. Eulo hawked in the back of his throat, slicking copper across his tongue.

Suspicion writhed in his belly like a cut snake. He should've been able to make sense of what he knew, but the more he reached for it, the quicker it trickled out of his grasp. Like hunting for a speck of gold in a desert of red sand.

The stench of rotting vegetables smothered him as he stumbled along the laneway, pressing his fingertips against the pub's stone wall. His belly lurched and he doubled over, gecking up. The sour taste of vomit in his throat forced him to retch again, bringing up another spray. He stared at the puddle of dismayed realisation between his feet. A long strand of drool hung off his lips, swaying in the breeze.

He'd been wrong.

This whole time, the great fucking hunter Eulo Juke had been chasing the wind. He'd been gammoned. Again. Eulo Juke, the great fucking idiot.

He scrubbed his mouth and nose against his shoulder, smearing wet muck on the brown shirt. He ached to have Tali's wry reassurance beside him while he found his way out of this mess. Shades, he missed her.

A quick check of his pack confirmed Lilla had walked away with the necklace he'd pilfered from Tali's cottage, and the trinkets he'd lifted from the various places he'd visited since arriving in Vernesia. Worse, Lilla also now had Eulo's flickerblade and the gold one he'd taken from the dead assassin weeks ago when he'd been here with Tali. Somehow, she'd missed the binding rings tucked in his shirt. Maybe it would've been better for her to have taken them, to bring his debt down even more.

Eulo lurched away from the chunder at his boots, setting off with fresh determination. Much as Lilla loved to brag, he didn't trust her to stay away from Tali. He had to get back to Glimmers Gap, and fast.

# Chapter 34

It had been so long since anyone had knocked on the front door, Tali almost didn't register the sound. Yawning, she turned the faded brass handle and swung the heavy wood inward to reveal whoever had come visiting in the middle of the night. The air fled her lungs when the person grinning on her doorstep came into focus.

"What in blazes are you doing here?"

He took her. Reaching out through the darkness to clamp a wet rag across her mouth and nose before she could turn to run, her reactions slowed by surprise. Strange: a sickly smell Tali knew from the one time she and Rith tried it in Silveraine. The drug subdued her too quickly, riding into her lungs on sudden, sharp gasps for breath. The night folded over her as she collapsed in the doorway.

Tali's thoughts bounced against each other as she grasped for the reality of her situation. The lingering Strange blurred her senses into a kaleidoscope of colour and smells. She'd woken to warmth pressed against her chest, a body moving in rhythmic tempo, rising and falling first at her chest, then the hips.

Terror sapped the strength out of her limbs. She fought for breath against whatever was jammed in her mouth, retching against the thick dryness on her tongue. Air whistled through her nostrils, sharp and rapid.

*Her nostrils!*

Blissfully working just as the goddess had intended. Tali struggled against the panic threatening to unravel the edge of her mind. Stale heat clogged her lungs, its hessian taste coating her gums. A familiar animal stench. Roughness on her cheeks, her forehead, her neck. He'd bagged her head.

The body pressed against her. Up, down. Up, down.

*Clip, clop. Clip, clop.*

A horse.

Tali must've been thrown over its loins like a slaughtered beast. Fire twirled through her muscles as she wriggled her limbs. She'd hung here for a while, then. Moving her feet apart, she waited for a rope to pull tight around her ankles. It didn't. Pain seared down her back to her bound hands, which hung below her head.

She strained her ears. An owl hooted somewhere way off, singing its nightsong.

*Clip, clop. Clip, clop.*

One horse.

No doubt he was sitting in the saddle that dug into her left arm, having bundled her onto his horse like a sack of potatoes going to market. The fucking bastard. Rage exploded through her body, scouring away her fear. Tali laced her fingers together, drawing tension into her limbs. This ended now.

She raised her arms, begging Lolani's forgiveness for belting her entwined fists into the horse's belly. The startled animal leapt forward and—as Tali hoped—out from underneath her.

Although she'd intended to land on her feet, her strained muscles failed and she collapsed to the ground below a melee of hammering hoofbeats and shouting. Tali pressed her knuckles into the damp earth, driving herself upwards, gritting her teeth at the pins and needles torturing her limbs. She grabbed a handful of the pigshit-scented sacking over her head and tore it free, along with a good hunk of her own hair. Trees loomed overhead.

The tall man launched at her, his limbs exaggerated by the play of shadows in the overcast night. His mouth gaped open in a close-cropped beard. Tali hissed through her teeth. Her heart raced as she ducked Darley Krike's outstretched arm. He caught her by the shirt, pulling her off balance.

"Now girlie," he gasped, his breath hot against her ear, "don't be difficult on me."

Tali flung herself around like a cat caught by the scruff, driving her heels back into his shins. She tangled her fingers together, clamping them against the stone she'd palmed when she fell. "You fucking coward."

"They're waiting," Krike said. "Debts to be paid."

"What debts?" Tali's world spun. When he clutched at her arm, she swung her bound hands at him with all the force she could muster.

He choked out a breath as her stone-weighted fists slammed into his throat. It wasn't his forehead, but it'd do. Swinging again, she hit his right temple.

Tali bolted, shouldering through the dense undergrowth. Thorns and branches clutched at her hair and clothes, threatening to hold her back for Krike to find. The air filled with the harshness of her laboured breath. One moment she ran mid-stride, the next, the ground fell away. She flipped with a belly-dropping lurch. Unable to splay her bound arms, she sprawled heavily onto her hip, coming to a halt in the leaf-litter. Honeyspiral sweetened the crisp air. Krike must've brought her east, towards the coast.

He hollered, his shouts getting louder while Tali lay like a hopeless drunk. Terror pressed against her bladder. She rolled over, scrambling to find her feet in the slippery grass. While she knew this country far better than Krike ever could, Tali cringed at the racket of her boots crunching through dead leaves and snapping unseen twigs in the darkness. Easy signs for a trained warrior to follow.

Whoever he was talking about obviously wanted kilili, and he meant to give her to them. Panic trembled through her whole body. Was Eulo part of this?

She left the undergrowth behind, able to run faster on the dirt road dividing the tree-covered hills on her right from low scrub to the left. The rich tang of green grass and cow shit skimmed her nostrils, somehow reassuring in its familiarity. The Heartbreakers stood tall against the star-spattered sky, their craggy cheeks confirming Tali hadn't been taken as far from Glimmers Gap as she'd first assumed.

No one else shared the overcast road. This land was too dense to farm or domesticate. Splendid isolation. Or not. She cried out, skidding to a halt as a figure blundered out of the forest in front of her. Panting, she edged away, then dashed towards a rift in the trees.

Tali's precious breath escaped in gasps and grunts. Colours burst through her head, filling her mind with flashes of starfire—Eulo's weapon. The gravel slid out from under her feet, sending her falling to her hands and knees.

"Mako's teeth, woman, would you fucking well stop?" Krike growled, stalking closer.

Twenty paces.

Nineteen.

Eighteen.

He advanced on her, a hunter determined to catch his prey, his mouth a slash across his face. She wouldn't survive to see morning.

Tali scrabbled at the blinders flowers growing at the roadside. She crushed them, petals and all, between her fingers. Her hand tingled. She lurched to her feet in time to confront him.

"What do you want from me?"

"The Scabmen want kilili. To trade for things. People. Eulo's debts," Krike blurted, panting. "I don't...Eulo should've...it weren't supposed to be this way," he growled, flicking his gaze sideways. His lip curled.

"It won't be," she hissed, driving her knee into him. He made an oofing noise, doubling over with both hands clapped to his crotch. She swiped her fingertips across his face, dusting the crushed blinders flowers into his eyes.

"Fuuuu–"

He roared, staggering back from her, rubbing both hands across his eyes and cheeks. Tali didn't bother telling him it would only make the blinders much, much worse.

Instead, she ran.

Into the cover of the forest, up the hill back to the road, where the goddess must've been smiling on her. Krike's horse grazed the roadside, waiting where he'd been left. Tali urged her aching body into the saddle, cantering west on the trail they'd just come down. Further along she came to a familiar creek—one on the road between Glimmers and Gullwing. The Scabmen must've been waiting in the port town for Krike to return with her.

When Tali was confident she'd left the immediate danger behind, she slowed the horse to a trot, using the stars and the far-off spine of the Heartbreakers to guide herself home. The rush of anger and panic ebbed away from her with each mile, leaving her body heavy with fatigue and her mind addled from the Strange.

She readily accepted that Krike wanted to trade her kilili to someone, but it was Eulo's involvement she struggled with. Over a week had passed since they'd untied their binding. Sifting through her Strange-veiled recollection, she had to admit Eulo would've acted before now if he was going to betray the secret of her silver tattoo. If he'd meant to dishonour their agreement, he would've robbed her estate and left before their first week was up. She never would've revealed the kilili to him in the first place if she believed he'd harm her.

With each mile that passed on the way home, Tali became more determined to grab Eulo Juke by the scruff of his neck and find out what in blazes was going on.

Her tattoo thrummed with indignation. No man would hold a Sarsega woman down. She wouldn't let anyone risk her family and estate, especially not now she was on the verge of seeing through her plans. When she got home, she'd go straight to Cyska and tell her everything, and together they'd figure a way out of this fucking mess.

Fatigue sharpened to a fine point of pain where she'd wrenched and wrestled her limbs during her escape. Fucking Krike. If he was lucky, the effects of the blinders flowers might be starting to wear off now. When it did, would he come looking for her again?

Her heart raced when she considered where he'd intended to take her. To someone she wouldn't have chosen to go to herself. Someone who valued kilili more than life itself. If Cove Vasker's Scabmen were hunting for it, every kililismith in Vernesia was in danger.

Smoke tinged the valley below the Starsfall Ranges, acrid in the forest air. Heaviness grew in Tali's belly as she neared home, spasming at the sight of a grey column rising above the eucalypts on the ridge. Kilili tingled on her shoulder, spurred by the dread in her bowels.

It took an excruciating time to reach the Glimmers Gap boundary, but Tali pressed Krike's weary horse on, cantering up the track to Cyska's. Blackness coloured the billowing smoke here. It felt wrong, *smelt* wrong—not the sharp campfire scent Tali knew so well. They'd barely passed mid-spring; far too early for bushfire to strike the lush undergrowth and pastures.

*We're safe here, aren't we?*

She crested Bald Hill, reaching Cyska's cabin. Gold flames stroked wooden slats, seducing the dry tinder to catch and burn. A figure lay across the doorstep, arms outstretched, black hair skipping over her bare torso and torn, blood-stained shirt. Cyska's bay mare, Vane, spun and wheeled in the yard beside the cottage, screaming out to Tali's mount, desperate to find reassurance with other horses.

Tali leapt out of the saddle, running up the cottage stairs on unsteady legs. Whimpering, she fell to her knees. Blood smeared Cyska's arms, painting her lips red where it had risen out of her mouth. Tali reeled. Someone had butchered her aunt's back, peeling a big square of skin off her ribs and muscles where a silverviolet tattoo should've covered the oozing flesh and white bone.

Cyska groaned, her eyelids fluttering.

"What happened? Who did this?" Tali demanded, cradling the woman in her lap.

"Men waiting for me...you..." Cyska's words rustled on her breath. Blood bubbled on her lips. "Don't...go...Eulo...don't trust...Iskarlians."

"Iskarlians? Which ones?"

Cyska's breath caught, stuck in her throat, making her gag. She keened for a terrible moment that didn't end until she sagged in Tali's arms.

Tali's grief echoed in the forest. She ran trembling hands over her aunt's body, wanting to soothe and heal. Unable to do either. She scooted backwards on her arse, falling onto her elbows, rolling over to vomit into the saltvines growing wild around the cabin. Leaves clamoured at her, revealing flowers crimson as blood. Tears trickled off her nose and chin.

"The sky for her soul," Tali whispered, the words bitter in her mouth. She pressed two fingers on her left eye then the right. "Safe home, Cyska."

Pushing through the squall of tired muscles in her limbs, she opened the gate, letting Cyska's bay mare, Vane, out of the yard. Tali dragged herself back onto Krike's gelding and spurred the horse into a gallop with her hands knotted in his mane, pleading him to be fast enough to reach the house before anyone else. He lurched down the home hill, his mane streaming over Tali's fists. Vane galloped ahead, holding her tail high. The wind whipped tears out of Tali's eyes, leaving her breathless.

Hoofbeats drummed through the morning. Another horse burst out on the track ahead, the rider's head and face obscured by a hood, but Tali knew who it was just by looking at the grey gelding. That fucking grey horse. She dug her fingernails into her palms. More trouble Eulo was notching up. He'd however be the one explaining to Loress Skylani why he still had Cloud, not Tali.

"You're alive. Thank that fuckin' bastard Mako," he called out.

She reined her horse back to a trot, her limbs singing with terror. "What the fuck is going on. What have you done?"

He pushed the hood back, revealing one blackened, swollen eye and a deep frown. "I got trouble with the Scabmen. I owe 'em money, and they want the debt paid in kilili."

A muscle rippled in his jaw, the hard ridge of bone she'd nuzzled and kissed. A mouth full of lies.

Dread leaked a vast, terrible sadness through Tali's chest. "Did you tell them about me? That I was here?"

Eulo's mouth dropped open in astonishment, or a good mimic of it. "No," he shook his head, "you got it all wrong. Soon as I found out, I came to help you."

"What in blazes makes you think you can help me?" Tali rounded on him, threads of greensilver steeling her words. "There's nothing safe about you."

A red flush crawled across Eulo's cheeks. Now, finally, his unrelenting stare broke. He glanced away, his voice low. "I made a mistake."

"Oh, I know all about mistakes." Scorn curdled her laugh. "Seems like I made an enormous one when I got bound to you."

"I'm sorry. I never meant for this to happen, for the Scabmen to show up."

Tali didn't bother picking apart his tone and words, to wonder if he meant it. Sorry was such a hollow word, something easy that people said to each other as though it excused them from being utter shits. She brushed her fingers over the knife hilt on her hip, seeking reassurance. "I never questioned you. Not once. Now I'm wondering, what might've been different if I had?"

"I ain't told a soul about your tattoo. I swear it in Mako's name."

"You swear it in the name of the demon god of chaos, who your people love so much?" She bared her teeth. "Because someone fucking well told them, and they set your idiot friend Krike after me." Was this blood-spattered man really the same one who'd charmed her in Port Garnet and slid into her life with unexpected pleasure?

Tali wheeled her gelding around, glancing back as she urged the horse into action. "My family need me. What I have left of them, anyway."

He followed her as she barrelled down from the forest into a skidding halt on the grass outside the house. Tali leapt up the stairs, holding her own flickerblade, which she'd found in Krike's saddle bags. She half-opened the door before common sense pulled her up. Her heart pounded against her ribcage. Moving one foot after the other, she strained to hear any hint of who was inside and what they were doing. Her hand trembled, making the blade waver.

Before Eulo had the chance to take the lead, she stepped inside, moving down the hallway as quietly as she could.

The dread butterflying inside her chest exploded the moment she encountered Huon Ahmela in the great room. Sunlight fell through the open front door, laying a golden band across his feet and legs. Crouching, Tali slid her clammy fingers onto his neck to feel for a pulse. She recoiled from a gelatinous sensation on her fingertips, staring from the red and grey slick on her skin to the shattered mess of what had until very recently been the right side of her stockman's skull.

"Shades," Eulo murmured, faltering to a stop beside her. He squatted over Huon, tilting the stiffening corpse to probe at the hole where the side of the stockman's skull had been.

Tali's belly roiled. "Do you have to do that?" No matter how hard she clutched her hands together, they wouldn't stop trembling. She looked up at movement coming down the stairs; a young Vernese and an Iskarlian woman. The woman's laughter tapered off as she registered Tali and Eulo's presence.

"Hello handsome," the blonde smiled, moving slowly now, coming down one step after another. "Brought the rest of your payment for me, did you?" Her brown gaze slid across to Tali.

"Fuck you." Eulo's blade slid free from its sheath with the dull sound of steel.

"You already did and you weren't that good." The blonde snorted. She gestured to his blade, crooning, "Come on Eulo, show your wife how you treat women. You're prepared to kill me to save her, aren't you, because she's bought your love with her fancy clothes and big house and money."

Eulo braced his shoulders. "She's a good person. Not like you, Lilla."

Without looking away from him, the blonde woman pointed one finger past her Vernese accomplice to the other side of the stairs. He nodded, moving away from her, forcing Tali to glance from one to the other, wondering who posed the greater danger. The blonde, Lilla, advanced on Eulo, wielding a flickerblade.

Its off-key kilili whispered a tune Tali knew too well, its silver-green colour darker in the patterns she'd smithed into it for Eulo mere weeks ago. Her tattoo hummed in return.

She stormed the woman, hoping to catch her unprepared. Kilili sang in the air, chimed through her right shoulder, rejoicing in her unbridled fear and fury, impelling her to attack another person—something she'd never done before. Her feet barely touched the floor.

A shadow filled her vision; Lilla springing forward, her shriek mingling with the whine from the kilili blade in her hand. Its silveriron edge cut towards Tali's head.

# Chapter 35

The flickerblade hit the air around Tali like a hammer on a huge bell, its impact dulling her hearing. She screamed as the weapon rebounded away from Lilla's hand, spinning over her shoulder straight at the Vernese accomplice.

The world slowed to a near-standstill, right down to the air flowing into Tali's open mouth.

The Vernese pitched face-down. Behind him, the flickerblade slammed into the wall hilt-first and fell to the floor.

Tali's ears rang from the crash of Eulo's blade hitting her...what? *Kilili?* She came to a standstill in front of Lilla, close enough to see sweat on the woman's forehead and black pupils flooding her blue eyes. Close enough to smell the reek of fresh urine.

"You started this like Iskarlian thugs. Let's finish it like Vernese women," Tali said. She shifted into the stance she'd practised with Eulo, holding her own flickerblade up in front of her throat. She'd never win a fight with anyone, but at least she'd die trying.

The Vernese man leapt into a crouch, snatching up Eulo's flickerblade. For a heartbeat, Tali thought he meant to try attacking her again, but he grabbed the Iskarlian woman's elbow, propelling her towards the door. His mouth opened, forming one shrill word.

"Run!"

Eulo moved in a blur, hurling one of Ranson's wooden horses across the room. The heavy sculpture ricocheted off the Vernese youth's shoulder into the wall. A resounding boom echoed through the great room.

The pair raced past Tali, their feet thundering across to the front door, leaving her alone staring at the Iskarlian woman's piss-puddle on the rug. Eulo sprinted after them, shoving the door wide open and disappearing into the sunlight.

"Vivica?" Tali's cry bounced back at her off the stone walls. Heckling her. She hollered, wanting the horror to stop, wanting to find her sister alive. Her pulse racing, she dashed down the polished floorboards from one end of the house to the next. Her desperate sobs filled empty rooms and hallways, to be met by echoing silence at every turn. If she'd gotten away from the forest earlier, she could've stopped this.

A whimper tugged the edge of her senses.

Tali froze, straining her ears, unsure if she'd imagined the noise or even made it herself. She bolted up the stairs, dizzied by the slant and slip of reality as somewhere a woman screamed, over and over.

She shoved open the door to Mema's rosewood-scented room with a hand that didn't seem like her own. A cry of anguish tore free from her lips. Mema lay in a spreading pool of red, lifeless as an autumn leaf. The old woman's back was a flayed expanse of flesh and knobbled bone, just like Cyska's.

Vivica squatted beside Mema, face buried in her hands. She looked up at Tali, blinking through a veil of tears and snot. Shocked, but alive.

"Nononononono."

Tali fell to her knees, jabbering a senseless disbelief, weakened by the whirlpool consuming her soul. Nothing she'd feared came close to the reality of what had happened here. Her face wet with tears, she crawled over to embrace her little sister. "We have to go."

Vivica shook her head, wide-eyed. "I can't." Her tone teetered on the precipice of hysteria.

"We have to." Tali forced a calmness she didn't feel. "I don't know where they are."

Whoever they were. It couldn't be a coincidence the woman called Lilla and her Vernese accomplice had slaughtered her family right after Krike tried to trade her off to them. Lilla, whose name Vivi knew, who was so familiar with Eulo, and carrying his blade. The blade that had swung toward Tali but been stopped *mid-air* by a force she'd heard but not seen.

This was all Tali's fault. For getting on the wifeship, for getting involved with Eulo and his past. A past that had come looking for him and taken her family instead.

She coaxed Vivica to her feet and they staggered away from Mema. Vivi pressed her fist against her mouth, moaning. Gouging her fingernails into Tali's arm, she turned a beseeching gaze on her. "Father?"

"I don't know," Tali admitted.

In a moment, they'd reach the top of the staircase, overlooking

Huon's corpse on the rug below. Her urge to get out of the house clashed with concern for how her sister would cope with seeing another maimed body but Vivica pushed forward with a death-grip on her arm, resigned by what she must've already known. She'd have heard everything—from the bootsteps of the intruders arriving to smash in Huon's skull, to their laughter as they'd hacked out Mema's kilili.

Had Huon come to the house to warn them? Tali opened her mouth to ask where Ranson had been, when Vivica let go of her arm. She ran ahead down the second flight of stairs, with her hair and skirt flowing out behind her, a ghost of the little girl who'd raced her big sister down the same staircase years ago. She stood over the stockman's corpse, biting her bottom lip.

Tali edged past Huon, her mind trying to deny the truth in front of her eyes. She pressed herself against the front doorway, heart skittering. Peering out in the sunlight, looking for any suggestion of what awaited them at the stables. Had Eulo managed to overpower them? Tali didn't want to consider the alternative.

Vivica wiped her nose on one silk sleeve. "What's happening? Why did those people come here?"

"Where's Cailene?"

"She went to town for supplies. Father was in the dining room when Huon came thumping on the door." Vivi rubbed her knuckles into one eye socket, releasing a fresh wave of tears. "He shouted for us to run. Those…people…came right on his heels. I was upstairs. Too late."

"How did you escape them?"

"I climbed out Mema's window onto the ledge. I was too frightened to move until I saw that pair leave with Eulo and heard you calling me." Her lip trembled. "I thought they'd killed you, too."

Tali sucked in a deep breath, bracing herself. She and Vivi ran hand-in-hand, crouching low to stay obscured by the shrubs and shade beside the driveway. Halfway to the stables, the thunder of approaching hoofbeats drove fresh fear into Tali's belly. She tackled Vivica to the ground, pressing her into the damp grass and leaves. They lay as still as they could, shivering against each other, their breath too loud. Tali peered through the foliage as the horses neared.

The nearest horse was an indistinct bay, ridden by a Vernese with a rat's tail. Lilla's horse bore a baldy face and four white stockings. Both riders crouched low in the saddle, more interested in escaping than checking for anyone hiding at random in the bushes.

"Who are they?" Vivica murmured, when the drumbeat of hooves faded.

"Scabmen," Tali said, pulling her up.

"I counted five of them. Four men and a woman. She laughed when they…while they were…" Vivica shuddered, wrapping her arms around herself. "I was sure they'd find me there outside Mema's room, hiding in plain sight. If just one of them had looked up at the front of the house…"

The stench of Cyska's burning cabin—her flesh—clung inside Tali's nostrils, its acridity thick in her throat, scouring her raw from the inside out. She squeezed Vivi's hand, wishing she wasn't dragging her into more danger. They needed horses to get to safety, though, and Tali had to account for Eulo and Ranson. She clenched her teeth. She'd stare the people who'd done this in the eye while she faced them with her flickerblade. If the Scabmen wanted kilili, she'd give them its full rage.

Tali frowned at Vivica's slipper-shod feet. They'd have to run the last two hundred paces to the stables in the open, hoping no unseen eyes watched or waited in the darkness inside.

Vivica dragged, resisting. Tali hauled her across the exposed yard without slowing. She gripped the flickerblade in a sweaty palm, holding it alongside her leg. Taking a moment to steel her nerves, she crept into the stable block.

Her breath caught in her throat as she tripped over an object in the doorway. Vivica yanked Tali upright, her face contorting as they clambered over a body. Tali glanced at the man long enough to satisfy herself it wasn't Eulo or Ranson. She pulled Vivica behind an open stall door and peered out down the breezeway. No one waited to surprise them. Figures moved outside the building, bellowing, striking out at each other.

Tali's tattoo prickled under her shirt.

A triumphant kililisong chimed above the racket of crashing metal. She licked her dry lips. She'd only made one flawed blade in her life. A flawed blade for a flawed man, Eulo said. How true those words were, if not for the fact that blade was now in their attackers' hands.

"Quick." Tali shoved Vivica in the back. "Into the tack room." She grabbed a nearby rake and rushed after her. The door's unoiled hinges shrieked, its splitting timbers groaning in protest when she shut it. It was the first time in Tali's life that she'd ever seen it closed.

Vivica peered through a mess of black curls at the rake. "What are you going to do with that—ask if they want you to clean up their shit?"

Tali thumped the end of the handle down between Vivica's boots. "I'm not doing anything with it. You are."

She tossed blankets and bridles aside, hunting for something to block the door. Not even piling the saddles against the rotten wood would keep a determined murderer out for long. Instead, she detached the stirrup leathers and irons from the closest saddle. She looped one leather over the door handle and buckled it to a wooden beam on the closest saddle rack, holding the door shut. At least she could use the second leather and iron from a distance.

Hefting the makeshift weapon in one hand and her blade in the other, Tali pressed herself against the bricks beside the door hinges. As much as she feared for Eulo's safety, he was a warrior trained to keep himself safe. She had Vivica to look after.

The timbers warped inwards when the first inevitable crash came, some splitting from the impact. The second blow landed straight after. Another, and another.

Vivica whimpered, cowering against the wall, her eyes huge over the prongs of the rake. The tang of leather and horse sweat filled the air. A Glimmers smell, of strength and tenacity. Tali ground her jaw, waiting.

The next blow shattered the door. A man's big foot booted away the broken timbers.

Tali raised her arm, readying the stirrup. With a roar of triumph, the man shouldered the old door right off its hinges and lurched through in its wake.

She swung at him with all her might.

The stirrup iron flung around on the end of its strap, colliding into Eulo Juke's bicep. He skidded across the stone floor, barely knocked off course by the blow. Glancing from Vivica to Tali, he lowered the flickerblade he'd been wielding, his scowl easing. "They're gone."

Tali gestured Vivica out into the breezeway, where their father was bawling out for her. Vivi edged past Eulo in her ruined slippers. She raised an open palm to Tali, who shooed her like a rogue steer. A spark of warmth glowed in her heart. Her little sister *did* care about her.

She glowered at Eulo's blood-spattered forehead, tamping her desire to smack the stirrup into it. Sweat rose off him, warm and heady. "You let her go, that woman?" The blonde with the sly smile.

He nodded, not meeting her eye. "Yeah."

"And?" She frowned, sensing his unease.

"Her name is Lilla Cutter. Her father's Sif Cutter, head of the Scabmen."

Tali threw the stirrup down to clang on the stone between his boots and stalked out into the breezeway. Two men lay out back of the stables, their lifeblood soaking into the dirt. Furrows at their heels showed they'd been dragged beside each other. One full and one part-Vernese, dressed in work-worn clothes. *Scabmen.* Here at Glimmers Gap.

She gagged against the bile rising in her throat, recognising the youth who'd confronted them in the homestead beside Lilla. Knowing Eulo killed people was different to witnessing him doing it. In the before, she'd let herself believe she'd brought a charming rogue to her homeland. Today, the same hands that had touched her with such tenderness had cut free the souls of these people.

Ranson sat splayed on the ground nearby, clutching his blood-soaked arm. Vivica sobbed into his neck, showing a tenderness Tali didn't know how to find for the man. Cloudiness wrapped around her head, like a nasty hangover she couldn't recover from.

"You know these men?" Tali said to Eulo, pointing at the bodies. "Or the one with the woman?"

"Scabmen thugs." He readjusted his grip on the flickerblade hilt.

"Thugs who just happened to have the blade I smithed you."

He grimaced. "I didn't give it to them by choice. As you can see, the lad wasn't real keen to give it back, either."

"Yet the other two still escaped." She folded her arms.

"I had no choice. There's more lives at stake." Lowering his gaze, Eulo crouched over each man in turn, rummaging through their pockets. Quick, practised, tossing his findings into a pile. Coin purses, a few knives, two felt pouches and a hip flask. Jutting his jaw, he unfolded a scrap of bloodied cloth he'd taken from the dead youth. A thin pink sheet rolled out and slapped onto the dirt between his boots.

Vivica gasped, covering her mouth with a hand. Tali curled her tongue against the vomit rising in her throat, knowing but not wanting to accept what Eulo had picked up. He splayed his hands under it. A skein of mauve ran through the gore-smeared material, tracing the white scars and wrinkles which told of a life long lived.

"Give it to me," Tali barked, snatching Mema's skin off him. She wrapped it up as carefully as her trembling hands would allow. "They killed Mema, and torched Cyska's cabin, with her inside." The stench of burning timber stuck to her clothes and skin. A band gripped her throat, bringing tears to her eyes. "Saltwater for their souls," she whispered, pressing the forefingers of her left hand over her right eye-socket, then the left.

"Oh, shades," Eulo murmured. He squeezed her upper arm, stroking it with his thumb.

"What do we do, Tali?" Vivica said. Beside her, Ranson nodded, lifting his hands in appeal.

Suddenly they were all looking at her, waiting for her to decide what to do and how to fix this. Tali's skull squashed tighter around her pounding thoughts. She pressed her lips together, unsure what emotion would break out first if she opened her mouth to speak.

"We need to get you and your sister somewhere safe." Eulo shifted his weight to one side. The rust-coloured stains drying on his forehead framed his intense blue eyes. "You won't survive without protection."

"If Eulo hadn't arrived we'd *all* be dead," Ranson said. He straightened, wringing his hat between both hands.

Wild-eyed, Vivi stabbed a finger at Eulo. "What did you do to my sister?"

"What did *I* do to her?" he said. "How about what you've done to her?"

Vivica hissed at Tali. "You started this, by bringing Eulo here in the first place. What happened here is your fault."

Tali's breath caught in her throat, bringing her roiling emotions to a sudden halt. "You're right, Vivi. You and Father are always right—it is my fault, and Cyska's." She threw her knife to the ground and peeled off her coat and vest. "Let me show you what those Scabmen are looking for." Stripping naked from the waist up, she turned to expose the silver green tattoo sleeking from her shoulder down her ribcage.

Vivi yanked Tali around, bringing their ferocious gazes together. "You never thought to tell me you have a kilili tattoo?"

Tali pulled her shirt back over her head. "I have to keep it a secret, to keep us safe." A whispered chunder of words she wasn't sure she meant anymore.

"But you didn't keep it safe, did you? You told fucking Eulo and then a bunch of lunatics attacked our family," Vivi shrieked, launching herself at Tali, pummelling the silver-shot muscle and bone of the new Sarsega matriarch. "They're probably the same fucking lunatics who killed that dignitine fool Lyselle."

Tali stood with head bowed, letting Vivica release the brunt of her snot-smeared fury. All with Eulo and Ranson witness. She bit her lip hard enough to taste blood, biting back an agony she hadn't suffered since her mother walked out. Vivi raged until strength left her, then collapsed into Tali's arms, sobbing tears into her collar. Tali held her and smoothed tangled hair out of her face, the way their mother used to.

"What is it, then, this tattoo?" Vivi drew back, dabbing at her nose.

"The legend of Lolani's Song," Ranson said, pushing himself upright against the wall. He eyed Tali, wary. But not surprised.

She nodded. "I sing the kilili into silver and metal. Into items like jewellery and flickerblades."

"*You?* Sing?" Vivi scoffed. "You sound like someone hitting a baby with a cat."

Pinching the grit of exhaustion in the corners of her eyes, Tali said, "Maybe so, but I have to do it."

"Or what?"

"It'll kill me."

# Chapter 36

"**B**lazes. It lives off you like a beautiful, expensive parasite." Vivi flattened her hands against her cheeks. "Mema had it too, didn't she? That's why they killed her."

"And Cyska."

Ranson shuffled closer. "But not your mother? Or Vivica, even though she's gifted with her voice?" He picked up Tali's blade between a finger and thumb. "You use it to make these tools of Mako. Bringers of death."

"Show it to me." Vivi gestured to the flickerblade in Eulo's hand. She stared at the symbols swirled into the metal. Everyone winced at the squeal when she flicked her wrist left and right. Eulo took it back, imitating her motion. The blade purred in his big hands.

"Your colour is green." Vivi's lips peeled apart. "Eucalyptus green."

Tali dug in her pocket. "We all have our own shade, which can be stronger or weaker depending on the smith's skills to craft it." She held her palm out, revealing a kilili disc. "Cyska and I discovered a way to meld our colours. We thought we'd be safer if we could obscure ourselves. These are unique, so they're worth more."

Vivi plucked the grape-sized disc out of Tali's hand. She held it up, marvelling at the play of dark green and purple smoked across the silver. "Like Lolani's Song captured in metal. If Lolani sang in Iskarlian symbols." She didn't give it back.

"Our buyers are Iskarlian," Tali said.

"You must make a lot of money off it." Ranson's accusation hung in the air like a black cloud. "Pays for your husband and all your pretty horses, does it?"

"More like pays for Vivica's academy fees," Eulo growled, banging the hilt of his blade against the wall, startling them all with the sound of kilili resonating through the yard.

"Eulo!" Tali protested, too late.

"No." He shook his head, moving to stand at her shoulder. "It's time you tell 'em. Time they start believing in you."

Vivi narrowed her eyes. "What's he talking about?"

"It's true," Tali said. "Cyska paid the last of your audition fee when she went to Silveraine this week. We did it, Vivi. You've got your chance to become a lyricene."

Eulo tapped the flat of his blade against one palm. "I can stop the Scabmen from coming here again if you tell me where to find more kilili. I'll sort out my business with 'em and put an end to this."

Tali rubbed both hands down her face. He still didn't understand. "Fine. Come with me and I'll show you exactly how the Scabmen take it."

"No," Vivica cried out, stopping her mid-stride. "Don't go with him." She glanced sideways at Eulo, wiping her nose with the heel of one hand. "Please, Tali, I'm sorry. I need you."

"You and Ranson need to saddle Sonata and Vane, ready for us to go when we're done here," Tali said. She set off for the homestead with Eulo beside her. Confronting him was the only way he could understand the danger she faced. For her to know if her family was safer with him around or not.

Their footsteps crunched a counter song to the shivering eucalypt leaves overhead. Blazes, she stunk, from the perspiration stiffening her clothes to the smoke tainting her hair, and the fear clinging to her skin.

The house loomed over them with the pall of smoke from Cyska's cottage staining the skyline black. How could Eulo compare his situation to her failing her whole family? She forced one foot after another up the front steps, dreading what she was about to face again. Wire barbs tangled around her heart.

She crossed the threshold from light into dark.

"We can't stay here," Eulo said.

"I'm not convinced about this *we* business," she said. Not yet, and maybe not at all. "Who sent you to Vernesia? And what the fuck did you do to cause them to do this? You owe me the truth."

Eulo looked away. "I had debts at home, money I couldn't pay 'cause I gambled on games that stupid, drunk Iskarlian warriors lose more on than they win." He ran a hand over his head. "The Scabmen don't like unpaid debts, especially not when the goon what owes them money travels the countryside for a living. I got back from a job with enough coin to pay half what I owed, except those bastards don't got much patience and they like changing the rules as they go." He breathed out through his nostrils. "I fronted up to 'em too late. Now they got a hostage."

Resentment prickled over Tali's scalp. "Krike's sister?"

"Oh, fuck no. Pirin Krike disappeared years ago. They took my little brother, Remmy. Said they'll trade him for a ransom of kilili."

"And that's why you bound with me to get across the border." Tali twitched. For his brother, not the imagined love of a long-lost girl. No wonder he'd kept asking where silveriron came from, about Blackrock Cove and the mysterious Skramos with his ship of contraband.

"Someone I'd reckoned I could trust suggested it," he said, curling his lip.

The betrayed betrayer.

"And here I was thinking you did it because you liked me." Tali jabbed at him, although hollowness eclipsed her chest.

"I do like you. A lot."

"Then why didn't you tell me about Remmy?"

Eulo looked her straight in the eye. "I saw how much you care about Vivica. What would you think of me if you knew how bad I let my brother down?"

"Who betrayed you?"

"This fucker Speer. I didn't reckon there was much to his suggestion I come here. Not 'til I found out he'd also gee'd Krike into getting on a wifeship to look for his sister."

Tali gripped the balustrade, its cold wood worn smooth by generations of her family's hands. Now, the house's scent of flowers and beeswax polish would always be undermined by death.

"The Scabmen gave me sixty days to get their kilili. Lilla Cutter caught up with Krike a few days ago, told him he might get Pirin back if he got some too." Eulo exhaled through his nose. "When I ran into Lilla yesterday, I copped this." He gestured to his bruised face. "Her men searched my packs and snatched all the silveriron I had on me. She took off, saying Krike reckoned he knew where to find a good kilili supply. I didn't know until now that the kilili is *you*."

His careful words sent a shiver down Tali's spine. She hesitated at the top of the staircase, gritting herself for the awaiting horror. The bloodied bundle she'd snatched out of his hands weighed heavy inside her shirtfront.

"Krike must've realised you were a kililismith after seeing the pieces in your mother's room, and the snarls board." The revelation spewed out of his mouth like a bad batch of rotgut. "He could've stole kilili out of your house, or his own, but he knew where to get something even better. A kililismith is much more valuable alive than dead." He glanced at Tali. "They don't want to kill you, they want to farm you. Your magic, anyway."

"Why was he taking me away from the Scabmen, if they were already here?" Tali asked.

"He must've wanted to use you to bargain with them. Maybe reckoned he could force them to show him Pirin first."

"Why in blazes would they have kept her hidden away for ten years?"

Eulo shook his head. "They didn't. They don't have her, probably never did. Lilla reckons Pirin saved up her money and left Iskarlia without telling anyone."

"She's very familiar with you, this Lilla."

He paused. "We were lovers, like she said."

"Of course you were." Tali snorted. Something ugly twisted inside her, at hearing these stories of missing siblings and vindictive ex-lovers. "Well, let me show you what your friend Lilla wants to do to me."

Pinching her top lip between her teeth, she shoved him into Mema's room. Even knowing what awaited, the half-naked, mutilated body lying in a lake of coagulated blood on the floor sent her reeling all over again. Cloud-like wisps of hair stuck up from her grandmother's head. The image blurred behind Tali's tears. Hair she'd never brush again, hands she'd never hold again.

"Fuck." Eulo's pupils widened. He pressed the heel of his hand against his forehead. "Mako's fuckin' teeth."

Tali extracted the rag bundle from her shirt. Unrolling it with care, she revealed the flap of skin Eulo had found on the attacker in the stables. A shuddering breath tore free from her. She lay the piece over Mema's raw shoulder, angered by how the edges curled away from the rest of the body.

"Vivica hid while they tortured Mema," Tali said, rolling her tear-flooded gaze to Eulo. "She listened to her scream while they hacked out her kilili. My grandmother died in agony."

The gorge in Eulo's neck bobbed as he swallowed. "I didn't know."

"My silveriron blades were in Krike's saddlebags." Sarcasm thinned Tali's lips. "Funny, isn't it, how he knew I had kilili? Or how he took me, not Vivica, because she doesn't have a drop of mystic on her skin."

Eulo worked his jaw. "I didn't know, I swear."

"I fucking knew. Right from the very first night when the two of you were fighting on the wifeship." She blustered the rawness away with more anger. "Do you think I'm stupid?"

"I never said a word about your tattoo to anyone." He tugged at the collar of his shirt. "And I never reckoned you were stupid."

Tali gripped his shirt in both fists. "Then tell me what Mema said to you the night Filia Tartula came here."

"Don't, Tali. It don't matter."

"It matters to me, and it ought to bloody well matter to you if you really give a shit about me trusting you."

Frowning at his silence, she crushed her knuckles into his chest, again and again. Eulo caught her by the wrists. Tender, the way he'd held her when he'd made love to her. His arms slid around her, their bodies moving like oil through water. Tali wanted to find comfort in his presence, his touch, but yet…

Stepping back, the moment broken, she looked him in the eye. "What did Mema say?"

"She told me"—he licked his lips as if to soothe his desert-roughened voice—"She told me I picked the wrong one."

Calamity reigned in Tali's mind, flashes of voices and images of the people she loved all lying dead. Huon and Cyksa—the two people who'd believed in her and her dreams. Numbness stole over her, except for the kilili tingling on her shoulder, stirring her anger.

Opening her eyes, she stared at Eulo, whose gentle hands still covered hers. "Your Scab bitch came at me with your flickerblade, and it nearly took her own head off. I'd say Lolani is sending her a warning, wouldn't you?" Even if Tali herself didn't understand it.

She left him cradling Mema's small, sheet-bound figure, which he'd insisted on taking while Tali gathered supplies for the road. First, though, she wanted to see her mother's room one last time. Maybe Lilla Cutter hadn't been as thorough as she'd hoped.

Tali emerged from the room with tears tracking down her cheeks, having salvaged a small bag of kilili jewellery and her mother's snarls set. Thank the goddess for Ranson's gift of crafting hidden compartments into his furniture, hiding at least a few valuables. The Scabmen had upturned drawers and boxes on the floor, pilfering their precious gems and kilili trinkets. The case of Sarsega flickerblades lay empty, too, its generations of family legacy were gone.

Tali fled to the kitchen, sidestepping the dark stain where the goddess had captured Huon's last breath. Eulo must've already returned to take his remains away. She shivered, unnerved by the silent house. It hadn't been this sombre since her mother left. Hovering on the kitchen doorstep, she saw Eulo's shirtless torso gleaming in the warm spring sun as he and Ranson lifted the wrapped bodies up onto an old cart.

Startled by a sudden noise, she cried out, leaping backwards into the bench. Renewed fear burst into her chest. Someone was in the house with her.

"**B**lazes, you snuck up on me." Tali rubbed the point of her hip where it had collided with the solid wood benchtop. She moved aside to let Vivica enter the kitchen.

"I couldn't stand it down there, watching them," Vivi said. She swept a tangle of curls off her face, securing them back with a leather tie, her demeanour hardened again by the typical Vivica Sarsega steel. Her eyebrow dipped at the bag in Tali's hand. "What's that?"

"Kilili. It was Mother's. What's left of it."

"I'm scared, Tali. I'm really scared." Vivi's façade slipped.

Tali held her by the shoulders, stared her in the eye. "We'll get help. The Kestrine's Goshawks will catch those people and punish them, I promise."

"What if they find us first?" Anguish crumpled Vivi's face. She bent over, gathering her skirt, then yanked it up, revealing her thigh. "What's happening to me?"

Tali staggered back with a gasp. "When did you get that?"

Pearlescent kilili shimmered on Vivi's skin, like someone had thrown a handful of liquid silver at her. "I think it got stuck to me when I touched Mema as she...after they..." She shuddered, flailing away without warning. "They'll kill me for it. Get it off me. Get it off me!" She gouged her long nails into her flesh, but it moved as one with the kilili.

Tali shocked herself as much as Vivi when she slapped her across the cheek. "Stop," she growled at her sister, who gaped with a hand to her face. "You can't tell anyone about this. *Anyone.*" Vivi nodded. "Good. Now, we need food. One package for us, one for Ranson."

"Us?" Vivica blinked at her through eyes red-rimmed and sunken in her puffy cheeks. "I'm not leaving. I'm staying to help Father with the estate."

"You and me can't stay here, and there's no way we can fight off those people by ourselves on the road," Tali said, swallowing her misgivings. Vivi was in as much danger as she was, now. "Eulo can help us get far enough north to find protection from the Goshawks."

"I wish Eulo was the man you want him to be. He isn't," Vivi said. "Hasn't he proved that by now?"

"I wish, for once, that you and Father had some faith in me," Tali said. "Go get dressed. You need riding clothes."

They headed towards Eulo and Ranson, carrying two hessian sacks packed with supplies. Eulo stopped to wipe his face, his gaze on Tali as she and Vivi approached.

Ranson came to meet them. He squeezed Vivica's hand but aimed his question at Tali: "Where are you thinking to go?"

"I have to get Vivi to the Academy. Once the b-b-bodies…" Tali bit her bottom lip, unable to speak.

"I'll take them up to the Sarsega Ave statue above Cyska's cottage," he said. "Lolani will find them on the lookout rock there. I'll manage it. You need to see Vivi to safety."

"I need you to look after the stock, too. If we lose them, we lose everything."

He frowned, hitching his pants up on his hips. "I'll have to drive them into the hills. It'll take a long time, even with the dogs." He scratched long fingers through his thinning hair. "I'm not happy about this. What if those men come back?"

"Then go to the safest place there is." Over the forested hills, to the grassy slopes and white beaches, and across the strait of aqua water, with its pockets of sucking sand and unseen currents. "Glassrock Island."

Ranson opened and closed his mouth, spoiling for an argument. "I can't." He rubbed his faded brown eyes, as though it could erase the memory of Adeline arguing about the Glassrock muster before she stormed out for the last time.

Tali folded her arms. "You bloody well will. Because if you don't, you'll have to explain to all of us why Huon was the one who got slaughtered in the house while you were at the stables looking for a way to escape." Leaving his daughter and an invalid to the Scabmen's mercy.

The colour drained out of Vivica's cheeks. She took a faltering step away from Ranson. "Father?"

Tali stared him down, relentless, unforgiving. The kilili tattoo tingled, provoked by her chagrin and anguish. "If you can sneak off like a coward, you can fucking well look after my horses and cattle."

He yielded with downcast eyes and slumped shoulders. "What about you?"

Tali might've asked Filia Tartula for help if Krike wasn't working with the Scabmen. The Taths wouldn't be so welcoming since she'd snubbed Rithisak, and she didn't much trust any of Vivica's acquaintances. "I have a friend in Oyster Point who might help us get to the Goshawks."

She readjusted the waistband of the too-big brown pants and fawn shirt she'd taken out of Vivi's wardrobe. Vivi had probably never worn the outfit. At least it didn't smell of smoke and death. "Please take Cyska to the Ave, too. I can't bear to think Lolani might leave without her."

Ranson nodded. "I'll take care of her." He opened his mouth. Closed it. Opened it again. "Is it the Myrtises who've done this?"

Tali gaped at him, stunned by an assumption so obvious she hadn't even made it herself. "I don't know if they're involved. Perhaps you should avoid them, just in case." Eulo blamed the Scabmen, but he clearly wasn't the only one tangled up with them.

Ranson sniffed. "I'll do my best to look after your horses. For when you come back."

"Good," she said, unsure what her father's best was anymore. She closed her eyes, too aware of the growl in her empty belly, and the grime already staining her skin. Knowing she had to keep going but not knowing when this would end. She'd tried her hardest, and it had left her family dead and fractured.

"Safe home." Ranson shocked Tali by clapping her into a goodbye hug. "Be strong, my girl. You have to be. And you will be."

She breathed in the sour reek of fear in his shirt, hoping he was right.

Riding out the gateway onto the Bintau road and away from Glimmers Gap took all of Tali's willpower. She didn't want to leave, but she had to. She rested her hand on Vane's wither, seeking comfort in the touch of silken horsehair. Vivi's horse strode out in front, leaving Tali back beside Eulo.

Once they'd passed the last boundary post, she spoke, unable to stand the silence any longer. "The goddess knows what those bastards did to my cottage."

Eulo said, "I asked Ranson to stop in and check on the cat."

"Yes. Just as long as the cat is alright, eh?"

"I like Chance, but you know that ain't why I'm here." Eulo rested one hand on his thigh, tilting his head at her.

"Why *did* you come back?" she said, irritated by the pitch of her voice. "I can't give you a way to force those people to trot your brother out."

"Mako's teeth. I wanted to explain to you, to ask if—"

"Explain what? How you and Krike are two thugs for hire who were blackmailed into coming to Vernesia to hunt down kilili?" Tali said. "And speaking of Krike, where is he? Galloping to your Scabmen with pieces of my aunt in his hands?"

"A thug for hire," Eulo echoed. A muscle rippled in his jaw.

Emotion pressed hard inside Tali's heart, cracking her finely bound self-control. "This isn't about you, or your brother. You and Krike are just tools for people who won't sacrifice their own skin to get what they want."

"I know what I am, and you do too, else you wouldn't have brought me here."

Brought, bought, there hadn't been any difference, had there? She met his furious gaze. "Our agreement didn't include people smuggling and murder." Was that what her life was worth to him—the buyer offering the highest price?

"Whatever else you reckon about me, I'd never wish anything bad on you. All I'm asking is for a chance to make it right between us."

Fire and stars spanned the damp roadway between them as Tali debated his words. One more chance was about all she could offer, now. She just had to decide if Eulo really deserved it.

# Chapter 37

Sweat rose on Eulo's palms. Tali had plenty of reasons to leave him in the roadway with his chest slit open by silveriron, but she'd chosen to ride on beside him. The kilili silvering her eyes sent a ripple down his spine. To have half a chance of earning her respect again, let alone her trust, he had to be honest with her.

So he told her about talking to Whitey, the Iskarlian captain in Gullwing, of Eulo's unanswered questions about the darkships coming into Blackrock Cove, of his doubts about ever seeing Remmy again. Admitting his stupidity to someone who was smart as a scrubcat didn't come easy to Eulo. He'd never been a man who seduced women with smooth talk.

Tali listened without speaking. The dappled sunlight traced shadows along her cheekbones and the hollows under her eyes. She hadn't touched her right shoulder once, though. At least the kilili tattoo wasn't troubling her anymore. It'd shone flawless in the stable yard, earlier, taking his breath away like the first time he saw it.

"So, it was pure chance that Darley Krike found me on his travels far from home, and discovered I had the very magic these sibling-stealing Scabmen are after?" she said. A razor edge of silver and steel danced on her question.

Eulo flicked a finger against his hat brim, pushing it up from his eyes. "I reckon the Scabmen knew about your kilili before me and Krike lobbed into that binding agency." He'd smash the big fucking idiot when he next saw him.

"Should I be worried about Krike sniffing around my estate again?"

He shrugged. "I doubt it. I reckon it'll keep him busy enough explaining to the Goshawks why he was at Glimmers at the same time as a mob of murdering thugs."

"How much is a sibling worth? One flickerblade? A pair of binding rings? You could've traded the ring for Remmy if you hadn't already sold them."

Eulo let the jibe slide. He stared at the rows of white tree-trunks lining the roadside like giant leg bones. She'd throttle him if she found out the rings were safely snugged in his pants pocket, six paces away from her.

"Obviously your Scabmen friends didn't trust Krike enough to drag a woman to them, so they came after my family themselves."

He cracked his neck left and right. A bruise was forming where she'd slammed the stirrup iron into his arm. Just as well she hadn't aimed higher and hit his nose. "They ain't my friends."

Tali's mare shied at a pair of parrots fleeing the trees above, screeching a panicky warning to their skymates in the surrounding trees. Anyone else might've admired her poise as she kept riding. Eulo knew her well enough to recognise the tension skewering her body. If he'd offered such a shitty explanation to Tambo Tarch, the great Iskarlian mercenary would've skewered *him* with his best knife.

"We were both too late," she said, her words whipping away on the breeze.

"You and Vivs are still alive, and your father," Eulo said, after a long pause. If Krike had managed to deliver Tali to the Scabmen, the big maggot would be lying dead beside her and Eulo. Shades, why didn't Tali see that sometimes it wasn't who'd been taken, but who was left that mattered? He rolled his sleeves down to cover his goosebumped forearms. The sun shone hot out in the open, but the shadows held onto a chill, keeping him uncomfortable no matter where he was.

"You know murder doesn't go unpunished in Vernesia, don't you? I want Lilla and her Scabs brought to justice. But four people also died by your hand."

"Five," he corrected, without thinking.

"Five?" She stonewalled him again with those greensilver eyes.

"Ah." Eulo scratched his unshaven cheek. "I had a run-in with a bloke in Gullwing, when we were at the markets. Caught him about to drive a knife into Flame's foot, and when I stopped him, he fought back a bit too hard."

"You killed him?"

"It wasn't my choice. Dead people aren't real good at sharing secrets. The maggot wasn't keen on having a chat, and in the end, it was him or me." Eulo didn't mention Huon's involvement. The stockman could take that secret to the grave with him.

Tali brushed a bug off her hand. "And you didn't think to tell me?"

He opened and closed the fist resting on his thigh. "You didn't need to worry about someone coming after me."

"Except *I* was riding Flame, a Sarsega horse." She jabbed a thumb against her chest. "That man wasn't after you; he was there for *me*."

Eulo had no remorse for killing someone who would've killed him or Tali. Or worse. Blackness leaked into his chest when he recalled the half-flayed old woman lying on the floor at Glimmers Gap, and the faded, sparkless scrap of kilili which Lilla's Scabman had hacked out of her.

He wished he could fix it all, for Tali. Right now though, they were chasing the wind. If he got close enough to reach out to her, she'd kick his plums straight up into his throat. He lifted his hat, resettling it onto his head, wishing for a solution he couldn't offer.

Ahead, Vivica reined her horse in, bringing them all to a halt. "You should've tied a binding with Rithisak, you know," she said to Tali. "At least *he* didn't nearly have you killed."

The Kestrine's stableman? Eulo raised his eyebrows.

"Rith?" Tali's voice took on an edge. "Honestly, Vivica."

"We don't need Eulo's help. He can just—"Vivica said, making a fly-shooing motion with one hand "—toddle off to wherever he came from."

He snorted, stung. "And what'll you do when the Scabmen come? You ain't exactly very good at sweet talkin' anyone, even if they could be bothered listening."

"Stop it, both of you." Tali clapped her hands together. The sound cracked the air. She sniffed with as much grace as a soldier clearing Iskarlian sand out of his nose. "Eulo's right, Vivi. We need to get to a properly staffed Goshawk's post. First, you have to warn Cailene to go to her mother's, and stay away from Glimmers," She waved a finger from herself to Eulo. "We'll ride along the creek, around the village, and meet you at the Broken Bridge."

Eulo scratched his jaw. Splitting up was stupid, but they had to tell others what had happened, so they could help Ranson with the dead Scabmen and their horses.

Vivica chewed her lip, eyes brimming. "I can't do this."

Tali pulled her into an awkward hug across the horses. "You can. I believe in you."

Vivica sat tall in her saddle, steadying herself with a deep breath. She looked at Tali for a long while, uncertainty swimming in her gaze. "I believe in you too, Tal. Safe home." Her liver chestnut mare cantered away, all long mane and legs.

"Alright, Eulo, we're going this way." Tali nudged her mare off the road into a belt of trees and bushes. "I hope you know how to jump."

Eulo's heart pounded in his ears as he dismounted, happy for his boots to hit solid ground after his and Tali's breakneck-paced detour past Bintau. They'd ridden at a flat gallop, jumping in and out of paddocks, swerving through trees with branches so low they'd scraped his back as he'd swung sideways out of the saddle just to stay on. The splintered boards of an old bridge spanned the creek here, where they'd meet Vivica.

Eulo tethered Cloud to pick at thigh-high grass while they waited. Settling against a dead tree, he stuck his legs out in front of him with his water flask propped on one side, and a bundle of food to the other.

Tali stood facing an Ave statue beside the bridge, wiping her sleeve across her eyes from time to time. She gripped the barely-shaped bluestone effigy of Vernesia's ever-present bird protector, working her fingertips into ridges and dents worn over an aeon of sun and rain.

Eulo swallowed. Legend said the pure gods and goddesses claimed Vernesia, Saltspit and the Threes, leaving Mako with Iskarlia's torn mess. This morning, the demon god had blundered into a place that hadn't deserved him.

The nasty twist of Lilla's sneer crept into his mind, quickly replaced by his shock from witnessing Tali repel Lilla's blow with the flickerblade. If Eulo hadn't seen it for himself, he never would've believed it. Tali hadn't mentioned it, so neither did he. For now.

"You ought to eat something," he said to her.

She drifted over to perch beside him. A trickle of water eased free as she tilted her chin to drink from the flask, tracing a pale track through the road-dust on her skin. An ember burnt low in Eulo's belly.

"Blazes, why is Vivi taking so long." She tucked her hands between her thighs, jigging her legs up and down. Rapping her knuckles against her heart, she said, "Do you still feel it in here, when you kill people?"

"Not when it's like this morning. I don't got room to feel for them kind of maggots, not anymore." And especially not when they killed innocent people.

He held out an apple to Tali.

"I'm not hungry."

"Eat it anyway, or you'll be no use to anyone." He'd spent enough time with his belly growling for days on end, and his mind tangled from lack of food. Hungry men made mistakes, and right now, they couldn't afford for anything else to go wrong. He tipped his hat to shade his eyes and slumped against the tree. Tension from his muscles loosened, ebbing from flesh into wood.

"I didn't think you'd stay on, riding the track back there," Tali said, interrupting the chirp and coo of parrots in the branches above. She ripped the skin off the apple with her front teeth.

"Why wouldn't I? Racing like maniacs through the forest only scared me a little bit shitless." It'd hardly been a track, just following the tumble-down fence-line.

"I needed to remind myself I was alive." She coughed as she realised what she'd said, not quite hiding a sob, staring at a leaf she'd shredded between her fingers.

"Don't you fuckin' dare. It ain't your fault what happened. They would've gone for your family anyway." He spat into the grass. Bloody Lilla. She was venomous as a snake, worse than he remembered.

Tali wrapped her arms around her knees. "I can't stop thinking about what they did to Mema and Cyska. What kind of person does that?"

He knew that kind of person well. Remorse slicked black around his throat. "They're people who're desperate for something. Money, praise, recognition."

*Kilili.*

"I can't imagine being so addicted to something that you'd do whatever you could for it."

"I can." Eulo stabbed a stick into the dirt beside his thigh.

"To gamble?" Tali studied him, absorbing his soft-spoken admission. She threw the leaf shreds up, scattering them like torn dreams on the breeze. "I saw how determined you were when we played snarls in the Bintau pub. You hate backing down."

"That's what got me into this whole palaver."

"What are the chances Remmy is still alive?"

"I don't reckon there's much chance at all." Each word caught on his traitorous bloody tongue. Saying it out loud was much harder than thinking it in his head. "That's what the Scabmen do. They disappear people." He clenched the flask hard enough to spill water out over his hand. "But I reckon if they were going to kill him, they would've done it in front of me, made a big display to everyone of what'll happen if you piss 'em off. I've seen it myself." Eulo swallowed back memories of men screaming as Sif Cutter slaughtered their wives and children like sheep, of blood running black on the red Iskarlian sand.

"Why didn't they just deal with you?"

"Because living with what I've done is worse. This way, they can keep blackmailing me."

Tali sat back on her heels, her knee pressing against Eulo's leg. "Why are you going to pay them if you think they'll keep using you like this?"

"So when I crawl home with my tail between my legs, I can tell my mother and father I did what I could to get Rem back, and I still failed 'em all." He squirmed under the intensity of her green gaze. "Vivs is taking too long. We can't keep waiting."

"We have to go find her."

"No." He got up to untie Cloud. "We got to keep going. Without her."

"They'll kill her."

Eulo paused with his foot in the stirrup. "From the way she said good-bye to you, I'd bet my life she put word out in town about what happened, then galloped back home."

Tali's eyes widened. "She never really intended to come with me, did she?"

"Let her go, darl. Sometimes that's what you got to do for the people you love."

"Right, so you *have* to save Remmy but it's fine for me to leave Vivica to fend for herself?"

"She's got your father, and the Academy. After everything you've given her, let her go take it." He forced his tone to soften. "Me and you are in this together, Tali. Everything you've worked for means nothing if you ain't safe. You owe it to your family." Swinging onto Cloud, he added, "Besides, the Scabmen won't be hanging around. They'll be heading to Gullwing, looking for Skramos to get 'em home before your Goshawks get a sniff of what's happened."

"I hope you're right." Tali frowned. "I'm also hoping Kardia Riole will give us refuge in Oyster Point until we can alert the Goshawks." She vaulted into her saddle.

He whistled. "We'll spend half the night getting there." Riding in the dark with Mako-knew-who in the vast forest around them.

Her eyes silvered. "We'll be there by nightfall because we're not going by road. We'll go directly down the Eagle's Drop escarpment."

Both the gleam in her eye and the path she'd named sent a slow burn from Eulo's chest out through his limbs. Galloping full pelt through the scrub might've been Tali's way, but it was his stealth and cunning that would keep them alive against the Scabmen.

# Chapter 38

Night shrouded their arrival in Oyster Point, as black and hopeless as the situation Tali found herself in. She rubbed at the exhaustion in her eyes. The day had been too long and traumatic to shift the grit on her skin and the weight on her shoulders. Thoughts slithered through her mind, snakes of reason slipping away from any attempts to make sense of it all.

The Riole family estates sat within grapevine-strewn hills edging the ocean and northern outskirts of town; a chain of properties housing Kardia's parents and siblings. Finding Kardia's house was easy. Getting in proved more of a challenge.

Tali stopped in the shadows opposite the house's tall, wrought-iron gates. She stood in her stirrups, peering at the walled estate. A breeze skimmed off the ocean, cool against her cheeks. She swallowed, grimacing at the staleness in her mouth.

"It's better if I go by myself first," she said to Eulo, sliding to the ground and handing her reins to him. They exchanged the same wordless smile they'd shared so many times working the farm at Glimmers Gap. This morning, she didn't think she knew anything about the man who'd spent a whole month under her roof. Now, though, she understood why he'd left their binding without a word.

Her anger had dissolved into fatigue. It would've been easy to blame Eulo for putting her at risk, for being too proud to tell her about his debts and the Scabmen. In reality, she suspected he'd happened to appear in the Scabmen's plan at the right time. Somehow, they'd cottoned on to her or Cyska smithing or sourcing kilili. Both women had taken risks which must've caught the Scabmen's attention, long before Eulo stumbled into Tali's life. Perhaps like poor, dead Lyselle. Did the broken-nosed man betray them—Cyska's lover?

She skulked into the lamplight around the Rioles' gateway. Aches pressed and pulled at her back and legs, her punishment for spending hours in the saddle. A woman rested both elbows on the edge of the sentry booth, one finger knuckle-deep in her nostril. She startled when Tali appeared, jerking her hand away like a naughty child.

"Move on."

"I need to see Kardia Riole."

"Is she expecting you?" The sentry tilted her head in defiance, crossing her arms across her chest.

"Why don't you go ask her?" Tali forced herself to take a slow breath, her patience having rubbed itself to nothing.

"Because she's not expecting visitors."

At least it sounded like Kardia was home.

"Please tell her Tali Sarsega is here." She gripped the iron bars.

The sentry sat taller, her arrogance dropping away. "Sarsega? As in Vivica Sarsega, the singer?"

"Yes, she's my sister." Tali forced the tight smile she used whenever she faced such an exchange. She preferred not to throw her family's name around, although seeing the response it got right now, she didn't mind so much.

"Wait here." The sentry scrambled to her feet and stepped out of the booth. She reappeared from behind the small building, mounted on a horse.

Tali sagged against the gatepost, resting her forehead against the cool bluestone. The hoofbeats faded into the darkness. Not many Vernese matriarchs had younger sisters who were better known than the matriarch herself, but Tali wouldn't have it any other way. She loathed the fawning attention that Vivica craved and won. Still, a shard of solidarity between her, Vivi and Ranson seemed to have risen out of the horror that had engulfed her family that morning.

Worry strummed her nerves. She prayed Eulo was right about Vivi going back to help Ranson at Glimmers, rather than falling into the Scabmen's hands.

She pulled her coat tighter around herself. At least the season flourished, from rainbows of blossoms to the lush grass covering Glimmers Gap. Her stock would find plenty of forage on Glassrock Island until she returned to put her estate in order. After so many months trying to look after her family, how in the skies had she managed to destroy what mattered the most to her?

Lifting her chin, she breathed in the salt air. An owl hooted nearby, its wings shearing through the night, seeking somewhere else to hunt.

Tali's nostrils flared. She steeled herself against a whitewash through her skull: fatigue, threatening to drop her on the spot. She needed to eat and rest, so she could give the Goshawks a clear picture of what had happened to her family. Right now, the fog of stress and exhaustion would make her sound as plausible as a spoony drunk.

Hoofbeats sounded down the hillside, returning from the house. Tali pushed away from the wall, peering through the gate. Two horses approached. She hoped to offer Kardia a semi-sensible explanation of what she and her ex-husband were doing here. The lingering fear of being turned away by someone she barely knew threatened to knock her over completely.

"Tali?" Concern rimmed Kardia's soft lilt. She swung off her horse, running to unlock the gate and lift the thick bar to open it.

*Thank the goddess.*

"Are you hurt?"

"No, but I need your help."

"Of course. Come on, let's get you inside." Kardia tugged her hand.

Tali's throat constricted at the sight of her friend's pinched frown and frantic motions. She couldn't predict Kardia's reaction to what had happened, and Alvic certainly wouldn't approve.

"Eulo is with me." She glanced down the road.

A moment's hesitation, then, "Bring him, quickly."

Tali worked spit across her tongue, put two fingers into the corners of her mouth and blew out a sharp whistle. Shadows moved across the way, forming horses and a rider.

"Well that's lovely, calling out to me like you're whistling Huon's dogs," Eulo's molasses tone oozed through the still night. They'd devised their own set of whistles when working the cattle in the paddocks, building on the ones Tali and Huon used with some extras from Eulo's Iskarlian hunting work.

Tali lowered her voice. "Kardia, I need to ask for your—"

"Discretion? You don't need to ask, from me or my employees. I trust them with my life and the lives of my friends. Which is why we need to get inside. *Now.*"

Fingers of ice traced Tali's spine. She reached to take Vane's reins from Eulo. He leant close enough for her to smell eucalyptus and mint on his breath. Something shone in him with the hard mystique of kilili, darkening his blue gaze, broadening his chest, wicked in the corner of his mouth.

"She's nervous," he said. "Someone's been here telling tales ahead of us." He squeezed Tali's hand, rubbing his thumb over the finger where her binding ring once sat.

Kardia caught Tali's eye, her brow creasing. Unsure what she tried to convey, Tali mounted her mare. They cantered to the house, where an older woman waited on the white gravel skirting the front steps. She took Kardia's horse and reached for Vane and Cloud. Tali pulled her saddlebags free, pleased to see Eulo do the same. Letting go of the horses troubled her but whatever happened now, they couldn't take their spent mounts any farther.

Kardia ran up the stairs, leading them through a foyer bigger than Tali's cottage and into a sitting room. "Please make yourselves comfortable in here. There's a washroom through the far door. I'll give you a moment." Her yellow skirt whirled around her legs as she went out, leaving them in the sudden silence.

Tali dumped her saddlebags in a heap and headed for the washroom, a stride ahead of Eulo. She plunged her hands into a steaming basin, agitating soap over her fingers, swirling black trails through the water, wanting to stick her whole head into its warmth.

She poured two mugs of kaif from a pot on the sideboard while Eulo washed up. He collapsed onto the sofa beside her. They sat without speaking, sipping their hot drinks, gorging down slabs of buttered bilah cake. Tali stared at the immaculate cream cushion below her thigh, sure she'd leave a dirt-smeared imprint of her legs and arse when she stood up again. Not a single cushion on the Sarsega estate was covered in pale, impractical colours like this.

After a time verging on painfully long, Kardia swept into the room. "The cook is serving dinner for you. You both look famished." Tension pulled the maimed side of her face into a grimace. "Mind, if what they're saying is true…"

She broke off, interrupted by her husband bustling through the doorway behind her, holding a plate of food in each hand. Alvic stopped short, gaping at Tali and Eulo. He rounded on his wife. "Are you mad, Kardia? Bringing them here?"

His high pitch ground away Tali's patience. She sprang to her feet, pushing the little man back with the force of her anger. Ignoring his startled reaction, she asked Kardia, "What's going on?"

Kardia prised the plates out of Alvic's hands, offering one to each visitor. Eulo dived into his without hesitation, glowering over the top of it at Alvic. Tali scooped up a mouthful of fish and vegetables, ashamed by their rudeness but desperate to placate the emptiness gnawing at her.

"I'm sorry to seem unfriendly"—Kardia slid a sideways glance at Alvic—"but this is—"

"This is preposterous," he interrupted, planting himself in front of Eulo, a ridiculous contrast against the mercenary's height and bulk. "These people cannot be here, Kardia. They're putting us in danger." He glanced at Kardia's belly.

Tali's mouth went dry. Blazes. Her friend was pregnant.

Kardia blurted, "The Goshawks are hunting for you, Tali. They're saying Eulo helped you kill your family."

"What?" Tali dropped her fork. Globs of sauce splattered out of the plate, tracking across her leg and the impractical pale cushion. All the pieces were taking shape in her mind, if only she could fit them together. She shoved the plate into Eulo's hands, pushing him away.

"It's not true," she said. "I saw the people who did it, and Eulo wasn't one of them."

"How can you be so sure?" Alvic said. "The man kills people for money. Why else would he come here?"

Eulo half rose, his mouth distorting into a ferocious snarl. "What the fuck would you know about it?" He readied his arm like he was about to hurl the plate at Alvic's head. Tali tsked at him, warning him back.

"I don't know who's spreading rumours, but they're not true," she said.

Kardia took a deep breath. "Two riders came through the Goshawk post this afternoon, claiming to be workers from your farm. They said Eulo went mad and killed everyone, and they didn't know where you were," she said. "They insisted the guards find you because you were also your husband's victim. Or accomplice."

"That's ridiculous," Tali said. The room blurred into a swirl of lights and colours.

Eulo's knee popped as he moved to stack their plates on the sideboard beside the kaif pot. "Drink this." He squatted beside Tali and pressed a cup of water into her hand. Low, quiet, like he was handling a nervous dog. "Now breathe. In, out."

She did, struggling to match the unhurried pace of his inhalations and exhalations. The spinning in her head faded. Fear seared her veins, rubbing her nerves raw, sapping what remained of her strength. Eulo rested his hand on her knee in unspoken support.

"Tell me how to help you," Kardia said. "I can give you fresh horses, anything."

Tali said, "All I need is a paper and a pen, please."

She wrote down a statement for the Goshawks, naming Lilla Cutter and the Scabmen as her family's attackers and killers. Eulo wrote his name in big, uneven letters beside her signature, without reading the statement. Emotion blocked Tali's throat, threatening to unravel her. She stamped the letter with the Sarsega brand she carried, the same entwined GG that marked her horses and cattle.

She stuffed the folded statement into a heavy envelope, which she passed to Kardia. "Please have this delivered to the Goshawks as soon as possible."

"Of course. And the horses?"

"Can you get the grey gelding to Loress Skylani? She'll be expecting him," Eulo said. "The mare is Tali's."

"I'll make sure they're returned," Alvic said, surprising Tali, despite his dour-faced disapproval.

"Appreciate it." Eulo nodded.

"Thank you for your hospitality," Tali said to the Rioles. "We won't impose on you any longer."

On the front porch, Kardia wrapped cold fingers around Tali's hands. "Are you sure about this? I wish we could do more for you."

"Almost everyone in my family was murdered, and the people responsible seem determined to destroy what I have left. I promise we haven't done what we're being accused of, but I can't put you at risk too."

"Please be careful." Kardia pressed her into an embrace. She shook Eulo's hand with the same dignified respect she'd shown him on the wifeship. "Keep her safe, won't you?"

Beyond the Riole estate, Tali and Eulo slunk through the unlit laneways. She twisted the strap of her pack in both hands, pushing her leaden limbs to keep moving.

"This is madness."

"There'll be troops crawling all over the place looking for us," Eulo said.

"The Scabmen had this all planned out. They're not stupid."

"Nah but they didn't plan on their plan going wrong, did they?"

"Shall we bet on that? Whoever is still alive at the end can be the winner."

"Shh." Eulo pulled her back against a warehouse wall. Two Goshawks paraded the waterfront ahead.

Her heart battered against her ribcage. How had the situation become so bad they couldn't even trust the Vernese guard?

"Head for the little ship there." Eulo pointed out a vessel bobbing in the water about thirty paces from where they stood. "Go, quick."

They ran, their boots slapping on stone, thudding up the wooden gangplank. No sooner had they stumbled onto deck than a sailor pulled the plank up behind them, calling his crewmates to cast off.

"Thank the goddess," Tali said, her chest heaving. She crumpled, dropping her packs on top of Eulo's.

Eulo shook hands with a man in a woollen skullcap. The man slapped him on the shoulder, his mouth forming a gap-toothed grin.

"Didn't reckon I'd see you again, lad. We'll be bloody close to catching the tide as it is," he said in Vernese, his words heavily accented with Iskarlian.

"How long 'til we get to Silveraine?" Tali said, glancing to the captain.

"Silveraine?" His laughter boomed out into the night. "We ain't staying in this land of glory, we're sailing across the straits."

"What?" Her jaw dropped, her tired mind grappling to understand.

"We're leaving Vernesia, my girl," he said slowly, like she was a simpleton. "Ain't no stopping now 'til we reach Iskarlia."

Behind him, Oyster Point's smattering of lights blinked across the water. Along with Vernesia's decency and civil order, its esteem for women and all the values Tali had taken for granted. All the work she'd done, left behind, scattered in the debris of her dreams. The people she cared about the most now gone.

Except for one.

Eulo lifted Tali's hand and pressed something into it. He curled his fingers around hers, closing them into a fist. A sharp edge bit into her palm.

"Don't lose hope," he said.

She unfurled her fingers. A small disc on her palm caught a glimmer of lamplight. "What's this?"

"A blue flyer scale. I hear they bring good luck." Eulo smiled, half-sheepish.

Tali blinked at it. Had he carried this ever since their first voyage together, on the wifeship?

He touched the back of his fingers to her cheek. "You got my heart, righto? Every little bloody bit of it." Engulfing her in a hug, he kissed her, warm and soft, this man who in his own way had just admitted he loved her.

But, as they stepped apart and she raised her face to the sky, she knew he was right, too, when he'd told her a man wouldn't ever change the colour of the sand in his veins.

She closed her fingers around the fish scale in her palm. Where she was going, she'd need all the luck she could get.